T0359923

INTRIGUE

Seek thrills. Solve crimes. Justice served.

Black Widow
Janice Kay Johnson

Safe House Security
Jacquelin Thomas

MILLS & BOON

Black Widow
© 2024 by Janice Kay Johnson
Philippine Copyright 2024
Australian Copyright 2024
New Zealand Copyright 2024

First Published 2024
First Australian Paperback Edition 2024
ISBN 978 1 038 93524 3

SAFE HOUSE SECURITY
© 2024 by Jacquelin Thomas
Philippine Copyright 2024
Australian Copyright 2024
New Zealand Copyright 2024

First Published 2024
First Australian Paperback Edition 2024
ISBN 978 1 038 93524 3

MIX
Paper | Supporting
responsible forestry
FSC® C001695
www.fsc.org

Published by
Harlequin Mills & Boon
An imprint of Harlequin Enterprises (Australia) Pty Limited
(ABN 47 001 180 918), a subsidiary of HarperCollins
Publishers Australia Pty Limited
(ABN 36 009 913 517)
Level 19, 201 Elizabeth Street
SYDNEY NSW 2000 AUSTRALIA

Cover art used by arrangement with Harlequin Books S.A.. All rights reserved.

Printed and bound in Australia by McPherson's Printing Group

Black Widow

Janice Kay Johnson

MILLS & BOON

An author of more than ninety books for children and adults with more than seventy-five for Harlequin, **Janice Kay Johnson** writes about love and family and pens books of gripping romantic suspense. A *USA TODAY* bestselling author and an eight-time finalist for the Romance Writers of America RITA® Award, she won a RITA® Award in 2008. A former librarian, Janice raised two daughters in a small town north of Seattle, Washington.

Books by Janice Kay Johnson

Harlequin Intrigue

Hide the Child
Trusting the Sheriff
Within Range
Brace for Impact
The Hunting Season
The Last Resort
Cold Case Flashbacks
Dead in the Water
Mustang Creek Manhunt
Crime Scene Connection
High Mountain Terror
The Sheriff's to Protect
Crash Landing
Black Widow

Visit the Author Profile page at
millsandboon.com.au.

CAST OF CHARACTERS

Jordan Hendrick—Years after she escaped her hometown of Storm Lake because of a rush to judgment, Jordan must face the past. Suspicion over the murders of two men she'd briefly dated follows her home.

Shelly Hendrick—Shelly has supported Jordan's choices...and her innocence. Her debilitating stroke is the catalyst that brings Jordan within easy reach of the family that hates her and the community that judges her.

Tom Moore—Rehabilitating after a shoot-out, Detective Tom Moore accepts a job in a quiet community. He dislikes the undercover role he's persuaded to take on: a friendly neighbor who is really staking out the notorious Jordan Hendrick. He knows better than to fall for a woman who will detest him once she knows who he really is.

Steve Dunn—Storm Lake's golden boy and football star, Steve responded to life's disappointments with violent outbursts. Could the people who'd adored him ever believe he had a dark side?

Kevin Dunn—Having worshipped his big brother, Kevin knows who to blame for Steve's downfall.

Ronald Bowen—Steve's uncle, now Storm Lake deputy police chief, shares the family opinion, although his long career in law enforcement gives him a moderating perspective. Or does it?

Prologue

The front door slammed. She straightened, the muscles between her shoulders knotting as her husband stomped toward the kitchen with a heavy tread that roused fear she hadn't felt in a while. They'd been doing so well! He'd been especially unhappy at work recently, though, and if his supervisor so much as mentioned he'd been impolite to a customer, it would have festered all day. If he'd been fired...

The pie! After grabbing pot holders, she hastily took it from the oven, shoving the door shut with one foot. He'd be happy that she'd baked it for him, wouldn't he?

A solidly built man who towered a foot over her average height, his hands were already tightened into fists when he came in sight and a dark scowl made his face ugly. "What's that?"

"It's...it's a raspberry pie." Hating herself for feeling timid, she held it out even though it was too hot for him to take into his hands. "Raspberries are just coming ripe. When I saw them, I thought about you—"

He advanced on her, menace in his body language. "Where did you see them?"

She retreated until her back came up against the kitchen table. "I...had lunch with Mom. We stopped at the farmers' market after."

"Who were you meeting?" snarled the man she had once

believed she loved and had been trying to convince herself she could love again.

"What?" Her tongue tangled. "I don't know what you're talking about!"

"Then why didn't you tell me you were seeing your mother today?"

He was so close now, she felt his spittle on her cheeks. Her hands shook. If she didn't set this pie down… "She called this morning—I didn't think—"

"You thought wrong!" he bellowed, fist already swinging. Connecting with her right cheekbone.

Crying out, she staggered and dropped the pie. The ceramic dish shattered at her feet, splattering its hot contents on her legs and his. As she cowered, she couldn't tell if her blurred vision was from the blow or from tears.

"You promised!" she cried. He'd *sobbed* when he apologized and swore he'd never hurt her again.

"You know the rules." His next blow struck her shoulder as she turned away to protect herself. "You tell me if you have to leave the house *before* you leave it."

She fell to her knees and then hands, which slid in the berry filling. Blood. It looked like blood.

He kicked her in the belly before she could curl into a ball to protect herself.

"No!" she cried. "I was trying to do something nice for you!"

"You think I'm a fool?" The blows kept coming.

After the time when she thought she might die, almost six months ago, she'd sworn that she wouldn't submit to this again. Now, fear awakened anger. She wouldn't be his punching bag because something had gone wrong today.

Even knowing it to be useless, she thrashed, kicking her feet out at him.

His booted foot slammed into her, over and over, as if her ineffectual struggles only enraged him more. Terrified, she looked up to see his gun in his hand. He always carried it somewhere on him. Nobody was going to tell him he couldn't. Not even his boss.

Now, it was aimed right at her, and she saw death in his eyes.

He was supposed to love her. And now…was it too late to stop him?

No. Somehow, she calculated distance and angle. Sliding to her back, she slammed both feet up as hard as she could, with such effort her butt left the kitchen floor. Those feet struck him right where it hurt him most.

On a guttural cry, he clutched himself, letting the gun slip out of his hand. It fell into the mess from the dropped pie. This was her only chance.

She flung herself forward and got her hand on that gun. He bragged about having one of those cop pieces with no safety, so she didn't have to think whether it was locked or not and take a chance of getting it wrong.

"You bitch!" he screamed, and followed that up with a string of the worst obscenities she'd ever heard. "I'm going to kill you. I swear I am."

Despite his pain, he kicked her head. Ears ringing, she slid a few feet, but still managed to lift the gun and point it at him. Trying to scrabble away gained her mere inches. Pain splintered through her head.

Through chattering teeth, she cried, "Leave me alone— Let me go, or I swear…"

He threw his big muscular body at her.

She pulled the trigger. Once, twice…and he crashed down on her. Her head hit the floor, and the whole world went black.

Chapter One

Jordan Hendrick stared up at the night sky, rapt, as impossibly golden fireworks melted while drifting in twinkling sparks toward the ground before vanishing. Her butt was sore, because she was sitting on a blanket spread over a rock-hard mowed soccer field, but that was a small price to pay for the fun of joining the townspeople to watch a really spectacular fireworks show. And she hadn't come with a casual group of friends this time, either; no, she was on a real date.

The music playing from giant speakers reached a crescendo, and a dozen fireworks at a time exploded into the sky in the grand finale. Everyone oohed and aahed, including her. The wonder on the face of a young girl sitting near Jordan was almost as entrancing as the fireworks. Jordan's heart melted just a little, but for some reason the sight of such open, uncomplicated joy also triggered a pang of sadness. When had she last let herself feel anything like that?

Unfortunately, she knew. She hadn't been that much older than the girl when she'd last been able to trust life to be full of possibilities.

As the display ended, she shook herself. All around her, people started gathering themselves and their possessions. The man she'd been sharing the blanket with did the same, and she stood to help him shake it out and fold it. A minute later, he held out his hand for hers so they could join the crowd clumped and waiting turns to mill through one of the handful of gates in the chain-link fence surrounding the field.

Being on a date at all felt surreal to Jordan, even though this was actually the second time she'd gone out with Elliott Keefe. He was a real estate agent at a Walla Walla Windermere office, where she dropped off mail daily. Pleasant chats had become a mild flirtation, and she'd astounded herself by agreeing to dinner last weekend at a highly rated restaurant that specialized in the local wines this area in eastern Washington was known for. Then came the picnic and fireworks for the Fourth of July this week. Nice as it was—he smiled at her just then and squeezed her hand—Jordan already knew this wouldn't go anywhere. For her, though, this was a venture into the strange new world of pretending she had something in common with her peers.

She was twenty-eight years old, and this was only the second guy she'd gone out with in the past eight years.

A whisper in her left ear that she couldn't quite make out had her turning, off guard when a moment later, a shoulder bumped her, hard. She stumbled and would have gone down if Elliott hadn't caught her. He glared, but from the way his head turned it was apparent he couldn't tell who'd been so determined to get ahead. By the time they reached the gate, she'd been jostled a couple more times, but the lighting wasn't good and anyone who bumped her could just as well have been pushed from behind themselves.

Or so she told herself. This past week, she'd felt uneasy, off and on, as if someone was watching her. The past couple of years, she'd had three distinct periods with the same creepy feeling that lingered for a few days, but nothing had come of it. Something was different this time, though:

Wednesday she'd have sworn someone had been in her half of a duplex, and *that* was new.

Except…it was all in her mind. It had to be. She hadn't actually *seen* anyone staring at her or following her, and just because her butcher knife lay out on her clean kitchen counter where she'd never have left it wasn't enough to call 911…and tell them what to investigate?

Ignoring that twinge she sometimes got between her shoulder blades, the one that whispered, *look around*, she gripped Elliott's hand and focused on keeping to her feet as they hustled in front of cars inching toward the exits from the lot. The headlights were too blinding for her to make out faces around her, anyway.

"I had a good time," Elliott said just then.

"Me, too." Jordan didn't protest when he wrapped an arm around her shoulders and steered her toward her car. She liked the warmth of his embrace as long as he kept it loose like this, but was also a tiny bit glad she'd insisted on driving herself.

"I wish I'd been able to pick you up," he grumbled mildly, "but it's not as if I won't see you sometime this week."

"Unless you're out showing houses when I drop by," she teased. "Which you should hope you will be."

"I do have some great listings right now."

Her diversion had worked, and his enthusiasm sparked. He kept talking, stopping only when they reached her car, and she unlocked it.

This kiss was more serious than the one last weekend, but not a lot. More…warm and pleasant. A coworker of hers who liked to talk about the constantly changing roster of men in her life would have said, *meh.* Jordan knew that in this case, it was likely because of her, not anything wrong with him. Given her history, letting herself relax enough to enjoy any kind of intimacy with a man might never be possible. They said their good-nights, and once behind the wheel of her car, she worked her way into the slow traffic dissipating onto the city streets.

At least she'd found the courage to *try* to start something with a man again. Even baby steps were something to celebrate, Jordan decided twenty minutes later, as she let herself in her front door.

JORDAN DIDN'T HAPPEN to see Elliott the next day when she dashed into Windermere with a pile of mail bundled with a rubber band. Some days she left it in their box at the street, but today the batch had been too bulky. The cheerful woman at the front desk looked up with a smile. "I haven't seen Elliott yet today."

Jordan flipped a friendly hand at her just before the glass door closed behind her and she trotted toward her postal vehicle. It was out of character for her to have ever taken the time to talk to the good-looking guy who'd shown an interest in her. Truthfully, she hustled all day.

Mail delivery looked a lot easier than it was. Her first day on the job, her grumpy supervisor had had to wait for her, the last person by over an hour to make it back into the office. But now that she was on her fourth year, she'd long since learned the tricks to allow her to move fast.

Even now, though, she hadn't gotten over being exhausted by the time she carried her empty trays into the back of the post office at the end of the day, sorted what mail had appeared in the interim to give herself a jump start in the morning, and clocked out.

Maybe she'd settle for a salad tonight. Or something out of the freezer. She was happier in her solitude than a young woman her age should be, but she had several episodes of a show she was streaming to watch and was eager to get back to it.

She hadn't gotten further than studying the contents of her freezer before her doorbell rang. Jordan jumped at the sound. Who on earth…?

She of all people didn't like surprises. She hadn't forgotten that the last guy she'd dated had been killed several years ago after surprising burglars in his house—or so the police believed. Violent crime happened everywhere, even in a nice town like Walla Walla, built around a high-end liberal arts college. Since there was no peephole in the door, she cracked the blinds to see a large, dark sedan in her driveway. It bristled with antennae, and the bumper didn't look like the one on *her* car.

Wary, she opened the door without removing the chain. A man and a woman stood on her small front porch. Both wore badges and holstered guns on their belts. Jordan had seen stern looks like that before.

"Ms. Hendrick?" the man said politely, but with no give in his voice. "I'm Detective Shannon and this is Detective Dutton. May we come in?"

Her fingers clenched on the door and her heart pounded in her ears. "May I ask what this is about?"

"It has to do with an attempted murder that took place last night. I believe you know the victim."

"Victim…" Her forehead creased. A coworker or— "Oh, God, not Elliott Keefe?"

"I'm afraid so." The words might sound sympathetic, but the expression on his face remained watchful.

No. How could that be?

She closed the door as her fingers fumbled with the chain to let the cops in. Not just cops—detectives. They had to be, didn't they, since they were plainclothes?

She evaluated them automatically. The man was bulky in the way of a former high school or college athlete, his hair graying at the temples. His wedding ring caught her eye. The woman had to be midthirties, lean like a runner. Her glance took in Jordan's small living room thoroughly before she met Jordan's eyes with a look that hadn't softened at all.

"Please, sit down." Jordan gestured at the sofa before her legs dropped her into the wooden rocking chair. "Can you tell me what happened? Is he badly injured?"

The man took the lead. "Mr. Keefe was found unconscious midday by a coworker who went to check on him. Apparently, he had appointments set up, but didn't come into work."

"He was...excited about some new listings." She almost continued, but of course they knew how real estate sales happened.

"A different coworker mentioned that the two of you were seeing each other. She said you're employed as a mail carrier."

With her hands twined together on her lap, Jordan's fingers tightened painfully. "Yes. Although seeing each other is putting it strongly. We've gone out twice, that's all. He's nice, but..."

Those implacable stares silenced her.

"When did you see him last?" the woman asked.

Jordan had no doubt that they already knew the answer to that question. Elliott had probably talked about his plans at work.

"Yesterday. Because it was the Fourth—" as if they didn't know about the national holiday "—he brought a picnic dinner, and we ate it at the soccer field before the fireworks started."

"And afterward?" Detective Dutton again.

"He walked me to my car, and we said good-night."

"Said good-night?"

Her cheeks heated. "He kissed me. It was brief because there were people all around."

"You had driven separately." The male cop—Jordan couldn't remember his name—picked up where his partner had left off.

"That's right. Even though it was a holiday, earlier in the day Elliott showed several houses to a couple who had trouble finding time. He offered to pick me up anyway, but…" She looked away for a moment, then made herself face them. "I preferred driving myself. I'm not in a hurry to take a casual relationship anywhere. It's easier if he doesn't see me to my doorstep at the end of the evening."

Something shifted on the woman's face that suggested she understood and had made the same choice in the past.

Jordan looked from one to the other. "You haven't said how he is now."

"I'm afraid he's in a coma." The woman cop spoke with surprising gentleness, given their attitude to that point. "We believe his assailant thought Mr. Keefe was dead. In fact, he's still in critical condition."

"Oh God." Jordan bent forward as if she had to protect herself. How could this be?

"Your name came up," the man said.

Of course it had. She waited with dread.

"Having to do with another man you were *seeing* at the time." The emphasis on *seeing* was unmistakable. "A Pete Shroder."

"He was killed during some kind of home invasion." Did she sound shrill? She took a slow breath to calm herself.

"Or at least, that's what I heard. That his house had been cleaned out, and he surprised them just before they left."

"That's true, but it's interesting that the physical assault on Mr. Keefe looks a good deal like the one on Mr. Shroder. A gunshot—two in Mr. Shroder's case—that probably brought each man down, followed by a brutal beating."

She had to face her peril straight on, even if she felt so nauseated she wanted to run for the bathroom. "And you think *I* could have had something to do with those attacks."

"I didn't say that," the man corrected her. "We're interested because of the fact that you had a relationship with both of them."

Mouth dry, she said, "Pete died three years ago. He and I went out only a couple of times, and I doubt either of us would have bothered to continue seeing each other. I hadn't seen him in several days before he was murdered." Jordan glared at them. "I don't see how you can have failed to find and arrest his killer by now."

Wooden expressions suggested she'd hit them where it hurt.

"Unfortunately, neither the bullet nor the trace evidence led us anywhere, suggesting the killer had not formerly been in trouble with the law."

Both raised their brows as they continued to look at *her*.

"You're wasting your time with me. I don't, and have never, owned a gun." She'd only fired one once in her life, and the memory so horrified her she shied away from it. "I'm law-abiding, polite and verging on timid. I rarely even date. I can't imagine any way these two attacks could have anything to do with me." She rose to her feet. "If you feel the need to come back with more implied accusations, I'll need to hire an attorney before I speak to you again."

A twitch in his face might have been a suppressed grimace. Both produced cards and handed them over.

"Thank you. Now, unless there's some other way I can help...?"

"Can you think of any other connection between these two men?"

"Only the obvious, which I trust you already know. Pete worked in property management, and very possibly crossed paths with Elliott." She swallowed. "Am I permitted to visit Elliott at the hospital?"

Detective Dutton—Beverly, according to the card—shook her head. "He's in the ICU. Only family is permitted in to see him, and even they're limited."

Jordan nodded, a sort of numbness creeping over her. Shock, of course.

Detective Shannon opened the door and held it for his partner, then turned back to Jordan. "I encourage you not to leave town."

She was still speechless when he closed the door behind him. A minute later, she heard the car out front drive away.

THE NEXT FEW days were agonizing. She couldn't stop thinking about Elliott—she called the hospital each evening to hear how he was doing, despite the fact that she was given only nonanswers.

The first time she had to take the mail into the real estate office, she said, "I heard about Elliott. It's so awful! You must all be shaken up."

Of course they were. At least no one looked at her as if it had occurred to them that she might have started knocking off men after she'd gone out with them a time or two.

She searched reviews online for a criminal attorney in the event she needed to hire one. The experience was new to her, even though she'd had one before. That time, her mother had decided who to hire while Jordan was still in the hospital.

However, she didn't hear a word from either detective in this case. The *Walla Walla Union-Bulletin* reported that police were investigating but had given no indication they were closing in on a suspect or suspects.

Friday when she handed over the mail at the Windermere office, the woman behind the counter beamed at her. "You probably already know Elliott has regained consciousness! It'll still be a few weeks before he can make it back to work, but that's such good news!"

A huge weight lifted off Jordan's shoulders. "Yes, it is."

"He's going to be mad that two of his listings have sold while he was in the hospital. He was so determined to be the selling *and* the listing agent on both of them."

"He talked about that." She hesitated. "I was told he couldn't have flowers in Intensive Care, but maybe I'll order some now."

"We're planning the same," she was assured.

Jordan felt wobbly with relief when she returned to her vehicle. For once, she didn't jog and leap in. Once behind the wheel, she just sat there for a minute. Nothing about the attack had been her fault, but still... Thank God. He was going to be all right.

A few days later, she received a stiff note thanking her for the bouquet—from Elliott's mother. Maybe he wasn't up to writing notes yet—but Jordan wondered. If one of the detectives had shared the *interesting* coincidence of her having dated two men who had almost immediately thereafter suffered similar attacks, wouldn't Elliott tell himself he'd be smart to stay away from her?

The continuing silence confirmed her guess. It stung,

even though he could just have sensed how tepid her interest in him was. He might well not have asked her out again no matter. She did her best to wedge mail into the Windermere box that she once would have carried in.

Jordan kept expecting to hear from the detectives again—they would surely have researched her background more thoroughly by now—but the call that came in just as she left the post office at the end of her shift, two weeks to the day after Elliott was attacked, didn't come from the local area code. She knew this one, though; she'd grown up in Storm Lake, Idaho. Only…she didn't recognize the number. It wasn't her mother's or one belonging to any of the few other people she'd stayed in touch with.

"Hello?" she said cautiously.

A woman said, "Is this Jordan Hendrick?"

"Yes, it is."

"I'm calling from Cavanaugh Memorial Hospital in Storm Lake," she said kindly. "I'm sorry to have to tell you that your mother has had a stroke."

Chapter Two

Mom is alive. Jordan had at least that much to cling to. Some of the rest of what the hospital representative had said wasn't as encouraging. The ER doctor had done everything he could for her, but Mom hadn't been found as quickly as would have been ideal, so there were noticeable and disturbing effects that, she was assured, would improve with physical therapy.

Jordan had no idea who had found Mom. Was it like Elliott, that she hadn't shown up at her job in the city auditor's office? Maybe. Probably. Although Mom had more friends than Jordan did. Any of them could have been concerned if Mom didn't call when she'd promised, or missed a garden club meeting.

Oh, she hated thinking of her mother collapsed on the floor, unable to grasp her phone or, if she had succeeded, make herself understood. Had she tried to crawl?

Jordan shuddered.

She didn't remember the drive back to the duplex, only flying in her front door. All she could think was to pack as fast as she could. Most of the furniture had come with the place; the rest, she'd abandon. Mom would need her for a long time. She couldn't let herself think that Mom wouldn't because... No!

Jordan didn't have enough boxes to contain her books, so she carried piles of them out and set them loose in the trunk of her car. Clothes and shoes, first in her suitcases, then in white plastic trash bags.

Coat closet. Couldn't forget that.

The doorbell rang and she jumped six inches. What now?

Mostly uncaring, she flung open her door. Of course it had to be the pair of detectives on her porch again, expressions unchanged from the last visit. She knew why they were back, but right now she didn't *care*.

Both of their gazes went past her and fixed on the suitcases sitting by the front door. That couldn't be a surprise, since they had parked at the curb this time, and walked past her car with the trunk and one door standing open, many of her possessions already loaded.

Detective Shannon raised an eyebrow. "Going somewhere?"

"Yes." She backed up. "You can come in, but whatever you plan to say, you have to make it quick."

The detective stepped inside, followed by his partner. "Hoping to get out of town before we came back to talk to you?" he asked sardonically. "Or did you forget I asked you to stay available?"

"I would have called." Her eyes burned from the tears she'd refused to shed. "My mother had a stroke. I'm going home."

"That would be Storm Lake in Idaho."

"Yes. Mom's in the hospital. It was a serious stroke. If— *when*—she makes it home, I need to be there to take care of her."

"Interesting timing."

Interesting had become one of her least favorite words.

"It's horrible timing. I've been sick about Elliott, and now this."

"Please sit down," he suggested. "You have a long drive ahead of you. I guess you're not planning to fly."

Jordan shook her head. "That would be so complicated, it would take longer than driving." And she'd have to leave way more behind, or figure out how to ship it, or…

"Well, then, ten or fifteen minutes isn't going to make any difference."

Of course it could! But she was law-abiding, and she understood why they had more questions. So she sat, even as she quivered with the need to leap up and keep packing, to get on the road.

"We found your fingerprints on file in Idaho."

"If you'd asked, I'd have told you they are. I know what you discovered, but there was never any suggestion that I was at fault for what happened. It was clearly self-defense. I was in the hospital for days after the…incident." Oh, why be squeamish? But she couldn't make herself be blunt.

"You're right," he conceded.

His partner hadn't said a word, but she was listening. Her gaze was trained on Jordan's face, too, reading the range of emotions that must be crowding each other.

"That said, it's hard to believe it's chance that you would have been involved in another man's death. That you fired the shot that killed him."

She shuddered and resented the vulnerability he'd exposed. "He would have killed me if I hadn't pulled that trigger."

"That seems to be the consensus," he agreed.

She bounced to her feet. "Please. I need to go. You didn't find my fingerprints or anything else pointing to me at either Pete Shroder's house or Elliott's because I'd never been to either one. There's nothing more I can tell you. You can call me anytime. I'll answer unless I'm in the hospital."

Detective Dutton touched her partner's arm. Only a brief contact, but he gave her a surprised glance. Then his mouth tightened, and he grudgingly stood.

"Very well. At this point, I can't compel you to stay in Walla Walla. Please get in touch with us if you think of anything that might be helpful. We'd appreciate it."

He'd think she was making up stories if she told him about feeling watched, about the whisper in her ear that she hadn't made out just before someone buffeted her, about the knife left out on her kitchen counter. A knife she hadn't used in days.

But even if they didn't doubt her credibility, none of that had anything to do with an attempt to kill Elliott. Jordan didn't see how it possibly could.

So she nodded, thanked them when they carried her suit-cases and a couple of bags out to her car, and got a tiny bit teary when stern Detective Shannon paused after opening the driver's side door of the unmarked car, looked at her over the roof, and said, "Drive carefully, Ms. Hendrick. You're shaken right now. You need to focus on the road." He sounded positively human.

She smiled shakily at him. "I'll do that. I've driven this route plenty of times."

He dipped his head and climbed in. A moment later, the unmarked police car drove away.

Kitchen. She couldn't leave food to spoil. Jordan hurried back into the duplex, making lists in her head of all the people she had to call, and everything that remained for her to do before she left.

Given the difficulty of her mother's recovery, Jordan

knew she'd be committed in Storm Lake too long to ever take up her job again or move back into this duplex.

THE FIRST THING San Francisco PD Homicide Detective Tom Moore knew was pain. The second was recognition of one of his least favorite locations: the hospital. He didn't even have to open his eyes to know where he was. The beeps of life-sustaining machines and the smells were all he needed.

Those beeps sounded close, as if it might be *his* life the machines were sustaining. Given the extremity of his pain, that seemed possible.

A firm voice spoke in his ear, and he flinched. He immediately regretted even that tiny motion.

"Detective Moore. Are you back with us?"

Where else would he have been?

He grunted.

"We're preparing to take you into surgery. I don't know if you recall what happened to you…"

He hadn't gotten that far yet, but now he did. Approaching a house with his partner to speak to a witness to a murder who was possibly a suspect. Reaching for his sidearm when the front door was thrust open unexpectedly. Max yelling a warning Tom hadn't needed even before gunfire erupted. Reeling as the first bullet struck him, losing some touch with reality as he felt as if a horde of yellow jackets were stinging him. Falling, falling, his nerveless hand losing touch with the grip of his Sig Sauer. That hand flopping on top of a dandelion. Strange that was the last thing he saw.

"Max," he mumbled.

"What?"

"Max." His mouth felt like sandpaper. "Partner."

"Oh." The pause stretched painfully long. "I'm sorry. Detective Cortez didn't make it."

Tom hadn't realized he'd opened his eyes until they fell shut. He couldn't have said what the woman looked like, except she wore one of those starched white uniforms.

"My fault," he managed to say.

Her hand touched his forehead like a benediction. "I very much doubt that," she murmured.

A bright light hung overhead. Somebody else started talking to him as they lifted his arm. Must be time... Yeah.

MACHINES BEEPED, although Mom was breathing on her own.

Jordan had stayed at her mother's bedside as much as hospital personnel allowed. The chair was comfortable enough that, with the addition of a pillow and a blanket, she could nap for stretches. She found her way at intervals to the cafeteria drawn by the smell of coffee, her feet knowing the way. Life had a surreal quality. Most of her breaks happened when one or the other of her mother's friends came by to check on her, or even asked for a turn to sit with her.

Mom's face was twisted enough to make her appear almost a stranger. Jordan wondered whether her mother's friends found that as disturbing as she did. The hand Jordan held so often was a claw; with the IV on Mom's other side, the chair had been placed so that visitors didn't get in the way of nurses and doctors coming and going.

Worst of all was when Mom tried to speak, and all that came out was a garbled mockery of her voice. She couldn't speak a coherent word.

Jordan swore Mom recognized her. Her eyes—one only partially open—stayed fixed on Jordan's face whenever she was in the room and Mom wasn't sleeping.

"I think she looks better," Bonnie Feller insisted as they met in the waiting room. A plump, attractive woman who was allowing a streak of gray to appear in her dark hair, she'd arrived for today's visit shortly after Jordan was banned from the room while Mom underwent physical therapy. Jordan couldn't imagine what that consisted of.

"You really think so?" she asked doubtfully.

"I do," Bonnie assured her. "She couldn't lie on her back at first, only curled on her side in this almost—"

Fetal position. That's what she'd been about to say.

Jordan nodded. It was true.

Hurrying to change the subject, Bonnie patted her on the hand. "Guy was so glad to hear that you're home again. I'm sure he'll call you one of these days."

Uh-huh. Sure he would. Personally, Jordan would rather hear from Detective Shannon.

Bonnie and Mom had been friends since Jordan's family moved to Storm Lake when she'd been a toddler. Bonnie's son Guy was a year older than Jordan. Apparently the two of them had happily been playmates into the early years of elementary school, when he'd dug in his heels one day and said, "She's a *girl*!" He'd been forced to attend one more of her birthday parties, but had been so appalled that he was the only boy, his mother gave up thereafter. By high school, they were casually friendly, but never having even a hint of romantic feelings. Back then, Jordan would have said they regarded each other almost as siblings.

Guy had been away at the University of Idaho during the years of Jordan's marriage. After a summer home, he'd left for Washington State University for a graduate degree in veterinary science. Jordan saw him a couple of times that summer, and wished she hadn't.

Mom, who kept her updated on everyone she'd known, had reported that a couple of years ago he'd bought into the only small animal practice right here in town. That knowl-

edge would be enough to keep her from adopting a dog or
cat. For all the years she and Guy had known each other,
he'd been one of the many people who'd had doubt, and
more, in their eyes when they'd looked at her that summer.

Did you really have *to kill your husband?*

How could Guy not have known her better than that?
But then, he'd played on the football team with Steve Dunn,
taken classes with him, gone to the same keggers. For all
that Guy was in an accelerated academic program, he
mostly hung out with his jock friends. Jordan had been to
those same parties as Steve's girlfriend, awed by his swagger and charisma even as she hovered unobtrusively to one
side, sipping at a single beer as long as she could make it
last. Astonished at her luck, wondering what the homecoming king and star football player with Steve's looks
had possibly seen in *her.*

Well, she soon learned. He'd seen a vulnerability she
didn't know lurked deep inside her. Having her father walk
out and never bother with her again did damage that she
hadn't really understood. Steve? He'd seen that he could
dominate and terrorize her, and thought she'd never fight
back.

He'd almost been right.

She could ignore people like Guy Feller. Mom had always been there for her when Jordan would allow it, and
she had every intention of doing anything and everything
she could to get her mother back on her feet, able to dead-
head the roses in her garden, have lunch with friends like
Bonnie and flirt with Mr. Enyart, who owned the plant
nursery. Most of her contemporaries in this town could go
to hell, though, as far as she was concerned.

The nurse appeared and beamed at Jordan. "You're welcome to come back again!"

Jordan smiled at her mother's friend. "Why don't you go first?" Only one person was permitted at a time. "I might wander out in the courtyard and see if there's still a sun in the sky."

Bonnie laughed and rose to her feet, clutching her handbag. "You take your time, dear. You know your mother wouldn't want you to exhaust yourself the way you have been."

"Thank you, Bonnie."

Watching her hurry away behind the nurse, Jordan slouched deeper in the waiting room chair. The sun would feel nice—but another cup of coffee might do her more good.

TWO DAYS LATER, more tired than ever, Jordan parked in the driveway—Mom's car occupied the single-vehicle detached garage—detoured to grab the mail from the box out at the street, and was flipping through it as she trudged back to the house. Not much today, thank goodness—mostly advertising flyers and a couple of what appeared to be get-well cards from people whose names Jordan recognized. Not until she glanced up as she put her foot on the first step did she see a bobbing movement right in front of her. She started, then realized a helium balloon was tied to the doorknob.

Several white gravestones featuring skulls-and-crossbones stood out on the black balloon. Standard Halloween fare, she thought, in the distant way one did at a moment like this. It was the bloodred words scrawled below the stones that chilled her.

Large letters spelled out *Welcome Home,* while smaller letters beneath added, *Where You Belong.*

Was someone watching, enjoying her reaction?

She spun on her heels but saw no one. Which didn't mean someone wasn't out there.

If she hadn't been so tired, the message might not have hit her so hard. As it was, hurt warred with rage. Rage won. Let whoever had done this *see* what she felt!

She already had her keys in her hand. She leaped up the steps and used the car key to stab the damn balloon. She wanted to keep stabbing, but it deflated fast with a hiss. All she could do was tear the ribbon from the doorknob and take the thing into the kitchen.

There, feeling vengeful, she cut it into shreds with scissors, wishing she could send them to whatever creep had been so determined to remind her of those shattering moments when she had to choose her own life or Steve's. Then she buried them—unfortunate pun—under some messy vegetable trimmings in the trash can.

Finally, she sat at the kitchen table, hands shaking, teeth chattering, and asked herself, *Why?* And, *Was this a threat, or only a needle jab to remind her what a terrible person she must be?*

Only belatedly did she wish she'd photographed the balloon before she destroyed it.

TOM ALMOST DIDN'T recognize the woman who stepped into his room at the rehab center, where he'd been moved after a ten-day stay at the hospital. Emilia Cortez looked as if she'd lost more weight than should be possible so quickly, her eyes were red-rimmed, and her skin no longer had that usual glow. Max had worshipped his pretty wife and been thrilled when she gave birth to the world's cutest baby girl six months ago. It would never have occurred to him that he'd be killed on the job. For all the drama injected in thrillers, movies and TV shows, detectives were far less at risk than front-line patrol officers.

She shuffled like an old woman to his bedside. "Oh, Tom." Her failing attempt at a smile told him how bad he looked.

Damn it, he was going to cry now. "Emilia, I'm so sorry. I should have guessed we were walking into a disaster. Max was depending on me."

She perched on the edge of the bed, tiny enough to barely depress the mattress. "No, you two worked together. Don't lie to me. He had no more idea than you did."

That was true, but—

"He shot that monster, you know." Actually, *monster* wasn't her choice of word; she used a deeply angry word in Spanish that Tom hadn't known until he paired with Maximo Cortez and expanded his own vocabulary. None of which he'd have expected to hear from this sweet woman. "At least he's dead."

"Yeah." He reached out for her hand. "Max saved my life." Another bullet or two hitting him, or even just a delay in getting him to the hospital, and he wouldn't be here now. "I wish it was the other way around." His throat felt clogged and his eyes burned.

"He would be glad. That's what I came to say. You were Max's best friend, not just his partner. If he'd had to choose—" This time, her voice broke.

"He should have chosen himself," he said harshly. "He had you and Lidia to think of. I don't have a wife or children. I wouldn't be missed the same way."

She tilted her head and studied him for longer than felt comfortable. "You've been given a chance to have all that. That's what I came to say. Live gladly, Tom."

His throat all but closed up.

"For now, Lidia and I are going to stay with Max's mama. She needs us, and it will be good for Lidia to have her *abuela*, too."

"Yes." He tightened his fingers on hers. "If you ever need me—"

She kissed his cheek lightly. "I'll always know you would come if I called, but…I have family."

He didn't, something he rarely regretted, but this was one of those moments. He had friends, sure, but they had lives and families of their own. He couldn't exactly go knocking and say, "Hey, can I move in for a few months? Just until I can walk and maybe grip a gun and even squeeze a trigger?"

No.

But lucky him. Barely ten minutes after Emilia had left him to a grim mood, a light rap on the door presaged the upbeat voice he'd come to dread: his physical therapist.

Tom had never backed off from a challenge before, though, and wasn't about to start this time. Whatever it took to regain strength in his damaged body, he'd do. So far, he tried to avoid facing the truth that returning to the peak physical conditioning required for his job with the police department in a major urban city was a long way off, if possible at all.

They had already let him know he could go on desk duty, which held zero appeal. Maybe he'd find a…transitional job. Yeah, that was it. Probably not for a couple of months yet, if not longer, but he'd bet there were smaller towns out there who'd hire him because of his experience, understanding he might not be prepared to run down a suspect and tackle him the first day of his new employment.

And maybe he'd be investigating the theft of equipment from a rental business, minor embezzling, a holdup at the tavern. Considering his goal had always been to work homicide, that didn't stir a lot of excitement, but it would beat shuffling paper and answering phones. When he was ready, he had no doubt SFPD would reinstate him after his time away to heal.

Growling under his breath as he laboriously transferred himself to the wheelchair, he thought, *Make it a small town on flat ground.*

Chapter Three

"You…gave…up…" Mom swallowed hard before she was able to continue working to shape her mouth and control her tongue to make her speech legible. "So…much."

Having no trouble understanding her anymore, Jordan smiled and gave her a side hug. "Don't be silly. I'm taking a long vacation because I don't have to pay any rent. My job wasn't very exciting, you know. I'd made friends, but none close enough for me to be likely to stay in touch. I've missed you so much. You gave me the excuse I needed to come home. I just wish it wasn't such a traumatic one for you."

They sat in the sun in the backyard of Jordan's childhood home, a white-painted clapboard house built in the 1940s and distinguished by the graceful porch that stretched the width of the front facing the street. One of the tasks she'd taken over as the weeks dragged on was maintaining her mother's extensive garden that wrapped from the sidewalk out front to the back of the property, gorgeous enough to have starred on several garden tours. It frustrated Mom to be able to do no more than watch her and occasionally try to give her a tutorial in such topics as dividing perennials and mixing the proper strength of fertilizer for hanging baskets, but she'd come so far in only a few months, Jordan had begun to regain an almost lost belief that her mother *would* rebound from the stroke.

After all, she was home, no longer confined to the rehab center, although therapists of various kinds and home health care workers still came daily. So far, Jordan wasn't thinking about looking for work; housecleaning and yard work, plus helping her mother as needed evenings and during the night, was all she could handle. When she said she was happy to be home and to be able to help, she was being completely honest.

She had *not* told her mother about the attack on Elliott or the phone calls from one of the Walla Walla PD detectives.

In fact, her phone vibrated right now and when she glanced down at it, she immediately recognized the number.

"You okay if I leave you for a minute to take this call?" she asked.

"Yah." Her mother's eyes held a speculative expression that she couldn't convey in any other way.

Jordan would rather Mom be suspicious that her daughter had left behind a boyfriend than realize the truth: that she couldn't shake two police detectives who really wanted her to be a viable suspect in an attempted murder.

She let the screen door slam behind her and went deeper into the house to be out of earshot before she answered. "This is Jordan."

The woman's voice told her the caller was Detective Dutton even before she identified herself and then asked, "How's your mom?"

Both detectives had softened up some, Jordan reflected.

"She's doing really well, considering. She needs help to walk and is just learning to shape intelligible words, but considering the severity of her stroke, it's amazing that she's sitting out in her garden right now and we were having a conversation."

"It sounds like this isn't a good time," the detective said stiffly.

"No, it's okay. She can enjoy the sun without struggling so hard to make herself understood. I think it must be frustrating beyond belief." Of all people to confide in.

But she wasn't as surprised as she should have been when Dutton agreed. "My grandmother had a stroke. She... didn't recover, but I remember worrying about whether her brain was working as well as ever while she'd lost the ability to express herself. What if you had an awful itch, or hated the food they were shoveling in your mouth? And I shouldn't have said that."

"No, I've been thinking the same. Fortunately, Mom *is* starting to be able to communicate some of her needs and thoughts. And no, you don't have to tell me that she's at high risk of having a follow-up stroke."

"I've seen people completely recover," the detective said.

If that was a lie, Jordan appreciated it. "This isn't why you called."

"That's...not entirely true. We're not heartless, you know."

Jordan stared blindly at the drawn drapes on her mother's front window. "I do know. I might not be taking your calls if I thought you were."

"Have you heard from Mr. Keefe?"

Her mouth twisted. "No." His silence said it all.

If only he'd heard or seen anything! Police were unsure whether he really hadn't, or whether he could have suffered from some traumatic memory loss. Supposedly, all he did remember was walking into the kitchen from the attached garage and dropping his keys on the counter just before the *bang* of what must have been the gunshot that sent him crashing to the floor. Something slamming into his head was his only other memory until he awakened in the hospital.

If he remembered going into the kitchen, that meant he hadn't forgotten the Fourth of July celebration, or her.

"You're an unlikely suspect," the detective surprised her by saying. "We'd have moved on if it weren't for your, er, history."

"I understand." A familiar, bitter taste filled her mouth. "It will haunt me forever. There's a reason I moved away from Storm Lake, you know. I could see people speculating, even old friends. If people locally hear about what happened to Elliott, wondering will become certainty. My husband—" Oh, how she hated saying that much. His name would be even worse. "He had a bigger personality than I did. He was a star on the football team, had half the girls in high school trailing him through the halls, was comical enough he could get even the teachers to laugh and let him off the hook when he was caught breaking rules."

Soon after their marriage, she'd started noticing his humor had a nasty edge. Or maybe it had changed when he'd begun to resent his first boss, then the one after that, until it became a pattern. He thought *he* should be the supervisor, even though she suspected he slacked off like he had in classes. She didn't dare to so much as hint that anything could be his fault.

She'd be embarrassed that she hadn't seen through him in the first months of her marriage, but she had. It was more that she'd convinced herself things would change, that she had to show her faith in him by sticking through the hard times. She understood that this life wasn't what he'd been so sure he would have. Even after he hit her a few times, then exploded once and came so close to killing her, she desperately convinced herself a family was supposed to stay complete.

Now she suspected that mostly she didn't want anyone to know her judgment had been so bad. She'd almost died because she had been too embarrassed to ignore her pride and say, *You were right, Mom. Help.*

Her mother had been appalled when Jordan announced after high school graduation that instead of going to college, she was marrying Steve Dunn. Once she discovered what a horrible mistake she'd made, Jordan had pretended everything was fine. Eventually, after the traumatic end to her not-quite-twenty-month marriage, she'd figured out that she'd gotten herself in that spot and stayed in it for a lot of complicated reasons she hadn't seen clearly at the time. What she hadn't guessed was how much her pretense would hurt her mother once the truth came out. The result was that Mom blamed herself for Jordan's mistakes.

I was so young, she thought sadly.

"There was nothing out of the ordinary in the weeks before Mr. Keefe was attacked," the detective said. Or was that a question?

"Shouldn't it have been him who noticed anything weird?" Jordan asked.

"He claims the only thing new was that he'd started to date you."

Thank you, Elliott. "He'd gotten a couple of listings that were an especially big deal for him," Jordan said. "He was excited, because he thought he'd taken a step toward being a top seller. He was seeing dollar signs. Somebody could have resented his success."

"We've considered the possibility," the detective said neutrally, "but haven't come up with any, say, sour grapes."

She was talking to Jordan, which was new. Jordan still

didn't believe anything that had happened to her could have led to Elliott being nearly killed, but after a hesitation, she said, "There were a couple of things. Nothing I could prove, and…it just doesn't make sense!"

"A couple of things?"

"I kept feeling like someone was watching me. You know? Just a prickling at the nape of your neck, but when you turn around, no one is there. And then a few days before the Fourth, I thought someone had gotten into my apartment."

"It was unlocked, or a window left open?"

"No. Or, at least, I'm pretty sure I unlocked the front door when I got home from work, but I can't swear to it. You know what it's like when you're juggling stuff you're carrying, including groceries, and you think you turned your key in the lock. The only sign someone had been there was that my butcher knife lay out on the counter." The memory still gave her the creeps. "I'd left the kitchen clean that morning. I swear I did. And I hadn't done any serious cooking, certainly not cutting up meat, for, oh, at least the previous week if not longer. But if I'd called 911, I knew a patrol officer would have stared at the knife and then said, 'Is that yours, ma'am?' I'd admit it was, and he or she would say, 'You don't think you could have been reaching in the drawer where you kept it for something else and maybe just set it aside without thinking?' Could I one hundred percent claim I hadn't? No, but the knives were in one of those wood blocks with slits in them to one side of a deep drawer where I kept linens. I wouldn't have *had* to take one out to reach anything else!"

She still thought it had been a threat, but everything she'd just said would sound so logical to Detective Dutton, Jordan didn't even bother to say that.

"That's it?"

"Somebody bumped me really hard when we were leaving the field after the fireworks display, and I thought whoever it was whispered something in my ear, but I couldn't make it out. And...there was a lot of jostling. You know what a crowd like that is like, even if everyone has had a good time."

There. She'd told them. It probably didn't look good that she hadn't earlier, except they'd have thought then that she had a wild imagination—or that she was trying to divert attention from herself. *Somebody was following her;* he *must have attacked Elliott.*

Sure.

"Well," the detective said with more tact than Jordan might have expected, "we can't check any of that out now. And it is a little hard to see why someone interested in you would go after a man you've gone out with twice. Now, if you had a possessive ex-husband or—boyfriend?"

"My ex-husband was very possessive," Jordan said flatly, "but he's dead. And no, there hasn't been anyone since who gave even an indication of that kind of behavior. Like I told you, I've hardly dated."

There'd been the other stuff over the years: the wedding—and funeral—anniversary cards, and, even worse a couple of times, bouquets that always looked as if they should be set beside a casket at a funeral, or perhaps left on a grave as an annual remembrance. Those would have been expensive, which didn't fit with any of Steve's friends. The handwriting on the cards wasn't always the same, either. The problem was, she could think of several people offhand who had outright accused her of murdering Steve, and then there were the uneasy or even narrow-eyed looks. Steve's brother and mother surely hated her. Maybe his sister; Jordan didn't know. He'd had a big circle of friends, the ones he continued to meet at the tavern evenings after their marriage, when he left her home. People probably thought they were being clever, tormenting her for taking away a man who had been bigger than life, much too good to be the abuser they refused to believe he'd been.

Jordan had given up even bothering to wonder who sent any particular card. She had tried to find out from florists who had ordered the bouquets, but the businesses were determined to honor their customers' privacy, so she gave up asking.

She trashed the flowers and cards alike, refusing to acknowledge how much it hurt to know that so many people in her hometown would rather detest her than believe what was in the police report. Steve had been Somebody, with a capital *S*. Her shyness and the self-doubt that took deep root the day her father had left and never bothered with her again had combined to turn her into a nonentity in most people's eyes. She even understood that; it had taken her years to discover who she really was.

Detective Dutton didn't comment on Jordan's teenage marriage that had ended so catastrophically after twenty months. She'd likely seen enough on her job to be able to read between the lines on that report. Unfortunately, she and her partner could have convinced themselves that, after being battered, Jordan might have nursed underlying rage and developed a taste for offing men who'd maybe said or done the wrong thing.

That was her, she thought: the angel of death.

The detective didn't try to extend today's conversation.

Jordan forgot all about it after she hurried out the back door to find her mother tipped so far in the chair, she was inches from tumbling to the brick pavers.

After gently helping Mom into the closest to a sitting

position she could achieve, Jordan caught her breath and vowed not to take her eyes off her mother for more than a minute unless she was safely tucked into bed with a bolster of pillows that kept her from rolling off the mattress.

So much for confiding in a supposedly sympathetic police detective.

AS WAS PROBABLY INEVITABLE, Shelly Hendrick's recovery slowed. Jordan was aware of very little that lay outside her childhood home, her mother's garden, the physical therapists, the city swimming pool where she took part in a water aerobics class aimed to help physically challenged people. The pharmacy—Jordan was on good terms with both the pharmacist and an assistant she'd known in school who seemed happy to see her and genuinely regretful about her mother's stroke. The grocery store, the several home care workers who came and went. Oh, and the couple of different doctors Mom saw on a regular basis.

The local hospital served as a regional center for specialists. Her mother had been lucky in that respect. A neurologist had taken over from the trauma team quickly. Mom's family doctor stayed in the loop, along with a cardiologist, a rehab nurse, physical and occupational therapist, a speech pathologist and a case manager. Jordan had been assured that a psychologist or even psychiatrist might be a big help once her mother's speech improved enough.

Jordan was grateful for every one of them, although she couldn't help being appalled by the bills. The many tests, from an MRI to a cerebral angiogram, did not come cheap. So far, Mom's insurance was paying the bulk of the bills, but taking care of what was left could still end up totally depleting her funds.

Her mother was currently undergoing an echocardiogram

for the second time, as the doctors had never been entirely satisfied that they had identified the source of the clot or clots that had traveled to the brain and caused the stroke. Jordan sat in the waiting room, scrolling through news on her phone without getting very engaged when she heard a voice.

"Jordan Hendrick!"

She looked up and recognized one of the ER doctors who'd checked in several times while Mom was still hospitalized to see how she was doing. She'd wondered at the time whether big-city docs ever did anything like that.

Now she smiled. "Dr. Parnell. How nice to see you. Mom's having another echocardiogram, thus me sitting here twiddling my thumbs."

"Make it Colin," he said, lowering himself to the seat right beside her. "I'm not your mother's doctor anymore."

She blinked. Was that a glint of interest in his brown eyes?

"Colin," she agreed. "Did you just happen to wander this way?"

He laughed, making her realize that he was an attractive man. When she'd briefly met him before, all she'd seen was the white coat and stethoscope. The physicians all blended together at that point.

"No, I heard your mother would be here and thought I'd say hello to you. Find out how you're holding up."

"I'm not the one struggling. That's Mom. People keep telling me she's progressing well, but…oh, she is. It's just so slow."

He laid a warm hand atop hers on the armrest of the chair. "I know. But it hasn't even been three months, and she's home. From what I've been told, she really is bouncing back faster than we originally expected. She was young to have a massive stroke."

"I know, especially when she didn't have any obvious risk factors."

His eyebrows rose. "She'd been ignoring her higher-than-ideal blood pressure and what we now know was atrial fibrillation."

Jordan made a face. "She was sure her symptoms had to do with the amount of coffee she drank."

"She's not the first person and won't be the last I've heard that from."

His hand remained atop hers. She didn't quite know how to react.

"I'd suggest we go get a cup of coffee, but I don't suppose you have time," he said.

Was that a tiny thrill of anticipation, or dread? "I'm afraid not," Jordan said. "She should be out pretty soon."

"Are you able to get away long enough to meet for coffee another time, or even to go out for dinner?" he asked.

"I…maybe?"

He laughed. "A solid answer."

How could she not laugh, too? Impulse seized her. "Sure. Why don't we start with coffee so I don't have to leave my mother for too long?" Good excuse.

"Tomorrow?" he said immediately, taking out his phone and pulling up the calendar. "Say, three o'clock?"

She did the same. "I can do that. Mom's physical therapist will be there, and then an aide takes over to help her shower."

"Great." He was especially handsome when he grinned at her and squeezed her hand before rising to his feet. "Clearwater Café?"

A trendy—by Storm Lake standards—establishment, the café was only a few blocks from the hospital and had both good food and coffee, so she said, "That sounds great. Thanks for suggesting it."

His name was called over the PA system just then. He shook his head in mock dismay and left at a brisk pace.

Not until he was gone did she wonder whether this was smart, given her recent history. She wondered whether anybody had told him she was at the heart of one of Storm Lake's most shocking tragedies, one that nobody seemed to have forgotten.

I should cancel, she thought—but the two of them weren't planning to go out on the town. It would be the merest chance if anyone who held a grudge against her happened to see her sipping coffee and chatting with a doctor she obviously knew from the hospital. And what was she supposed to do? Quit trying to have a semi-normal life because of the assault on Elliott Keefer? The one Jordan couldn't believe was connected to her?

No, that was ridiculous. She'd been home for months. Wasn't she entitled to start *some* kind of social life?

Still, she circled back to thinking maybe going out with anyone right now wasn't a good idea, then feeling mad because there wasn't any good reason she shouldn't…until a nurse pushing her mother in a wheelchair came through the double doors.

"She's all set to go home!" the nurse declared. "Dr. Taylor says she'll give you a call to talk about what she saw. Why don't you go get your car, and we'll meet you at the portico?"

"I'll do that." Jordan bent to kiss her mother's cheek, then hurried toward the main entrance so Mom wouldn't have to wait long.

Chapter Four

It was one date. No need to panic.

Still, Jordan sat stiffly in the passenger seat beside Dr. Colin Parnell and thought, *I shouldn't be doing this.*

She also wished she could drop the "doctor" part in her mind. She would *not* let herself feel the inadequacy that had haunted her as a teenager. She was working toward a BA. It was just taking time.

What if he didn't see her as an equal and was thinking about nothing but getting her into bed?

He'd be in for a big disappointment. She'd worked hard on herself to accept that, while she'd made one massively bad choice, she'd also proved her strength by surviving. Heck, she bet her personal life had been more colorful than Colin Parnell's.

"What are you thinking?" he asked just then.

"I'm giving myself a pep talk," she admitted. "This will be the longest I've left Mom since she had the stroke." Nice excuse.

"You said you found an aide to stay with her."

"Yes, and Mom's doing really well. She kept telling me she didn't need anyone, but even with the cane she walks so unsteadily I keep being afraid she'll fall." Jordan sighed. "Enough about Mom, already."

He laughed. "I can agree with that, although if you need to talk about her, I'm available."

"Nope. I'm ready to expand my horizons." Just…not too far.

He'd asked her if she liked Italian food, and minutes later they walked into a small restaurant in a space that had been a dry-cleaning business in her day. The smell was amazing, and her first quick scan of diners didn't identify anyone she knew. She let herself relax.

After shedding their coats, they were seated at a table in the corner. The fat candle added to a romantic ambiance created in part by dim lighting. After they ordered and their waiter poured a red wine Colin had chosen, he lifted his glass and said, "To getting to know you."

She lifted hers as well and smiled. "To getting to know *you*."

They'd covered some ground over coffee last week. Jordan knew he had grown up in Idaho Falls and had always intended to come back to the area to practice medicine. What she didn't know was whether anybody had whispered to him about the scandal that had shaped her life.

"Do you plan to stay in town once your mother is more solidly on her feet?" he asked now, dipping a slice of bread in the spiced olive oil. His mouth quirked.

She frowned a little at his question. "I actually haven't even thought about future plans. I was so focused on being here for Mom, and then the slow pace of her recovery makes it obvious that at best I can't leave her anytime in the foreseeable future. So…I don't know." Her frown deepened. Strange she hadn't let herself think about this. Being home in Storm Lake stirred up a lot of complicated stuff, much of it bad, but she was rediscovering how much she loved, too, starting with the wooded, mountainous setting on a beautiful lake. It really did feel like home. "Some of the issues I didn't like here have probably changed," she said slowly. "Right now, I can't see myself moving out of the area and leaving Mom behind. I mean, realistically…"

He obviously knew what she was thinking.

She got him talking about why he'd chosen trauma as a medical specialty and found he could be really funny when confessing to his youthful exploration of adrenaline-inducing activities, from jumping onto a backyard trampoline from a second-story window in his parents' house to amateur bungee jumping.

She was laughing when the restaurant door opened and a couple entered. She froze mid-breath. Guy Feller, with a woman who was probably his wife.

Maybe because she was staring, he saw her right away and met her eyes.

Surely he'd be civil, if he spoke to her at all. Crossing her fingers out of sight, she wanted to believe that.

In fact, once he and the woman had been shown to a table, he murmured something to her and steered her toward Jordan.

Tall and lean, he'd matured well, she thought. She could see the boy she'd known best only because they'd gone all the way through school together.

"Guy," she said pleasantly. "How nice to see you. Your mother talks about you."

Colin stood and the two men shook hands, introducing themselves as well as Guy's wife, Autumn.

"I know I've told you about Jordan," he said to her as she smiled politely.

Determined to keep it light, Jordan asked, "Did you tell her about the birthday party when I turned—what was it?

Eight? Nine?—and you stayed with your back to a wall staring at your feet for something like two hours?"

His laugh appeared genuine. "Yeah, I was paralyzed. All those *girls*."

Jordan grinned.

"In fairness, I did bring a present—"

"Which your mother undoubtedly chose and wrapped."

"And I ate cake and ice cream."

"Hunched over it while you pretended no one else was there."

"C'mon." He appealed to Colin. "How would you have felt about being the only boy at a birthday party with a gaggle of girls all dressed in pink and giggling nonstop?"

"I'd have been out of there," admitted the man who'd just told her how much he enjoyed risking his life.

Jordan rolled her eyes.

"Pleasure to meet you," Guy told Colin, then looked steadily at Jordan. "I wasn't as good a friend to you as I should have been. I...regret that."

Stunned, she bobbed her head.

He didn't give his wife or Colin a chance to ask what he meant, and even though she saw questions in Colin's eyes, he didn't pry.

Instead, they returned to the "getting to know each other" conversation that Jordan tried hard to keep superficial.

Still, she was surprised to realize what a good time she was having with the doctor and didn't feel too nervous about him delivering her to her doorstep. Dr. Colin Parnell wasn't a man to be pushy, she felt sure. To the contrary, she suspected he wielded patience, that charming smile and his innate kindness to achieve his aim when it came to women.

He did kiss her on her front porch, but gently. "I have this feeling you've been burned," he said quietly, confirming her belief when he raised his head. "I had a good time tonight."

"I did, too," she was able to say honestly.

He pressed his lips to her forehead, said, "I'll call," and strolled back to his car.

She waved before she let herself into the house. The evening had left her with way too much to think about—but that would have to wait until she'd seen the aide out and reported to Mom.

JORDAN SLEPT BETTER than she had in a while. Getting out, laughing, forgetting for a couple of hours the main preoccupation of her life, was better than a sleeping pill. Mom must have made it through the night, too.

Wait. What if she'd decided to get up to go to the bathroom on her own? She was definitely starting to rebel against the "don't move without someone standing beside you" rule. In one way, that was good news, but in another...

Jordan leaped up, feeling some relief because she didn't find Mom lying in the hall or the bathroom. Mom's bedroom door was always partially open, and...there she was, awake and reaching for the bell that sat on her bedside stand.

Jordan stepped into the room. "Good morning! Do you need a hand?"

"No." Her ever-stubborn mother slowly pushed herself into a sitting position, albeit twisted to accommodate her weak side, then swung her feet onto the floor. Her walker waited to give her support standing. Once she was upright, she said, "Hah! Told you."

"Yeah, you did." Jordan grabbed her robe and draped it over the walker as Mom shuffled toward the bathroom. Thank goodness this was mostly a one-story house, the attic reserved for storage. Stairs would have been impossible for Mom to navigate now.

Ear cocked for any worrisome thuds or crashes behind her, Jordan went on to the kitchen, letting her mother follow. Loss of independence was a big trigger for depression in stroke victims. She didn't want to contribute.

They both had coffee. Jordan sliced the banana that went on top of each of their bowls of cereal, since her mother's right hand was still both weak and frozen into an unfortunately clawlike position. It had improved noticeably, though, after a whole lot of PT. Life would be easier for Mom if the stroke had crippled her left side instead of her more dominant right.

"How...was...your date?"

"Good," she said. "Do you remember Dr. Parnell?"

"Yah." Mom's tongue still refused to form the *S* sound. Mostly, Jordan's brain simply filled it in. "Nice."

She chatted about dinner, how good the food was—Mom had lunch with friends regularly but had never been to the restaurant—and mentioned seeing Guy Feller. The two of them laughed again at the memory of the birthday party that had severed the friendship. Jordan still remembered the doll his mother had picked out to give her, and the beet-red color that crept over Guy's cheeks while she was opening it.

An hour later, the doorbell rang and Jordan let in the aide who helped Mom take a shower. Later today, Mom's hairdresser was going to drop by, too, which she was excited about.

Jordan took advantage of the time to work outside, starting by raking leaves. After checking to find an occupational therapist with Mom, she continued her ongoing task of cutting back brown stems of perennials and annuals and then

mulching flower beds—sort of like piling on the comfort-
ers—in preparation for the really cold weather to come.
Late October teetered between the heat of summer and the
bitter cold of winter in mountainous Idaho. The electric
bill was climbing by the day, she reflected, but at least the
water bill had plummeted now that she was no longer laying out soaker hoses for the forty-something roses in Mom's
garden. In fact, the hoses were now curled up neatly in the
garage; if left out, they'd crack over the winter.

Jordan had grown up rolling her eyes at Mom's over-the-
top enthusiasm for gardening. Since she'd gotten home, she'd
taken on the work so that when Mom made it home from
the hospital, her garden would be brilliant with bloom and
welcoming. Now…maybe it was odd, but Jordan had become invested.

Lunch was sandwiches, applesauce and chips—so
imaginative—and Jordan had put the pillow bolster into
place once her mother had lain down for a nap when the
doorbell rang again.

Who on earth? Jordan had bought a whiteboard calendar to keep track of her mother's many appointments. Had
she forgotten to note one?

She didn't even think of looking to see who was here
before she opened the door. All-too-familiar shock struck
her at the sight of two uniformed police officers on the
doorstep. And, dear God, wasn't one of them Cody Bussert, better known in high school as Buzz? Jordan had had
no idea that one of Steve's good buddies had become a cop.

Apprehension had her clutching the door. "I…how can
I help you? My mother is—"

Cody interrupted without apparent compunction. "It's
you we need to talk to, *Ms*. Hendrick."

The other officer glanced at his partner in what appeared

to be surprise and possibly warning. Had to be the sneer in *Buzz's* voice.

It made her mad enough that she was able to say coolly, "And why would that be?"

The second cop said, "I'm Officer Wilson. This is—"

"She knows me," Buzz snapped.

"May we come in?"

Jordan glanced over her shoulder. "Can we talk on the porch? My mother had a stroke recently and is napping."

"I'm sorry," Officer Wilson said. "That's tough. Yes, we can sit out here."

Thank goodness the day was cool but not bitingly cold so she didn't have to ask them in. Buzz leaned a hip against the porch railing while his partner perched on an Adirondack chair, obviously not wanting to slide far enough back as to impede his being able to leap up to...? Tackle her? Pull his weapon?

Pulse racing, she sat on the swing hanging from chains. "What is it? I haven't been back in town long—"

"And another man is already dead," Buzz said with a razor-sharp edge in his voice.

Her fingernails bit into her palms. "What?"

Officer Wilson looked reprovingly at Bussert, but said, "We're speaking with people who knew Dr. Colin Parnell well."

Knew. Past tense. It couldn't be.

"You mean, he's... Something happened to him?" That sounded mealy-mouthed, but she couldn't even let herself picture—

"I'm afraid he was murdered last night, Ms. Hendrick."

"Oh my God." This couldn't be. She heard herself whimpering, "Oh...my God."

"I believe you and he went out together yesterday evening."

Panic clogged her throat. She couldn't let them see anything but the grief, not now, not until she had time to think about what this meant. "Yes. We...had dinner. He dropped me here afterward."

Why hadn't she said no? Why, *why*?

"Do you know what time?"

"About eight thirty." The pressure behind her sternum *hurt*. "I'd hired an aide to stay with Mom and promised not to be out late."

"Someone was here when you arrived."

"Yes. She...was in the living room. She saw Colin and smiled and waved. He wished her good-night, too. I guess their paths have crossed before."

A small spiral notebook had materialized in Officer Wilson's hand. *Small town, low tech.* "Her name?" he asked.

"Uh... Patty Younger. She's one of Mom's and my favorites."

The questions went on and on. How had she met Colin? Hospital. How long ago? Three months. Had they been dating that entire time? No. She explained about the most recent encounter with him at the hospital while she waited for her mother who was undergoing a test, about the casual invitation to coffee, then dinner. Yes, she'd seen someone she knew at the restaurant. Buzz obviously recognized Guy's name.

Colin had kissed her lightly on her doorstep. Yes, that was the first time. No, except for the two occasions, she'd never seen him outside the hospital. She had no idea where he lived.

They didn't tell her. But how hard was it these days to find someone's address online?

Only at the end did they allow her to ask, "Was he killed at home? Or…or did he stop somewhere else?" Had a bullet from a high-powered rifle struck him as he was driving? As horrible as all this was, she prayed his death didn't resemble the attacks on Pete and Elliott. Because if it did…

She would have to tell these cops before they found out on their own.

"He was attacked in his own home," Officer Wilson said stiffly.

"You mean…someone was waiting for him?"

"It appears he'd been home long enough to make a cup of coffee and settle down in a home office to work on his laptop."

Had his assailant already been in the house? Hidden, so as to muddy Jordan's alibi? Oh, that made sense.

She could see the attack with painful clarity. Had he been shot first, or had a blow to his head that came from behind taken him down? Weirdly, that was the moment when grief struck like a lightning bolt. She saw him, kind eyes, handsome face, the dimple that formed in one cheek when he laughed, which she thought he did often. His stories, a quality she could only think of as joy in life.

Had he really been killed because of *her*? How was she supposed to live with that?

"The caliber of bullet that killed Dr. Parnell was the same as the bullet that killed your husband," Buzz said, and the expression in his eyes spoke for him. "What happened to that gun after his death?"

Even though she was afraid hot tears were dripping down her cheeks, Jordan held her head high and spoke with as much steel in her voice as she could summon. "I have no idea. I never wanted to see it again. That's something you should be able to look up. What's more, as a police officer, you have access to reports about Steve's death. Not a single person, from responding officers to the doctors, believed I shot him for any reason but self-defense. He had been abusive in different ways almost from the beginning of our marriage. And yes, I should have left him before it came to that, but you have no right to hear the reasons I didn't. The man you knew was not the man I had to live with."

His glare didn't soften.

She transferred her gaze to the other officer. "Was Dr. Parnell...beaten, too?"

Wilson's expression sharpened. "Yes."

If they threw her in jail, what would Mom do? But she had to tell them. They'd inevitably find out anyway.

"I told you I don't know where Colin lives." *Lived.* "Except to save my life, I have never committed a violent act in my life. But..." She took a deep breath. "I think his murder may have to do with me."

Chapter Five

The interrogation that followed was a nightmare. It made her realize how incredibly lucky she'd been with the detectives in Walla Walla. They, at least, started as impartial. Once Detectives Shannon and Dutton heard from the Storm Lake PD, though, their opinions about her would probably do a one-eighty.

Thinking of them, Jordan asked, "Shouldn't I be talking to a detective?"

The two men exchanged a glance. Wilson answered, "In a small department like this, we all step into major investigations. I'm...expecting a promotion to detective anytime, so I'm sure the chief will leave me on this anyway."

It wasn't him she wanted to get rid of. It was Buzz, who made no pretense of hiding his opinion of her.

She had her chance when he asked an especially offensive question. Rising to her feet and completely ignoring him, she looked at Wilson.

"As you may have gathered, your partner holds a grudge against me because he was friends in high school with my husband. Apparently—" now she allowed herself a scathing glance at the jerk "—he still believes because Steve was a football star, the life of the party and a popular man on campus, he couldn't have had a darker side. I will not speak with Officer Bussert again."

Buzz said nastily, "What makes you think you have any choice?"

She raised a hand, her gaze once again on Officer Wilson, who stood, too. "I won't talk to anyone again without having a lawyer present. I did not commit these crimes. As I told you, I believe I've been stalked on and off all these years by someone who blames me for my husband's death. Someone—" she made this stare incinerating "—who has a lot in common with Officer Bussert."

Officer Wilson winced.

"Yet you kept no evidence of that stalking," Buzz sneered.

"Now, you'll have to excuse me—"

"Wait! You said you'd give me the names of the investigators in Walla Walla and their phone numbers. I'm sure I could track them down, but…"

"Give me a minute." She hustled into the house, careful not to let the screen door slam, grabbed her phone, and pulled up the names and numbers by the time she was back out on the porch.

Wilson scrawled the info on his pad. "Thank you. I'll be in touch."

At least he'd said *I* rather than *we*. She kept her mouth shut, just watched as they retreated to their patrol unit and drove away. Then she waved a weak hand at a neighbor who was out raking—but mostly watching the excitement—and retreated back into the house.

No, a sob was building in her chest. She'd wake her mother. She hurried out the back door, a hand clapped over her face. Only after she dropped into a bench as far from the house as possible did she let the wail erupt.

"I'M NOT REAL happy about this," said the Storm Lake police chief, Tom's new boss. His call had come in while Tom was packing his last possessions to vacate his condo, which he'd let out for the next year. "Even though we're past the tourist season, we need you fully on board, but this case is a strange one."

Hip and thigh aching, Tom pulled up a barstool that he was leaving for the young couple moving in. "Tell me about it," he said.

Chief Guthrie had decided it was ideal that Tom would be moving into town now, knowing no one. "Place this size, we couldn't usually pull off any kind of undercover operation. But the house almost across the street from the suspect is up for rent. Decent place, too—you might want to stay in it."

Tom had done a couple of undercover stints in his career and hated both of them, so his first feeling wasn't positive. That said, this might give him a little longer before he had to participate in any hard physical operation—say, a search and rescue.

So he made an inquiring noise.

The facts Guthrie presented about a woman who seemed to leave dead men behind everywhere she went created a strange picture in Tom's mind. The chief wasn't kidding. Jordan Hendrick, age twenty-eight, had married right out of high school. The husband had allegedly been abusive. She'd shot and killed him to save her own life. In fact, she'd spent days in the hospital recovering from the damage he'd done to her in that struggle.

"At the time, I believed her story," Guthrie admitted, before continuing.

She moved away, first to Great Falls, Montana, then to Walla Walla, a smallish city in eastern Washington, staying off the radar until roughly three years ago. At that point, a man she'd just started dating was killed in an apparent home invasion. Five months ago, she started seeing another lucky guy, who after the second date was attacked and nearly killed in his own home. The investigators there couldn't pin anything on her but were uneasy. Her mother had a stroke, and this Hendrick woman rushed home to take care of her. Unlikely she'd had time for any social life at first, the chief said, but just recently, she'd gone out with a doctor from the hospital. A week later, they had dinner— and he was attacked and killed in his own home later that same evening.

"We have no witnesses, no trace evidence leading to her, but I'm not a real big fan of coincidence," Chief Guthrie said. "We don't have a ballistics report back yet, so we don't know if the same gun was used here and in Walla Walla. The detective I spoke to there said different guns were used in the murder of the one man and the attempted murder of the other."

Coincidence didn't sit well with Tom, either. Still, a woman in her twenties made an unlikely serial killer. Unlike the classic black widow, she apparently hadn't gained a thing from any of these deaths. She claimed a stalker but had zero proof. Somehow, she'd never been disturbed enough by the strange messages left on her doorstep and in her mailbox over the years to bother calling 911 to report any of them.

The two men threw around the possibility she'd left behind other victims who hadn't been linked to her. There were some big gaps in time to be accounted for.

"It was hiring you that gave me the idea," Guthrie said. "You'd be in a good position to watch her. Not saying you should push it too far, but with a little luck, you might make friends with her. I can't think of any other way to be proactive."

What he meant was, at thirty-four, Tom was close enough in age to their target to potentially appeal to her. In the end, Tom agreed. It sounded like a soft assignment, but intriguing. After ending the call, to give himself something to go on, he looked up Jordan Hendrick's Washington State driver's license, since she didn't appear to have gotten one in Idaho yet, but the photo didn't tell him much. Blond hair— although he squinted and wasn't so sure that was quite right, brown eyes, five feet five, 120 pounds. Weight on a driver's license was almost always about as accurate as a carnival psychic's predictions. She was a pretty woman, he thought, but given the quality of DMV photos, he couldn't even be sure about that.

He had a feeling Chief Guthrie was hoping for more than a casual friendship sparking between his new detective and this black widow. If he could persuade her into a date or two, a trap would be a logical tactic.

Then he'd only have to worry about surviving a relationship with Jordan Hendrick.

JORDAN IDLY NOTICED a moving truck in the driveway of a house on the other side of the street that had been vacant and for sale since she'd come home. Men unloaded, but she didn't catch sight of anyone who was an obvious new homeowner. No children were running around, anyway. She didn't see a woman.

She wouldn't have paid any attention at all if not for her mother, who could hardly wait to find out all. Mom knew everyone on the block, and despite Jordan's new notoriety, most of them stopped by to chat when Mom was out front or dropped by with offerings of baked goods on a pretty regular basis. Mrs. Chung, a tiny woman in her eighties who was almost as ardent a gardener as Jordan's mother, had been the first to visit her in the hospital.

They'd all carefully stayed neutral where Jordan was concerned, for which she was grateful. Despite rampant gossip, in the days following the murder, they continued to stop by for her mother's sake. They smiled even at Jordan, commented on the weather or asked in low voices how her mother was really doing before spending time with Mom. But Jordan knew *they* knew she was being investigated by the police, and neither they nor she could ever forget that.

The facade of normalcy was almost unbearable.

The Storm Lake police had made it clear they expected her to stay put and available. Not like she'd flee anyway; she couldn't leave her mother. What she knew was that her life had taken another hard left turn. Steve's death, she'd come to terms with. But what happened to Pete Schroder, Elliott, Colin was a horror that weighed on her every waking minute.

Whenever she had an idle moment, she tried to remember everyone who might possibly be responsible for trying to set her up as a murderess, but how could she separate the burning stares that might have held hate from the snubs that might have grown into more if she'd stayed around? Then there were the doubtful glances, the avid ones, the... She shuddered every time she circled through her memories of those expressions, those faces.

She would never dare again have even a friendship with a man. Unless and until the police identified and arrested the killer—and how likely was that when they focused on her?—the future she'd still sometimes imagined, in which she had a husband and children, had faded from sight like an oasis in the desert that never had been real.

Desperate for occupation, she began to wish there was more to do in the garden, but she'd already divided perennials. With it now November, in the next few weeks she could plant more bulbs, but that was about it. The next big job wasn't until March when she'd be pruning roses for the first time in her life. If she wasn't in jail by then.

She'd started running again but could only do that when someone was here with Mom. Today was relatively balmy for the season, so she'd put on a parka but didn't bother to zip it, and sat on the porch with a book on her lap. With fragmented concentration, she was easily distracted by the sight of a man emerging from the house recently visited by the moving truck. He gave her something new to think about.

He walked down the driveway, his head turned as he seemed to ponder where he wanted to go, and then he ambled along the sidewalk toward his next-door neighbor, going up to knock on the door. He disappeared inside for long enough to suggest he'd sat down for a cup of coffee. When he reappeared, he progressed to the next house on his side of the street.

Jordan rolled her eyes at her nosiness, but what else did she have to do? Once Mom was up from her nap, she'd want every detail Jordan could glean about this new neighbor.

On a block occupied mostly by senior citizens who'd been in these houses as long as her mother had, this guy stood out by his youth alone. Youth being relative. Jordan guessed him to be in his early to midthirties. He was also tall, broad-shouldered and…not quite handsome, at least from this distance, but something. Quintessentially male, she decided—and, after all, she had plenty of time on her hands to watch him. She'd have guessed him to be athletic except that his walk was noticeably stiff even though he didn't let whatever bothered him shorten his long strides.

After sitting on the porch with Mrs. Chung for an interval, he apparently caught sight of Jordan, because he strode across the street directly toward her, his gaze intent on her.

She didn't move, just waited until he reached the foot of the porch steps. Short, unruly brown hair and piercing blue eyes added to her impression of a man who didn't have to be model-handsome to catch any woman's eyes.

She wouldn't let *any* man catch her eye.

"Hi," he said. "I just moved in across the street."

There was no reason not to be polite. "The moving truck made you the talk of the neighborhood. People were starting to wonder if the house would ever sell."

"It didn't. I guess the owners gave up. I'm renting, although if I like my new job and the town, I have the option to buy." He paused, looking up at her. "I'm Tom Moore."

"Jordan Hendrick. This is actually my mother's house. You may not see much of her, because she's recovering from a stroke and still doesn't get around very well. I'm in town to take care of her."

He smiled, planted a foot on the bottom step and leaned a hip against the railing. "She's lucky you could drop everything and come home."

He had a deep, resonant voice that Jordan did not want to find appealing.

"Mom's always been there for me," she said simply.

He nodded as if he understood.

The pause became a little awkward. Obviously, he was in no hurry to move on. It appeared he didn't yet know he was speaking to a murder suspect. She'd have to thank Mrs. Chung and Mr. Griffin later for not giving him a heads-up.

"What's your new job?" she asked.

"I'm with the county parks. I moved here from San Fran-cisco, a city I enjoyed, and which has fantastic parks, but like your mother I'm recuperating, although in my case from an injury. The hills in San Francisco, not to mention the beaches, challenged my physical capability. I thought this would be a change of pace, and I could look forward to some hiking and climbing down the line. Maybe take up cross-country skiing."

She didn't feel like she should ask *how* he'd gotten hurt. He could volunteer that if he wanted her to know.

When she didn't comment, he finally withdrew his booted foot from the step.

"I'll let you get back to your book. Just wanted to intro-duce myself. If I can give you a hand anytime, I'm close by."

"Thank you, but we have a constant stream of health aides and therapists of one kind or another coming and going."

"You an only child?"

Her mouth tightened, but she saw no reason not to say, "Yes."

She was being rude not to take him up on his conversa-tional gambits, she knew she was, but Jordan wasn't trying to make new friends, and particularly with a man. *Any* man.

A flicker in his eyes told her he knew she was just wait-ing for him to go away, and he bent his head. "I may see you around."

"I'm sure you will," she said, sounding stilted.

He studied her for another few seconds, smiled faintly and turned to walk away.

Message sent and received.

WELL, HIS FRIENDLY introduction had pancaked. Ms. Hen-drick was not receptive to a new neighbor who wanted to become buddies. Tom would like to think she'd been as aware of him as a man as he'd been of her as a woman, but he was honest enough with himself to admit he had no idea. The whole conversation had been forced.

She was probably wondering why a guy his age was trying to get chummy with all his neighbors. Which was actually a good question. He'd never done more than nod with most of his neighbors in the tall brick warehouse in San Francisco that had been converted to condominiums. A guy his age met people at work, bars or the health club.

He had to assume she was watching, which meant he went on to talk with an old guy next door who either needed hearing aids desperately or didn't bother wearing them when he didn't expect a caller. After tearing himself away and bellowing, "Nice to meet you!" Tom crossed the street and let himself into his own new home.

He'd brought most of his furniture, but that familiarity didn't make the house feel homey. Furniture wasn't in the right place. Neither were light switches, or the dishwasher, which was strangely placed an irritating distance from the kitchen sink.

He liked the era of the house—1940s, at a guess, along with the others on this block. There was a solidity to it. If he were really to buy it, he'd want to do some serious remodeling, though, starting with the bathrooms. It might be worth spending the money, at the very least, to get a plumber out here to replace the showerhead so he could have a satisfying shower.

Tom sighed and walked far enough into the living room to allow him to stand mostly hidden by the drapes but be able to look across the street and down one house. He thought his target hadn't moved.

Frowning, he mulled over his impressions of the woman. *Stricken* was the first word that came to mind. As he'd

approached, he had the impression she wasn't really reading. She looked like someone emotionally paralyzed. That
could be true whether she was guilty of these crimes or not.
Being under scrutiny by law enforcement wasn't a lot of
fun. There were plenty of times he'd done his best to lay
on the pressure, waiting for his suspect to crack.

Tom winced. Wasn't that what he and Max had done
with that last investigation? Jared Smith had cracked, all
right, and come out firing.

Tom thought what he'd seen in her eyes was pain, but
he couldn't put any weight behind what might be a trick of
the light. Preliminary impressions were just that.

Fortunately or unfortunately, he wasn't sure which, he
could say with certainty that she was more than pretty. The
delicacy of her features hadn't been shown to best advantage in that DMV photo. Her slender wrists and graceful
neck made him think she was fine-boned overall. He'd been
right about her hair, thick and shiny, sort of a streaky dish-
water blond that she wore bundled in a knot on the back
of her head. Curves, undetermined. Her brown eyes were
more caramel than dark chocolate. He felt sure she hadn't
worn any makeup at all, and in his opinion didn't need it.

He didn't like the complication of having his body stir
just because he was picturing her. On the other hand, he
wasn't good at faking attraction, and he couldn't expect a
reciprocal response without laying it out there.

Frowning at where she sat, still unmoving, he tried to
decide a next step. Asking her out…yeah, no. As a renter,
he was expected to keep up the yard, but it was pretty bare.
Casual encounters would be tough. He had no flower beds,
like the ones that wrapped her house, and several of the
others on the block, too. He definitely needed to rake the
leaves blanketing the lawn out front, which would make

him visible from her house, but he'd save that for tomorrow. Actually, a couple of old fruit trees in the fenced backyard had dropped most of their leaves, too, but he'd be out of sight working there.

He had to keep active, Tom reminded himself. He'd brought weights and a treadmill, and was thinking of buying a rowing machine, too. If there were any indication Ms. Hendrick belonged to a gym, he'd have taken that route, but Chief Guthrie said no. Maybe she'd turn out to be a runner, and he could casually meet up with her.

His main intent was to stay alert so he could be sure she wasn't slipping out once her mother slept come evening. He doubted that would happen, given the police scrutiny, but he bet she hated feeling watched.

His number one priority was making sure she didn't notice that she had a new watcher—right across the street.

And he needed to be patient. There was no big hurry here, not unless she got involved with another man.

Chapter Six

Didn't it figure that Mom decided she had to meet the new neighbor?

"We should do something to welcome him," she declared—or at least that's how Jordan translated her speech. "Bake cookies."

Bake cookies. Okay, she couldn't misunderstand that.

"Mom, I'm sure it's not necessary."

Her mother firmly disagreed. Taking a casserole or cookies to a newcomer was part and parcel of belonging in this neighborhood.

In fairness, Jordan had seen others on the block knocking on Tom Moore's doorstep and handing him something.

All she could do was make a face behind Mom's back before pulling out a cookbook with familiar tattered pages.

Snickerdoodles, she decided, after determining she had all the ingredients.

The baking part actually turned out to be fun. She let her mother do everything she could while seated, even if that took way longer. A double batch meant they could enjoy home-baked goodies. Uh, not that they'd been short of them thanks to Mom's friends and neighbors, but still.

Once the cookies had cooled and Jordan had climbed on a step stool to unearth some round tins with lids to hold them, Mom also announced that she wanted to walk over to deliver the "welcome to the neighborhood" cookies.

"Mom! That's farther than it looks."

Her mother's facial muscles had recovered enough to let her almost raise an eyebrow. And it was true that the therapists were encouraging her to walk. Jordan checked to see that Tom Moore's big black SUV was parked in his driveway. Probably his single garage was too small for a monster vehicle like that.

Today was chilly enough, Jordan bundled her mother up as if she were a toddler, threw on her own parka and led the way. The first obstacle was crossing the threshold with the walker. That the recently built ramp was at the back of the house meant it took them a good ten minutes to reach the front walkway.

Down the driveway, onto the street. The pace slowed. Taking mini-steps, Jordan looked from one direction to the other and hoped no teenager would rocket down their block right now.

"Doing okay, Mom?"

"'Course."

Okey doke.

The new neighbor must have glanced out a window because he appeared on his porch, grabbed a rocking chair and carried it down to the walkway. Evidently sharing her concern, he turned his head sharply at the sound of a car engine not too far away, but no vehicle appeared.

He called, "I hope this means you're coming to see me, Mrs. Hendrick." Smiling eyes met Jordan's. "And you, Jordan."

"We are. Mom, this is Tom Moore, who I told you about." She touched her mother's back. "Let's get out of the road, why don't we."

Mom shuffled forward. Jordan noticed how, without making a big deal out of it, Tom moved in close on her mother's other side, probably as ready to grab her as he was. That was...nice, she couldn't help thinking.

Mom sat with obvious relief and a little help in the chair he'd provided.

"I can get something for us to sit on——" he began, but Jordan shook her head.

"Ground's fine for me." She did hand over the tin of cookies. "Snickerdoodles. I hope you like them." She sat cross-legged on the cold but fortunately dry grass.

"I love them." He sat, too, but stretched out his long legs. He grinned. "Friendly neighborhood. I may have to let out my belt if people keep bringing food."

He asked her mother how long she'd lived here, and at least pretended to understand her answer. Jordan stayed, watchful, to one side. Mom struggled to ask something, and he told her he'd never been to Idaho until a week ago; he'd grown up in northern California—McKinleyville in Humboldt County, which Jordan recalled had once been famous for illegal marijuana farms—then gone to college in San Francisco and worked there ever since.

He opened the tin of cookies and offered them each one. Mom took one with apparent pleasure. She tended to dribble crumbs when she ate, but Tom gave no sign of noticing. Fortunately, Jordan had a tissue in her pocket.

She broke up the party so they could be home by the time an occupational therapist arrived. Tom looked quite seriously at her mother and said, "I'd be glad to drive you."

"Supposed to walk," Mom told him—minus the first syllable.

Again, he clearly understood and said, "Then let me

walk you two home. You have quite a garden, Mrs. Hendrick. I wish I'd seen it when all those roses were in bloom."

Somehow, he managed to continue gently chattering as Jordan's mother labored along at a snail's pace. He admired the ramp, and suggested they add an arch over it by spring. "With a climbing rose, it'd look like it's been here forever."

They parted at the back door on a cordial note, Jordan relieved when he left with that long, confident and yet slightly stiff stride. Could he possibly be as nice a guy as he seemed?

Jordan was disconcerted by her suspicion. Of course there were decent men out there. That didn't mean she wanted anything to do with one who showed up on her doorstep.

Now all she had to do was listen to Mom talk about what a gentleman he was, and how perhaps they ought to have him over so he and Jordan could get to know each other.

Not a chance. The very fact that she found Tom Moore to be attractive—never mind his *niceness*—punctuated the importance of keeping her distance. Really, that shouldn't be a problem now, with him apparently having started work. He'd soon find friends.

What she should do was quit sitting out on the front porch.

Twice in the next week Tom saw Jordan heading out for a run. The second time he was able to change to sweats and athletic shoes in time to trail some distance behind, waiting until she'd circled to head back to finally catch up with her maybe half a mile from their homes. He didn't mind the hanging back part, given that he had plenty of time to appreciate how good she looked in stretchy women's running pants and top. He'd been right about her build—long, slender legs could give him plenty of fantasies, and he liked the curvaceous hips just as much, although they wouldn't serve a dedicated runner.

They were fine by him.

Once he stepped it up, she heard his approaching footsteps, looked over her shoulder and half tripped before catching her balance. She appeared startled to see him, and not really pleased, but slowed down when he did and asked civilly, "Don't you have to work?" Her face gleamed with sweat, but she wasn't gasping for breath which meant she was in decent condition.

"I'm doing some work remotely." He was intensely relieved to slow from a jog to a walk. He pushed through pain every day but didn't enjoy it. "I'm…not so much the guy you'll see mowing the grass at the park or cleaning the public restrooms." He grinned. "Can't say I mind that. I'm mostly in administration, which means endless reports. The county is like any form of government—they're fond of rules and regulations. I'm acquainting myself with all of them and issues the parks department has had in the past as well as ideas for expansion." He paused, glancing out of the corner of his eye at her. "I'll be called out for any public disturbances or crimes, too. If you see me carrying a weapon, that's why."

"Oh." She didn't look at him. Had she just slotted him into place with the cops who were making her life miserable?

Officer Wilson and Deputy Chief Bowen, recognizable to Tom from photos, had stopped by together twice this week, keeping the pressure on but learning nothing new. Tom had no idea how much Jordan's mother knew. He hoped not much.

"If my truck is in the driveway and you want company on a run, give me call," he suggested. "In fact, how about

I give you my phone number in case you need a hand with your mother?"

Her glance struck him as suspicious, but she took out her phone and entered his number. She had to know that if her mother took a fall in the middle of the night, say, he could get there quicker than anyone else.

They parted ways, Tom smiling, Jordan merely nodding. He'd believed he'd made some inroads the other day, when she and her mother visited, but Jordan must have been faking it for her mother's sake.

This was his investigation now, but the department was pretending he didn't exist. He was working remotely, all right, reading every scrap of information he could find about her.

Yesterday, he'd killed hours researching violent crimes that occurred in Great Falls, Montana, during the couple of years she'd lived there. A city of over 60,000 people, Great Falls was impacted by a lot more tourism than he'd have suspected given the distance from Yellowstone to the south and Glacier National Park to the northwest. The police department and county sheriff's department stayed plenty busy, he determined, but he also hadn't hit on any murder or violent assault that jumped out at him. He might circle back later, but had decided to take a look at the couple of years she'd stayed here in Storm Lake before moving away, and her first year in Walla Walla and then the two-year gap between the deaths of the two men so far linked to her. He assumed the Walla Walla investigators were doing the same, but he preferred to do his own research. In fact, he felt some uneasiness about the competence of his new department.

Call him credulous, but he was having trouble envisioning her as a killer. He kept seeing patience and tenderness with her mother. The small touches that spoke louder than words. He'd felt some tightening in his chest that was unfamiliar.

He was also perplexed as to how to build trust between himself and Jordan. She was conspicuously *not* hanging out on the front porch anymore. Four days after the cookie delivery, he succeeded in setting out on a run only minutes behind her, but when he caught up, she came right out and said, "If you don't mind, I like running alone." After a pause, she did make an effort to soften the rejection. "It's the one time my mind can free float."

"I understand that." That might even be true, but he suspected that wasn't why she'd slapped him down. "See you," he added, and turned on the afterburners to leave her behind.

When he passed a small neighborhood park, he turned to round the block it occupied and saw Jordan continue on ahead. Probably running to the lakeshore and maybe a distance beyond it. The minute she was out of sight, he slowed to a walk and bent over with his hands on his hips.

Damn, damn, *damn*. He felt as if his left femur had snapped—again.

Walk it off, he told himself, and did. He chose a route that wouldn't intersect with Jordan's and finally was able to ease into a jog again. Yeah, he definitely wasn't ready to run a perp down, unless it was a six-year-old who'd just lifted a candy bar from a convenience store.

The chagrin he felt for the slowness of his physical recovery might be the cake, but Jordan Hendrick had supplied the icing. His ego insisted her attitude had nothing to do with *him*, and everything to do with her predicament. Unfortunately, he couldn't be sure.

He'd gotten home and showered before he saw her walk

into sight and head up to the front door. A minute later, a smiling fellow came out, lifted a hand and left in a sedan parked in the driveway. He looked familiar and was presumably one of the aides or therapists that came and went.

Tom brooded. Maybe this wasn't going to work. So far as he could see, the pressure the cops were applying wasn't working, either. She was a strong woman. So strong, he'd like to know what had happened in her brief marriage.

He'd read the reports from first responders, including the eventual interviews with her, and he'd seen the photographs. The one of her brutally battered face sickened him. He reminded himself that she had only been nineteen and in the marriage for a year and a half. Teenagers weren't famous for common sense. Hadn't she felt she could turn to her mother?

He didn't think it'd go well if he dropped by and asked, "Hey, can we talk about your marriage? Didn't end so well, did it?"

To cap an unsuccessful week, he was out in front raking up what he hoped were the last leaves from that enormous maple when a police car pulled into her driveway. The front door of the house opened, and Jordan stepped out. She looked straight at him, and for a long moment that look held. He couldn't be sure from this distance but thought her cheeks reddened. She turned to Officer Wilson and didn't let herself so much as glance at Tom again.

Damn. Now she knew he knew if he hadn't already. Unless he pretended to worry and knocked on her door later to ask what was up, and imply he'd be glad to listen?

That little fantasy lasted about five seconds. She'd hold her chin high and say, "This doesn't concern you," followed by, "No, thanks."

What he'd do was keep investigating without talking to

her. He'd spoken once with a Walla Walla detective. Since then, he had thought of additional questions. Surely it had occurred to those investigators that, if she were a killer, there might be other victims?

So far, he hadn't dared talk to anyone here in town, in case his name got back to Jordan. He was itching, though, to get a better idea why she didn't seem to have friends who welcomed her back to town. There might have been red flags about her personality all along that had been ignored. And what about her dead husband's friends and family? He bet they could give him an earful. As it was, the only relatives he knew about for sure were the mother, sister and brother. Small town like this, there might be others.

For now, he'd keep his cover here in Storm Lake. With time, Jordan might soften. Given the apparent lack of friends, if she were innocent, wouldn't she be desperate for someone to listen, to maybe believe in her?

Here he was, ready and waiting to be that guy.

WHAT DIFFERENCE DID it make that Tom Moore must now know what police suspected about her? She hated the humiliation that washed over her when he saw the cops arrive and his eyes widened. It wasn't as if he was anything more to her than a new neighbor who disturbed her for reasons she refused to analyze. So what if he immediately concluded he'd associated with one of the rare female serial killers?

The police were leaning hard, but it hadn't occurred to Chief Guthrie that including the deputy chief would just get her back up. Wilson was too young to have been around then, but knowing Bowen could have been in a position to see her unconscious and battered made her skin crawl now. Plus, Steve had really liked the man, who had stepped in some once Steve's dad died. They'd gone hunting together but took their trophies to Steve's mother instead of Jordan, who couldn't have dealt with a dead deer or a wild turkey complete with feathers. Of course, that was a small town for you. She knew several other of the officers from school, or because she'd gone to school with their kids.

In the next week, she tried harder not to notice Tom when he set out for a run or washed that big black SUV in his driveway even though it already looked shiny to her. She should probably do the same to her mother's car, and hers, but that would leave her exposed out front, where anyone could see her and wander over for a friendly conversation.

Better not.

Mom had become more time-consuming, not less, as she became more active, her natural determination and stubbornness surfacing. She became testy when Jordan hovered. She had enough of that from the therapists and the aide who still didn't think she should shower by herself. She could handle enough tasks now, she thought she ought to be unsupervised while she did so. Jordan could only be grateful that November had brought plunging temperatures. If it had been high summer, Mom would have insisted on working in the garden, and just try to stop her! As it was, she watched like a hawk while Jordan planted bulbs, handing out a few at a time because only *she* knew what she wanted where.

Mom's garden, she reminded herself. *Not mine.*

Mom didn't like the row of pillows that kept her from rolling out of bed, either.

"I feel like I'm in a crib," she complained.

Increasingly, Jordan found she'd kicked a couple of them onto the floor by morning. Mom was getting stronger by the day now, but slowly, not by great leaps. Jordan understood her frustration. She'd started demanding to see the bills, too, and didn't appreciate having them withheld. *If anything was likely to give her another stroke*, Jordan thought, but really, Mom's insurance had covered a surprising amount.

Even so, Jordan was starting to think it might be a good idea for her to find a job. Mom wouldn't be going back to work anytime soon, and one of them should bring in some income. Oh, no—at what point would Mom lose her health insurance?

Thank God she owned the house outright.

Jordan had barely fallen asleep one night after her usual hour-plus of worrying when she snapped awake again. What...?

She frowned at the darkness. Mom hadn't cried out. No, she'd heard a thud. Something hitting the side of the house, or someone falling.

Pulse accelerating, she leaped from bed, stumbled over the rug and regained her balance before she reached the hall. If it was Mom, she hadn't turned on a light. Jordan switched on the light in the hall. She immediately saw her mother's bare feet and legs lying on the floor just inside the bathroom.

"Mom! Oh my God, what happened?" She rushed forward to see her mother lying on her side, absolutely still on the bathroom floor. Blood ran over her face and darkened her newly washed and styled hair.

It was all Jordan could do to straddle her mother's body— no, no, to straddle her *mother*—and to search for a pulse. For a frightening minute, she couldn't find one, but then did. It seemed...steady, but her mother was unconscious.

Had she had another stroke? Or overestimated her strength and fallen? It appeared she'd bashed her head against the toilet going down.

911.

Jordan scrambled backward and raced into her room, snatching up her phone and dialing with a shaking hand. The woman she spoke to projected calm.

"If you'd like to stay on the line…"

"No." Tom. He'd come. However resistant she'd been to him, she knew he'd come.

He answered on the third ring, voice muzzy.

"My mother fell… Or…I'm not sure. This is Jordan," she remembered to explain. "Across the street. I…actually don't know why I'm calling you."

"Have you called 911?" Was that clothing rustling in the background?

"Yes." Tears seeped from her eyes. "I'm sorry. I shouldn't have—"

Any vestige of sleep had left his deep voice. "I'm on my way."

He ended the call. Jordan hurried to stand by her mother's feet, then realized she'd have to let the medics in anyway, so she raced to the front door and flipped the dead bolt just as a knock hammered on the door. She flung it open, and Tom stepped in.

The next instant, his arms were around her and he gave her a hard hug that was immensely reassuring for no reason she could determine.

Because someone else is here, she decided. *I'm not alone.*

"Down the hall?" he asked, and she nodded.

Without another word, he moved fast. Jordan left the front door wide open despite the cold air rushing in and followed. She found him crouched in the bathroom, obviously taking Mom's pulse with his fingertips. He abandoned that to gently probe her head. He must have some medical training. Maybe that was a requirement for people working in parks.

Seeing Jordan, he said, "She's definitely developing a bump. Until she wakes up, there's no way to determine whether she just got too ambitious and fell, or whether she had an attack of dizziness, or—"

"Another stroke," she said dully.

She'd been hearing a siren, she realized, which grew in volume. Within minutes someone rapped on the open door. "Hello?"

"Back here," Tom called, and feet sounded on the steps.

Jordan retreated out of the way. When the pair of EMTs or paramedics or whatever they were came in sight carrying packs of equipment and a backboard, she stepped into a bedroom.

"It's my mom. She's been recovering from a stroke. I don't know what happened. She's supposed to ring a bell if she needs to get up in the middle of the night."

"All right."

Tom stepped out of their way and went right to Jordan's side. She didn't resist when he wrapped an arm securely around her again, or when after a few minutes he said, "We'll want to follow them to the hospital. Why don't you get dressed?"

She looked down at herself wearing a sacky T-shirt and faded flannel pajama pants. At any other time, she'd have been embarrassed. As it was, she snuffled and backed away. "Yes. Of course. Thank you."

The medics took her mother out with stunning speed. Jordan had barely donned jeans and a sweatshirt when they passed in the hall. Mom looked so frail Jordan's fear ratcheted up.

She heard Tom saying something about them being right

behind the ambulance. She pulled on socks and thrust her feet into a pair of boots she could zip, then rushed to the living room.

The siren still wailed when she reached the front porch where Tom waited. Lights on the rear of the ambulance receded. Neighbors had come out on their porches, but she couldn't acknowledge them.

"Wait," she said. "I have to get Mom's wallet with her insurance card." Her own bag with her keys, too.

She found both quickly. Still on her porch, Tom displayed no sign of impatience. "Let me drive," he said. "You shouldn't when you're so rattled."

Oh, heavens—he sounded like Detective Shannon. He was right, though. In retrospect, she didn't know how she'd made it so many miles home with her thoughts racing and only a couple of phone updates to let her know that her mother was still alive.

Now…she tried to calm herself. "I can make it on my own," she said. "I'm…okay. But… I'm really glad you came. Thank you."

Those blue eyes never left her face. "You're welcome. I'm not letting you do this alone, either."

"You hardly know us," she argued, even as he watched while she locked the door, then hustled her across the street.

He simply bundled her into the passenger side of his massive vehicle without bothering to argue. The engine roared to life, and she huddled there, grateful. So grateful.

Chapter Seven

In the excruciating hours that followed, Tom barely left her side. His presence felt...surreal. Who was he? Why was he here? He couldn't possibly *want* to be. Could he?

And yet, at some point, she realized he was a sturdy bulwark she'd never had before. Not once did she see so much as a flicker of discomfort in his eyes. For a stranger, he had a remarkable ability to figure out what she needed before she did.

Most of the time, they sat side by side on chairs in the waiting room. His feet stayed square on the floor. He didn't fidget the way she did. When he moved, it was to get her a cup of coffee, or to lay a strong arm around her shoulders when he guessed she was close to shattering.

A doctor or nurse appeared a few times to pull down a mask and give them an update.

"We don't believe she had another stroke," was the first and most heartening.

"Our worry is that she could have broken a hip."

Oh God; something else to terrify her. Recovering from a broken hip could take months that would set Mom's recovery back immeasurably.

"No broken bones," was the next report, "but she hasn't regained consciousness. We'll do an MRI as soon as the staff get in."

Regional hospital or not, it wasn't huge. They probably didn't need MRIs run in the middle of the night very often.

Nodding her understanding, Jordan felt herself sag. This time, when Tom wrapped her in a reassuring embrace, she let herself lean into him and shed a few tears against his sturdy shoulder. What would she have done without him?

Called one of Mom's friends, she supposed. Bonnie would have come in a heartbeat, for example, but she'd have needed to talk and talk…and a hug from her wouldn't have been the same.

Maybe, Jordan thought, she'd isolated herself from old friends more than she needed to. The thing was, their lives had moved on, and she'd been conscious of how little they had in common with her on those occasions she'd encountered one or the other at the grocery store or post office.

She could just hear herself say, *You haven't been interviewed by a police detective? Why, you haven't lived until that happens!*

Plus, she bet the few female friends who weren't married could go out with a guy they'd met as many times as they wanted without condemning him to death.

Speaking of police…she wondered why Tom hadn't asked about the cops he'd seen on her doorstep. Or did he already know from neighbors or people at work?

More people filtered into the waiting room when morning arrived. Jordan kept a wary eye out for anyone who looked familiar. What if Steve's mother had some health blip and Kevin brought her to the ER? Oh, Lord—she'd been lucky not to see either of them so far. Of course, that would be because she left the house only to accomplish essential errands, and to drive Mom for checkups and tests here at the hospital.

And to run. But why would Kevin Dunn be in her neighborhood by happenstance to see her go by? One thing she had done when she first came home was look him up to be sure he didn't live nearby.

Unless he knew she was home and was keeping an eye on her? Creepy thought. He and his mother and plenty of Steve's friends had made it known that they believed Jordan had murdered her husband, who would never have attacked her. Not the sainted Steve Dunn.

She sighed, made herself straighten, and went back to staring at the closed double doors she had yet to be allowed to go through.

TOM HAD FORGOTTEN he was a cop, far less a detective investigating this woman, from the minute her call had pulled him from sleep. He had hated hearing how frantic she was. Given that he had medical training to deal with many emergencies, he'd shot out of bed and across the street. Seeing fear in those warm brown eyes that had to be genuine, he wouldn't have left Jordan's side even if their acquaintance was as casual as she believed it to be. She needed someone, and he found he didn't at all mind being that person.

She smelled good. Shampoo, maybe, but he liked the sweetness. He'd come close to burying his face in her hair several times during the night. He liked her slender bone structure, the generous breasts he was careful not to inadvertently glance at, and the strength that ensured every time a medical professional appeared, she sat or stood straight up on her own.

He wondered if she questioned her decision to trust him this far.

They'd sat together in near silence for a lot of hours when she turned those troubled eyes on him and asked, "Are your parents alive?"

He hesitated long enough for her to say, "It's none of my business. You don't have to—"

He interrupted. "I don't know."

Her eyes widened. "How can you not know?"

"I grew up in the foster care system. There are plenty of us in this country who did."

"But...weren't you told about, I don't know, your mother at least?"

"They guessed she was a teenager who couldn't keep me. I was dropped at a fire station. Since I was obviously premature, I had to stay in the hospital for a couple of months. There were concerns that I'd have ongoing health issues, which kept me from appealing to adoptive parents who wanted a baby."

Her mouth fell open. "That stinks!"

She wasn't thinking of her mother now. Maybe that's why he forced himself to go on, talk about something he usually kept to himself.

His mouth twitched in a half smile at her vehemence. "You're right. It does. I also understand. When people have a child with problems, they usually deal. Taking on one that isn't yours is different."

Jordan snorted.

He laughed. "It wasn't that bad. After a few short placements, I ended up in a really solid foster home for years until my foster dad had an early heart attack. One of those things where he just dropped dead on an outdoor basketball court where he was playing a pickup game. There was a flaw in his heart, and it kicked in."

Her gaze hadn't once left his since he started talking. "How old were you?"

Had she even blinked?

"Twelve."

"Oh." She seemed to wrench her gaze away at last. The pause drew on long enough, Tom began to think it was up to him to fill it, but then she said, "That's how old I was when my parents got divorced."

"Tough age."

"Is any age good to lose your father?" Anger and something else infused her voice.

The background info he was given hadn't mentioned her father. Now he wondered whether that gap didn't hold critical insights into her psychology.

She shook herself. "Oh, I don't know why I started this conversation."

"Hey, what else do we have to do?" He managed a wry smile. "It's...natural to think about your parents when one of them is in the hospital." The way his foster father died, he'd only attended the funeral. "Did you keep seeing your father?"

"No. I never saw him again, and he didn't even really say goodbye." She was back to staring at the doors into the ER, but probably wasn't actually seeing them. "I...grieved for a long time. I built him up into something he never was. It took me forever to admit that he hadn't been that great a parent." She shrugged. "He became a long-haul truck driver, which meant he was gone a lot. That would have been okay if he'd been more *present* when he was home, but he tended to drink a lot of beer and watch sports. Maybe it was different when I was younger, but...I don't remember. I'm pretty sure he wasn't much of a husband, either. I guess one day he just announced he could find a better berth between hauls and walked out."

She did turn her head then, and the pain in her eyes was very apparent. "Mom never faltered, and I always knew it was for *me*. I know how lucky I was. Because...because she tried so hard, I felt protective of her, too. You know?"

Tom didn't say anything—platitudes wouldn't help—but he took her hand and held on. That was one question answered. She could well have felt she had to hide the problems in her marriage from her mother.

"I can't lose her." Her eyes swam with tears for only the second time of the night. "I can't."

"Hey." He bent far enough to kiss the top of her head. "Here's the doctor again."

"Oh, God." Jordan swiped frantically at the tears and straightened. "Dr. Pratt?"

This time, the middle-aged woman was smiling. Jordan shot to her feet, but the doctor came to them and sank down in a chair.

"I'm glad to say, your mother has regained consciousness. Aside from the concussion itself, she has a headache and some bruises, but that's all. We want to keep her for at least another twenty-four hours, but you can come back and see her now if you'd like."

"Please." Jordan quivered like a deer in that second before it sprang away.

Weariness on her face, the doctor laughed. "Only you," she warned, and Tom nodded his understanding.

Jordan whirled to face him. "I should have thought of this. If you want to go home, I can—"

"No, Jordan." He took her hand again and squeezed. "I don't mind waiting. Take your time."

The shimmer of tears in her beautiful eyes gave him a kick in his chest. Damn, he had to watch this. If she found out—no, *when* she found out—there'd be no forgiveness, even though tonight hadn't been about his job at all.

Uh-huh. He hadn't volunteered information on his own background just so she'd open up about her own? That wasn't about the job?

Weirdly, he wasn't sure it had been, but she wouldn't believe that, would she?

He felt a little sick as he watched her walk away and disappear through those doors.

JORDAN WALKED ALONG when her mother was moved upstairs to a room. She'd gotten used to the physical damage from the stroke, but now her awareness of Mom's fragility shook her.

She tried to hide that. When her mother grabbed her hand—the one Tom had held for so much of the night—and said in that slurred voice, "I was so silly! All I did was make more trouble. I'm so sorry!"

"You have no reason to be sorry," Jordan said sternly. "I don't want to hear it. You're a smart woman who thought she could do something as simple as go to the bathroom by herself. You just haven't adjusted to your muscle loss. And with the help of all those evil therapists working you so hard, you'll regain your strength before you know it."

"If I just hadn't worn my slippers. One of them got tangled up, and…"

Jordan vaguely recalled seeing a slipper lying in the hall. The other must be in the bathroom. "How about we buy you a new pair that aren't so floppy?"

A sound startlingly like a giggle came out of her mother. "*I'm* floppy!"

A laugh burst out, and the two of them kept laughing long enough to let go of some of the awful tension.

Mom settled down after that and was asleep within minutes. Jordan sat there for another twenty minutes, but she felt guilty about leaving Tom waiting, and anyway… She was exhausted.

She slipped out in the hall and told the nurse who'd

settled her mother that she was going home for a nap but would be back this afternoon.

Then she went back downstairs and found Tom in the same chair, seemingly engrossed reading something on his phone. When he heard her footsteps, though, he looked up with a smile.

"Everything okay?"

"Yes!" Then she made a face. "Except I need a nap."

"You and me both." His grin presumably wasn't intended to be sexy, but she couldn't help noticing the way it deepened a crease in one cheek and flashed even white teeth. Foster kid or not, he'd obviously had excellent dental and orthodontic care.

Or had been born with perfect teeth.

She had to be giddy.

The daylight startled her when they got outside. He rested a hand on her back as they walked out to where he'd left his truck in the parking lot. She noticed the contact, but it felt normal after the last twelve hours when he'd been touching her much of the time.

His hand *almost* touched her butt when he boosted her up into the passenger seat before slamming the door.

When he got in, she said, "Why do you drive something so humungous?"

His sidelong grin was even sexier, if that was possible. "Because I like big trucks?"

She blew a raspberry.

He laughed. "I bought it new after I accepted the job here. It seemed sensible for hard winters. Looks like a fair amount of snowfall is the norm."

He was right. She should upgrade her tires.

Warm air barely had time to start blowing before they pulled up to the curb in front of her house. He turned off the engine as she reached for the door handle but turned to face him.

"I don't know how to begin to thank you."

He shook his head. "I'll walk you to your door."

"You don't need—"

He hopped out before she could finish her sentence and circled around to meet her. "Feeling better?"

"Yes!" She was going to crash anytime, she knew she was, but right now she buzzed with giddy energy. "I want to dance!" A tune came to her, and she started to hum "I Could Have Danced All Night," from *My Fair Lady*. She didn't remember the rest of the lyrics, but she held out her arms as if she had a partner and began to twirl across the driveway.

To her astonishment, Tom bowed formally and held out a hand. "May I have this dance?"

Laughing, she laid her hand in his, and they began to waltz, albeit in a very confined space. Only for a few minutes, but her heart had swelled by the time they slowed, and he smiled down at her.

"You can waltz."

"Took ballroom dance in college." This smile was more wry. "To impress a girl, of course. Haven't done it since."

"Most people our age don't." Wow. She had to blink to bring the world into focus. "Thank you again. I think I need to lie down."

He ushered her to her front door, kissed her forehead and gently pushed her inside.

She was crossing the kitchen when it occurred to her the front door hadn't been locked. No wonder, in the frenzy of getting out of here. She did lock it behind her, thinking only about her bed...until she saw it. She froze in the doorway, staring. The covers were pulled invitingly back…and a butcher knife lay on the pillow.

She rushed to search the house, including her old bedroom upstairs. Once sure she was alone, she fell to her knees in front of the toilet and surrendered to the nausea.

Afterward, she considered photographing the scene, but what was the point? She could so easily have set this up herself, who would believe her? So she returned the knife to its place in a drawer in the kitchen, changed the sheets, dragged a chair from the dining room to brace her room door, and fell into bed. She'd think about this later.

Along with the fact that anyone at all could have seen her dancing on the driveway with her handsome neighbor. How could she have been so careless?

TOM MANAGED TO sleep for a few hours, but was awake to watch from his front window when, midafternoon, Jordan drove away, presumably to the hospital. A part of him wished he was going with her, but of course that was ridiculous. Unwise, too. He'd felt more for her since that middle-of-the-night call than he could afford. It wasn't like him to feel these stirrings.

Black widow, remember? Lures men into her web, then kills them.

He believed that was true even less than he had before. That said, he couldn't forget that plenty of general scumbags—*and* killers—also loved someone. Jordan obviously didn't blame her mother in any way for what happened with the husband, so her loyalty remained solid.

Last night, the cop in him had briefly wondered whether she might have gotten tired of taking care of her mother. The scene hadn't supported anything like that. Mom's only injury, as it turned out, was the blow to the head, which had clearly been from contact with the toilet. Not a very sure way to knock anyone off, and the risk was there that her mother would wake up exclaiming that she'd been pushed. Jordan had to know eyes would turn her way.

Plus, Jordan had called him and let him see her fear.

She couldn't be that good an actor, could she?

Damn, Tom hated knowing how she'd feel if she learned he had even briefly suspected something like that.

Circling back to the marriage, Tom might have doubted that the husband—Steve Dunn—was abusive, except that about six months before the blowup when she shot the guy, he'd taken her to an emergency room. Not here in town; he'd driven her a ridiculous distance to a hospital across the state line into Washington, presumably not wanting anyone who knew either of them to see her. The injuries were classic: spiral fracture of both lower arm bones on the left side—typically caused by violently twisting the forearm—along with a broken collarbone on the right side of her body as well as bruises and a burst eardrum. There had to have been bruises. It would have taken quite a blow to burst the eardrum.

Even if Jordan had lied to protect her husband, how had nobody asked serious questions and red-flagged the visit? As a patrol officer and detective, Tom had dealt with enough domestic violence to recognize the particular injuries.

Thinking about the complex, damaged woman he was getting to know, he had a feeling that any man who tried to lay his hands on her that way now would be deeply sorry. He was also beginning to understand why she'd been susceptible to abuse at such a young age.

Father walked when she was on the cusp of womanhood, probably leaving her lacking some confidence. Handsome, popular guy wants *her*—of course she'd be dazzled. Then the slow progression to turn her into an abused wife—a slap, a blow, apologies and even gifts, a teenage Jordan dazed enough to wonder if it all wasn't her fault.

What she'd said tonight had given him a clue about why she hadn't left the guy early on and gone home to mommy. Pride, first. Who wanted to make their first big decision as an adult and have to admit within months that it had been a whopping mistake? But worse, in her case: she wanted to protect her mother from upsetting news. She'd likely been afraid her mother would blame herself because of her own failed marriage and the impact it had had on her child. No, Jordan had told herself she could deal with it—and maybe she'd even believed that, if good ol' Steve was still apologizing and doing his best to convince her that theirs was a love match, he'd just been under a lot of stress, it wouldn't happen again.

By the book.

Unless, Tom thought, *I'm fooling myself because I like the woman.*

Entirely too much.

Yeah, her marriage had been a disaster, but it sounded as if she'd given the man she'd initially loved every chance. Tom's reaction to that was complicated, given that he'd spent a lifetime wondering why his biological mother hadn't made even the smallest effort to keep him.

He was usually good at detachment, necessary for a homicide detective and coming naturally to a kid who'd been tossed around in the foster care system. If he'd ever needed it, it was now.

He had to reserve judgment. Investigate, instead of trusting what information he'd been given. Try to draw Jordan in, sure, but only because he was undercover for that express purpose. Any kind of relationship would not end well, no matter how his investigation turned out, but he couldn't worry about that. Instead, he'd take ruthless advantage of the opening her mother's fall had given him.

He'd start with a call this evening, a simple *How's she doing?* Couldn't go wrong with that.

He shook off the memory of sweeping Jordan around in a briefly magical dance and paced off some of his restlessness. Time for some PT, he decided, including weights. A dose of pain and suffering might get his head in the right place, too.

Chapter Eight

Jordan had never fallen into friendship so fast. She wouldn't even let herself *think* that it might be more. Unless and until the police, here or in Walla Walla, arrested a killer, she could never *have* more. She wasn't even sure she was capable of more.

Yet Tom was just *there* when she wanted to talk. After Mom's doctors decided to keep her a second night, he insisted on coming with Jordan to pick her up the next morning—although they took her car, given the height disadvantage of his SUV.

Jordan hovered closer to home for a few days, but once the awful bruise on her mother's face began to fade and she insisted the headache was gone, running seemed like a good option to de-stress and get out of the house. She hesitated the first time, but it would be rude not to call Tom and find out if he wanted to come, wouldn't it? Honestly, she was surprised he was home—he seemed to work remotely most of the time—but, after all, an increasing number of Americans did work remotely these days.

She'd actually looked up the parks and recreation department to find there were a whole lot more parks than she'd realized, including trails, picnic grounds and ball fields. The rangers apparently had the power to issue anything from a ticket to taking someone in custody for a misdemeanor offense. Who knew? She didn't see his name listed, but the site probably hadn't been updated recently.

The air was crisp and cold when the two of them set out. Their breaths puffed out in clouds. It seemed to her he was moving with less stiffness, although she could tell he hurt by the time they got back to their block. Whether it was true or not, Tom insisted doctors and physical therapists assured him that running was a good exercise unless he pushed it to the point of excessive pain.

"Oh, I've had plenty of PT," he said ruefully. "Your mom and I have more in common than she knows."

After all he'd done, it seemed only decent to invite him to dinner.

As they trotted to a stop mid-street between their houses, he gave her a surprised glance.

"You sure? I don't want to make more work for you."

"I cook every night. I won't guarantee fine dining."

His devastating grin came close to buckling her knees given their already weakened state. "I'm not a fancy guy."

"But you know how to waltz," Jordan teased.

He laughed as he walked away.

She'd never tell him that she'd put more effort into the meal than she did on an average day. Mom ate like a bird, so cooking for her benefit wasn't very satisfying.

Jordan felt uneasy when she watched Tom approach from across the street and come up to the front porch even though there was no reason anyone would think he was here for her. Whoever hated her so much couldn't be watching *all* the time, and neighbors had always come by this house even before Mom's stroke.

Unless they'd also seen him running with her.

We're not dating, she told herself firmly, and let him in before he even had time to ring the doorbell.

She felt as if she were in a lull—maybe the eye of the hurricane would be a better analogy. Every time she opened the mailbox, she expected to find a rattlesnake coiled and ready to strike, but nothing threatening came. Until the knife, the helium balloon was the last suggestion someone was watching her, and that had been months ago. If she hadn't so carelessly left the front door unlocked, she wanted to think the knife thing wouldn't have happened. Was her enemy mostly satisfied because, once again, the police suspected her of a murder? But so far, the investigation seemed to have stalled, probably because there was no physical evidence to connect her to the crime, just as there'd been none back in Walla Walla.

What would happen if this murder dwindled into a cold case? Would some guy she'd chatted to briefly at the grocery store be killed?

Or—oh, God, the nice guy who lived across the street from her? The one she'd spent more time with than she had any of the men she'd dated before their deaths?

But she wasn't dating Tom Moore, and she wouldn't. She convinced herself that's what mattered. What relationship she had with him didn't fit the pattern.

Over the course of the week, they ran again together. He showed up unannounced once, tools in hand, to work on the railing framing the front porch steps. He'd noticed one side wasn't quite solid.

"I know your mother goes out the back," he said, "but that'll change." When he was finished, he left without saying anything.

Jordan invited him to dinner again. He was all but offering to let her and Mom, too, lean on him. She owed him.

Plus, he had devoured that first meal, making her suspect he might normally subsist on microwavable meals from the frozen food case at the store.

That evening, Jordan served a spicy vegetarian chili that she and her mother both liked and added corn bread and defrosted home-baked oatmeal and raisin cookies that had come from Mrs. Welsh in the house on the corner.

As they ate, Tom asked Mom about her physical therapy. What she didn't mind doing, what she dreaded.

"Like exercising to make me stronger," her mother said after a moment. Her speech had noticeably become clearer, but so slowly Jordan was surprised in that moment at how easy she was to understand.

Certainly Tom understood her, because he nodded. "I felt that way, too, even if it hurts sometimes."

"What…happened to you?" Mom asked.

Would he answer?

His hesitation was noticeable, but finally he said, "I was shot. Multiple times." Seeing their expressions, he grimaced. "Yes, it happens to park rangers occasionally, too, especially in a big city. I approached a guy we'd been keeping an eye on. He didn't want to talk. He opened fire instead." His voice thickened. "A friend was killed, too."

Another ranger, presumably.

Her mother lifted a shaky hand and reached out farther than Jordan had known she could with her weak arm. She laid the hand on Tom's arm. He looked down, up quickly at Jordan, letting her see how moved he was, then pressed his own hand over her mother's.

"Thank you," he said quietly, that deep resonance in his voice giving Jordan goose bumps.

Once everyone had time to take a couple more bites, he

smiled at her mother. "We got sidetracked. Which PT do you like least?"

This answer required Jordan to translate, although she tried not to make it obvious that's what she was doing. "Occupational and sometimes speech? I didn't know that, Mom."

Her mother's frustration trying to explain distressed Jordan and, she thought, Tom, but the gist became clear. Therapists often assumed she didn't know *how* to do something, when in fact she did. She just *couldn't* do it because of limited physical ability. "I'm not a child."

When Jordan walked Tom to the front door, she said, "I know I keep thanking you, but I have to do it again. I never thought to ask whether she felt all her PT was useful. I'm glad you got her talking."

"There may still be reasons why her doctor will insist they keep on," he warned.

"But at least I know to talk to them." She lifted a hand and realized in horror she wanted to lay it on his chest. Curling her fingers, she snatched the hand back.

His eyebrows rose, and there was a peculiar pause, the kind where oxygen seemed to be lacking. It must be the way he was looking at her, his blue eyes so intent she had to fight the desire to sway toward him.

No, no, no! She couldn't afford a complication like this. They were becoming friends, that's all.

Suddenly, he shuttered his expression. "Good night, Jordan," he said in a low rumble, and let himself out.

She hustled to the window and watched him cross the street in reverse, his passage obvious thanks to the light at the corner.

For a second time in a matter of minutes, the very air

seemed to be stolen from her. What if somebody had let themselves into his house and was waiting?

Her rib cage tightened. She should back off. Make it coolly apparent she and Mom didn't need him.

Only, she hadn't felt alone this past week the way she had for so many years. She'd never tell him that; it would be completely normal for him to make friends through work, start seeing a woman, and as Mom regained her normal capabilities, do little more than wave at her or Jordan when he saw them coming or going.

Would it be so bad to soak in his strength and calm good nature while he offered it?

CHIEF GUTHRIE WAS of the opinion that the recent lack of the kind of threats Jordan had claimed she'd gotten previously made it pretty plain she'd made them up...or was responsible for them herself. Otherwise, why nothing since the helium balloon, which she'd destroyed and thrown away without giving a single thought to saving it to show police?

"If she has a stalker, he or she could be satisfied by the intense scrutiny Ms. Hendrick has been under after the latest murder," Tom suggested in their latest face-to-face. He'd have preferred not to chance ever being seen with the police chief, but Guthrie liked a more concrete connection.

Now pulling out his wallet to pay for the lunch they had shared at a hole-in-the-wall café, the chief grunted his dissatisfaction at Tom's point. "Just don't get soft on her."

Tom raised his eyebrows. "You seem to have made up your mind about her, which is just as dangerous."

Guthrie nodded genially at a constituent as they walked out. Only when they paused before parting in the parking lot did he half complain, "Doesn't seem like you're getting anywhere with this."

"Being undercover has advantages, but also a lot of disadvantages. I can't do any investigation into people from her past who might be targeting her. I've compiled a list from social media and started researching backgrounds, but that's the best I can do. Even if she is the black widow you want to think her, these deaths have occurred several years apart. No, the latest was, what, six months after the killing in Walla Walla? Still a break. What makes you think she's going to change that? It wouldn't be smart, not when she knows you're suspicious. In fact, it might be a good tactic if your investigators appear to be backing off. If we're looking at someone besides Ms. Hendrick, he might be angry that she's not being punished the way he thinks she should be."

Guthrie scowled. "My guys won't like it, though. Everyone hereabouts has an opinion about her. But yeah, fine. They're not learning a damn thing, anyway."

Maybe because there was nothing *to* learn from Jordan? Tom carefully didn't say that. He did question whether anyone had looked into the doctor's background, as would be standard. His murder could be completely unrelated to the assault on Elliott Keefe.

The chief snapped, "Of course we did. You concentrate on the Hendrick woman. Push her a little. Dating a man is the trigger, for her or for someone else. You're ideally situated, just the way we planned."

"And she's wary."

"Tempt her then!" Guthrie walked away.

Irritated, Tom watched him go before going to his own vehicle. *Tempt her.* Damn it, *he* was dangerously tempted by *her*. The identification of the killer aside, the idea of setting himself up to be shot again had a cooling effect every time he thought about doing something as foolish as kissing the woman. What's more, that felt like crossing an ethical line that repelled him.

Growling under his breath, he headed over to his office at the parks department. The one he'd been assigned to maintain his cover, just as everyone who worked there knew to take messages for Head Ranger Moore.

So far, there'd been not one. Even the local newspaper remained unaware of a new hire who didn't actually do anything except spend time on the internet in that otherwise pristine office.

He brooded for a while about the pushback he was getting from the chief. *Everyone hereabouts has an opinion about her.* What did that mean? Had Guthrie included himself? Tom sure wasn't satisfied with what details from the investigation he'd been fed. Or maybe it was more what *hadn't* been done or had been left out of reports. Whatever Guthrie claimed, this department hadn't seriously considered the possibility that Jordan was a secondary victim. Because that meant the killer was a local? One of those people who had "an opinion about her"?

He didn't see Jordan or her mother that evening, although he kept an eye on the lights in their house. When he'd first moved in here, he hadn't thought there was a chance in hell that Shelly Hendrick had any chance of truly recovering from what had clearly been a devastating stroke. Now, he was impressed by her. Inspired, too; he knew how hard she had to be working, how discouragement must feel like a high wall in front of her, one she had to knock down brick by brick. She was a gutsy woman, he'd concluded— as was her daughter.

He was always an early riser no matter what time he'd gone to bed. Tom made a habit of starting his mornings with coffee—and, these days, a look out the window at the Hendricks' house. He didn't know what he expected to see—A moving truck backed into the driveway? An ambulance? Fire bursting from every window?—but he had a growing sense of disquiet where his investigation was concerned.

Did he just *want* to believe she was the victim, not the killer? Max had always accused him of being too soft on women. Was it true? Tom would have given a lot to be able to toss around ideas about this investigation with Max.

Growling under his breath, Tom carried his first cup of coffee and strolled into the living room where he had the best view of the houses across the street.

The kitchen was at the back of the Hendrick house, so if the light was on, he couldn't tell. Jordan typically seemed to get up mornings as early as he did. Otherwise... He frowned.

There was...something on the front window. And the garage door?

He set down the mug on a side table, let himself out of his house and trotted at a slant toward Jordan's. He didn't like not carrying, but his cover wouldn't last long if he always wore a shoulder or ankle holster. The back of his neck prickling, he wasn't halfway when he made out the addition to the garage door: spray-painted in bloodred, all in capital letters, the single word *KILLER*.

Swearing, he switched his gaze to the glass of the front window. Smaller of necessity, *KILLER* was spray-painted there, too.

And then he saw the same word sprayed on the driver's-side window of Jordan's car.

He took the steps two at a time, pausing only long enough to touch the paint and determine that it wasn't going to wipe off easily, before he knocked lightly on the door. He hoped Jordan's mother was still asleep. Quiet footsteps approached, there was a pause while Jordan likely checked on who the visitor was through the peephole, and she opened the door.

"Tom?"

He ignored the momentary hit the first sight of her often gave him. He especially liked seeing her first thing in the morning, when she looked less closed up, softer, as if she hadn't donned her armor.

"You need to come out here," he said grimly.

Those caramel-brown eyes widened. "What…?" But she didn't finish the question, instead stepping over the threshold. Her gaze followed the direction of his outstretched hand and she saw the lettering.

"Oh God. Oh God!" She sounded frantic. "I have to clean it off! If people *see* it—"

With her horror so convincing, he hated to say this, but did. "It's on your garage door, too. And your car."

Shoulder brushing him, she ran down the stairs, almost falling on the last two. She was still barefoot, he saw, following her as she ran far enough down the walkway to be able to see both her car and the detached garage.

"Oh God," she said again. "Everybody will see. This will never end!"

"You need to call 911. I don't know what's going on here—" the hell he didn't "—but this is a threat."

Her shoulders sagged as she stared at the two-foot-tall lettering. "Yes. I'll do that." She almost laughed, but without any humor whatsoever. "For what good it'll do."

"You need to get some shoes on, too. It's cold this morning."

Jordan looked down at her feet as if she wasn't sure what he was talking about, then nodded numbly. "I'll have plenty of time before an officer responds."

He could get a faster response for her, but that wouldn't be a good idea. Instead, he walked her back to the porch and said, "I'll circle the house. Make sure the vandal didn't bother with any other surfaces."

A pained sound escaped her as she opened the door. "Thank you."

"Jordan?"

She went still, her back to him.

"You going to explain this to me?"

It was a long moment before her shoulders stiffened again, and she said, "Yes, but...not now."

He made sure he spoke gently. "Okay."

His last glance back saw her on the front porch, phone in hand.

SOMETHING ABOUT THE paint job on her car disturbed her most. The other lettering was sloppy, but this was more deliberately done; one leg of the *K* almost looked like an arrow pointing downward. She was sure she'd locked the car door, she always did, but when she tried it, it opened. Probably she shouldn't be touching the car, but—

Was that her driver's license lying facedown on the floor in front of the gas pedal? How could it be? She bent and picked it up, gave a stifled cry and dropped it. That wasn't *her* license—it was Colin Parnell's. Her teeth chattered. That it was in her car was meant to implicate her further in the murder. And, oh God, it now had her fingerprints on it.

Tom would reappear any minute. *Pocket the license...? No. Push it out of sight under the seat. Lock the door. Close it.*

She had barely done so when she saw the first police unit coming down the street. At least there were no sirens. Jordan had to be grateful for that. She'd asked, but sometimes thought cops all loved drawing as much attention as possible.

Otherwise, Tom determined there was no paint in her garage to cover the writing, so he volunteered to go pick some up, as well as any products he could find that would clean the paint off glass.

While he was gone, it seemed as if every member of the Storm Lake Police Department, from the newest rookie—who'd been the first responder—to Chief Allen Guthrie showed up to take a look. She watched, stiff as a porch upright, scared to death.

Detective Wilson—yes, he'd evidently received his promotion—and Deputy Chief Ronald Bowen finished studying—or were they admiring?—the spray-painting and interrogated her. As always, Wilson sounded almost pleasant, but with a hint of "don't think you're going to fool me" thrown in. The deputy chief balanced him by the contempt overlaid by a veneer of civility. Other people might not notice, but his attitude wasn't much better than Buzz's. She could just imagine the result if she demanded a replacement for him, too.

Jordan responded to questions by rote. No, neither she nor her mother had heard a sound all night. No, she didn't own any cans of spray paint—or cans of any kind of paint, for that matter, unless there were some old ones in the back of the garage. If they found the can of red spray paint, it wouldn't have her fingerprints on it because it wasn't hers.

Detective Wilson asked what she thought the point of the vandalism was. Beside him in the living room, Deputy Chief Bowen raised his eyebrows in challenge.

"Whoever is doing this must be frustrated," she said wearily. "You haven't arrested me. It's a nasty accusation for me, but it's also aimed at you. He clearly thinks he's set me up so well, you're incompetent because you haven't arrested me."

She could tell they didn't like that assessment. If she hadn't hidden the driver's license and locked the car door before they got here, she was chilled to know they'd have had reason to arrest her.

Tom walked into the living room as she finished.

"Mom's in the kitchen," she told him. "The occupational therapist is staying until, well, we're done."

He nodded at her, then at both cops, and went straight through the house toward the kitchen. Thank goodness—Mom was so upset by the events, she was gabbling more than actually speaking, and mad because her tongue wouldn't keep up.

Looking back at the two cops, she said, "I can't tell you anything else. Please let me go to work cleaning and painting."

They glanced at each other. Bowen grunted and heaved his weight to his feet. "I believe we have adequate photographs. Unfortunately, because your driveway and walkway are both paved and the past few days have been dry, there are no visible footprints. We haven't found the spray can, either, which isn't surprising."

She could see in his eyes what he was thinking: because they didn't have a warrant to search the house top to bottom, there were plenty of places she could have hidden an object that size until she saw an opportunity to dispose of it.

Standing to let them out, she felt exhaustion settle down on her as a crushing weight. She even swayed slightly. How much more of this unrelenting suspicion could she bear? It wouldn't stop. Whoever hated her this much wasn't done.

She stood out on the front porch for a moment, watching as the couple of remaining official vehicles drove away.

After she soothed Mom again, she'd do her best to obliter-
ate those messages. Too late, of course. She had no doubt
everyone on the block and plenty of passersby, drawn by
the police presence, had already seen the accusation everyone knew was aimed at *her*: KILLER.

A hand came to rest on her shoulder. She hadn't heard
Tom approaching, but she felt his warmth at her back. He
was being supportive…so far.

"I'll take care of the garage if you want to tackle the
window," he said.

Even though, when she turned, she saw questions in his
eyes, she said, "Thank you for staying."

He only nodded and loped toward the back of his SUV,
now parked in her driveway.

Swallowing the lump in her throat, Jordan wondered
how much he'd hang around once he heard her story…and
got to wondering which parts of it were true.

Chapter Nine

It ranked right up there with the other longest mornings of her life. And gee whiz, they were all ones when police officers had shown up at her door.

When lunchtime rolled around, she found another cause for intense gratitude. Instead of ordering out—Tom must have guessed Mom would have had trouble with pizza—he took the time to make egg salad sandwiches on soft bread in their kitchen and sliced a blueberry cheesecake Mrs. Chung brought over when she came knocking to be sure Mom was okay.

"I don't understand any of this," Mom fretted at the table, although she'd calmed down some. "How could anyone think...?"

Jordan patted her mother's hand. "The police will figure it out, Mom. It's just...a nasty trick."

It occurred to her that *she* was now treating her mother like a child—maybe had been in some ways ever since she came home—but at the moment, she didn't have the energy to do anything else.

She coaxed Mom into lying down for her nap, and sneaked several peeks into the bedroom until she was sure she was asleep. Then Jordan returned to the kitchen, where Tom had efficiently cleaned up and put the remaining cheesecake in the refrigerator.

Hearing her, he turned and met her eyes. "You look like you could use a nap, too."

Her attempt at a smile had to be pitiful. "Except I'd never fall asleep." She wondered if she'd ever again be able to relax into sleep without a care. Who knew what would happen while she was oblivious?

"Why don't we sit in the living room?" he suggested.

She desperately wanted to put this off, but knew she couldn't. Imagine how he'd wonder if she sent him home, then hustled out with a hand vac and dustcloths to frantically clean the *interior* of her car, like that was the most urgent thing she could do. No, no. The police were gone, satisfied for now. Getting the driver's license out of the car and hidden could wait.

She just wished she could forget for a second the knowledge it was sitting there, a trap with sharp teeth.

She took some deep breaths for calm before focusing on the conversation she had to have with Tom. Outside would have been better, but on the front porch they could be seen, and really, it was too cold today to sit and chat outside. So she nodded.

He sank down at one end of the sofa, and after a hesitation, she chose the other end, curling one leg up. The wing chair wasn't all that comfortable, and Mom's upholstered glider...no, it was *hers*.

Tom shifted to better face her. "This isn't really my business."

"You deserve to hear about it. Anyway, you must have heard some of the background."

Gaze steady, he said, "Not enough to put the pieces together."

"*I* don't understand it. It's... I think someone is determined to ruin my life. Only, that person has to be beyond obsessive." She couldn't keep meeting Tom's sharp blue eyes. She looked down at her hands instead. "It has to go back to my marriage. I married right out of high school, even though Mom tried to talk me out of it." Her laugh sounded broken. "Because why wouldn't that be a good idea?"

She skated over the abuse, because she didn't want this man to see her as someone who'd put up with it. Jordan did tell him, briefly, about the disastrous scene where she'd truly believed he would kill her if she didn't kill him first. When she pulled that trigger.

"I was in a coma for twenty-four hours, in the hospital for days. Eventually I learned he'd been fired from his job that day. He…seemed to be in trouble at work a lot. He didn't like to be told what to do, and he had a hair-trigger temper." This laugh wasn't any better. "How could I not know this about him? But I didn't. The thing was, at school, he didn't care much about grades and shrugged off the bad ones, and the football and baseball coaches worshipped at his feet. He really was a talented athlete, but he didn't get recruited by any top colleges. I wonder if they could tell by his grades that he didn't have the discipline they would expect? I don't know. *He* wasn't going to play for some second-tier program that might be willing to take him, so he went to work in construction right out of high school. I don't think he expected the comedown from being admired, girls flirting, guys wanting to hang out with him." She gave a short laugh. "This is a small town. Everyone came to games. I vaguely remember seeing the mayor and most of the members of the police department in the stands, or slapping Steve on the back in congratulations after a game. Everyone wanting to blame *me* for what happened isn't a surprise."

Tom didn't comment, just listened.

She shrugged awkwardly. "Our marriage started great—I thought so, anyway—then went downhill. There was one big blowup, and I was prepared to leave him, but he cried and begged me not to. I had no idea that's the way it goes with men like him. I believed he had it in him to change if I forgave him and stood beside him."

"Did you talk to your mother?"

She blinked away the water in her eyes. "Not the way I should have. In fact...most of it, I didn't tell her. Anyway, not everybody in town was convinced that I had to shoot and kill Steve, even though none of the responding police had any doubt. I was...hurt really badly. But afterward, I'd see these looks. Later, a few people came right out and said hateful things. I tried to avoid running into anyone in Steve's family, or any of his teammates and best buddies. Even with friends, I could see doubt. That's why I finally moved away."

She told him about the couple of years in Montana, getting most of an AA degree but scraping by financially, deciding to try somewhere else and moving to Washington State. "I finished the AA, started taking a few classes with a goal to eventually get a bachelor's degree, and was lucky enough to get on with the post office. The pay let me have a decent place and be able to tell Mom honestly that I was okay and didn't need financial help."

He nodded. She waited for him to ask what she'd majored in, tell her what *he'd* majored in—he had to have a degree for his level of work, didn't he?—but he didn't offer anything.

For an instant, Jordan wondered why she was being so open with him. Chances were good he'd pretend to believe her side but pull away. Why wouldn't he? Everyone else had.

But what was she supposed to do? Say, *See, three men I got involved with were attacked, two are dead, and the police think I did it.*

"I didn't date for years after...you know."

"You didn't trust men?"

"Or myself." She shrugged awkwardly. "Maybe mostly myself. How could I? I married a man who, when he was in a bad mood, thought of me as his punching bag."

Tom's mouth tightened.

"After I moved to Walla Walla—I guess that was the first time I stayed put and didn't apartment hop—I started having some weird stuff happening. Bouquets delivered on the day Steve died. Some creepy cards. I figured Steve's brother or one of his closest friends—maybe even his mother—was holding on to enough anger to need to lash out. It wasn't like they needed to remind me. How could I ever forget that day?"

She waited a little anxiously for his nod of understanding, which comforted her more than it should.

Then she continued, "But a little over three years ago, a nice guy asked me out. I wasn't really attracted to him, but, see, that made him safer. We had two very casual dates. I doubt he'd have suggested we go out again. It was kind of a mutual shrug. Except, three or four days after we had dinner, he apparently walked into his house when some men were stripping it. He was beaten, shot and killed. A detective talked to me a few days later, but briefly. It seemed pretty obvious what happened, although there's never been an arrest."

"So they didn't associate the attack with you."

"There wasn't any reason to. I think there'd been some other similar home robberies. The homeowners just didn't walk into the middle of it. As far as the police were concerned, I was just someone who knew Pete." She sighed. "Maybe a year later, the creep campaign stepped up. Every so often I'd have this feeling someone was watching me. There'd be raps on my windows. The letters and bouquets, of course. My car got keyed. Just enough to keep me on edge."

"I didn't try dating again for three years. Elliott was a Realtor. He started flirting with me when I dropped off mail, and when he asked me out, I thought, why not?" She met Tom's eyes even though he probably saw her despera-tion. "I'm ashamed to say I wasn't so much interested in him as I wanted to feel *normal*. I was a twenty-eight-year-old woman with hardly any social life."

When the man who'd gone from neighbor to, maybe, best friend so quickly reached out and took her hand in his, she gathered strength from the contact.

"We had dinner once. The next week we took a picnic to the city fireworks display. I'd driven myself, so we parted ways in the parking lot. Next thing I knew, two detectives are on my doorstep. Elliott had gone home and been at-tacked. Maybe shot first, they're not sure, then beaten. Po-lice think he was left for dead. He was in a coma for days, but he did survive and recover. Unfortunately, he doesn't remember anything that happened. But my name popped up associated with the victim whose attack was similar."

Tom frowned. "Except for the burglary."

"Right." *Get this over with*, she told herself. "The detec-tives in Walla Walla pushed pretty hard, but they couldn't place me at the scene because I didn't even know where he lived, and we hadn't dated long beside that. They didn't let up, though, because they had no leads at all. In the middle of all that, Mom had her stroke and I came home. Those two detectives called a couple of times after I came home, but…they were mostly decent."

He nodded.

"Then, just recently an ER doctor who'd treated Mom when she was first taken to the hospital asked me out. I knew I shouldn't say yes. I *knew* it." She was probably crushing Tom's hand. "But I was still deluding myself. I kept telling myself the attack on Elliott didn't have anything to do with me. How *could* it?"

Emotions, or maybe thoughts, flickered over Tom's face. "Anything else going on back when this Elliott was attacked?"

"Yes, but I was big in denial about that, too. It was one of those weeks when I felt like a spider was crawling up the back of my neck. I kept whirling around, but there was never anyone there." Then she told him the rest of the weird stuff.

"I'm sure it goes without saying that the detectives there weren't interested in any of that."

"And here in Storm Lake? Have you noticed anything like that?"

"I get the creepy-crawlies sometimes, but people are always staring at me. Steve's death was like the biggest tragedy and scandal in Storm Lake history. There was plenty of controversy—he'd had so many friends, or really fans—that everyone thought they knew him. Football star, champion baseball pitcher? Prom king, knocking a woman around? Steve Dunn? Everyone thought I had to be lying. So I've been slinking around avoiding people I knew in high school or while I was married." And doing her best to avoid looking anyone in the eyes. "And remember, for the first month or two, I pretty much lived at the hospital. I ate three-quarters of my meals in the cafeteria. I wasn't on public display until Mom improved enough to come home and I actually started heading out on a regular basis to the grocery store, the pharmacy, the plant nursery, and working in plain sight in Mom's garden."

"I take it that brings us to the murder of the doctor. Colin Parnell?"

"Yeah. We had coffee, then a week later, dinner. He was killed that night after he got home."

Tom's gaze sharpened in a way that made her uneasy. "Someone was waiting for him?"

"They don't know, except whoever it was got into his house somehow. After arriving home—they also haven't figured out whether he went straight home or not—he apparently had time to make himself comfortable. He got a cup of coffee and was on his laptop in his home office. So it could have been half an hour after he got home, or two hours." She frowned. "Maybe the medical examiner nailed down the time closer than that. Like they'd tell me. All *I* know is that, bang, I'm the central suspect. One of the two cops who showed up the first time was a teammate and buddy of Steve's. He made his feelings about me crystal clear."

"I hope you pointed out that he was seriously biased."

"I did." She grimaced. "Not that Deputy Chief Bowen is much of an improvement. No, he is. He isn't rude, at least. I was going to lawyer up, but I haven't. What's the point? I didn't do it. I had no idea where Colin lived. I didn't know him that well. Except...he was funny and *nice*. He didn't deserve that. No one does. I can't keep my head in the sand anymore. I have to accept that he died because of *me*. Pete, I don't know. And thank God Elliott survived. But of all people to be killed, Colin was a compassionate doctor who followed how Mom was doing long after he was responsible for her. Why him?" She shook her head. "I have to believe now it was because I went out with him. He barely pecked me on the lips when he walked me to the door that night. There was no big romantic or passionate scene to make someone mad. It just doesn't make any sense!"

No, IT DIDN'T. Seeing her emotional fragility, Tom wanted to tug Jordan across the cushion that separated them and wrap her in his arms. Instead, he had to keep that distance. She'd expect him to maintain some doubt and might even be suspicious if he announced he was completely on her side and ready to fight the world for her. He had to hold back for his own sake, too. Because he had a job to do.

He had to *prove* this woman hadn't attacked any of those men. And that wasn't easy to do, mainly because they hadn't found the forensic evidence they needed either to clear her or point to other suspects. That was unusual in and of itself.

These attacks had to be meticulously planned after Jordan showed interest in a man. They were damned cold-blooded, and also clean. The killer knew how to avoid shedding trace evidence—although thanks to the plethora of cop shows and thrillers out there, everybody had some idea what not to do. Still, Tom didn't like the idea that one of Steve's best buddies was a cop who'd have learned on the job everything he needed to know to accomplish the perfect murder.

"Back to Elliott—?"

"Keefe."

"He doesn't remember whether his assailant appeared as soon as he walked in the door?" Shouldn't have used the word *assailant*, he thought, but she didn't seem to notice.

"No. He remembers parking in the garage, then going into the kitchen. After that, nothing. The head injury was bad enough, it could have wiped out hours from his memory. He wasn't discovered until the next day when he didn't come into work for some appointments." Jordan's forehead creased. "Why do you ask?"

"Just struck me you'd have had to drive like a bat out of hell to beat him home and be waiting for him."

"If only a neighbor had *seen* something. Maybe Colin would have survived, too, if he'd been found right away."

Given what Tom had seen in the autopsy report, there'd been no possibility of that. He only made a sympathetic sound.

He asked more questions, delving into the creep campaign, as she described it.

Her mouth twisted. "As things turned out, you don't know how much I wish I'd called the police. But…can you imagine what kind of response I'd have gotten? An anniversary card that you take as subtly threatening given the date you received it? Mightn't you have an admirer sending the bouquets, ma'am? Or could someone be expressing sympathy? One of your own knives left out on your counter? How can you be positive you weren't thinking about something else and took it out for some reason, then got distracted?" She made a soft, pained sound. "Even if I'd kept those notes, what are the odds they'd have any fingerprints on them except for the mail carrier's and mine? From the attitude I'm getting from police officers, they'd be sure I sent them to myself so I'd look innocent." She disentangled her hand from his and sat up, putting both feet on the floor. "The police want to blame me. They might as well be wearing blinders. Plainly, I can't trust that they'll really investigate without bias. In fact, I can't trust anyone wearing a badge. No matter what happens, I may never be able to again."

She might as well have punched him. It was all he could

do not to reel at the blow. She didn't know she'd taken aim against him, but she'd hit her target all the same. Tom couldn't even blame her. He had the impression from his couple of conversations with the detectives in Walla Walla that they really were looking for other possibilities. Chief Guthrie wasn't. He'd hired Tom to go undercover because he was so damn sure she was a killer. Tom wished he'd understood sooner how biased the police chief was. He might not have taken the job, or at least not agreed to go undercover.

Now…he wouldn't go back for a redo. Jordan too badly needed someone on her side—or at least impartial.

He turned his thoughts back to the latest event. Whoever had painted that word on Jordan's house and car last night was getting impatient. But was that because he believed passionately that she was guilty? Or was the killer trying to influence the local police department because she deserved to be punished for what he saw as a crime she'd gotten away with?

The obvious was the death of her husband. But even with family, it was hard to imagine anyone fixated enough on his or her grievance to be willing to murder several people in hopes of sending Jordan to prison. Steve Dunn had died almost nine years ago. Long time to hold on to this level of rage.

Tom still believed that was exactly what was happening, but had to circle back to the hard reality that nailing down her innocence to everyone's satisfaction wouldn't be easy. It was one of those conundrums: proving someone had done something was a snap compared to proving they *didn't*. That was the very reason the US justice system insisted on the concept of without a doubt.

If he succeeded, he could be Jordan's hero—until he confessed to lying to her from the beginning.

She was withdrawing before his eyes. In fact, she rose to her feet and said, "You've wasted a lot of time on us. I appreciate it, but I won't keep you anymore."

His stomach coiled. *"Wasted?"*

"Thank you for being here again today, but I think you should go home. You do have a life."

No, actually he didn't. As things stood, *she* was his life, but he could hardly say that. What he did say was, "Don't hesitate to call," and left because that's what she wanted.

IF MOM'S ROOTS weren't thirty years deep in this town Jordan positively hated at the moment, she would have seriously considered packing Mom up and moving with her. Selling the house, finding a community where not a soul knew them.

Peering through the blinds at a car that slowed down in front of the house before abruptly speeding up, she thought, *Uh-huh.* Because starting over had gone so well for Jordan before. If someone hated her enough to kill men he didn't even know, probably hadn't met, he could find her anywhere.

Anyway, she had a number of blessings to count. Number one on her list would be Mom's many friends who kept rallying around, whatever they thought about Jordan. The hospital and care workers had been amazing, too.

Tom Moore was on that list as well. Higher than he probably should be given what a short time she'd known him—and how much about him she didn't know—but from the night Mom took that fall, he hadn't failed her. How could that not scare her?

Thank heavens, the next morning she saw him back out

of his driveway and his big SUV disappear. Jordan wasn't sure how much longer she could have waited.

She told her mother what she was up to—minus her actual motivation—then assembled what she needed to detail the interior of her old car, unlocked all the doors and the trunk, and set to work. She searched the trunk first, in case another little surprise had been left for her, then vacuumed the thin carpet that covered the wheel well.

Classic avoidance: she started with the back seat, ashamed of the trash she'd ignored, then took out the floor mats, and vacuumed thoroughly.

Front seat, passenger side next. Ditto. More vacuuming, and she used a spray bottle and clean cloth to clean the door and dashboard.

She'd just wiped the glove compartment when she thought, *can't skip that*. Fortunately, there wasn't a lot in it except for the official papers, a flashlight and a few receipts.

By this time, her heart was hammering. Around to the driver's side. What if the license was *gone*? No, that would negate the whole purpose.

She took out the floor mats, shook them and vacuumed them, then groped under this seat, too. The first thing her hand touched on was Colin Parnell's Idaho State driver's license. For an instant, she let herself look at his face. He was one of those rare people who looked good in a DMV photo. Along with his warm smile, a hint of humor showed in his eyes.

Jordan shuddered and whisked it into her jeans pocket.

Just to be thorough, she kept searching. There was less trash here; she supposed she too often tossed receipts, paper napkins, whatever, on the passenger seat. But then she touched something stiff that might have kept the seat from sliding on its track if she ever had reason to move it.

She knew, even before she pulled it out. Another driver's license, this one from Washington State. Elliott looked straight at her from the photo.

Chapter Ten

Had this license been left on the seat, too, right after Elliott was attacked, but she'd hopped in with her arms laden and unknowingly brushed it off? Thank God there hadn't been any evidence that would have allowed those detectives to get a warrant. Why hadn't anyone ever said that each man's driver's license was missing? Maybe Elliott hadn't noticed until way later and hadn't associated it with the assault, but *someone* should have seen that Colin's was missing from his wallet.

She pushed this license into her other pocket, hurriedly finished her cleaning job, and dashed inside.

Who would believe her if she admitted finding these? But she shook her head instantly. Nobody.

The next question was, where best to hide them?

Because it had momentarily crossed her mind that Tom was the one person she might be able to talk to, she set about avoiding him. She waited until she saw him leave in his huge SUV before she set out to run, and once she pretended not to hear the doorbell when she knew it was him standing on the welcome mat. It wasn't right to keep depending on him when there was so much wrong with her life. Face it: she'd become a Jonah. Bad luck followed her. No, be honest: *deadly* luck followed her.

A few days after the vandalism, a photo of Mom's garage made the Storm Lake weekly newspaper. Thank goodness Jordan had carried the paper into the house along with that day's mail before she opened it to see the front page. In black and white, the words didn't have quite the same impact, but it was bad enough. The caption read, *Vigilantism in our town?*

At least it didn't say, *A killer in our town?*

The editor wouldn't have dared. That would have been inviting a lawsuit.

The article was brief, every word carefully chosen. The writer did remind any reader who'd forgotten that Jordan Hendrick, a graduate of Storm Lake High School, had killed her husband in self-defense eight and a half years ago. They didn't say, in *possible* self-defense, but the reminder alone whispered, *A killer does live in that house.*

Jordan slumped in her chair, aware of the murmur of voices from the kitchen where a speech therapist worked with Mom, but focused on her own whirling thoughts. There was no hope of hiding the paper from her mother. Poring over every page including the classifieds was part of her routine. She'd demand Jordan go buy another copy if this week's had apparently failed to be delivered. Anyway, someone would have a big mouth.

Not like Mom hadn't shuffled out onto the porch to see "KILLER" painted on her front window anyway.

Feeling sick, Jordan bent forward and rested her forehead on the table. Would this ever end?

The doorbell pealed, and she jerked. Maybe she'd be lucky and this would be a neighbor instead of cops back for round six or eight. She'd lost track.

It was Tom on the doorstep, and he looked mad. "Did you see your newspaper?"

She smiled wryly. "How could I miss it?"

"I'm sorry," he said simply, and stunned her by pulling her into his arms.

For a moment, she stood there stiffly…but then she collapsed against him. Not to cry, just because she *needed* his strength and solid body. She flung her arms around his waist and held on for dear life. That had to be his cheek resting on her head. His chest rumbled with words she didn't even try to make out. This felt like more than reassurance.

Jordan kept clinging even as awareness of him as a man, not a friend, stirred in her. His powerful thighs pressed hers, and her breasts were flattened on his broad, muscular chest.

She couldn't let him see what she was feeling. She didn't dare *feel* any of this. But when she finally summoned the will to step away, that involved lifting her head and looking at him.

His gaze flickered down to her mouth, and she knew: he was thinking about kissing her.

And right this second, there was nothing in the world she wanted more than that.

TOM DIPPED HIS HEAD, as he'd wanted to do almost from the first moment he set eyes on Jordan. He wouldn't have been surprised if she'd yanked away, or at least pretended she didn't know what was about to happen, but instead she parted her lips and—damn, was she rising slightly on tiptoe? Yes!

Her lips were soft and sweet, the hum in her throat exciting him. He pressed and nibbled, and waited while she did the same back. And then, God help him, he slid his tongue into her mouth, rubbing sensuously against hers. He didn't sense any resistance, but she met the kiss awkwardly, as if she didn't quite know what she was doing. Had it really been so long—?

She had to know how aroused he was. His hands had been moving without conscious thought on his part. One cupped her butt and lifted her. The other had slid up to her nape. He plunged his fingers in hair as silky as he'd imagined and held the back of her head so he could improve the angle for deep, long kisses that grew in urgency.

Jordan whimpered, and he thought he might have groaned. He needed to think this through...but right now, he wasn't capable of that kind of reason.

He ground his erection against her softer body and nipped her lip. She tried to climb him. Fine by him. He could help with that—

Background voices seemed to be gaining in volume.

"You're doing so well, Mrs. Hendrick! I don't think you're going to need me for much longer."

Tom tried to process that. He knew who *he* needed, but that didn't make sense. Then, suddenly, it did. Oh, hell! He and Jordan weren't alone.

He lifted his head, made himself lift Jordan away. "Sweetheart. Your mother is coming."

Her lashes fluttered. "What?" Then an expression of horror crossed her face and she backed into the doorframe with a bump. "Oh, no! What are we *doing*?"

Stung, he said, "We kissed. That's all."

"We can't let anybody *see* us," she cried...and his brain kicked back in gear.

She was right—and not only was the therapist coming, but also judging from the tap of the cane so was her mother. Worse yet, he and Jordan still stood on the threshold. Front door wide open, *any*one could have seen them.

"No, no!" Jordan keep retreating, expression panicked,

cheeks flushed…her eyes holding both shock and the remnants of passion. He hadn't been alone in that firestorm.

"Oh, Jordan," her mother called. "Is somebody here?"

Tom said, "Just me, Mrs. Hendrick. Wanted to check on you two." Remembering suddenly what he had come over for, he looked down, disconcerted, to see that he'd dropped the damn newspaper. In fact, he'd crumpled it beneath the sole of his boot.

"Did anybody drive by?" Jordan whispered urgently. "Or…or…"

Walk by? How would he know? He'd been that unconscious of their surroundings, something that hadn't happened to him in years. Cops couldn't *let* themselves be oblivious.

A lump in his throat, he said, "I don't know. But I'm taller and wider than you are. I doubt anyone could see past me."

"It wouldn't have been hard to tell what you were doing. And you wouldn't have been—"

Kissing her mother? Yeah, no stretch for an observer to guess his partner in that steamy embrace.

In a low voice, he said, "I'm not as vulnerable as the men who'd been attacked. You know I carry a gun." Would it make a difference if he'd introduced himself as a cop from the beginning?

Sure it would have—she wouldn't have given him the time of day.

After one wild look at him, she stepped to the side, giving a less than convincing smile to the middle-aged woman waiting for them to quit blocking the doorway. "Nora, thanks for coming."

Nora beamed, said goodbye to her patient, and trotted down the porch steps and to her car in the driveway as if she hadn't noticed anything.

Jordan's mother had been behind her, and probably hadn't, either. No, she was fussing because he was trampling on the newspaper, crumpling pages.

"This is my paper," he assured her mother. "I guess I dropped it."

Jordan took a deep breath. "Mom. There's a photo of the house on the front page. You know, with the spray-painting on it. That's why Tom came over. He wanted to be sure I'd seen it."

Mrs. Hendrick stared at them in bewilderment. "Why would they put something awful like that in the paper?"

Tom glanced at Jordan, who seemed speechless, and said gently, "I guess they think it's news. There was quite a fuss here, you know. I can't remember the last time I've seen so many official vehicles in one place."

Actually, in his world, that kind of gathering was common, but usually provoked by a shooting with fatalities. He could only imagine what the scene had looked like after he and Max had been gunned down. Funny, he'd never thought to ask who had called it in. As if it mattered…except that if there had been any greater delay, he probably wouldn't have survived.

"Why don't you sit down, Mom? Our copy of the paper is on the table."

Jordan wasn't meeting his gaze, or, really, looking at him at all. Shyness? Or something else?

"Tom," she added, "thanks for telling us. It's too late for us to do anything about it, but everyone in town is already talking about me anyway." Resignation dulled her voice. She was trapped and enduring. Her only way out would be to abandon her mother, and his gut said she'd never do that. That absolute loyalty tapped something vulnerable deep in him. He'd had friends, but never anyone he knew with complete certainty would never abandon him.

He had to clear his throat. "Give me a call if you want to take a run in the morning," he said, backed the rest of the way onto the porch, gathered up the torn pages of his newspaper and left.

As he ambled across the street, pretending nothing was out of the ordinary, he scanned sidewalks, lawns, the depths of front porches. If any of the neighbors were out front, he didn't see them. That didn't mean some hadn't seen the show, then scuttled out of sight to call everyone they knew.

There wasn't a lot of traffic on this street, especially at this time of day, but casual passersby weren't what worried him. What he had to wonder was how much time her stalker was able to give to spying on her, and where he hid. At this moment, utterly exposed, Tom knew exactly what Jordan meant when she described this feeling: as if a spider was crawling up his neck.

Even more disturbing was his realization that he couldn't have staged that kiss any better if he had plotted it. Chief Guthrie would be slapping him on the back in congratulations.

After the last guy she'd dated had been murdered so recently, Tom doubted she would be willing to be seen in public with any man, even if she felt something strong for him. In fact, the more she liked him, the *less* likely she'd be to agree to a date.

Unless, of course, she was the killer. Little though he believed that, his job required him to add the usual addendum.

Either way, Tom had just accomplished much the same purpose as a date at whatever restaurant in town was most popular...assuming that embrace had been witnessed by the right—or wrong—person. Or that gossip reached that person.

There was a certain relief at letting himself into his rental house and locking the door behind him, even though somebody could be in the house already, waiting. That was improbable, but still he stooped and pulled his backup weapon. He listened to the silence before clearing the house, room by room.

He did feel just a little paranoid now. He'd already been sleeping with his gun close at hand, but he thought it might be smart to take other precautions.

Speaking of traps, he hadn't set this one…but he was very willing to take advantage of it.

TOM WAS ABOUT to set out to spend a couple of hours in his fake office before picking up groceries when his phone rang. Jordan.

"Hey," he said, going for relaxed, "you up for a run?"

He hadn't seen her leave that morning, but he'd sure as hell seen her coming back, tearing down the street as if a pack of vicious wolves was snapping at her heels.

There was a short silence. Then, "I've already been. It was weird. I thought… Oh, never mind." She drew a shuddery breath. "I'm seeing shadows, that's all."

"Why didn't you ask me to run with you?" he asked gently.

"You know why. I can't be seen with you."

He felt a wrench in the vicinity of his heart. He didn't mind being needed; he'd protect her in any way he could. He wished he believed she trusted him—even though she shouldn't.

"I'd rather you did ask me," he assured her, marveling at his calm voice.

Damn, this had him as dizzy as if he were staggering off the kind of carnival ride that was fun when you were a kid but that he wouldn't be caught dead on anymore. Up, down, all around.

He cared about Jordan Hendrick more than he wanted to admit, even—maybe especially—to himself. He could fall for her. But always, the cynical side of him that he'd learned as an unwanted kid and honed as a cop murmured, *There's no way to prove she was followed. Did she just want to throw that out there?*

"This one of those times you felt that spider crawling up your back?"

"Something like that." She chuckled, although he didn't buy it, said, "Maybe we can run Wednesday," and pretended she needed to help her mother with something unnamed.

Tom closed his eyes. He shouldn't have agreed to this. Originally, it had seemed straightforward, as undercover work went. Keep an eye on the woman living across the street from him. Befriend her if he could. Prevent anyone from attacking her even as he tried to trick her into going after *him*.

Don't feel too much.

And lucky him, his plan for the day was to spend a couple of hours in his fake office, then break for lunch with Chief Guthrie, who insisted again on a face-to-face. Fortunately, one woman without much of a social network was unlikely to hear that he was hanging out with the police chief.

JORDAN WOULD HAVE been happier not to leave the house again today, but Mom started fretting about one of her medications due for a refill.

"I forgot to ask you to call it in yesterday. I'm sorry."

"It's fine. Are you completely out?"

"No, not until tomorrow, but…" Mom would worry until she had a nice, full bottle safely tucked in her medicine cabinet.

"I'll call and then go pick it up." Jordan smiled. "Won't hurt me at all." She could go while the caregiver who helped Mom bathe was here.

An hour later, she went out to her car. She didn't see any hint of movement up or down the street. Tom's big vehicle wasn't in his driveway. She should quit noticing if it was there or not, except…she couldn't help feeling reassured when she knew he was close and would come running if she called.

The pharmacy was downtown, and she had to park a block away. Once inside, she fidgeted as she waited in line while pharmacy techs searched, seemingly in slow motion, for the prescriptions people ahead of her had come in for.

Once her turn had come and she'd paid, she glanced at her watch and realized that hadn't taken as long as she'd thought. Being on edge all the time—swiveling her head constantly to see who came in the door, who was in each aisle—seemed to stretch the minutes torturously.

Maybe she'd treat herself to a latte. Betty's Café had served nothing but plain coffee when Jordan lived here before, but was apparently doing a booming business once an espresso bar was added.

She could treat herself, even if the caffeine wasn't ideal given her state of mind. But, heck, she wouldn't get the jitters until she was safely home again.

The booths and tables were mostly occupied, she saw at a glance, not surprising at around one o'clock. She walked briskly past several tables to the bar, careful not to look at anyone.

She'd given her order and was waiting when a deep but

low voice coming from a nearby booth penetrated. Was
that Tom? Why wouldn't it be? By this time, he must have
made other friends.

Unable to resist looking, she saw only the back of his
head. But across the table from him...that was Storm Lake
Police Chief Guthrie. Uniform, badge and all. An empty
plate pushed away, he appeared intent on his conversation
with Tom.

For some reason, her heart thudded in a heavy beat. They
might know each other because Tom was responsible for
law enforcement in the county parks. They might—

"I think I've set myself up." Tom's voice filled a lull in
the overall chatter. "She'll never be willing to go out with
me—she's afraid even to run with me in case we're seen together too often, but we did have a...moment on her front
porch. If anyone was watching..."

The chief leaned forward. "A moment."

Frozen, she waited. Tom wouldn't say. He wouldn't—

"A kiss."

She didn't analyze what she heard in his voice. It didn't
matter.

"This is our chance," he said.

Behind her, the barista called, "Jordan!"

As if everything around her had gone into slow motion,
Jordan saw Chief Guthrie's gaze pass Tom to lock on her.
Tom turned to look over his shoulder and met her eyes. His
expression was appalled.

Jordan backed away. One step, another. She bumped into
a diner seated at a table, then whirled and ran.

Chapter Eleven

"Well, damn. There's a good plan down the tubes." Guthrie sounded annoyed.

Every muscle locked into battle mode, Tom just looked at him. He'd never in his life wanted more to say *I told you so*, but he did currently work for this man.

Sliding out of the booth, he stood, said, "I'll see what I can do to patch things up," took the tall cup labeled with Jordan's name from the barista and walked out.

Yeah, who was he kidding? Everyone knew that no glue ever made could patch trust, once broken.

Convince her we're on her side. Spying on her to protect her.

Stomach roiling, Tom wished he hadn't eaten that burger and greasy fries.

He drove home on autopilot. He'd try to talk to her, but then what? Start wearing his badge and gun openly, maybe walk into the police station and introduce himself as the new lieutenant heading investigations? Or would Jordan let him continue passing under the radar as far as the rest of the world was concerned?

Talk to her first.

Turning the corner, he saw her car in the driveway. He parked in his own, sat unmoving for too long, then grabbed her drink and got out. Somehow, he knew she'd hear the slam of his door. His knock wouldn't be a surprise.

That she answered the knock *was* a surprise. Her face was cold and set as she stepped out on the porch and shut the door behind her.

"Your mother is napping?"

She didn't bother responding to that. She did take the cup from his hand and set it on the broad railing. Then she crossed her arms.

"This is the last time I'll open that door for you or speak to you. I'll ask you not to try to bypass me and go to my mother for any reason whatsoever." Pure ice.

"Jordan, will you listen? Give me a chance to explain?"

"That you were hired to wriggle your way into my life and find evidence that I'm the killer the police want me to be?" She made a harsh sound. "Given their tunnel vision, I should have suspected. Are you a PI or a cop yourself?"

Voice rough, he said, "Cop. I'm a detective."

"Of course you are. Well, you can tell Chief Guthrie that I'm through speaking to you or his detectives without an attorney being present. I was a fool."

The flash of pain in her eyes had him stepping forward. "Will you listen?"

She studied him with contempt. "You've lied to me from the beginning. Every word. Why would I believe anything you say? Isn't what you're saying now a lie, too? Just a new, expedient story." She shook her head. "Please leave, and don't step foot on this property again. Do you hear me?"

"I can help you. Keep you safe." Damn, was he begging? "I don't believe you ever hurt anyone."

"But I did, didn't I?" The one sentence was both scathing and filled with pain.

"I mean it," he said to her back.

She grabbed her to-go cup and opened the door.

Before she could shut him out once and for all, he said, "Don't tell anyone I'm a cop."

Jordan went still.

"Help me keep my cover so I can catch the scum who murdered the doctor."

She hesitated before giving an abrupt nod and disappearing inside. Tom heard the dead bolt slide shut with steely finality.

FORTUNATELY, MOM APPARENTLY hadn't heard the knock.

When she appeared after her nap, she used a cane instead of the walker, demonstrating her increased steadiness. She must have brushed her hair on the way, too.

Jordan was struck again by how much she'd improved. In the absence of another feared stroke, Mom might not truly need her for that much longer.

Dishing up leftover potato salad, she wondered if it was too late to apply to the University of Idaho or other schools for fall semester to finish her BA. If she stayed in Idaho, she could claim in-state tuition and be close to her mother, too. She wanted so much to believe she had a future.

Except, moving on was a fantasy until the killer trying to set *her* up was arrested, tried and convicted.

I can help you. Help me keep my cover so I can catch the scum who murdered the doctor.

Could he? Would he?

Anger seared her. *Sure. You betcha. Mr.—no, Detective Trustworthy.*

The one who'd kissed her as if he meant it, then bragged about it to his boss because really, he'd positioned her where anybody might see and done it because a date wasn't happening, and he was getting desperate. Not desperate for *her*, but for a triumphant closure for his case.

Thank God she hadn't told him about those driver's licenses.

Her eyes and even sinuses burned, but if tears were responsible, she wasn't about to let them fall. She joined her mother at the table and helped herself to servings of potato and fruit salads she didn't want.

For the second time in her life, she'd let herself fall for a man. Jordan had to marvel at her own judgment. *Fool me once*, she thought, but she hadn't learned anything. Look how spectacularly she'd been fooled the second time.

Never again.

She went through the motions of a normal afternoon and evening. She vacuumed, scrubbed the downstairs bathroom, made and pretended to eat dinner, watched a streaming show Mom liked without hearing a word herself, showered, and helped Mom with bedtime tasks. This was why she'd come home. For now, she was needed, and always loved as long as her mother lived.

But no matter what she did, no matter how firm her vow, her thoughts spun.

How could Tom Moore live with himself? Or was that even his real name? He'd pretended ignorance about her, then listened to her story with compassion and intelligence. Fake compassion, probably real intelligence. Too late, it was easy to imagine Tom weighing her every word, slotting pieces into place and seeing the gaps. His kindness the night her mother fell. Was that real, or had he been on the clock the entire time, gloating at the chance to build trust with her?

Was he a runner at all? Had everything he'd told her about the parks been gleaned from the city and county websites and maybe a few career articles: So You Want to Be a Park Ranger. San Francisco? For all she knew, he'd visited the city once or twice.

Of everything he'd said, Jordan was most inclined to believe he'd been shot. His stiffness and grimaces of pain looked too genuine. She'd bet cops were shot a whole lot more often than park rangers.

His strength when he held her, his tact and kindness with Mom, those hurt to remember. The part she'd never forgive him for was the heat in his eyes when he looked at her. Either he had somehow faked it, which she doubted given his erection—or he'd have been happy to take her to bed because, hey, she was a woman, he was bored, why not? She'd be mad at him when she found out the truth anyway, so what was one more betrayal?

Jordan pulled down the covers and sat on the edge of her bed, exhausted but knowing what would happen when she lay down and closed her eyes. She'd keep picturing Tom's every expression, the way amusement crinkled the skin beside his eyes, the deeper groove in his left cheek when he laughed or gave her a wickedly sexy grin. His impatience with the unruly waves in his hair, his funny stories, the warm clasp of his hand.

Him.

Two nights later, she was still going through the motions. Sleep remained elusive, her dreams disturbing. About to get into bed, she heard her mother call, "Jordan?"

She found Mom dumping out the contents of the drawer from her bedside stand on her bed.

"Mom? What are you doing?"

"You know I have asthma. I suddenly couldn't remember—"

Oh God—was she struggling for breath? She was definitely breathing hard.

"Isn't it usually brought on by allergies, or when you get a cold?"

"Yes, but—I'm going to have an attack! I know I am, and I can't find my inhaler."

Jordan felt almost certain that her mother was getting worked up only because she'd suddenly thought about the asthma that hadn't once reared its head since Jordan came home, and then got to thinking about where she left her inhaler.

Almost was the key word. What if…?

Jordan joined the hunt, finding and searching her mother's purse, the bathroom, the kitchen junk drawer, between cushions anywhere Mom might have sat in the living room. Under the bed. She delved into the pockets of her mother's coats and bathrobe, checked an old purse. By the time she had to concede defeat, Mom was panting for breath.

"I'll call your doctor."

"It's the middle of the night!"

"He's part of a clinic. I bet they have someone on call. If not, we'll go to the ER."

There was indeed a doctor on call, who agreed to phone in a prescription to the hospital pharmacy. Jordan just had to go get it.

Her mother had calmed, and Jordan became even surer that this was all unnecessary, but it was also true that Mom had lost control of so much of her life. She'd definitely become fixated on her medications, as if they were the armor that kept her from disaster. Who could blame her?

"I'll call Jennifer Pierce," Jordan decided. The Pierces lived three houses down. Jennifer wasn't as close to Mom as several other neighbors, but she was considerably younger.

Getting up in the middle of the night and making it over here wouldn't be as big a deal for her as it would for Mrs. Chung, for example. "I won't be gone long."

Jennifer's husband answered the phone, and Jennifer immediately agreed to come over. He came with her and said he'd stay, too. Of course he did. After all, this was the house where an accused killer lived.

Jordan thanked them and said, "I think she's okay now, but if breathing really becomes difficult, call 911."

While waiting, she'd already scrambled into her clothes, and she hustled out now. Something moved in the darkness between the house and garage, so she threw herself into her car and locked the doors. As she stared in a vain attempt to see a person or dog or cat that might have jumped onto a garbage can, she turned on the car to warm it up.

Shivering, she knew she'd been imagining things. She did that a lot these days. She was not being watched 24/7, no matter how it felt.

Annoyed at herself, she drove the all-too-familiar route to the hospital. Fifteen minutes, she'd be home, Mom could take a couple of puffs on the inhaler, and they'd all get some sleep.

RESTLESS, TOM TRIED to stay too busy to brood. He sat at the kitchen table working on his laptop. Maybe he *should* break cover. That would allow him to seriously investigate everyone close enough to Jordan's deceased husband to hold a grudge. Given that he hadn't been able to interview anyone, what information he'd gathered from databases had been more sparse than he liked.

The best he'd been able to do today was peruse the high school's yearbooks, which were online. He'd already seen DMV and news photos of Steve Dunn, but studied these of the guy who was, as Jordan had said, obviously a star in the eyes of his classmates. In the senior yearbook, he was in at least a dozen photographs aside from his class photo. Football and baseball teams, live action photos during games, being crowned homecoming king—no sign of Jordan there, Tom noted—even student council. Chosen most likely to become famous.

Really?

The kid was good-looking in an unfinished way, buff but probably not big enough for major colleges looking for linemen, and he had a grin that would have impressed Tom more if he didn't know what a piece of you-know-what he'd turned out to be.

Of course, Tom looked up Jordan in the several yearbooks. She was just as pretty as he thought she was now, but noticeably shy, or maybe just reserved. Didn't wear a lot of makeup, didn't look polished the way more confident girls did.

Tom searched out Steve's sister and brother, too. The sister, Carolyn, was a year older than Steve. She had some of the reserve, even watchfulness, that Jordan did, making Tom wonder what her home life had been like.

Kevin Dunn was two years younger than his brother and had some of the same shine but not quite at the same level. He played football, too, running back because he wasn't as big as his brother. Not as many photos in the yearbooks. No prom crowns. Question was, did he resent his big brother, or idolize him? Or both?

Tom wondered if other people would know. Man, he wanted to talk to the guy.

He noted the names of boys on the sports teams, underlining the ones who seemed especially buddy-buddy with

Steve in candid photos. Bussert—or Buzz, according to a caption—fell into that hanger-on category.

The list he made of girls who posed with Steve, or appeared to be part of his crowd, was shorter. Tom didn't see a single picture of the great and glorious Steve Dunn with the girl he'd married months after their high school graduation.

He started by searching for information on those people in the intervening decade plus. A few popped up with criminal records, including Kevin Dunn. He'd had a couple of DUIs and been tagged for bar fights, although he hadn't actually done time. So—a short temper, like his brother. He'd worked for four different roofing companies since he graduated from high school two years behind Steve and Jordan. Maybe moved around for a better salary or because of layoffs, maybe not. He'd married a couple of years after high school, and his wife had been active on Facebook but seemed to have gone quiet, without a post in the past eight months.

Sister Carolyn was married, waited tables at a restaurant Tom hadn't yet been in, and had two children, according to her Facebook page, which was only sporadically updated.

Buzz had a sealed juvenile record, which interested Tom a good deal given his speculation about the pristine crime scenes. He'd ask Guthrie about it.

Tom starred names that jumped out at him for one reason or another. Eventually, his eyes began to cross and a headache defied the painkillers he took. He still had some of the heavy-duty stuff, which he rarely used anymore because it knocked him on his butt. Right now, he particularly had to be on his guard. If the kiss had worked as bait…

He flinched, ashamed of himself. Okay, yeah, purely by accident that kiss had presented an opportunity in this investigation. But there were things a man kept his mouth shut about, and this was one of them. Jordan had plenty of reasons to be furious, even if she didn't care enough about him to be hurt—and he thought she had been.

Damn it, he'd *known* it would come to this, one way or another, but hadn't expected that he'd feel as if he lay bleeding on the ground again. How could he have failed so spectacularly in letting himself forget that nothing between them was real? That was especially ironic, considering how stunned he'd been by a kiss that felt so damn perfect. For a fleeting instant, he'd felt as if he had held everything he could ever want in his arms.

He was afraid he knew where that had come from.

You have been given a chance to have all that. He'd known exactly what Emilia was talking about: a wife, kids, happiness. With her words in the back of his mind, had he wanted to see something with Jordan that wasn't real? The unexpected byway his life had taken might be responsible for that hollow inside that wanted to be filled.

Or had he just blown the chance he'd never expected to have?

With a groan he closed his laptop, slid it into a sleeve and then in a cupboard with pans and lids where it wasn't obvious.

He turned off the light above the stove, reached for the switch for the overhead light but frowned at seeing the only other light he'd left on was in the bathroom. He'd cleared the house, but the window locks in particular were inadequate and the one on the back door less secure than he liked.

Note to self: even if this was a rental, add a dead bolt to the back door tomorrow.

Frowning, he flicked off the light and started down the short hall to the bedrooms and single bathroom. He wondered if he'd be able to sleep at all—or whether he dared.

The air behind him stirred. If he hadn't already been in a heightened state of awareness, he wouldn't have moved fast enough. As it was, he jumped sideways and a club—no, a metal bar—slammed into his shoulder instead of his head. He started to spin while falling into the open door to an unused bedroom.

Pop.

Shot fired!

Tom dived for the floor and pulled out his backup piece, rolling to face the dark doorway. He had to see his assailant. The dark shape gave him no answer.

"Drop it!" he yelled.

Pop, pop. Suppressor.

He pulled the trigger of his own weapon. Once, twice. Running footsteps told him he'd delayed too long.

He shoved himself to his knees, intent on pursuing when he heard the back door hitting the house, but his left arm hung uselessly at his side and he staggered into a wall once he reached his feet.

He couldn't decide if the iron bar had dealt the worst blow, or the bullet. Or, hell, had there been two?

Tom carefully lowered himself to his knees again, propping his good shoulder against the wall to keep himself from going all the way down, and pulled his phone from his pocket.

Chapter Twelve

Two blocks from home, Jordan saw flashing lights. Mom! Oh, no. Had she really had a major asthma attack, after Jordan hadn't believed her? Or had worse happened since Jordan called Jennifer from the hospital?

Terrified, she strained to see. There was a police car with flashing lights in her driveway, but the ambulance was in Tom's, another police unit at the curb in front of his rental. For an instant, she didn't understand, but then a cold trickle entered her veins.

He'd been assaulted, just like the men she'd dated. What if he was dead?

Given how he'd betrayed her, she didn't expect the anguish. She braked hard at the curb in front of her house. She'd barely jumped out and reached the sidewalk when a police officer planted himself in front of her, gun held with his arms outstretched, and yelled, "Freeze! Hands in the air! Drop whatever you're holding!"

The cold turned to ice. The small paper bag holding the inhaler fell to the concrete. Shaking, she said, "I live here. This…this is my house."

"Turn around!" he snapped.

Turning let her see Tom's house where medics were carrying an unmoving patient out to the ambulance. The anguish heightened, as did her fear.

"I don't understand." But, oh, she did. The police here had made up their minds about her long since. Her mind flickered back to what she'd thought was motion, and now she knew she'd been right. *Someone* had seen her leaving the house, oh, so conveniently.

The memory was wiped out when, next thing she knew, the cop had grabbed her left hand and wrenched it down. A metal cuff snapped closed on her wrist. She struggled instinctively as he forced her other hand down and cuffed it, too. He grabbed her by the scruff of her neck and shoved her forward. She stepped off the curb without seeing it and fell hard onto the street, trying to take her weight onto her shoulder but ending up with her face skidding on the gritty pavement. She was momentarily dazed.

"What's going on?" another voice called. This one she knew—Deputy Chief Bowen, who had a conscious or unconscious swagger to impress onlookers with his authority even when he didn't wear a uniform, like tonight. He'd probably been getting ready for bed, she realized, or even *in* bed when the call came.

"Ms. Hendrick just arrived home. Real convenient timing."

He loomed over her, staring down with typical contempt. "What's she doing on the ground?"

"Fell after I cuffed her."

"Okay. Hoist her up. We need to take her in."

"Why?" she cried. "What happened?" Her view of him was distorted, just a tall figure rearing over her.

"Oh, I think you know exactly what happened. Once you get her loaded, search her car," he ordered.

Scared as she was, anger sizzled, too. "Do you have a warrant?"

"I have probable cause." And oh, how smug he sounded.

"I can prove where I was. But I'm not saying another word until I'm given the opportunity to call an attorney to be with me. And if you search my car without a warrant, count on a lawsuit."

The silence didn't tell her whether she'd intimidated them in the slightest or whether they were only pausing to watch the ambulance back out of the driveway and accelerate in the same direction she'd come from.

Despite herself, she pictured Tom smiling at her, and prayed, *Don't die. Please don't let him be too badly hurt.*

Another of the SUVs the Storm Lake PD liked rolled up to the curb, the lights blinding her. Jordan turned her head away to rest her other cheek on the road surface. When she did, salty blood trickled into her mouth.

A door slammed. "You arrested Ms. Hendrick?" the police chief asked.

"Ah...not officially. Just made sure she couldn't go for a gun."

"Does she have one on her?"

"Doesn't look like it." The original officer sounded nervous. "I haven't patted her down."

"Well, help the woman up!" the chief growled. "Then do it."

They essentially had to pick her up and set her on her feet. She closed her eyes and held herself rigid as a strange woman officer's hands groped her.

"Nothing, sir. I was going to look in her car, but she said she'll sue if we do."

Chief Guthrie snorted, but said, "We'd best have a talk with her first. What's that on the sidewalk?"

"I don't know. I made her drop it."

One of the men walked over and picked up the small sack. Paper rustled. "Uh, I think it's an asthma inhaler."

"What?"

She refused to look at them, but from the sound of it they were passing the sack around and peering inside.

Mad as it made her to ask for anything, she finally said, "Would one of you please take that to the house? My mother was short of breath. It's for her."

That elicited some discussion, but after a minute, one of them moved away.

"Well, let's take Ms. Hendrick to the station—"

"No," she said.

"Don't think this is your decision," the chief remarked.

"I called a neighbor to sit with my mother. She and her husband can tell you when I left. The receipt in that bag will tell you when I paid for the inhaler at the hospital. I drove straight home. I didn't have time to do whatever you think I did." Should she have even said that much? "Now, I want to call an attorney."

"Plenty of time for that," Bowen declared. "You can use the phone once you're at the station."

Bowen and the officer she didn't recognize muscled her into the back of one of the vehicles. The chief had apparently walked away, maybe to talk to another officer across the street at Tom's house.

With her arms wrenched behind her, Jordan's shoulders ached, the pain sharper in the right one she'd fallen onto. Her head hurt, too. It must have bounced when she went down. No wonder her brain felt rattled.

She stared at the back of the officer's head while he drove her the ten minutes to the city police station. He wasn't any gentler pulling her out, even though she didn't fight him.

She was aware of some stares as she was hustled to a windowless room and propelled into a wooden chair. There she sat for what felt like an hour, but probably was more like fifteen minutes. It was Chief Guthrie and Deputy Chief Bowen who walked into the room then.

She turned to look at them, hoping her stare incinerated them.

"You have *no* evidence connecting me to these crimes. After the way I was treated tonight, I'm going to bankrupt this city. I swear I will. Now, uncuff me and give me a phone."

They remained solid instead of crumbling into the hot cinders of her fantasy. The muscles in Chief Guthrie's jaw did flex before he circled behind her. A moment later, her hands fell to her sides. She stifled the groan.

A phone and the skinny local phone directory appeared on the table in front of her.

"Leave me alone." They'd be able to listen from outside the room, she felt sure, but right now she wanted the illusion of privacy.

The selection of local attorneys was skimpy, but one name leaped out at her. Susan Throndsen was an ardent gardener and longtime friend of Jordan's mother. She also happened to be a criminal attorney who'd moved here, if Jordan remembered right, after her partner died, and she'd practiced for ten years or more in Portland, Oregon.

Given the time of night, she was surprised when a woman picked up on the third ring. Jordan fumbled an explanation.

"This is Susan Throndsen," she said. "I remember you, Jordan. Where are you?"

"At the police station."

"I have to throw on some clothes, but I'll be there in twenty minutes or so. Don't say another word to anyone until I get there."

Jordan struggled with a lump in her throat. "Thank you."

TOM WAS AWAKE through the ordeal in the ER, unlike last time. They sedated him while a surgeon dug out the bullet, but he felt clearheaded surprisingly fast. They must have used a local instead of full anesthesia.

Suddenly a doctor stood above him, surgical mask pulled down to reveal the face of a man in his forties, at a guess. "Mr. Moore, we've removed a bullet from your shoulder, and cleaned and bandaged a slice on your thigh that must have been a bullet graze. I believe you suffered a head injury, too, although any concussion doesn't appear serious. We'll be keeping you for the night, though." He hesitated. "Either you make a practice of living dangerously, or you were struck by a barrage of bullets at some point."

"Barrage," Tom managed to say through a dry mouth. Was he still supposed to be undercover? Clearly no one had told the surgeon that he was a cop.

The surgeon's eyebrows climbed, but he said only, "You'll be doing some rehab for that shoulder. I doubt that's a surprise to you."

"No."

The man patted his good shoulder, said, "Glad it wasn't worse," and departed.

A nurse took his place a minute later and slipped some ice chips into Tom's mouth. He was moved from what looked like recovery to a curtained space in the ICU. He desperately wanted to talk to Guthrie, to know what happened after he went down, but the man didn't show up.

Tom would have given a lot to be able to say, convincingly, *It wasn't Jordan*, but unfortunately he couldn't. From what little he'd seen, his assailant was shorter than him, and could conceivably be a man or woman. Man, he thought, from the breadth of shoulders, but it had all happened so fast.

God, he hoped they hadn't jumped to the conclusion that

it was Jordan who'd attacked him and come down hard on her. Either way, she hadn't rushed to his side.

And why would she do that?

He let his eyelids sink closed and realized how much he wished she *was* here, firmly holding his hand. Her scent was distinctive enough he'd be comforted even when he couldn't keep his eyes open. Last time, his lieutenant had been the first person he saw after regaining consciousness, and Yates had assumed Tom didn't need anyone sitting at his side. Nothing in Tom's background explained why this time he ached for someone—not just someone, Jordan—to care enough to come right away and stay with him.

Instead, he saw her face when she understood that he had betrayed her.

SHE AND SUE sat in that claustrophobic room for some time while a police officer drove to Jordan's house to retrieve the receipt from her purchase at the hospital pharmacy. For all she knew, Jennifer had dropped it in the wastebasket, but at least she had been able to locate it.

Chief Guthrie sat across the table from Jordan and her attorney and said woodenly, "Mrs. Pierce had the time of your call on her phone, and took a guess at how long it took her and her husband to get dressed and get to your house. She said you talked for a couple of minutes about what to do if your mother had a crisis."

Jordan didn't speak. All she wanted was to go home, take a hot shower and crawl into bed, after reassuring her mother. The only positive she could think of right now was that, while Tom had been shot, the chief said his recovery was likely to be swift.

"Mrs. Pierce also mentioned that you called later to check on your mother, saying that you were sitting in the parking lot at the hospital." His eyes narrowed. "You could just as well have called while you were driving. That opens the possibility you had a few minutes more than the timing you're claiming, but I'll admit that gap isn't a large one."

"It's ludicrously small, and you know it!" the attorney snapped. "Have you yet interviewed Detective Moore?"

He clearly didn't like that Jordan had given away the true identity of the wounded man, but had no right to complain.

"Deputy Chief Bowen spoke to him briefly. He didn't see his assailant well enough to give a description."

"What was this assailant wearing?" Sue asked drily. "Did it bear any resemblance to what my client is wearing? Or is she supposed to have managed a quick change in that infinitesimal *gap*, too?"

Guthrie transferred his gaze briefly to Jordan, who wore a Seattle Seahawks sweatshirt over leggings. Her bright blue parka had been torn in several places when she slid on the pavement.

"Ah…it was dark."

Sue drilled him with her gaze. "I'm placing you on notice that I will be pursuing remedies for the treatment doled out to Ms. Hendrick for no defensible reason by your officers. She would have willingly answered questions and did not in any way resist, yet she was held at gunpoint, cuffed, manhandled and injured although no arrest was made. I will be taking her to the hospital on the way home for a shoulder X-ray and to get her face and hands cleaned up." She stood, an athletic woman who might be fifty. Her graying dark hair was disheveled enough to suggest she hadn't stopped to brush it on the way out the door. As she helped Jordan stand up, she said quietly, "I thought better of you, Allen."

Jordan shuffled out the door ahead of her attorney, wishing she'd taken the time earlier—an eon ago—to put on socks as well as the wool felt clogs she wore as slippers. Although being cold for a few minutes going out to the car, into the hospital and out again was nothing compared to everything else about this evening.

During the drive, wishing the car heater would hurry to warm up, Jordan said, "I threatened to sue them."

"Their treatment of you was abominable. I think we need to follow through on that threat just on principle."

Thinking about Dr. Parnell, Jordan winced at having to walk into the ER. Did people working here know her name, and that she was a suspect in his murder? But Sue stayed at her side, insisted on an X-ray even though the physician felt sure Jordan's shoulder had only been wrenched, and watched as her face, hands and, yes, ankle, were cleaned, bits of gravel picked out, ointment applied and then bandaged.

Jordan almost opened her mouth and asked about Tom, who must have come through the ER, but restrained herself. He didn't *deserve* for her to care about him or worry about his injuries. She couldn't imagine he'd welcome a visit from her anyway. For all he knew, she'd been the one to shoot him. Although you'd think the police would have spent more time wondering what gun she'd used, and what she had done with it. Couldn't they have done that gunpowder residue test she'd read about in mysteries? Too late now, she thought, looking down at her hands, swathed in what seemed like an unnecessary amount of gauze.

Once Sue started the car again, Jordan said, "I don't think the Storm Lake department has a clue how to investigate a murder. Or an attempted murder. Assuming Detective Moore has the experience they need, they were dumb enough to put him in a position where he couldn't do anything but cozy up to me."

"Will you tell me more about that?" the attorney asked.

Jordan hesitated, then did, but kept her account abbreviated. Guthrie hadn't mentioned that passionate kiss in front of Sue, and Jordan would just as soon keep that to herself. The humiliation dealt to her tonight was bad enough, but admitting she'd fallen that far for his act was another story.

Sue walked her in at home, waiting while she fervently thanked the Pierces, who had stuck with Mom despite what they must be thinking about Jordan, and saw them out.

At last, Sue left, too, and Jordan thankfully locked the door, checked every window and the back door, and finally peeked in Mom's room to find her mother sound asleep.

And, no, according to Jennifer Pierce, Mom hadn't needed the inhaler. None of this needed to happen, not tonight, anyway. Once she knew Jordan had left to pick one up, she'd calmed down.

She had heard the to-do outside, meaning Jordan had a lot to tiptoe around come morning, but right now…the shower sounded blissful.

DISCHARGED, TOM ENDURED the ride in a wheelchair out of the hospital, then got stiffly into the back of a taxi. One of only two in town, he'd heard. Lyft and the like hadn't made it to a town this size. Guthrie had sounded a little embarrassed during his call that morning when he suggested that Tom make his own way home so as not to undermine his cover.

"Assuming it stays intact," he added. "We'll reimburse you for the cost of a taxi if you don't have anyone else who can pick you up."

Big of him, Tom couldn't help thinking.

"I don't want it to stay intact," he said. "It's time I investigate the way I should have from the beginning." He ended the call, not letting the chief argue. He didn't think there was anything else the subterfuge could accomplish.

The taxi driver offered to help him into his house, but Tom declined and limped up to the front door. Guthrie had thought to grab Tom's car keys and wallet last night, so Tom was able to let himself in. His backup piece had been taken into evidence in case he'd succeeded in wounding his assailant and the bullet turned up. Hard to imagine anyone lying in wait for him now, after the night's drama, but he still moved as quietly and cautiously as he could through the house, peering behind doors, making sure he was alone. Then he took his Sig Sauer 9-mm from the gun safe. He'd keep it close for comfort.

Back in the living room, he separated the blinds enough to peer out. The facade of the Hendrick house told him nothing. Worry sat like an indigestible meal in his belly. Guthrie had admitted in this morning's conversation that they'd hauled Jordan in last night to interrogate her, but that they'd ended up having to release her for lack of evidence. He'd been reluctant to say more.

Something in the chief's voice made Tom wonder. Had Jordan answered the door in her pajamas, hair sleep-mussed, maybe a pillow crease on her cheek? If so, how had they justified taking her in? Had they searched the house for a weapon and failed to find one? How far had they gone in their determination to nail her?

Did she finally hire a lawyer?

He found himself hoping so. She'd been naive in believing she could continue to answer questions so that the police would eventually rule her out and pursue other possibilities. Tom wished he'd looked deeper before he took this job. Yes, the murders clearly had some connection to Jordan, but Guthrie had jumped right on her as the only possible suspect. Tom hadn't let himself question that the way he should have. The job was convenient for him, the timing good for him to do this undercover gig.

He just hadn't understood what he'd be doing to a woman who might be innocent...and terrified.

Or that he'd be pathetically grateful if she'd just walk across the street, knock on his door and say, "I'm still mad at you, but I hope you'll be okay." If she'd give even a hint that she felt for him a fraction of what he felt for her.

The blinds in the front windows of *her* house didn't even twitch. And, damn, he needed to lie down, where he'd cuddle up to his handgun and, he felt sure, dream about another stint of agonizing physical therapy.

Chapter Thirteen

The squeak of a grocery store cart right behind her was enough to tighten the muscles in the back of Jordan's neck. Ridiculous, when she'd almost become used to unexpectedly coming face-to-face with people she'd hoped never to set eyes on again. That's the price you paid for a homecoming.

Annoyed at herself for cowardice, she glanced over her shoulder fully expecting to see someone she'd never met in her life grabbing a box of macaroni and cheese off the shelf. But no such luck.

Steve's mother stared at her, eyes blazing with hatred. The knuckles of her hands gripping the handles of the cart showed white. She'd aged drastically.

"You!" she spat, faced flushed red.

Jordan held her head high. "Hello—" Not "Mom" as she'd called this woman so briefly. "Nancy," she settled on.

"How dare you come back to this town and strut around as if you belong! I was glad—*glad*—to see that picture in the paper and to know someone had the guts to remind everyone that you *are* a killer. You should be serving a term in the state penitentiary, not going on with your life when Steve is dead because of you!"

Rustles from behind gave Jordan a bad feeling they had an audience now. Although what difference did it make?

"I know you loved your son," she said, as gently as she could. "I did, too. I tried—"

Last time they'd met face-to-face, Steve's mother had blamed Jordan for the fact that he hadn't had a chance to go on to play college ball and ultimately end up in the NFL. In her version, Jordan had demanded he marry her and give all that up.

Jordan had no idea where the woman had come up with that fantasy version of her son's life.

Now, of course, she all but shouted, "You shot him!"

Jordan continued as if she hadn't heard. "I tried to keep loving him even when he hurt me. You had to know what an ugly temper Steve had. I always wondered if he got it from his father. Whether you had to cower when he was alive, hide your bruises, pretend everything was fine when you watched him raising his boys to be just like him."

The nearly gaunt face drained of color.

Guilt flayed Jordan. From things Steve had said, she was almost certain about what this woman had endured. But, no matter what, she'd loved her child. How could she let herself believe he was as bad or worse than her husband? Steve had been her golden boy and always would be in her memory.

Did I think I could puncture her illusions? Jordan wondered.

Face now bone-white and lips thinned to reveal the unhappy lines that had worsened since Jordan knew her, Nancy Dunn's eyes flicked to whoever was eavesdropping behind Jordan.

"You're the monster," she whispered, voice shaking. "You've fooled everyone. Even now you killed another man, a good, respected man. I don't know how you keep getting away with it, but sooner or later, they'll see through you, and you'll be cuffed and behind bars. For Steve's sake, I can't wait."

She wheeled her cart around and rushed away down the aisle.

Jordan gritted her teeth and turned to see who had been avidly listening.

Three other shoppers averted their eyes and grabbed, probably at random, for items on the shelves. One was a woman who looked familiar, probably from high school. The others Jordan didn't offhand recognize, but clearly they all knew who *she* was.

Heat seared her cheeks, and she wanted to abandon her own half-full cart and flee, but pride and practicality wouldn't let her. She and Mom were low on groceries, and she didn't want to have to do this all over again. Maybe next week she'd drive to the next town that had a decent size store instead of shopping here in town.

Ashamed that she'd let herself become embroiled in a scene, she moved fast, barely glancing at her list. She didn't see anyone else she knew except one of the checkers. She chose a checker she didn't recognize, paid and left the store. Just outside the doors, she paused and looked carefully around before she dared venture into the parking lot.

What a way to live.

"I'VE KNOWN BUSSERT since he was a kid," Chief Guthrie said. He already sounded cautious. Possibly offended, too. "What are you suggesting?"

Phone to his ear, Tom lay back on the workout bench that had been one of his few additions to the furnished rental. "I'm saying he may have been one of Steve Dunn's best friends in high school. When he and Wilson knocked on Ms. Hendrick's door after the doctor's shooting, Bussert didn't even try to hide his hostility for her. When I started looking into the backgrounds of Dunn's close friends, the fact that one of your police officers has a sealed juvenile file leaped right out at me. You must have known it would."

It was difficult to interpret a silence. Was the chief trying to figure out how to finesse his way out of answering the question?

But instead of a curt response, Guthrie sounded chagrined. "To tell you the truth, I'd forgotten he and Dunn were friends. Got into trouble together a few times," he admitted. "Nothing big—just pranks."

Uh-huh.

"Kid had a temper. No surprise, his family was a mess. There were half a dozen domestic violence calls to that address, but Cody's mother was never willing to speak out against her husband. Sad woman. Cody attacked his own father in defense of his mother. I suspect it was justified, but he spent some time in detention and then a group home. By the time he earned his AA degree, I believed he'd turned himself around, and nothing's ever happened to make me doubt that judgment."

"He pretty clearly harbors anger at Ms. Hendrick."

"You taking her word on that?"

"You made sure he didn't go back to talk to her again," Tom said mildly.

"You've got me there. Wilson suggested he sit this one out."

"Normally, I'd want to interview Officer Bussert," Tom said. "But as things stand, I'll step back and let you do it."

"You're seriously considering him for this?" the chief asked incredulously.

"You have to know he's a possible. I want to know if anyone else in the department had a close relationship to the Dunn family as well."

"What the hell?"

Another call was coming in, and Tom recognized the number.

"I need to take a call," he said. Without compunction, he cut off Guthrie and answered. "Lieutenant Moore."

A woman's voice said, "Lieutenant, this is Detective Dutton from Walla Walla. Thought I'd update you and find out if anything has happened on your end."

The detective and her partner knew Tom had been working undercover, hoping to attract the attention of this perpetrator. He told her about the assault, and his regret that he'd neither gotten a good look at his assailant, nor taken him down.

"You still suspect Ms. Hendrick?" she asked.

"I don't, but the chief does. Just between us, I think he's reluctant to believe anyone in town he might have known for years could be this obsessive."

"Ms. Hendrick is a local, too," Detective Dutton pointed out.

"But hasn't lived here in some years. When she did, she stayed in the background." She'd apparently excelled at that. "I doubt Chief Guthrie ever met her."

"Ah."

"You said you have an update?"

He'd be glad for any new tidbit he could chew on—or that might lead to the real killer.

"You know Ms. Hendrick caught our attention because a man she'd dated briefly was murdered only days after she'd last seen him."

"Pete Shroder." That was the guy who had seemingly

interrupted a burglar, or a team of them, in the act of cleaning out his house.

"Right. Well, a couple of days ago, a fingerprint we ran from the scene finally popped." She sounded quietly satisfied. "Belongs to a man named Bill Bannan." She spelled the last name. "He and a partner were just arrested in the act of carrying a fancy big-screen TV out of a house in Eugene, Oregon. Real nice house, apparently. They'd pretty well emptied it, and once local police had addresses, they found both the men's garages filled with stolen items. We're hoping they'll find something that came from Shroder's house, although after all these years, that would be a stroke of unexpected luck. Nonetheless, I think we can assume they—or at least Bannan—were responsible for Pete Shroder's death."

"So only the assault on Elliott Keefe can be linked to Jordan—Ms. Hendrick," he corrected himself.

"That's correct. We'd probably have done no more than interview her once if it hadn't been for Shroder's unsolved murder."

"Was her name mentioned publicly in connection with that investigation?" Tom asked.

"I'll have to check, but yes, a reporter from the *Walla Walla U-B* got her name somehow." She offered to email the article to him.

They parted on that promise, and his reciprocal one: he'd let her know when or if they got a big break here in Storm Lake.

Detective Dutton didn't dawdle. Within fifteen minutes, Tom had his laptop open and was reading the relevant article about what was apparently a rare, mysterious murder for the college town. And yes, there was the name, Jordan Hendrick.

He sat staring at it, highlighted in his imagination. What-ifs could be pure fantasy, but this time, he thought he was onto something.

What if the real killer had happened on this article, maybe because he'd hated Jordan all along and done regular Google searches for her name? What if the murder gave him an idea? The police had spoken to her because she'd so recently dated a man who was then murdered. What if it happened again? And maybe again? What if the police could be convinced to arrest her? She hadn't been held accountable for Steve Dunn's death, but wouldn't the next best thing be setting her up to serve a long, long sentence in prison for murdering another man?

If so, the idea obviously took a while to firm up. Might have initially been no more than a kind of revenge fantasy. Only then, because his rage grew for some reason, that fantasy became a real possibility to him.

As a scheme, it was diabolical and in some ways impractical...but Jordan had been a hairbreadth away from being arrested for Dr. Parnell's murder. If Tom had died—

She'd never been in his house. Her fingerprints wouldn't have been found. But sooner or later, this killer might come up with a way to be sure her fingerprints or even something that belonged to her *was* found at a crime scene. Or the other way around; suppose cops found something from one of the men's homes, as if she kept trophies. Planting an item wouldn't be difficult. He thought uneasily about her car, sitting unguarded in the driveway.

Then he thought, hell, had she handled anything *he'd* taken home? The newspaper that had fallen to their feet came to mind, but he was sure she hadn't touched that. Anyone could root in the garbage or recycling cans, though.

If it wasn't too late, Tom would have searched his own

house to be sure that hadn't already happened. He'd have heard by now if anything connected to Jordan had been found, though.

Thank God, he thought. Time to have a talk with Chief Guthrie. Turned out there was good reason for him to hide his real job here in Storm Lake after all.

He wanted some cooperation in checking the work schedules and vacation time of anyone in the department who'd had a connection with Dunn. Even while he was following that thread, assuming Guthrie didn't balk, they could goad the killer with a newspaper article that discussed the doctor's murder and the attempted murder of park ranger Tom Moore, but had no mention of Jordan's name at all. The police spokesperson—who might well be Guthrie himself—could imply that initial leads had fizzled and they were left with a real puzzler, but felt confident that sooner or later they'd solve the case. They could even hint that they were pursuing a new possibility.

Wouldn't *that* enrage someone trying to pin these crimes on Jordan?

The danger was that this would push this nutcase to give up on the idea of making Jordan's life hell by getting her sent to prison and fall back on a more certain alternative—sending her to her grave instead.

TO BE PROACTIVE, Jordan took a different route each time she went out for her run and found with the bitter cold and sometimes icy or snow-covered streets that she had to abbreviate her runs. Midmorning, she'd scarcely see a soul out and about. No matter which direction she went, though, she always upped her wariness quotient when she approached her house.

Today the streets were still slushy despite having been

plowed. From a couple of blocks away, she recognized Tom walking toward her. Not running—he probably wasn't up to that yet. The stiffness she remembered in his gait was back.

Turn at the corner and circle around to approach the house from the other direction? No, she decided. She'd just ignore him.

Sure, because being snubbed by *her* would deeply wound him. She grimaced, then forgot Tom at the uneasy realization that a vehicle was coming up behind her. A glance over her shoulder told it was a pickup truck she didn't recognize.

She wasn't half a block away from Tom when the truck came even with her, then swerved and braked in her way. She scrambled a couple of steps back. The driver's-side window rolled down, and she saw Steve's brother for the first time since he confronted her after she got out of the hospital.

His expression was as ugly as she would have expected. "Well, well. Mom was right. Here you are."

He had a friend with him—Ryan Carpenter, teammate of Steve's and, later, one of the buddies he frequently met at taverns several nights a week. Leaving her, of course, behind. At first, she'd been hurt, later grateful for the time to herself.

Ryan glared at her, and for a moment she gave herself the luxury of glaring right back.

Not wanting to give them the satisfaction of any other reaction, she spun to circle behind the truck.

Kevin slammed it into Reverse, and it skidded back. Jordan had to dodge, slipping as she did and barely staying on her feet.

She pulled her phone from her pocket. "I'll call 911."

"'Cuz the cops are your best friends," he sneered. "Just what did you do for them when they hauled you in? Has to be some reason they can't see what's in front of their faces."

She would not engage with him. She turned again, this time toward the sidewalk. The truck rolled forward again to cut her off.

Another man called sharply, "What's going on?"

Relief swelled in her. Tom. She'd forgotten he was so close and coming this way. Stepping off the sidewalk, he flicked a glance at her. "Called 911 yet?"

She lied, "Yes."

Kevin looked angry. "We're just having a little talk. This is my sister-in-law. None of your business."

"I'm making it my business," Tom said with an assuredness they lacked. "What I saw is harassment edging toward assault. If she'd fallen when you backed this truck toward her—"

"Took you a while to get here, didn't it? What's the matter?" Kevin's gaze raked him as he mocked, "Did someone *hurt* you?"

Tom gazed calmly back but didn't sound as stunned as she felt. "Interesting you know that's exactly what happened. You wouldn't have had anything to do with it, would you?"

Ryan muttered, "We should get out of here."

"This guy deserves to be taken down a notch." Kevin started to push the driver's-side door open.

Tom stepped forward and with a slap of his hand slammed the door, then reached through the open window and grabbed a fistful of Kevin's coat and shirt right at his throat. "I'm faster and smarter than you are, and don't forget it." He still sounded unnaturally calm. "Now, I think your friend has the right idea."

The hate on Kevin's face eclipsed even the way his mother had looked at Jordan. She stepped back involuntarily.

The next second, Kevin jerked the gearshift into Drive

and stepped on the gas. The truck shot forward, rocked and slithered as he swerved to avoid a parked car, and spat dirty slush back at Tom and Jordan.

Tom looked at her, his eyes not at all calm. "I don't hear a siren."

"I didn't finish the call. After you arrived, I figured you could deal with him. You're a cop, after all."

The muscles in his jaw bunched. "Good thing for you, too."

"Is it?" She started to turn away, but he grabbed her arm.

"Wait. I need to talk to you."

"I've talked to almost everyone in your department." Her expression was as devastated as any he'd seen on her face. "I'm done."

"I'm trying to keep you safe," he said to her back.

He might as well have ignited an explosion.

Chapter Fourteen

"Safe?" Blazing angry now, she swung back to face him. "Is that what you call being handcuffed, knocked down, shoved into a police car? That's the least safe I've ever felt!"

"What?" His eyes darkened as he focused on her cheek and jaw. The scrapes were mostly healed, but the bruising lingered like a yellow stain. "How did that happen?"

She wanted to stay mad, but his obvious outrage made that hard. "Did I mention 'knocked down'?"

"Who did that?"

"An officer who never introduced himself. I was more focused on the gun he was pointing at me than seeing his name tag."

Tom growled an obscenity, thrust his fingers into his hair and yanked. "What were they *thinking*?"

"Same thing you think." A harsh reminder. Still…she owed him for what he'd just done. "Thank you for…intervening. I mean, with Kevin. But I need to get home."

"I'll walk with you."

She had to cool down anyway after standing here so long. "Fine."

Despite obvious pain, Tom stretched his legs to match her speed.

"They said you were shot," she said after a moment.

"Shoulder." He touched his fingers to what must be

his wound beneath the parka. "Less serious wound to my thigh."

"I'm sorry."

Those turbulent eyes met hers. "Not your fault."

"But it is!" she cried. "Some way, somehow, it has to be."

"You need to know that you're no longer considered a suspect for Pete Shroder's murder."

She stopped.

"I talked to one of the detectives in Walla Walla." He told her about the fingerprint, such a small thing, that identified one of the burglars.

Not sure what she felt about news that would have been earthshaking if not for the other attacks, Jordan resumed walking.

"Who was the other guy in the truck?" Tom asked.

Switching gears took her a minute. "A friend of Steve's. One of his closest friends. Ryan Carpenter."

"Huh. Not quite the hothead Kevin is."

She fixed her eyes on her mother's house, half a block ahead. Almost there, thank goodness.

"Kevin implied that he'd just heard from his mother that I'm back in town. She and I met in the grocery store. But he couldn't have missed hearing about the vandalism."

Tom frowned. "No."

"What did you want to talk to me about?"

"I had an idea I just discussed with Guthrie. There's a big downside to it, though."

Jordan stopped where she was on the sidewalk, free of snow because several men on the block regularly came out with their shovels the minute a few flakes fell. "What?" she asked apprehensively. How could her life get *worse*?

He told her, and she immediately saw what he meant by downside. *She* would become the target if the murderer was made to believe that, after his attacks on three men associated with her, the cops *still* refused to believe she might be guilty.

Feeling lightheaded, she realized she'd quit breathing and made herself start up again. "But... Mom. She's so vulnerable."

"Jordan," Tom said quietly, "I mean it when I say your safety *and* your mother's is my number one priority."

Why was she even listening to this? She squared her shoulders. "I told you I wouldn't believe a word you said again, didn't I? I'll buy a gun. Keep myself *and* Mom safe." She walked away, not hearing the crunch of his footsteps behind her.

Then she had a thought. Would a gun shop sell one to her after she'd shot and killed her husband, even if the police labeled the act justified?

She quaked, glad Tom wouldn't be able to tell from behind. She was the one to lie to him now; she never, *never* wanted to touch a gun again.

NOT UNEXPECTEDLY, Guthrie didn't entirely buy into Tom's theory, but he did concede that eliminating Jordan from Shroder's murder introduced some doubt.

With Tom having nixed any more meetings, this conversation was taking place on the phone. He stayed silent, letting Guthrie think.

"Okay," he said finally. "It's worth a try. As often as reporters get in our way, it'll be good to manipulate them for a change."

"You'll handle it?" Tom asked.

"They're used to me giving the press conferences, so yes."

Tom had watched clips of a couple of those press conferences before he accepted the job here. They were pretty standard for small towns or rural counties: the sheriff behind the mic, a couple of other uniformed officers at his back to emphasize his authority.

The two men talked for another ten minutes, pinning down exactly what they wanted to see in print and on the news.

"We'll do our best to get TV here as well as print reporters. We catch the interest of stations out of Coeur d'Alene, Moscow, even Missoula or Spokane on a rare occasion. A follow-up on the shocking, unsolved murder of a respected ER doc who worked at a regional hospital might do it."

"I want to look at vacation and leave times for last summer for everyone in the department." Guthrie had dodged Tom's previous demand. "Unexplained absences."

"Why would you be arrowing in on other cops?" The chief sounded genuinely puzzled—or he was a hell of an actor.

Tom explained why. "Some of the obvious suspects don't strike me as patient or organized enough to plan, wait for the perfect moment and leave such clean crime scenes." He'd said this before, but the chief didn't want to hear it. "There may have been friends of Steve's or the family who got taken on at other departments. We can pursue that. But first, this is a small town. You could well be unaware of officers in your department who have a connection to the Dunn family. I'd like to be sure Bussert wasn't out of town the week leading up to the Fourth of July, for example."

This silence told him the answer before the chief said reluctantly, "He was on vacation. A couple other members of the department were, too. For people with families, it's natural to want time off around the holiday."

A couple other members.

"Who else?" Tom hoped he sounded as grim as he felt.

Guthrie named two young officers whose names hadn't caught Tom's attention before. "Bowen, too," he threw out with more reluctance.

"He has a wife and kids?"

"Ah, no. Lost his wife a little over a year ago. Freak thing. They'd never had kids. Wasn't himself for a while. Thought he needed some time."

Tom had already felt uneasy about Ronald Bowen without quite being sure why. Maybe he just hadn't liked what he'd seen and heard about the guy's attitude toward Jordan. That could be his usual style—intimidate anyone he interviewed—but there could be something personal, too.

Bussert's feelings for Jordan were definitely personal.

By evening, Tom was second-guessing himself. Had he just painted a target on Jordan?

Wasn't that the point?

Keeping her safe was his number one priority. How was he supposed to do that? Did he start patrolling around Jordan's house from dusk until dawn? Doable, except the intermittent snowfall was a problem, given that footsteps in it would be all too obvious. Also…reluctant as he was to admit it, that was an arduous schedule and activity for a man now recuperating from two separate shootings. Would Guthrie lend him someone? Could he trust that someone?

What Tom wanted was to be inside the Hendrick house. If he could achieve that, he'd have a lot more confidence in his ability to protect Jordan and her mother. Maybe once she saw the newspaper or the press conference on some local TV station, she'd give in.

He grimaced. Pride was a powerful force. He'd betrayed her trust, and he didn't see her forgiving that.

Once he'd checked all his locks and set his handgun on the bedside table, Tom lay back against his pillows, feeling residual pain in every single one of the places on his body that had taken bullets. Worse was the sick fear that he'd screwed up. He should have made a protection detail for Jordan a requirement for this plan, but he'd been too cocky. *He* could keep her safe.

What if he couldn't?

AFTER A LOUSY night's sleep, he called Jordan. Repeatedly. She didn't answer.

He talked to Guthrie again. Clearly he wasn't the chief's favorite person anymore. That man eventually growled, "I'll see what I can come up with. You know what a small department I have. Adding you to the payroll when you're not contributing day to day is straining my budget already."

Tom wouldn't have been surprised if one of his molars cracked.

Nonetheless, the chief pulled off the press conference, although attendance wasn't what he'd hoped to see. Tom didn't give a damn; this killer didn't live in Spokane or even Coeur d'Alene. He or she lived right here in Storm Lake. Tom would bet on it.

He watched the sheriff giving his statement online. He appeared deeply concerned and sincere. When the reporter from the local paper asked about the suspect he understood had been taken into the station for questioning—he was careful not to name her, Tom noted—the sheriff managed to look earnest and regretful.

"That was someone we had to look at, but there was a solid alibi. I can't say more than that."

A couple more questions followed, mostly interested in future steps in the investigation. Might the chief request assistance from the Idaho State Police Investigations?

Guthrie dismissed the question with a curt, "We're not at that point yet."

Tom tried to picture the people on his suspect list—almost all men—watching the nightly local news. He also wondered how much the chief had confided in his second-in-command.

He took a late-afternoon-into-evening nap, then spent the night sitting by his front window, staying alert. His instinct said this was too soon for the killer to make a move, but his gut roiled at the same time with the fear that he was wrong along with the knowledge that someone could slip into the back of the Hendrick house entirely unseen.

The article appeared the next day on the front page above the fold in the skimpy daily newspaper. The headline: No Suspect in Doctor's Murder. Tom winced, but read on. The body of the article might have been written using his script as an outline. He was both satisfied and unnerved. The implication was clear: police no longer suspected Jordan Hendrick...even though that wasn't actually true.

It seemed to Tom that the killer had a couple of best options.

One: murder someone else linked to Jordan, and this time make sure there'd be evidence of her presence at the scene. The problem there was she'd been careful to keep to herself since the doctor was killed—with the exception of Tom. Knowing now that Tom was armed, would the perpetrator try for him again? Was there any chance the perpetrator knew he was a cop? Guthrie had sworn to keep quiet, but who knew?

Two: go for Jordan. Tom liked that option the least, even though he had set it up himself.

Was Jordan really so stubborn she'd go it alone? Even

risk her mother's safety? He hoped not, since he had a plan
to ensure Mrs. Hendrick was safeguarded.

Maybe he should buy a down sleeping bag and start camping out on her front porch nights. Wouldn't help if someone broke into the back of the house...except he'd be close
enough to hear wood or glass breaking.

"JORDAN? IS THAT YOU?"

Uh-oh. Jordan had been trying to be so quiet. Mom had
read the article in Wednesday's *Storm Lake Tribune* and had
been relieved that "those police officers" had finally come to
their senses. How could they have thought for a minute that
Jordan was capable of such awful things? Jordan had managed to smile, pat her mother's hand and say, "I just hope
they figure out who killed Dr. Parnell soon. He was a really
nice man who dedicated his life to saving other people."

Mom agreed and had seemingly put the whole thing out
of her mind. She'd started browsing gardening magazines
and catalogs that showed up in the mailbox, planning orders for new hybrids. Mom found the local nursery to be
disappointing since it carried only the usual standbys. Her
optimism in planning for spring lifted Jordan's spirits, too,
especially since Mom had made such significant strides to
full recovery.

Her own worries about the effect stress might have on
Mom seemed like a good excuse to keep her intense anxiety
to herself. That she spent half her nights creeping through
the house, listening for any sound that didn't belong, wasn't
something she wanted to share with her mother.

But apparently the floorboard had creaked.

"It's just me, Mom," she said. "I'm sorry if I woke you."

Her mother's voice carried from the bedroom. "What
are you doing?"

"Oh, I—" Cell phone, that was it. "I think I left my phone in the kitchen, and I need to charge it."

"You've been sneaking around for the last half hour," Mom said tartly.

The few times Jordan had tried to sneak out of the house as a teenager, her mother had caught her. Why had she assumed a stroke diminished Mom's excellent hearing? She sighed.

It was weird talking in the darkness. "I'm having insomnia, and I keep thinking of things to fuss about, that's all."

"You think someone's going to do something else like the vandalism, don't you?"

"I guess that scares me a little," she admitted. A lot, actually, since it wasn't anything as innocuous as spray paint that worried her.

"I wish you would talk to Tom. He was so kind and helpful. I don't understand why you've cut him off."

Mouth open as she tried to come up with a believable excuse, she was suddenly hit by the realization that she'd underestimated her mother's acuity. Clearly, Mom had a lot better idea of what was going on than Jordan had wanted to believe. A stroke could cause cognitive damage, but there'd been no indication it had in Mom's case. The difficulty with forming words wasn't the same thing.

"I'm turning the hall light on," Jordan said. She followed the rectangle of light into the bedroom and sat at the edge of her mother's bed. Mom reached out and took her hand in a surprisingly firm grip.

"I…thought he was becoming a friend," Jordan said. "Maybe—"

"Even more?"

"Yeah. Then I overheard him talking to the police chief and learned that he'd been pretending all that time so he could get close to me. They did think I could have committed murder." She swallowed. "Tom is a cop, Mom. A police detective. He was hired to cozy up to me and catch me red-handed." That implied bloodstained hands, didn't it? She shivered.

"Are you sure?" her mother whispered, her fingers tightening on Jordan's.

"He admitted it."

Mom stayed quiet for a minute, then said, "Does he still believe you could have killed someone?"

"He claims he doesn't, but how can I believe him? He lied about everything."

"I saw the way he looked at you. Is it possible he started by doing his job, but also came to care about you?"

"How am I supposed to know?" Jordan asked simply.

"Maybe...you have to go with your instinct."

Like you did with Dad? Jordan wanted to ask, but that would have been cruel. They never talked about her father.

"I've always worried," Mom said softly, scarcely any slur in her voice. "After your father left, you changed. I think you've never been able to trust."

"I trusted Steve."

"Did you really? Or were you trying desperately to make a family, because that was something you wanted so much?"

Shocked, Jordan stared at her mother's face. "I...you knew?"

"Of course I knew, but you were so set on marrying him. Nothing I could have said would have stopped you. I just prayed he'd turn into a better man than I feared he was."

"But you were right about him."

"I didn't want to be."

Were those tears trickling down her mother's face? Jordan leaned over and rested her head on her mother's shoulder, accepting comfort she'd denied herself for so long.

"I didn't want to admit that I never let myself see who he really was," she whispered. "I kept thinking if I pretended—"

"It doesn't work that way," her mother said sadly. "I... tried that, too. Eventually I realized that for all the grief I suffered after your father left, he'd given me more joy. You."

Jordan lifted her head slightly so she could see Mom's smile.

Jordan cried, and knew as her mother cradled her, she was doing the same.

She sat there a long time, until she was sure Mom slept. Then she got up, turned off the hall light, waited until her eyes adjusted to the darkness, and crept to the living room so she could peer out the front.

Nothing was moving. No light shone in Tom's house. Was he awake, too? Watching? Afraid for her?

What did her instinct say about him?

Chapter Fifteen

Two days after the press conference, Tom accepted how much he hated his current role, and decided the time had come to shed it.

He started by crossing the street and ringing Jordan's doorbell. A car he recognized was parked at the curb, which told him a therapist of some kind or other was here keeping Jordan's mother occupied. He couldn't be positive that Jordan hadn't slipped out the back for one of her risky solitary runs, but—

Wearing skinny jeans, clogs and a sweater that hung to mid-thigh, her hair in a high ponytail, Jordan opened the door. She'd never looked more beautiful to him even though he saw no welcome on her face. Instead, she gazed at him in astonishment. "Really? You can't take a hint, or ten?"

"Please," he said, sticking out a booted foot so she couldn't slam the door. "I need to talk to you."

Tiny furrows formed on her usually smooth forehead. He still couldn't tell what she was thinking, but some emotion had momentarily darkened her eyes. Whatever it was, she chose to step back so he could enter, although she sounded distinctly sardonic when she said, "Disturbed that your plan hasn't worked?"

His plan. To goad a cold-blooded killer to go after *her*.

"Yes and no," he said. "I've been watching. I'm the one

getting impatient even though I didn't expect immediate action."

"Why?" She waved him to the couch and sat down in an easy chair.

"Because he follows his rules. You have to go out with a man—normally twice—before he acts."

She gazed at him expressionlessly. "Except for you."

"It may have become apparent to him—I say *him* for convenience's sake—that you were unlikely to date a man anytime in the next decade or two. *Especially* while you were in Storm Lake."

"I didn't date you at all."

"We spent quite a bit of time together. Running, at the hospital…and kissing."

"We kissed once." Each word froze into an icicle.

"We did. In plain sight."

Her eyes narrowed to slits. "Like you planned."

"No—"

She went on as if he hadn't opened his mouth. "So this guy was eager to go for it, but when that was a flop, he decided to be…patient?" Her eyebrows had a quirk to them.

The muscles in his jaw flexed. "I've decided I need to investigate, not keep sitting around waiting for another attack on me, or one on you."

Jordan just waited.

He pulled his phone out of his pocket, called up his list of suspects, and said, "I want you to talk to me about these people. Whatever comes to you."

She closed her eyes momentarily, then said, "All right."

He started with the women: Steve Dunn's mother and sister, and a former girlfriend who'd gotten the boot when he became interested in Jordan.

"Kendra Gruener? I can't imagine. I mean, they were

only sophomores when they dated for a few months. She should be grateful she *didn't* stay with him."

"She should, but that doesn't mean she is."

Jordan sat thinking about it for a minute. "I don't think it can be Kendra. She was shy. I heard her dad was an alcoholic and her family life was a mess."

"Making her vulnerable," Tom said slowly.

"Right." She opened her mouth, then closed it. Had she been about to admit the monster she'd married had chosen her, if only subconsciously, for the same reason? Too bad Dunn couldn't see the gutsy woman she'd become, the one who'd had no problem holding off the cop who'd lied to her.

"Any suggestion he had an affair?"

Jordan shook her head decisively. "I can't swear one of those nights he was out at the tavern he didn't take a woman in back, but I don't think so." She focused again on his list. "Steve's mother... She hates me. She, um, thinks it's my fault he didn't go to college and continue his glorious football career, because she can't blame *him* for anything. I ran into her at the grocery store not long ago. Did I tell you? I pointed out that she had to know what Steve was, that I was willing to bet he'd learned from his father and that *she* knew what being married to an abusive man was like. I'm pretty sure from her expression I was right. I felt hateful for reminding her."

In retrospect, the sister reminded her a little of herself, too. "She almost seemed...skittish around Steve. Trying to please him, you know?"

"Kevin?"

Jordan frowned. "They weren't the kind of family that held Sunday dinners. And with him the youngest... I didn't see them together that often."

When prodded, she gave impressions of Steve Dunn's

friends. Most, she thought, hung around him for the reflected glory. He had her study the list again to trigger
memories. She knocked some names off his list. One guy
had gotten a full ride to college with a baseball scholarship;
another had moved away and died in a motorcycle accident.
One lived in town, but was working with his dad in an auto
repair business and doing some custom paint jobs on the
side. Married, too, according to Mom, with at least one kid.

Cody Bussert, she'd disliked intensely. "After Colin—
Dr. Parnell—was found dead and Cody came to the house,
I could see he *wanted* to blame me."

"Or to make sure you were blamed?"

Jordan bit her lip. "Maybe. His level of anger didn't
make sense after all these years. I mean, Steve and he were
friends, but…"

"Unless Steve had done something extraordinary for
him. I hear Cody's family was seriously troubled, too."

"Yes, I vaguely remember that he went to juvie for a
while, but what could Steve have done to earn loyalty so
strong, Cody would kill innocent people to get revenge
on me?"

That was the problem, wasn't it? The motivation was so
damned twisted, Tom had trouble assigning it to anyone,
even the brother, who had earned a spot at the top of his list
after the way he looked at Jordan the day he confronted her.

"Kevin," she said, reverting to the brother. "He desperately wanted to *be* like Steve. I used to wonder if Steve had
stood up to his dad for his little brother. Maybe took some
blows for Kevin's sake." Her eyes met Tom's with sudden
alarm. "I don't know anything like that. I'm not even sure
their father was abusive. I…guessed. That's all."

"What happened to the father?" Now, if *he'd* still been
alive…

"Killed himself and another motorist when he was driving drunk. I saw him at games, and around, but he died when Steve and I were seniors, so I never met him." She wrapped her arms around herself.

Comforting herself? Tom wondered.

"Steve blew up because his father was being blamed. He insisted the other driver must have flashed her brights at him or something like that. Couldn't have been the booze. Didn't matter how much he had to drink, he was a good driver."

"Lot of denial in that family," Tom commented.

Jordan's crooked smile was sad enough to perturb him. "I guess it was contagious."

Or her own SOB of a father had damaged her as much as an abusive drunkard had his family.

There were a couple of other names they discussed that Jordan seemed more uncertain about. Tom mentally shifted them to his B list.

He tried to sound offhanded when he asked about Deputy Chief Bowen. "Sounds like he's given you a hard time."

"He shouldn't have been allowed to be part of the investigation," she said, instantly angry. "But I suppose the department is too small to rule out two officers."

Tom stiffened. "Why shouldn't he have?"

"He was around back then. Steve called him Uncle Ronnie. I'm not sure whether there's really a blood relationship, or whether he and Steve's dad were friends. Steve and he talked pretty often, and they went hunting and camping together a few times while we were married. I'd see him out by his truck when he picked Steve up, but he never came to the door and we never had anything I'd call a conversation."

Tom had some incredulous and profane thoughts. *Knowing* the guy had that kind of relationship with Jordan's dead husband, Guthrie had still thought it was fine and dandy to let him be involved in an investigation into her possible complicity in two murders?

That said, the guy had been a cop for a lot of years. His promotion to second-in-command suggested that he hadn't had uncontrollable anger management issues. How likely was it that he'd go off the deep end now?

Still, Tom couldn't believe the chief had been shielding an officer and maybe old friend. Maybe going so far as to steer the investigation to Jordan to be sure no one looked at his deputy chief?

If all of this been conscious on Guthrie's part, he needed to be fired—probably along with Bussert and Bowen. If that happened, Tom wouldn't be real popular in this department. Right now, he had one reason why he'd consider sticking to the Storm Lake PD after this was over: Jordan.

He didn't say any of that to her, but he moved Bowen up to his A list. Kevin Dunn was still up there, but their one encounter had introduced some real doubt into his mind. Was the guy capable of being coolheaded enough to pull off these murders? Bussert was still an unknown. Bowen, though, had experience and an ego on display. He was capable of the planning and execution of these crimes. Didn't mean he'd done it; even if he'd had a warm relationship with a real or surrogate nephew, why would he harbor so much rage over the course of years?

Still, a scenario was already playing out in Tom's head. What if Steve's mother told Bowen to butt out? Hadn't she implied that? Carolyn married and started her own family. Maybe Kevin was too angry to turn to his uncle. But there was Steve, the golden boy, the son Ronnie hadn't had.

And what if there was some guilt because Ronnie hadn't stepped in soon enough to keep Steve from sharing his father's anger and brutality? Hard to accept your own failing, Tom thought. But there was Jordan, who'd killed Steve. Blame *her*.

It made sense, even if Tom had just made the whole thing up.

Finally, he said, "I'm going to track everyone down. Find out where they are now, where they were when the doctor was killed, and where they were on the Fourth of July. Were any of them footloose enough to be able to go to Walla Walla for a few days or a week without anyone noticing?" He didn't mention that he already knew two of the people they'd discussed had in fact been free and unaccounted for that weekend.

"Kevin's married."

"Appears his wife left him. Don't know exactly when yet, but last summer. He lost his job about the same time— bad attitude, not his work ethic—and that could have triggered him to want to blame you for all his woes." Would have left him free for a side trip to Walla Walla, too.

For a moment, they just looked at each other. "Thank you," he said. "For talking to me."

"I should have done it sooner."

He tucked away his phone and rose to his feet, gazing down at her. "Do you know how much I hate nights? Knowing by the time I hear or see something, I could be too late?"

She gave him a wild look, then bowed her head for a moment, letting him see the fragile vertebrae on her nape. "I…didn't try to buy a gun."

He didn't know whether to be glad or sorry. The idea of her having to kill somebody, with all the horror that would stir up, disturbed him almost as much as knowing she and her mother were defenseless every night.

"I know you're angry with me." He sounded hoarse.

"I don't blame you. But I'd give a lot to spend nights over here. I could bunk down on the couch. You'd barely know I'm here."

"I can't remember the last time I really slept." She gripped one hand with the other, white-knuckling it. "I keep thinking, pride goeth before a fall."

When Jordan paused, he quit breathing.

With the faintest tremor in her voice, she said, "I don't want to fall. And especially…"

She was afraid of anything happening to her mother.

Exultation ripped through him. She hadn't forgiven him…but she'd taken the first step.

Plus, once he introduced his plan to get her mother out of the house, Jordan embraced it. Mom was going to have a fake crisis and be transported to the hospital, after which she'd be shifted to the rehab facility where she'd been before. She could continue to get therapy there. He'd made calls today to arrange all this—subject to Jordan and her mother's agreement. Tom was careful not to let her guess how much fast-talking he'd had to do to set this up. It might have been impossible if he hadn't encountered such fondness for Shelly Hendrick and her daughter. Plus, he'd been able to use Dr. Parnell's name.

It was hard to keep his hands to himself when he saw the relief on her face. "I'll persuade her." She met his eyes. "Thank you."

LATE AFTERNOON, Tom called. After she said hello, there was a long pause. "You answered," he said finally.

"I let you in the house," she pointed out.

"Not necessarily the same thing. Ah…be ready for the ambulance. Probably another hour or two. I'll make sure I'm not around. Better if you look scared and on your own."

Jordan agreed.

The whole operation went incredibly smoothly. Mom obligingly helped the two medics settle her onto a gurney. Jordan ran outside holding Mom's hand and watched as she was loaded into the back of the ambulance. The male medic winked at Jordan, who tried to sound frantic. "I'll follow you to the hospital."

Mom barely paused in the ER, where a clearly complicit doctor immediately admitted her. Had Tom gained so much cooperation because hospital personnel were angry and grieving about Colin Parnell's death? Did the administration know what was happening?

After sitting with Mom, she left to be home in time for dinner and to take half a dozen calls from friends of her mother and neighbors who had heard about the new crisis. She assured them that Mom was doing fine; it had just been a scare, but the doctor wanted her to spend a few days in rehab again where she could be watched closely. Nobody asked her to detail exactly what symptoms had led to the supposed 911 call.

Tom had let her know that he planned to slink through a few backyards well after dark and get to her house without openly crossing the street. Hearing no sounds out of the ordinary, Jordan waited at the kitchen table for his knock on the back door. She couldn't concentrate enough to browse news online or read. It was the first time she'd let herself fully realize that all of this had been designed to leave her ostensibly alone.

No, *really* alone for a good part of the day.

She thought about getting out a blanket and comforter and a pillow and piling them on the sofa to make it obvious where she expected him to sleep, except then it occurred to her that maybe he'd want Mom's bed so someone breaking in didn't see him right away. She plopped back down at the table.

He didn't rap lightly until almost nine o'clock. When she let him in, he asked how the transfer to the hospital had gone today.

"Like clockwork," she admitted. "I don't know how you talked so many people into cooperating. I mean, she's taking up a hospital bed tonight that somebody else might need!"

Tom smiled. "No, they have plenty of room right now. Everybody there knows your mother. They'd do anything for her."

That made Jordan's eyes sting. This was all so elaborate, it was hard to see how it could be a ploy to catch her in the act. Yet whatever her instincts insisted, she hadn't a hundred percent settled into believing he had faith in her innocence and really was here for her.

"I'm so grateful. I guess you figured out that right now, Mom's my weakness. If somebody hurt her..."

"Hey. Let's go sit in the living room."

She nodded. Tom checked the blinds to be sure they were all closed before he sat down with a sigh, stretched out his legs and patted the sofa cushion beside him.

Too close to him. She perched in the wing chair.

He watched her thoughtfully, except that wasn't entirely it. Her fingernails bit into her palms. Okay, thoughtful might be right, except she'd never had anybody focus on her so relentlessly. And *what* he was thinking so hard about was open to question.

She scrambled for something to say. "Did you learn anything today?"

"I talked to Kevin's ex-wife. She left him a few weeks before the Fourth, and says he got canned from his latest roofing job right before that. She said she'd had enough. She agreed he hates you but says he doesn't use a computer much. She can't picture him following you online long-term."

She blinked. "I guess that's what happened."

"Given that you lived in a different state, nobody from back home just stumbled on an article about Shroder's murder and your association with him."

"I didn't have—"

"You had enough to merit a visit from a detective," he said grimly. "And potentially to provide a model for future killings."

Jordan found herself curling forward. "But three years later?"

He leaned toward her, any suggestion that he was relaxed gone. "Here's what I think happened. I think the killer *was* following you online. Could have been only occasional. Maybe he just hoped to find out you'd been killed in a car accident, or murdered a second husband and were in jail. He wasn't really motivated to take action until some bad stuff happened in the late spring or early summer. Whatever it was, that was the trigger. He couldn't fix his marriage or bring his wife back to life or time travel so he wasn't fired, but *you* gave him a focus for all his rage and grief."

He'd explained this before, without mentioning the trigger part. Shivering, she almost wished he hadn't been so graphic. "Bad stuff," she murmured.

"I have some doubts about Kevin, but he fits the pattern in a lot of ways. Job loss, wife leaves him, he's feeling humiliated, powerless, and his big brother isn't around anymore to shore up his ego."

"If Steve ever did," she mumbled. "I heard him be really sharp with his mother, but Kevin…maybe that was different. They were close."

"Did Kevin go hunting with Uncle Ronnie, too?"

"I don't know."

His jaw set before he added, "Carolyn says Bowen really was Steve's uncle, her mother's brother. She remembers him being nice when she was little, but he and the dad clashed. She thinks he might not have been that welcome."

"Clashed. Like two bulls?"

Tom grinned. "Ronnie didn't have his own herd, so maybe he was getting a little too possessive with another man's."

"But what does that have to do with *me*?" Except she knew. She did. She'd killed Steve, the shining boy.

Back to that watchful thing, Tom said, "Bowen took his own hit not that long before the Fourth of July. His wife died. Guthrie called it a freak accident. She fell down a flight of steps into the basement of their home. What if she was pushed?"

"You mean, he was abusive, too." Her stomach had tied itself into knots. If she'd known more about Steve's family, would she have married him however excited she'd been by his attention?

"No domestic violence calls, so I can't say. Either way, with Steve gone, too, he was suddenly left alone."

"Does Bowen know you're a cop?"

"If he didn't, he does now. Everyone will be talking. Whether Guthrie opened his mouth sooner... I don't know." He sighed and, as if he'd said all he intended to, he lifted his arms above his head and stretched. Winced, too, as if he'd forgotten his newly wounded shoulder wasn't going to cooperate and he wasn't as limber as he thought he was.

"I'll get you some bedding. Unless you want Mom's room?"

"No, the couch is fine."

It didn't take her a minute to produce a pillow and a couple of blankets. Then, hovering, she said, "I should think about bed, too. Do you plan to slip out early tomorrow?"

"Yeah."

"Okay." Jordan let herself look at him, really look, and said shakily, "I'm glad you're here. Thank you."

She was ready to flee when he rose to his feet and said abruptly, "You may never believe me, but...I didn't kiss you as part of the act."

Chapter Sixteen

He hadn't meant to open his mouth.

Jordan looked as stunned as he felt. "You bragged to him. I heard you."

"I know. I can't even explain. I was ashamed the minute the words left my mouth. Kissing you for the first time… it should have stayed private. You have to know I've been drawn to you since our first meeting. Not until after it happened did I realize it was a good setup if the right person had seen us."

"I wish I *could* believe you," she whispered.

"You can," he said hoarsely. "About this. I swear." What he wanted was to reach for her, but instead he didn't dare move.

She pressed her lips together, hesitating while he held his breath. This was like being back in junior high when you thought your life would end if she said, *Get lost.*

Only…she didn't. She took the smallest of steps forward and said in that same, soft voice, "It just happened for me, too. I should never have let myself even think about a man like that, only there you were."

"Will you let me kiss you again? Nobody can see us." Had he ever begged a woman in his life? He was pretty sure not, but that's what he was doing now. What he was asking for was a level of trust, and they both knew it.

Jordan gave a tiny nod and stepped forward. With a groan, he engulfed her in his arms and kissed her with ravaging hunger and very little tenderness. She whimpered, threw her arms around his neck and kissed him back as if she was as hungry for this as he was. As if she'd lain awake nights aching because she couldn't quit thinking about him.

He broke off long enough for them both to suck in air, then nipped her earlobe. "God, Jordan. I've been so afraid…"

The kisses got deeper, more passionate. Somehow he'd sprawled back on the sofa with Jordan straddling his lap. He pushed his hands up inside her shirt and under her bra, groaning at the feel of firm, ripe flesh topped by hard nipples.

"I have to see you." He was in the act of ripping her shirt over her head when he felt her stiffen.

"Wait!"

Wait? He was dying here.

"This is…awfully fast." She sounded as agonized as he felt, but she went on, "Hearing what you said to the chief… That *hurt*."

Because she'd been falling for him, the way he was for her.

But there was another reason she was right. This wasn't a good idea. He had a disquieting memory of that other kiss, when he'd been utterly—and, as it turned out, almost fatally—unaware of what was happening around them.

Easing his hands from beneath her bra, sliding them down her slim belly, he tugged her down to rest her forehead on his. "Once I get my hands on you, I get distracted. I'm supposed to stay alert."

Tom knew he shouldn't make love with this woman now that their trap had been set, not the way he wanted to. "God, I don't want to let you go."

"I know." She kissed his neck, then climbed off him as he pried his fingers from her butt and nape. Her lips were puffy, one cheek red from the stubble on his jaw, but a hint of her wariness had returned.

She'd been right to put on the brakes. If they made love, it might kill him to see that expression in her eyes again.

But what did he do but blurt, "I've never felt anything like this before." Yeah, that was it; roll over and expose his bare belly.

Her face softened, but what she said was, "I...haven't either. But...I swore I'd never let myself be that vulnerable to a man again. You reinforced my vow when you lied to me."

"You're saying you can't get over that."

"No." She apparently tried to smile, but it didn't fly. "Just...asking you to be patient."

He took some deep breaths. There was only one answer. "I can do that. Whatever you need. However long you need."

Her lips trembled, her eyes shimmered, and she said, "Thank you," before backing away. It was all he could do not to stop her.

Tom could hardly wait for his night on the too-short sofa while living with the knowledge that she was only a couple of rooms away.

A DETECTIVE'S TOOL kit included the ability to stay calm and outwardly nonjudgmental. Tom didn't remember ever struggling the way he was while he listened to that jackass Kevin Dunn explain why he hated Jordan Hendrick.

"Isn't 'obeying' part of the wedding vow? Steve let her get by with not taking his name, and what's that say about her? What kind of marriage is it when she's defying her husband before the ring's on her finger?"

"Your wife seems to have gone back to her maiden name," he observed mildly.

Kevin sneered. "She knows she won't get a second chance with me!"

The two men stood on the porch of the shabby house Kevin rented. Both kept their hands in their pockets and thanks to the cold were puffing white clouds as if they were sucking on cigarettes between every breath. Kevin hadn't issued an invite for Tom to step into his place. Tom preferred to stay in the open.

He pointed out that every cop and medic who saw the scene after Jordan shot Steve felt sure she'd made a life-or-death decision.

Kevin's response was to spit onto the porch boards, just missing Tom's foot. "*Every* cop didn't think that. Probably not every medic, either. Else there wouldn't have been so much talk after."

Tom raised his brows. "Do you know a cop who disagreed?"

"Sure! My uncle Ronnie. He was one of the first guys there."

Actually, he hadn't been a first responder. Interesting that the deputy chief had let Kevin believe he was.

"Looked like a fight to him," Kevin claimed, "maybe both of 'em beating on each other, 'til that woman went for Steve's gun."

Tom had to remind himself that Kevin may have heard what he wanted to hear from Bowen. Nothing in the police reports indicated any such opinion.

Kevin continued to spew his vitriol, insisting, "A guy's got a right to know what his wife is up to. Don't seem like too much to ask."

Tom's jaw had begun to ache with the effort of holding

back. Even now, he stuck with conversational, not necessarily disagreeing with this SOB. "I understand he lost his job that day. Went home steaming."

The sneer was imprinting itself on Kevin's face, the lines deep. There'd come a day when he wouldn't be able to erase the expression. "Who's to say *she* wasn't the one got mad because they might have to tighten their belts a little? He didn't like that job anyway. He'd have done better, but I guess she didn't believe that."

After another five or ten minutes, Tom worked his way around to asking whether Kevin had ever wondered where she was or what she was doing after she recovered and made the decision to leave town.

He shrugged. "Didn't have to."

"Because?"

For the first time, he displayed some caution. "I know people who don't do nothing but follow social media time wasters."

"Anybody in particular keep you updated?"

"Not one person especially. And I'm done talking to you now. Uncle Ronnie got to arrest her. He can tell you stuff."

Tom didn't bother to mention that "Ronnie" hadn't actually arrested Jordan, because he'd had no legal justification. It was unlikely Bowen had ever actually told Kevin any such thing. Tom nodded politely enough, and felt sure Kevin watched as he walked back to his vehicle and drove away.

His cover was definitely blown now. He was still driving his own SUV, but he'd shown a badge to Kevin, whose shock had been apparent. Tom had no doubt Kevin was on the phone with Uncle Ronnie right this minute.

How did Bowen feel about the subterfuge, assuming he

hadn't known about it all along? Hell. Tom had never exchanged a word with the man.

Deciding to tackle Bowen next, he went by the police station, getting lucky when he saw the man walking across the parking lot. He didn't see any resemblance to Steve; Bowen had to have been shorter than both his nephews and his sister's husband, but was bulked up enough to suggest he did some weight lifting.

When Tom approached him, Bowen's eyebrows rose. "Well, aren't you the surprise. I hear Guthrie's letting you call the shots these days."

Tom held out a hand. "He hired me to initially focus on the one investigation."

They shook, Bowen not looking happy but not hostile, either.

"Yeah," he agreed, "Steve Dunn was my nephew. Far as I saw, he was always a good kid. I thought of him as a son."

"What about Kevin?"

"I offered to give him time, but he tried my patience." The deputy chief shook his head. "I thought I could get my sister to leave that SOB she'd married, but she wouldn't break up her family. Better for everyone if she had."

Tom agreed wholeheartedly but didn't say so.

The two men chatted for a few more minutes. Not so much as a flicker of response seemed off. If Tom had been more trusting by nature, he'd have crossed Bowen off his list. He'd also made note of how much of what the deputy chief said fitted in perfectly with the scenario Tom had come up with.

Not needing GPS to find anyplace in a town this size, he drove to Mama Dunn's place next. She was a cook and waitress at a truck stop just outside town, and he hadn't checked on her work schedule, but he found her home.

She even asked him in and offered a cup of coffee, which he declined.

Surprisingly, Nancy Dunn didn't give any sign she knew a thing about Tom beyond his introduction. Certainly not that he'd been in town for a few months now, playing a role. She was a lot more careful in her answers to Tom's questions than her son had been, but she expressed a significant amount of anger at Jordan, too.

The longer they talked, though, the more the anger dwindled into wrenching sadness.

"Steve was a good boy!" Her eyes strayed to the fireplace mantel, where Steve appeared to have received star billing, from a grinning toddler picture through his graduation photo. "Everyone always looked up to him."

"I understand he was a heck of an athlete," Tom remarked, to keep her going. Seeing that row of images, he found himself annoyed again at his private acknowledgment that her oldest son had been an exceptionally good-looking young man. Jordan had had good reason for her attraction.

The father, he noted, had been a big, burly guy, undoubtedly handsome in his day.

No surprise, Mrs. Dunn was a pretty woman for her age. He'd have wondered about why she hadn't remarried had it not been for his memory of Jordan's speculation. If her husband had been as abusive as his son, this woman must, on some level, be rejoicing in the ability to live without fear, without having to worry about pleasing anyone.

He chose to be blunt with her about Jordan's medical records. He started with the ones from the ER across the state border. "The fact that Steve recognized she needed medical care but didn't want her to receive it here in town where he and she were known is a real red flag."

She stared at him, then faltered, "I...I didn't know about that."

Truth or lie?

He laid out what he knew about Jordan's injuries in that final confrontation before saying, "I understand you loved your son, but you must have been aware of his temper."

Her cheeks flushed, a color especially unattractive when accented by the blush she'd applied, but he also saw her grief. "I...knew he could get real mad." More softly, she added, "Like his daddy did. I hoped, well, that he'd never hit a woman, especially one he loved." She looked down at the hands she'd woven together on her lap. "I guess I didn't want to know. Once or twice I didn't like the way he talked to Jordan, but, well, his daddy could be hard on me and the kids, too."

"You put up with it."

He hated to see the shame in the eyes she raised to meet his.

"I was raised to think that's what a woman does. I never could've done what she did." Her hands writhed. "I shouldn't have said what I did to her."

He pretended ignorance. "When was that?"

"Oh, a few times. Right after, and then when we came face-to-face not that long ago. She was doing the right thing, coming home because her mama needed her, and I was downright nasty."

"I suspect she understood," he said gently.

"If...if you talk to her, would you tell her I'm sorry?"

He thought, *Why don't you do that yourself?* but only nodded. "I will."

After giving her a moment to regain her composure, he said, "I get the feeling Kevin and your brother are still fixed on blaming Jordan."

"Steve was...well, you know. Special. The best-looking,

the best athlete this high school has ever had. Kevin wanted to be just like his big brother. Ronnie and I never did get along that well, but I have to give him credit for making himself available to both boys, but especially Steve. When Steve didn't get the kind of football scholarship he wanted, I hoped Ron would talk him into going to the police academy. That would have been a good career for him."

Tom hid a wince. He hoped psychological testing would have eliminated Steve Dunn before he was ever issued a badge.

When he asked about her son's friends, she said, "Oh, there's some who might speak out if they came to run into her, but that's all. Not like they'd attack her or anything."

"You know there's a possibility that a couple of men have been murdered with the intention of making it look like Jordan committed the crimes."

"I heard, but who would do that?" she cried. "No one I know."

He didn't say, *Oh, I'm sure you know someone who has done exactly that.* Instead, he thanked her for her time and went home to make himself lunch.

Somehow, he wasn't at all surprised to hear a deep-throated vehicle approaching entirely too fast and braking hard enough to skid on the icy pavement of his driveway even before he had a chance to heat up the frying pan to grill the cheese sandwiches he put together.

What did surprise him after a prolonged burst of *bongs* from his doorbell was the identity of his visitor. Kevin wasn't the only hothead; Officer Cody "Buzz" Bussert had been shaped by the same cookie cutter.

TOM SHOWED UP substantially earlier that evening, although he had waited until full dark. Still, his knock on the back door scared Jordan. He'd no sooner stepped inside, closed and locked the door, than he pulled her into his arms.

"Damn. I sit watching your house from my living room window *knowing* you could be in trouble, and I wouldn't know." He pressed a kiss to the top of her head before he loosened his grip. "I bought some timers for the lights today if anybody is watching my place. Which I don't expect now that everyone knows I'm a cop."

No, *she* was the bait.

After a couple of shaky breaths, she recovered her poise. "Have you had dinner?"

"I did." Without discussion, they went to the living room, where Tom carefully lowered himself to sit at one end of the sofa.

Jordan hesitated, then chose the sofa, too, but with a cushion separating them. "Can you tell me about your day?"

"Normally, I wouldn't," he said bluntly. "There are things a cop can't disclose. And honestly, when you've seen terrible things, sometimes you don't want to talk about it. That...can lead to problems in a relationship."

She nodded her understanding. Being stonewalled by your husband would be frustrating when you knew he was open with his coworkers but not you.

He continued, "That said, everything I'm doing right now, everyone I talk to, has to do with you. You're entitled."

He didn't say, *I know I don't have a hope in hell of gaining your trust if I hold back*, but if what he'd said last night was true, he had to be thinking that.

Watching her, he moved his shoulders a little, and she saw a nerve twitch in his cheek. Because he hurt? Was he doing physical therapy for this new wound? If he wasn't finding enough time, that *would* be her fault, she thought.

"Did you see Buzz come roaring up to my house?"

"No. Really? I must have been with Mom."

"Oh, yeah. He was mad as hell to find out that his talk with Chief Guthrie—the one I recommended—wasn't a fatherly chat, it was really what Bussert called a grilling. He blamed you, of course. After all, he was embarrassed by getting cut out of any calls or investigations concerned with you. Now he knows it's my fault. That anybody could suggest he'd have murdered complete strangers to get revenge on you shocked him. He's a good cop, and nobody is going to say he isn't. Especially *you*."

She rolled her eyes. "Back to blaming me."

"Yeah, but he resents me, too." He grinned. "Apparently Guthrie left Bussert with the impression that I'm next thing to a cripple, which is fine in case he plans to sneak into my house one of these nights."

"I guess he hasn't seen you running."

He smiled crookedly. "Or maybe he has."

She gave him a reproving look. "You were getting better until you got shot *again*."

"Bussert couldn't believe anyone would look at him for something like that. Yeah, he and Steve were good friends, but I could see some doubt when I laid out the facts for him. I got the impression no one had ever encouraged him to look at your medical records or the photographs from the scene."

His matter-of-fact comment made Jordan want to cringe, although she refused to do so. She was done being ashamed in any way about her brief marriage or its ending. Still, she didn't love the idea that Tom was stirring new talk about her. She could just imagine the whispers. *Do you know how long she was unconscious? I hear she had spiral fractures. Oh, and a broken collarbone, and...* She hated even worse to know police officers like Cody Bussert could look at photos of her, battered and pathetic.

"Has telling people about my medical records changed a single person's mind?" she asked.

"Yeah." His voice dropped to a deep, velvety note. "Steve's mother. She…asked me to tell you she's sorry for the things she said to you."

Jordan held herself very still. "You're serious."

"I am. I think she was sincere."

Having confirmation that "Buzz" Bussert still blamed her for everything up to and including climate change—assuming he believed in that—wasn't even a faint surprise. To know that her ex-mother-in-law had changed her attitude that drastically felt… Wow, Jordan didn't even know.

"Jordan?" Tom asked, in that same tone. One she could almost call tender.

"I think I feel even worse about what I said to her."

He held out a hand. "Any chance I can talk you into scooting over here?"

How could she resist? She wanted to cuddle with him, even if much more than that still scared her. Once she came in reach, he wrapped an arm around her, and she soaked in what she barely recognized as happiness.

Her happiness expanded as Tom talked more about where his investigation had taken him. Detectives Dutton and Shannon had been helping him canvass hotels and Airbnb and vacation rentals in search of any of the names on his list. No luck so far.

"Most of these men would have been fine camping out," he grumbled.

He even talked about his disappointment and anger at Chief Guthrie and Deputy Chief Bowen.

"Should you be telling me things like this?" she asked.

He tipped his head so she could see his smile and the expression in his vividly blue eyes. "Like I said, you're entitled. Besides…"

"You think you have to earn my trust."

"Don't I? But that isn't what I was thinking. I trust you. I'd like to see you less guarded, but no matter what, I know you won't open your mouth when you shouldn't."

The lump in her throat took her aback. Did she really still think he might betray her again—or was she just afraid of taking a risk?

He hadn't known her when he took this job. He was set up to suspect her, and she couldn't blame him for that. But unless the instinct she'd been listening to was completely wrong, he had since shifted to an intense focus on protecting her and finding out the truth, just as he'd promised. Couldn't she forgive him for his initial lies and misdirection?

If what he was implying was true—that he might even be falling in love with her—how could she *not* take the chance?

For all the hurts she'd suffered, the times she'd lost confidence in herself, she felt an unexpected certainty that he was much the same. He'd said enough about his childhood and, more recently, losing his friend, she knew that was true for him, too. They *matched*…if she could erase her last doubts. Or were they fears?

"What are you thinking?" he asked, voice husky.

She couldn't say. Not yet. Her mouth opened, closed, then opened again. "I was conducting an internal debate."

His expression of satisfaction struck her as sexual because he might look like that after—

"So, okay, I was hoping you'd kiss me again."

There was that wicked grin. "Oh, yeah."

Chapter Seventeen

Jordan had never known how much she detested waiting. Funny, when that's what so much of her life had come down to since she raced home to sit, yes, waiting at her mother's side at the hospital. Would she live? Could she recover?

This was as bad. She'd spent the past three days wanting to scream, feeling like a rubber band stretched until it had to snap any minute. The bone-deep terror because somebody wanted to kill her would have been plenty on its own. But then there was Tom Moore.

Yes, she drove every day to visit Mom at the rehab facility. In theory, she could relax there. Tom discouraged any other activities, though, especially running.

"But shouldn't I be safe with you?" she'd asked. Or was that "whined"?

An expression she didn't like crossed his face.

"If he thinks the kind of attacks he's accomplished before are too high-risk, he has another option."

Jordan had instantly understood what he meant. Most of the men in town were hunters and were capable of shooting her with reasonable accuracy from a couple of blocks away, and then be on their way.

No wonder her skin crawled every time she stepped outside! Tom did believe nothing would happen daytimes—

too many potential witnesses were out and about—but why take a chance?

Sun shining outside the windows or not, Jordan hated being alone all day. She just sat waiting and listening. She lived for the moment she heard that light knock on the back door and let Tom slip in.

Depending on how late he came, they might keep a light on until a reasonable bedtime for her. After that, they'd sit together in the dark for a couple more hours. She was deeply reluctant to sleep. When she did lie down, it wasn't in her bed, but rather curled up with a mound of bedding in her closet. She'd gone upstairs, dug through the stuff she'd left here, and found her softball bat, which was now her constant companion.

Most often, in the hours she and Tom had together, they talked quietly. Favorite bands, movies, sports. Topics gradually became more personal. Tom's reminiscences weren't so much reluctant as rusty, she diagnosed, as if he had blocked a lot out for a long time. His childhood had been much tougher than hers, she quickly realized, but when she said so, he nuzzled her cheek and murmured, "Different. When I was young, I didn't expect anything else. It was tough when my foster dad died, but—"

"He died. He didn't leave you on purpose."

"Yeah," Tom said in a quiet, gravelly voice.

Jordan didn't know about him, but she'd never in her life talked to anyone as honestly. He'd reach out and take her hand; often they cuddled. Nothing in her life had ever felt as good as his solid, strong body, always warmer than hers.

He told her about the frustrations of working homicide in a large city, when separating good guys and bad guys from each other was rarely simple.

"Protecting you," he said one night, "feels clean in com-

parison with some of my investigations." He told her about
the friend who'd been killed, how much he missed him, then
about his wife and young daughter. Almost choking up,
he said, "Emilia says he'd have chosen to save me and die
himself. I think it should have been the other way around.
He had more to lose."

Jordan understood, but...she would never have met him.
She held him for a few minutes after that, although she
knew he didn't do anything like cry.

They laughed, too, also quietly. Kept dipping into shared
tastes from food to ideas for a bucket list. Sometimes she almost convinced herself they were just two people getting to
know each other—but then she'd wish desperately she could
see his face, and would remember why they sat in the dark.

And oh, she wanted him to make love with her. Every
single night, when she gave up and whispered, "Good
night," he kissed her. Those kisses grew more and more serious, deeper, hungrier, until breaking off was almost more
than she could bear. She didn't even know if he backed off
every night because of his promise to be patient—or because he really did fear he wouldn't hear a small tinkle of
glass breaking or thump that wasn't a normal night noise.

So on the fourth day, when her doorbell rang at two in
the afternoon not long after she'd gotten back from seeing
her mother, she flinched. Would she dare open the door
to *anyone*?

She did creep like a mouse to peek through the blinds.

There was Tom, holding a pizza box.

She flung open the door. "What are you *doing*?"

He grinned and stepped inside. "Visiting. Bringing you
lunch." His smile faded. "I promised I wouldn't lie to you
again. The truth is, I want to see you in daylight when we
don't have to be so on edge. But I'm also hoping that seeing us

openly socializing will make our target mad." He shrugged. "We haven't exactly been subtle about being friends and maybe more. It might have looked strange this past week, me not showing up during the day now and again."

She couldn't decide whether to laugh or cry. She'd been miserable, bored, lonely, scared, and now here he was. With pizza, no less!

"Especially now that he knows I'm a cop, he's got to be wondering what I'm doing nights," Tom told her, as they reheated the pizza in the microwave. "My best guess is that he'll believe I'm sitting at home waiting for him."

"So we want to convince him I'm also alone at night." Bait.

He didn't even try to deny that he'd set a trap with a goal of convincing this monster that Jordan was here at home, on her own and defenseless. He did give her a hard hug and say, "I'm sorry."

She smiled with difficulty. "How else can we end this?"

TOM HAD SPENT the morning doing what felt like never-ending research. His effort to find out where the killer had stayed during the week he'd potentially stalked Jordan in Walla Walla had hit a dead end. He'd searched for traffic tickets on either side of the state border. He'd prowled databases until his eyes were crossing after it occurred to him that someone who enjoyed murder might have committed the crime at other times and in places unrelated to Jordan. Nothing jumped out at him.

"That's because you're not seeing what's right in front of you," Guthrie had the nerve to say. He snorted. "That woman has you cross-tied."

Tom didn't know what his expression had given away, but the chief seemed to shrink a little and kept his mouth shut when Tom stalked out of the office. He'd been even more ticked when he'd passed Bowen lurking in the hall probably eavesdropping. The SOB had grinned.

Walking out to his vehicle, Tom decided there wasn't a reason in the world not to expose his relationship with Jordan to the world, as long as nobody had reason to think he was staying nights. It wouldn't be a bad thing if his friendliness to her served as a goad to someone angry at the idea of the police investigator potentially romancing the woman the killer hated so much.

Tom believed an attack was just a matter of time. He pictured somebody who wouldn't be able to resist, whatever the risk. Somebody driven by deep, hidden anger. Somebody who thought he was smarter than everyone else. Look how much he'd gotten away with so far. And for how long.

Because all that was true, Tom ground his teeth at the thought. Jordan had been through hell because cops had looked for the easiest answer. He wasn't letting himself off the hook.

Increasingly, he leaned toward believing the killer *wasn't* someone who vented to anyone who'd listen. Like steam, every time you let go of some of the anger, the pressure lessened. But if you let the rage eat at you, that made for an explosive buildup.

Today, eating across the table from Jordan in broad daylight, Tom stopped thinking about much of anything but how beautiful she was. How he loved seeing emotions flit across her face, the purse of her lips, the way the weight of her mass of hair emphasized the delicacy of her neck. He loved the range of her smiles, too, from impish to wistful to true happiness. He wanted to think he was responsible for that smile.

He let her talk about her mother, who was eager to come home and claimed those darned physical therapists were working her harder there than they ever had here, in her home. "She's not complaining, though. I think she's on pins and needles as much as I am."

Her mother couldn't possibly be feeling the tension Tom did, with sexual frustration twined with fear for Jordan.

He'd put the leftover pizza in the refrigerator and was leaning against the counter wondering whether he shouldn't get out of here before he did something he shouldn't, when Jordan looked at him.

"You really think we're safe right now? That he won't go for me during the day?"

"I really think," Tom agreed. Damn. Was his body betraying his thoughts?

"I...suppose you need to go?"

"I never want to go," he said, grit in his voice.

Her lips parted. "Then...would you kiss me?"

Every time she asked, it just about killed him.

"Is that all you want?" he had to ask, knowing how thin his self-restraint was.

But miracle of miracles, she shook her head. "I want you," she said softly.

He was on her so fast, she let out a startled squeak, but she also met him with open arms.

This kiss went deep and frantic within seconds. She tried to climb him, and he helped even as he tasted her, drove his tongue into her mouth, squeezed her butt and got her sweater halfway off.

Lifting his head for a breath, he took a look around. Blinds drawn and doors locked or not, the kitchen felt too open. Besides, he had to get a grip on himself. She deserved tenderness. One of his worries all along had been about what her sex life with Dunn had been like. Abusers weren't likely to be patient, gentle lovers.

But if the guy had turned her off men, it wasn't apparent now. As Tom hustled her down the short hall and into her bedroom, Jordan slid her slender hand up beneath his shirt, kneading muscles, trying to reach his belly and chest.

At her bedside, he set about stripping her with maximum speed, and her cooperation would have made it happen even faster if she hadn't also been wrestling with *his* clothes. It being winter, they were both wearing too much, in his opinion. He especially hated having to sit down to take off his boots.

But when he lifted his head, she'd just kicked off her jeans. He stared. "You're beautiful," he said hoarsely. "Perfect."

"Not compared to you." Pink-cheeked, she inspected him. He loved the way she nibbled on her lower lip.

He lunged, bore her back laughing onto the bed, and sucked her tender lip into his mouth. They kissed some more, until he couldn't wait and shifted his body lower so he could lick and suck on breasts even more gorgeous than he'd imagined. He slipped his fingers between her thighs, finding her slick and sensitive. Things sped up when she got her hand on him, squeezing and stroking until he had to roll away before this all came to an abrupt end.

His hands shook as he got the condom on. Tom didn't remember ever having that problem. He intended to slow down again as he lifted his weight over her, but her legs were splayed wide, and her arms wrapped tight around his torso. The temptation was too great. Any worry he was going too fast disappeared when she whispered, "Now," and arched her back in a spasm as he pushed inside her.

She was tight, welcoming, everything he'd ever needed. Her hips rose to meet him; she dug her fingernails into his back and came with what would have been shocking speed if he hadn't been teetering on the edge so that he fell with her. His shuddering release went on forever.

Stunned, struggling to pull air into his lungs, he could only think, *Yeah*. With Jordan, he could live gladly.

"I'VE UNDERESTIMATED THIS BASTARD," Tom growled two days later.

"You're the one who said he's not impulsive, that he's patient."

"Yeah, but—" He made a sound in his throat and pulled her close for a quick kiss. When he lifted his head, he said, "That last bit of slush melted today."

"I noticed."

Tom only nodded. The fact that it would have been next to impossible not to leave footprints was a good reason for this guy to hold off.

"I may have misjudged his intentions," he added. "He could still be zeroed in on me. If he's gotten his hands on something of yours he could plant in my house…"

With impressive calm, Jordan said, "Should we move to your house?"

"No. Then your fingerprints would be all over it." Tom sighed.

"You look awfully tired." Now she sounded tentative. He must really look haggard. "I could stay awake for a while now so you could get some sleep."

He studied her drawn face. "You're not getting much more sleep than I am."

"No, I… I suppose not."

Tom shook his head. "If he comes in shooting, you wouldn't have time to wake me up. I'll be okay." How many more nights would he be able to make that claim? If this nightmare dragged on much longer—

Quit worrying about tomorrow, he told himself. What he needed was to be sharp tonight.

Something told him when Jordan said good-night, she wouldn't be heading off to slumberland any more than he would. When that moment came, he kept the kisses gentle but unhurried. Whether she got the message he was trying to convey, he didn't know.

He did know that once he was alone in the dark, his eyelids felt as if they had ten-pound weights on them, and he had to keep getting up to walk through the house just to stay awake. Tonight, he was conscious of a level of pain he usually blanked out. No, he really didn't want to get shot again. He already felt like a damn pincushion.

Sinking back on the sofa, he listened to the silence. Jordan was in her mother's bedroom tonight. Not in the bed, in case bullets were fired right through the window.

More silence.

If I wanted to break into this house, he asked himself for the hundredth time, *how would I do it?*

JORDAN JERKED OUT of a shallow sleep threaded with nightmares.

Glass breaking had to be at the back door. By the time she understood, a distinctive *snap* told her the lock had been unengaged, and an intruder was in the kitchen.

A cry of fear escaped her before she could stifle it. She shrank deeper into the closet, shoving shoes out of the way. Tom!

Pop, pop. Those were shots, she knew, but not usual ones. A silencer? Whatever it was called. Her thoughts flew feverishly. She'd seen Tom's gun, and it wasn't fitted with anything special.

Creak. He was already right outside her bedroom door.

The next shots struck her bed, which bounced. Oh God. She tried to will herself to be part of the wall at the back of the closet. Invisible.

Except…

Pop, pop, pop. He was firing farther away now, probably into the living room. Or Mom's room. Who knew? *Please God let Tom have been awake but not have leaped out to make a target of himself.*

Then she heard his voice.

"Drop the gun!" Tom yelled. "You aren't getting away this time!"

A snarled "You're a dead man" came to her.

More shots, some louder that had to be return fire. Terrified, she knew there was nowhere in the living room for Tom to hide. What if he was gunned down? She couldn't bear it.

Jordan steeled herself to crawl out of the closet, grab her wooden bat with shaking hands, and creep toward the door.

It was like being in battle. More shots. Plaster flew, bits hitting her face. Did she dare venture into the hall? Would either man have time to change out a magazine? The killer was running out of time, Jordan realized in some remote part of her brain. Neighbors must have called 911 by now. It hadn't even occurred to her that she should have.

Bang, bang, bang. Pop, pop, pop. How could they *not* be running out of ammunition?

Suddenly there was a massive crash, and guttural, animalistic sounds. She tiptoed into the hall, wishing it wasn't so dark, but saw enough to know the two men grappled with each other, one slamming the other against the wall. One body crashed to the floor.

What if she turned on the hall light? Only…it would blind them both.

Closer, closer… Oh God, Tom was down. The man with

a knee in his belly wore something black over his head. Tom was holding on to the other man's wrists, keeping a handgun from lowering to aim at him.

Another pistol lay on the floor where she might be able to snatch it up. Only...what if Tom or this monster had discarded it because it was out of ammunition?

Whatever her vow, she'd have picked it up if she'd been sure it had bullets left. Instead, Jordan summoned rage at the man who'd used a tragedy to try to destroy her life.

She jogged the couple of steps. His head turned, but his eyes were only black holes. Now he started to wrench that gun toward her, but Tom twisted his arm, drawing it back toward himself. The killer bellowed with pain or fury, and the gun barked again. Tom's body jerked from the impact. Both brimming with adrenaline and weirdly calm, Jordan readied for her swing, just as if she stood at home plate, and took it with everything in her.

The impact was hideous, like shattering a pumpkin, but she didn't care. She let the bat drop with a clatter, turned on the light, and fell to her knees beside Tom...and the man who lay unmoving, sprawled half atop him.

TOM HEARD HIMSELF swearing as he shoved the SOB off, rolled, tried to sit up. "Jordan—"

"Did I kill him?" She sounded...he couldn't decide.

"I don't know." Damn, he hurt. Yeah, he'd been shot again despite believing he was prepared. Would he have won the battle for the gun in his assailant's hands if Jordan hadn't intervened? He couldn't be sure and could never regret taking a bullet meant for Jordan.

"Sweetheart," he managed to say. "Come here."

Sirens were so close, he didn't know how he'd missed hearing them approaching.

"I have to let them in." Her voice was high, but she was hanging in there.

"Yeah. Okay."

He'd recognized the voice and not been surprised. He'd just as soon Uncle Ronnie was dead, but for Jordan's sake, it might be better if the bastard survived to be convicted to a lifetime in the penitentiary—the sentence he'd wanted *her* to serve. He could think about her every day for the rest of his life.

Tom couldn't quite make himself try to stand up.

Within seconds, they were swarmed with cops and medics.

"Take some photos before you move either of us," he snapped. Damn, was that Bussert looking so shocked?

From then on, events passed like a series of slides. As they loaded him to take him to the hospital, he heard Jordan again asking if Bowen was dead. Saying, "I hit him. He was trying to kill us both."

Then she saw that they were hustling Tom out, and tried to follow. When she got close enough to grab his hand, he tried to squeeze hers but failed. "S'okay," he said. "They need to ask questions."

"I'm sorry! So sorry!" Tears ran down her face, now that it was over. That's the picture he carried until, damn, he was under a bright light and a woman with a mask covering her face threatened to knock him out again. His last thought was comforting: this time, he believed Jordan would be waiting for him when he woke up.

Epilogue

Jordan had never envisioned the fallout beyond her small circle.

At first, once Tom recovered consciousness, she was occupied squelching his determination to beat himself up. He hadn't been asleep when Bowen broke in, but had been a step too slow. He should have rebounded faster from his previous injuries. Were all men like that? Jordan wondered.

She'd silenced him by insisting he was her hero, although he was determined to deny that. *She'd* saved him.

"I wish you could have seen yourself," he said. "Warrior woman. Although I hope I never see that expression on your face again."

She'd been trying to convince him he didn't have to pretend he didn't hurt, but in truth, his surgeon had encouraged him to get up and move. So now she and he were walking the hospital corridor just as she'd done with her mother a few months ago. He wore a sling, the bullet having struck the same shoulder as the previous wound. The surgeon had an air of reserve talking about what he'd done that made Jordan wonder how much of a mess it was in there.

Now, pausing at a rare window to look outside, Tom told her that ballistics had already established that Ronald Bowen had used the same gun to shoot Elliott and kill Colin Parnell—as well as wound Tom *twice*. They had him cold…if he lived. Bowen hadn't yet regained consciousness. Jordan didn't feel as squeamish about that as she would have expected to.

Tom also told her that the mayor had stopped to speak to him that morning while she'd been meeting a contractor who would have to erase evidence of the gun battle in Mom's house before Jordan could bring her home. She'd rather her mother not see the torn plaster and wood, bullet holes in the front window and blood staining the floors.

"Guthrie has resigned. I don't know if it was under pressure or not." Tom's voice hardened. "If he hadn't, I'd have pushed for it."

"But…why?"

"He had to know about Bowen's relationship with Steve. It was bad enough that he let Steve's uncle investigate you, given his partiality, but he should have understood that Bowen was a potential suspect in the murders. He either didn't, which is inexcusable, or he did and was complicit in two murders and several attempted murders." Tom shrugged his good shoulder. "Either way, he had to go."

"So why you?" she asked, although she had a suspicion.

"He wants me to take over the department. No one else is remotely qualified."

Since they had reached his hospital room again, which fortunately he had to himself, she waited until he had laboriously stretched out in bed again, stifling only a few groans, before asking, "What did you say?"

"I agreed on an interim basis." He watched her with familiar intentness. She basked in the rich blue of his eyes.

When he tugged, she sat on the bed. She didn't remove her hand from his warm clasp.

"Do you *want* to be police chief?"

"Right now, yes. This department needs a major housecleaning. Officers are inadequately trained, haven't been reined in the way they should be." He grimaced. "After that… I don't know. I think it's realistic to guess I've been shot a few too many times to ever plan to go back to an active job."

She wished she could tell how he felt about that. He had to regret not being able to pack up and return to San Francisco, didn't he?

Was he trying to read her, too? She wished she had as much confidence as she'd like, but did feel as if she had bubbles in her bloodstream. That had to be hope, didn't it? After the way he'd touched her, held her, the driving urgency of his lovemaking, she wanted so much to believe he could be falling in love with her.

When she stayed silent, he continued haltingly, "This is really soon, but as far as I'm concerned, where I work has to do with you."

The beat of her heart quickened.

"As long as you're here for your mother, as long as you want me around, I'll stay. But once your mother doesn't need you on an everyday basis, if you decide to go back to school to finish your BA or to grad school, I can get a job wherever we go."

We. He couldn't have used a more powerful word. No, he hadn't said, *I love you.* Anyone with sense would say it was too soon. Except Jordan knew that as far as she was concerned, it wasn't.

He was holding himself very still, she realized. He wasn't sure of her.

She swallowed. "I would…really like that."

His breath came out ragged. "Do you remember what I told you about my friend Max's wife?"

Jordan nodded, feeling a painful swell of pity for a woman

who'd lost the man she loved in exactly the way Jordan had just almost lost Tom.

"She knew about my background. That I'd become used to being alone. She all but whacked me over the head and insisted that, thanks to Max, I'd been given a chance to have everything. A wife, children, happiness. I mostly put what she said out of my mind until I met you. It was like a door opening, except after all my lies, I could see you closing and locking it. I couldn't imagine you forgiving me."

His raw, emotional admission brought the sting of tears to her eyes. With a cry, she bent forward to press her cheek against his, prickly from lack of shaving. She didn't dare hug him. He had to hurt everywhere.

"You were wrong," she whispered. "Of course I forgave you. And…and I want children and happiness, too. With you."

Tom's one good arm closed around her tightly enough to suggest he didn't intend to ever let her go, and she smiled and cried both. How had events so terrible led to this kind of joy?

* * * * *

Safe House Security

Jacquelin Thomas

MILLS & BOON

Jacquelin Thomas is an award-winning, bestselling author with more than fifty-five books in print. When not writing, she is busy catching up on her reading, attending sporting events and spoiling her grandchildren. Jacquelin and her family live in North Carolina.

Books by Jacquelin Thomas

Harlequin Intrigue

Guardian Defender
Safe House Security

Love Inspired Suspense

Sorority Cold Case

Love Inspired Cold Case

Evidence Uncovered
Cold Case Deceit

Love Inspired The Protectors

Vigilante Justice

Harlequin Heartwarming

A Family for the Firefighter
Her Hometown Hero
Her Marine Hero
His Partnership Proposal
Twins for the Holidays

Visit the Author Profile page at
millsandboon.com.au.

CAST OF CHARACTERS

Nova Bennett—A dedicated US marshal assigned to the witness protection division. She holds the Mancuso cartel accountable for her father's tragic demise and wants to make them pay.

River Randolph—DEA agent on a relentless quest for justice, driven by the mission to avenge two fallen comrades as he endeavors to dismantle the formidable Mancuso cartel.

Arya de Leon—Seeks to escape from the tangled web of consequences ignited by Mateo, which now threatens to engulf her.

Mateo de Leon—Defies the WITSEC program, opting for one last daring negotiation with the Mancuso cartel—an attempt that unfolds in deadly results.

Ramona Lazano—Arya's mother.

Pablo Lazano—Arya's father.

Johnny Boyd "Johnny Boy" Raymond—Top lieutenant within the formidable Mancuso cartel, whose guiding principle is that "dead witnesses can't talk."

Kenny Latham—River's partner.

Poppy Mancuso—The head of the Mancuso cartel.

Chapter One

Deputy Marshal Nova Bennett stepped out of the elevator and walked quickly to her boss's office. She'd received an urgent call from her supervisor, Roy Cohen, almost as soon as she'd arrived at work this morning. Nova didn't know what this was about, but whenever they discussed sensitive information, they did so within the confines of his office.

She took a deep breath before knocking and letting herself in.

"Juan DeSoto was found in the trunk of his car. Shot in the head," Roy said as soon as she stepped inside.

Filled with disappointment, Nova sighed and dropped into the nearest chair. With that news, what had started as a good day in the Witness Security Division of the US Marshals Service had taken a sudden turn. According to police reports, Juan had left his office five days ago and never returned home. Nova had been hoping for a better outcome for the missing brother of her latest witness, Mateo de Leon.

Mateo, whose real name was Manuel DeSoto, was close to his brother. He'd owned an accounting firm with offices in Los Angeles and Mexico, a perfect cover for laundering money. He was a prominent, trusted member of the Mancuso cartel, overseeing many of their financial transactions—until they discovered he was stealing from them. Poppy

Mancuso, the head of the cartel, had ordered his death, and Mateo had since joined WITSEC. Nova had been his handler for the past eight months.

She tapped the oblong-shaped table before her, her nails beating a staccato rhythm with increasing intensity. Her eyes bored into Roy's as she said, "Mateo has been nothing but a thorn in our side since he entered WITSEC. Demanding a six-figure stipend, a mansion in an exclusive neighborhood, and all the country-club privileges. But now, with Juan's death, he might go over the edge. He was already angry with his brother for refusing to join him in the program."

Despite Mateo's constant complaining, she was his handler. And she'd wanted this case because of the connection to the Mancuso cartel. She wanted to help bring down the organization to avenge her father's murder. Her dad's killer, a lower-level hit man, had been arrested but died before he could stand trial. Nova would not be satisfied until Poppy Mancuso was arrested and imprisoned.

Her cell phone rang.

Recognizing the number, Nova said, "It's Mateo. I'd better take this…" She braced herself for what was to come.

As soon as she answered, the man on the other end yelled, "Johnny Boy had my brother killed! Juan didn't have nothing to do with this. The cartel…they just went and murdered him. As far as I'm concerned, it's an eye for an eye… I'm going to find Johnny Boy myself and make sure he pays for this."

John Boyd Raymond, also known as Johnny Boy, was Poppy's right hand. Before Mateo joined WITSEC, he'd placed a call to the DEA. He'd agreed to testify against Poppy and a few other prominent cartel members—including her top lieutenant—in exchange for protection for him and his wife. No doubt Johnny Boy was behind this murder, trying to lure Mateo out of hiding.

Nova heard sobbing in the background and spoke calmly. "Mateo, you can't do something reckless. I'm so sorry for your loss, but there's nothing you can do to help Juan now. You did everything you could to convince him to come to WITSEC, and he refused. Go comfort Arya. Your wife needs you."

"You expect for me just to let this go?" he demanded. "Juan was innocent. His murder must be avenged…" Mateo lapsed into Spanish as he continued to vent. "I gave up millions for this…"

Nova kept a gentle demeanor as she listened to Mateo's rant about seeking revenge for his brother's murder and how he'd given up everything to join witness protection. The news of Juan's death saddened her. She understood his grief and his desire for revenge.

"Arya's afraid for her parents, Nova," Mateo said. "And I don't know what to tell her. It's my fault that she's in this situation, but it's not like I can do anything about it. Johnny Boy and Poppy aren't gonna rest until they see me dead for betraying the cartel. I never shoulda gone to the DEA. I shoulda just kept my mouth shut and disappeared."

"You went to the DEA for help because you embezzled money from the cartel. They found out and were going to kill you," Nova stated, reminding him that it wasn't some selfless act on his part. "You wanted protection. You still *need* that protection, Mateo."

"I know that," he muttered, his tone filled with resignation.

Arya must have taken the phone from Mateo, because Nova heard her voice next.

"My parents need to be in witness protection." Her voice

faltered a moment. "That horrible Johnny Boy is going after Mateo's family. He'll kill my family next. My husband's told the DEA everything he knows about the cartel. Why hasn't the FBI or DEA—whoever—why haven't they arrested Johnny Boy and locked him up already? You all know that he's a murderer. I'm not understanding why he's still walking around free. Why are we living like…like this…? We're the ones in *prison*."

Nova clenched her jaw, trying to contain the small wave of frustration. Mateo was overcome with grief at the moment, but he couldn't forget his situation, she thought to herself, taking a deep breath to calm her nerves.

"You call this living?" Arya asked. "We gave up everything, while Johnny Boy is free to do whatever he pleases."

Johnny Boy had been a close friend of Poppy's for years. After her husband Raul's death, Poppy had taken over the Mancuso cartel, which was one of the largest importers of drugs smuggled into the United States through elaborate land and air distribution channels. She had handpicked Johnny Boy to control a large part of the cartel operations after her former lieutenant, Calderon, was arrested two years ago. Tall and dark-skinned with long dreadlocks, Johnny Boy was an unassuming man. However, his unremarkable appearance was deceptive. He was a skilled marksman with an uncanny ability to elude capture for the past ten years. He needed to be stopped.

"Arya, would you put Mateo back on the phone, please?" Nova asked.

After a pause, Mateo's voice came on the line. "Juan's death is on me, and there's nothing you can say to change that, Nova. It's up to *me* to make sure Johnny Boy and Poppy Mancuso pay for having him killed."

She listened with rising dismay before saying, "Mateo, I

can't keep you in WITSEC if you want to leave, but understand that we can't protect you if you abandon the program." Frankly, they couldn't let him walk. The DEA needed Mateo to testify in court against the cartel.

"My b-brother is dead, and I can't even attend his f-funeral." His voice broke.

"I'm sorry, Mateo."

"It bothers me that this is all my fault," he said again. "If I'd kept my mouth shut, then maybe Juan would still be alive."

"I know this isn't easy for you," she responded. She searched for something to say that might offer a small comfort to him.

"No, it's not. If it weren't for my wife, I'd go after Johnny Boy myself. But I'll let the law handle him." He released a sigh of resignation. He sounded much calmer. "I don't feel like going, but I better prepare my mind for my work shift. I'm due at my new job at three o'clock." Mateo paused momentarily, then added, "Nova, you don't have to worry. I'm not going to leave the program."

She expelled a breath. "I'm glad to hear it."

They finished their conversation and hung up.

"I'm not sure what they're mourning more—Juan or the money they had to give up," Nova said.

She stood up and walked around the table, navigating toward the door. "I'm thinking both. Mateo's a little calmer now, so I'm going to get myself a cup of tea, then try to clear some of the paperwork off my desk."

Nova stopped in the break room to make herbal tea, then walked to her work area. She sat down at her desk, eyeing the wood-framed photo of her father. A pain squeezed her heart as she thought of him. "I miss you so much," she whispered. She was thirty-three years old but still yearned for the haven her father's arms had once provided.

She placed a finger as if to stroke his grayish-blond hair. Special Agent II Easton Bennett was a man she'd always admired. He'd fallen in love with a Black woman and stood up to his parents when they voiced their disapproval. Her father didn't care. He loved her mother and had married her. It was her father's passion for his career that had inspired her to become a US marshal. He had been dedicated to his job, but it was that same dedication that ultimately led to his death at the hands of the cartel while protecting a witness.

She whispered to the face with deep-set blue eyes, "I wish I could talk to you, Daddy. I've got such a bad feeling about this… I know Mateo's going to do something stupid. Something that will get him killed." Mateo wasn't the sort of man who would let his brother's death go unanswered. She understood this particular feeling. Luis, the cartel member who'd murdered her father, died before his conviction, leaving Nova still hungering for justice.

She'd considered before that Mateo hadn't told Homeland Security and the DEA everything he knew about the cartel. A man like him, who wanted to be in control, might keep crucial information if he thought it would give him an edge. She felt terrible for his poor wife. Arya was innocent in all this. Now she was doomed to spend the rest of her life in witness protection.

Her Apple Watch notified her that it was time for movement.

Nova exited her desk and strolled outside her 9 x 9 cubby to a nearby window. She stared at the busy street down below, bustling with automobiles and people going about their business in all directions. This September weather was the perfect temperature. Not too hot or cool.

Nova had left Wisconsin two years ago in search of a place that wouldn't remind her so much of her father everywhere she went. She loved Charlotte, North Carolina, but she still missed him dearly.

Her heart filled with grief, Nova turned away from the window and returned to her desk.

She'd learned that her father's absence would follow her no matter where she went.

Nova gave herself a mental shake. She had a stack of paperwork that required her attention. Although focused on her tasks, she couldn't escape the ominous feeling swirling around in her gut.

If Mateo violated the rules of the program, then he risked having to leave WITSEC, and any criminal actions on his part could land him in prison. Nova often had to remind Mateo and Arya of the importance of this chance they'd been given.

It was an opportunity to stay alive—something the cartel would never offer them.

Los Angeles, CA

DEA SPECIAL AGENT RIVER RANDOLPH and his partner entered the federal building on East Temple Street. He and Kenny, along with a few other colleagues, had just concluded a knock-and-talk with a suspect and were returning to the office.

"I hope the rest of the day won't be as exciting as this morning," Kenny said as they strolled across the lobby.

River chuckled. "Can you believe that guy? He welcomes us into his house and then tries to run."

Earlier that morning, they'd met up with a team of ATF agents and police officers in an empty warehouse fifteen minutes away from the suspect's home.

While the team remained out of sight, River and Kenny had brazenly walked up, knocked and asked if they could search the house. Surprisingly, Rico Alfaro had given them full access, claiming he had nothing to hide.

The man had no idea he'd been under surveillance for the past twenty-four hours.

Not long after, Rico Alfaro was apprehended and brought downtown in handcuffs. River's team had found massive quantities of chemicals in the garage, just as River had suspected. They'd also found stashes of cocaine, fentanyl and amphetamines in one of the bedrooms.

River felt a sense of purpose after the bust—the weight of his fallen partner's badge hung heavy on River's chest, a constant reminder of the vow he'd made to keep illegal substances off the streets. But now, with his partner's blood staining those very streets at the hands of the ruthless cartel, it was no longer just a sense of duty that fueled River. It was pure vengeance, a burning desire to bring down every member of that cartel and make them pay for what they had taken from him.

His new partner, Kenny Latham, was an experienced DEA criminal investigator, having worked in the field for more than fifteen years since River came to the agency. At forty-two, Kenny was the type of man who faithfully went to the gym three times a week to maintain his athletic build and never touched alcohol or cigarettes. It was something they had in common. River also worked out several times a week to keep in top physical shape for his job. Both men were over six feet tall, although Kenny was a few inches shorter than River.

They walked past an open area with potted plants and chairs down a hallway to a room filled with desks grouped in clusters of four, surrounded by a wall of offices belonging to the superior agents.

River could hear the voice of a news reporter on television coming from one of the offices—the one with the open door. His attention was immediately drawn when he overheard the news of Juan DeSoto's death. River had recently inherited the file on Manuel DeSoto from his former coworker, who'd decided to leave the agency. Manuel DeSoto and his wife were in WITSEC as Mateo and Arya de Leon.

River stood at the door outside of his supervisor's office, knocked and waited for a response.

"Come in."

Special Agent in Charge Jared Rush was seated behind a large desk.

"I just heard the news about Juan DeSoto as I walked by," he said, strolling inside. He sank down in one of the visitor's chairs facing him.

"Yeah…certainly wasn't the outcome we were hoping for," Jared said. "I'd hoped we'd find the man alive."

River nodded in agreement. Mateo had handed over important evidence to the DEA—it was a shame Juan had lost his life because of it. "The cartel must be desperate to try and flesh out his brother this way."

River didn't doubt that Juan was murdered because of his brother's criminal dealings. He had reviewed several pages of notes on the man and his family. To their knowledge, Juan had been a law-abiding citizen with not so much as a speeding ticket; he'd attended church regularly and seemed devoted to his wife and children. Juan's death was meant to send a clear message to his brother. To silence him.

River's main concern now was whether Mateo would still be willing to testify against the cartel. If Mateo wavered in his decision, River's job was to convince him that testifying was still in his best interest. And if necessary, remind Mateo that he'd become a dead man when he decided to steal from Poppy Mancuso.

River would make a trip to Charlotte to see Mateo in a couple of days. Before exiting the office, he discussed a few final particulars about his trip with Jared. He was looking forward to meeting Mateo and Arya de Leon. Less so, their handler. River had stopped short when he'd learned the name of Mateo's case agent with the US Marshals.

Nova Bennett.

He shuddered inwardly at the thought that they had to interact and work another case together.

He'd read Mateo's dossier and understood the type of man he was. There wasn't much on his wife except that she denied knowing her husband's criminal deeds.

River didn't necessarily buy it as the gospel truth but decided to reserve judgment until after he met the woman. The previous agent had also noted that he believed Mateo was withholding information from the DEA. He knew more than what he'd shared with them.

Mateo had been distraught when he'd learned that he would have to turn over all the money he'd stolen to the DEA. The report said they'd recovered over three million dollars in cash hidden in his office's walls. There was nearly a hundred thousand more in two safes at his house. He'd called it his emergency fund. The man was furious when the DEA had seized his house, business and other properties.

They were a pair of high-maintenance witnesses... He wondered how Nova was faring with them. He shut that thought down. He would come face-to-face with her soon enough.

A flicker of apprehension coursed through him. It had

taken him eighteen months to erase the pain of a broken heart after she'd left.

He'd met Nova while working with her agency on a prior case nineteen months ago. When the two weeks of working together ended, River couldn't help but feel a sense of longing. They had shared countless laughs, inside jokes, and even a few blissful moments together.

He woke up one morning and was met with an empty bed and the realization that Nova had left without a word. All their memories now seemed bittersweet, knowing it was just a temporary passion fueled by late nights and adrenaline rushes until it became more profound.

River's heart ached as he remembered their stolen kisses and whispered confessions of love. River couldn't deny that what started as a fling had become genuine and meaningful. He had fallen hard and fast, and now he was left to pick up the pieces alone. But now he couldn't shake the emptiness that consumed him. As he went through the motions of his day, River couldn't help but think about Nova—the one woman he wanted desperately to forget.

He couldn't understand why Nova had disappeared without a word to him. Was it something he'd said or done? Had he imagined the connection they'd shared? Doubt crept into River's mind, clouding his memories with uncertainty. The more he dwelled on it, the more his heart sank.

His pride wouldn't allow him to chase after her. It had been easy to avoid further contact with the woman he never wanted to see again.

Until now.

THE NEXT AFTERNOON, Nova learned that another member of Mateo's family had been assassinated outside his home. She braced herself for the phone call she knew was coming.

As expected, Mateo was enraged and spouting threats.

"I'm coming out there tomorrow to see you and Arya." Perhaps she could better reassure them in person. She spent the next thirty minutes on the phone trying to calm them.

"My cousin was just murdered! Johnny Boy is gonna kill my entire family unless somebody does something to stop him. If DEA or Homeland Security don't do something, then I will."

From what Nova had learned of Johnny Boy, he was a ruthless foe and seemed fated for the drug trade. He was the son of Chilton Raymond, a drug kingpin in Jamaica, and had become involved in the family business at the age of thirteen. Johnny Boy had risen to prominence in the cartel quickly. However, he'd been forced to leave his birthplace when his father violated a pact with a Sinaloa cartel and was assassinated when Johnny Boy was eighteen years old.

Johnny Boy had come to the US to live with his uncle at age twenty. He and Poppy had connected at a party in Miami, and she'd introduced him to Raul Mancuso. Johnny Boy soon began working for the cartel, rising quickly through the ranks.

"We're taking the threats seriously, Mateo," Nova said. "However, family members not part of the program don't receive the same level of protection. Still, we're taking appropriate action to address and investigate any threats or concerns of your relatives."

"So, what does that mean?" Mateo asked. "Do they get some type of protection or not?"

"Various measures will be taken—surveillance, law enforcement intervention, and other protective measures to mitigate potential risks. I want you to know that the safety of your family members is a priority. Law enforcement will assess and respond to threats accordingly. I want you to know that their well-being is a top priority."

As she spoke those words, her mind raced with possible scenarios and plans to protect those under her care. She couldn't afford any mistakes or lapses in security, not when the lives of her witnesses were at stake. Nova was determined to do everything she could to keep everyone safe.

"As long as you stay put, he won't find you," she said. "Do not contact any of your family members, Mateo. This is what the cartel wants. They want you out of hiding."

"I hear you," he responded.

"Do you *really*?" Nova asked. She couldn't shake the dull ache of foreboding that had persisted since Juan's murder. "Don't do something stupid, Mateo." She felt like her words were falling on deaf ears.

It's gonna be a long day, Nova thought to herself after her conversation with Mateo ended.

Her phone rang for a second time, and her heart began to race as she saw the caller ID. The Los Angeles area code flooded her mind with memories of River.

"Hello," she answered cautiously.

"Nova, it's River," he said, his voice bringing back all the emotions she had tried to bury the past couple of years.

"River...hey..." she managed, her heart pounding. "What can I do for you?"

"I'm coming to Charlotte," he announced without preamble. "We need to discuss your witnesses. I'm sure you're aware that Juan DeSoto was killed. I need to speak with his brother. Make sure he's still going to testify."

"Another member of his family has been murdered. His cousin Julio. Neither he nor Juan had any cartel affiliations."

There was a pause on the line. "They're trying to get Mateo out of hiding," River responded.

"That's what I told him. I will try to get protection for his aunt and Juan's family. Have them moved to a safe house."

"Any other family members in Los Angeles?"

"No. The rest of his family is in South America," Nova stated. "When will you arrive?"

"Tomorrow."

"I'm…I'm planning to see Mateo and his wife in the morning." She hesitated, her heart racing at the thought of facing him again. Would he even want to see her? "I'll send you their address, and you can meet me there." Despite the excitement and nerves coursing through her, Nova couldn't deny that seeing him after all these years would bring up a mix of emotions—both longing and fear of the unresolved conflicts between them.

"That's all I need from you," he replied flatly.

She felt a twinge of disappointment at River's lack of emotion. Part of her wanted him to show some enthusiasm that they'd be working together again.

As the clock struck quitting time, Nova considered canceling out meeting up with her best friend, Jersey, at the Golden Pier, a popular spot in uptown Charlotte where local law enforcement went to unwind over drinks.

By the time she reached her car, Nova decided she needed to unwind. She needed to take her mind off the case for a bit.

Her friend met her at the door.

"Perfect timing," Nova said in greeting.

"Hectic day?" Jersey asked after they sat at a table near the bar area shaped like a boat.

Nodding, she responded, "It's been a trying few days, to say the least."

Nova ordered a glass of red wine, and her friend chose white.

While waiting for their drinks to arrive, she said, "I'm

so glad it's Friday." It didn't mean much that it was the weekend, because she'd be driving out to Burlington first thing in the morning to check on Mateo and Arya. But she needed the short reprieve.

"So am I," Jersey murmured as she released her long reddish locs from the hair band that held them hostage. "I'm glad I'm not on call this weekend. I've had a busy week." Her friend was a homicide detective for the Charlotte-Mecklenburg Police Department. "I wore my murder boots more than my heels."

"You're the only person I know who has murder boots," Nova said with a chuckle. "And bright yellow ones at that." Jersey always wore rain boots whenever she visited a crime scene.

"I'm not messing up a good pair of shoes while looking for evidence," Jersey responded. "I can just rinse off my boots and keep it moving."

A couple of middle-aged men sat at a table across the room. One worked with the Marshals Service, while the other was an assistant district attorney. The assistant DA made eye contact with them and gave a slight nod in greeting.

"What's up with you and Matt?" Nova asked in a low whisper as their drinks arrived. "He can't seem to take his eyes off you."

"He keeps telling me that he wants us to try again," Jersey answered, turning her face away from him to Nova.

"How do you feel about it?"

"I don't know." Jersey shrugged. "I still love him, but I'm just not sure we belong together. Sometimes it's best not to revisit the past."

Nova picked up the menu and opened it.

Jersey sipped her wine, then asked, "What about you? Have you met anyone interesting?"

"Not really."

"You're a borderline workaholic, Nova," Jersey stated.

"You're probably right," she responded with a slight shrug.

"What about that DEA agent, River?"

Nova gave a choked, desperate laugh. "What about *him*? It's been *two* years. I'm pretty sure by now he's found someone else and is incredibly happy." She tried to keep her expression bland, but she couldn't ignore the ache in her heart whenever she thought of him. She wouldn't tell Jersey just yet about the call they'd had—or the fact she'd see him tomorrow.

Jersey studied her for a moment before replying, "I can tell by the look on your face that you don't really mean that. Don't you think it's about time you and River had a conversation?"

Nova placed a hand over her face convulsively. "About *what*?"

"Well…the way y'all left things, for one."

"You just said that sometimes it's best not to revisit the past—I agree," Nova said smoothly.

"I was referring to *my* situation."

"I know that. But it can apply to my personal life as well."

Jersey's greenish-gray eyes rested on hers. "There's just one huge difference with you and River. Y'all left a lot unsaid on the table."

"I told you that things moved at an alarming pace between us, Jersey," she stated with a hint of sadness in her voice. "It was overwhelming and I couldn't keep up." She paused, her eyes clouded with memories. "We spent every waking moment together for two weeks straight. It was all-consuming and it scared me. I needed to take a step back and figure out what I really wanted."

"Maybe for you," she responded. "But how do you know that he feels the same way?"

"Jersey, I know you mean well, but what River and I had is over and done with," Nova stated. "I admit I could've handled things better with him, but I can't rewind the clock. Besides, I spoke with him earlier. He'll be in town tomorrow to discuss a case."

Jersey's eyebrows shot up in disbelief. "How was it? Talking to River after all this time?"

"It was just business," Nova responded. "He told me he was coming to Charlotte. I said okay."

Although Nova continued to put on a facade of nonchalance for her friend, she felt an acute sense of loss deep down.

She shoved that aside as they gave their food order to the server who'd come to their table.

Jersey stood up. "I'm going to talk to Matt for a few minutes. I'll be right back."

"Take your time," Nova said.

She glanced around, taking in her surroundings. The servers were dressed in nautical uniforms. Nova soaked in the laughter and the various conversations that danced upon each interval just a tad higher than the soft musical notes playing in the background. She studied the muted colors of the bottles behind the bar.

A platter of hot wings was delivered to their table.

Nova placed six on her plate but waited for Jersey to return to dive in.

"Sorry about that. I didn't mean to be gone so long," her friend said when she sat down ten minutes later.

"I was just about to get started without you."

"Well, I appreciate you." Jersey stabbed her fork into

a wing, placing it on her plate. "Oh, I ordered us another glass of wine."

"Thanks," Nova said. She dipped a lemon-pepper drumette into ranch dressing, and the conversation turned to lighter topics.

After eating, Nova left the restaurant, heading home while Jersey stayed behind with Matt.

They are so getting back together, Nova thought to herself.

She tried but couldn't remember the last time she'd been on a date. Her focus for the last year and a half had been advancing her career. However, Nova was slowly realizing she was ready for a new career challenge.

There was a time when she didn't want anything other than to walk in her father's footsteps as a US marshal, but it hadn't been the same for her since Easton's death. She still wanted to go after the Mancuso cartel but had been thinking about switching law enforcement agencies to have a more active role in the fight against drug trafficking.

Nova glanced over at the clock on her nightstand. In a few hours, she would come face-to-face with River. Her heart raced as memories flooded her mind, the weight of regret pressing against her chest. She had always been a free spirit, drifting wherever the wind took her. And two years ago, when River had hinted that he wanted a future with her, she couldn't bear the thought of being tied down. It wasn't in her nature.

So, Nova ran.

But now she found herself questioning her choices. Had running away indeed been the right decision?

She sat in the middle of her bed, contemplating what to say when she saw him.

Nova had to prepare emotionally for facing him again. She didn't have a solid explanation for why'd she done a disappearing act. She cared deeply for River, and those feelings had scared her.

If someone asked her why, Nova couldn't provide an answer.

The clock ticked relentlessly, its sound echoing through the quiet room.

Nova couldn't understand why she struggled with commitment. The lingering doubt of what could have been if she hadn't run away that fateful night consumed her thoughts. It was a question that haunted her, even though she had accepted long ago that it would never be answered.

Deep down, Nova knew that the real reason for her reluctance stemmed from losing her father. His sudden passing had left a hole in her heart and a fear of getting too close to anyone else for fear of losing them, too. This realization only added to the weight of her doubts and fears, making it all the more difficult for her to let go and open up to love.

Chapter Two

Chapter Two

Nova got up early to make the hour-and-forty-four-minute drive to the quaint town of Burlington. She was vigilant, making sure no one was following her. Not that she expected to be followed, but one couldn't be sure. She always took extra precautions whenever she went to a witness's house.

She exited off I-85 and took Freeman Mill Road to a small neighborhood near the Friendly Center.

Ten minutes later, Nova pulled into the driveway of a modest two-story house on a corner lot with two sizable, colorful rosebushes adorning the front.

She took a deep, calming breath before walking to the porch. Mateo and his wife were going to find a way to work her nerves.

Nova admired the two giant Boston ferns in hanging baskets before ringing the doorbell. Arya had gifted hands when it came to plants and flowers.

She found the door unlocked—the lock looked like it had been tampered with, putting her on instant alert.

Nova entered the house, hand on her duty weapon.

The tiny hairs on her neck stood to attention, and her pulse raced. Her internal warning system screamed, but she couldn't abandon her charges.

After thoroughly searching the main level and finding

no one, she went upstairs, relieved she hadn't stumbled across their bodies.

Nova was about to walk into the master bedroom when she heard a sound behind her. She glimpsed a shadowed figure in her peripheral view. She prepared to defend herself when another masked intruder shoved her back into the hall. Taken by surprise, Nova managed to get her gun in hand, but before she could get a shot off, the intruder's gloved fist slammed into her face, making her eyes water.

He went for her gun and ripped it out of her hand.

Dizzy and disoriented, she used every ounce of strength to land a punch to the intruder's gut; the force of it loosened her gun from the man's grasp and sent it sliding across the floor.

Lightning flashed before her eyes as another fist hurtled into her. Nova fought off her assailant with her full might. She scratched, pummeled and kicked, then grabbed the lamp off a hall table and smashed it down on her attacker.

The second intruder hit her on the head with something, causing white-hot pain to flash through her brain before everything went black.

As River approached his destination, his heart began to race and his palms grew sweaty. He had avoided seeing Nova for the past eighteen months, but now he couldn't escape it. As he pulled into the driveway, his eyes landed on a black SUV. His thought was that it belonged to her.

Dread filled his stomach as he parked next to the vehicle. Seeing Nova again after all this time made him realize how much he had missed her, but also how much he feared her presence.

He took a deep breath and exhaled slowly before getting out to walk up the front steps.

River had barely touched the door when it swung open. Warning prickled at the back of his neck as he stepped over the threshold. He could practically hear his heart beating over the silence.

He pulled out his duty weapon, raising it at shoulder level as he cautiously entered the house.

River checked out the kitchen and dining area. Faded traces of sunlight penetrated through the large window along the opposite wall, casting shadows in the living room.

"Mateo?" he called out. "This is Special Agent River Randolph with the DEA… Deputy Marshal Bennett…?"

The sense that something was off felt even stronger now. River's eyes darted around, searching for the slightest movement. He moved deeper into the house, then walked back to the front door. He looked upward to the second-floor railing before making his way slowly up the stairs.

As he approached the landing, River saw Nova crumpled on the floor outside of a bedroom. Unconscious.

His heart leaped to his throat as he knelt to check her pulse. *Please let her be okay. She's got to be fine.* Her pulse beat faintly against his fingers. River called for paramedics and the police.

He examined Nova while waiting for the EMTs to arrive. He wanted to make sure she was still breathing. River couldn't bear the thought that she might be seriously wounded. Someone must have been here when she arrived.

After Nova was taken to the hospital, River stayed behind with the two police officers who were processing the house as a crime scene. He walked slowly through the house where Mateo and Arya had lived for the past several months, scanning his surroundings.

The living room looked fine, except for the bookcases. It

looked like someone had rummaged through them, searching for something.

When he entered the master bedroom, River found the space in disarray. Items of women's clothing were strewn across a chair in one corner. Several drawers were left open, and it looked as though someone had rifled through them. The closet door was ajar, revealing empty hangers and abandoned shoeboxes.

He walked over and peered inside to get a closer look. There was only one piece of luggage inside. Indentations in the carpet showed there were at least two suitcases missing. *Looks like someone packed in a hurry,* he thought to himself.

There were signs of forced entry when they examined the back door. Someone had broken into the house, but he didn't think they'd found what they sought. When he found no vehicle in the garage, River was pretty sure that Mateo and Arya were on the run. And he wasn't happy about it.

He went back to the bedroom for a second, more thorough observation.

The room was in disarray, with drawers and cabinets left open as if someone had frantically searched for something. River knew it wasn't just a coincidence. The intruder must have been looking for something specific, and they likely heard Nova enter the house. They knocked her out and quickly disappeared, leaving behind a trail of destruction in their wake. It was clear that they were determined to find whatever it was they were after.

An hour later, River was at the hospital checking on Nova. He stood outside her room, silently debating whether to go inside. He'd been told her injury wasn't life-threatening, which was a relief to him. Despite how he felt about her, he didn't want any harm to come to her.

He peeked inside.

Nova lay on her side, buried under a couple of blankets.

River noted that she was more beautiful than he remembered. Lying in that hospital bed, a bandage on her forehead, Nova looked much younger than her thirty-three years. When they'd first met, she wore her hair in a cute pixie cut, which had grown out, reaching well past her shoulders. The warm brown tendrils and golden highlights complemented the glow of her honey complexion. Faint freckles were speckled across her nose.

Unexpected and disquieting thoughts raced through his mind; River's heart rate increased every time he pictured Nova's smile. His mouth tightened as he remembered how she'd treated him at the end of their assignment.

After a romantic evening filled with talk of a possible future together, River woke up to find himself alone. He had left his room foolishly searching for Nova, only to discover she'd already checked out of the hotel. She didn't even bother to leave a note behind. He'd witnessed firsthand the way she handled herself in dangerous situations, so River had never thought Nova was the type of woman who would run away.

Nova moaned softly, then shifted her position slightly.

River eased back toward the door.

She had hugely gotten under his skin, and when she'd left, she'd disappeared when he needed her the most. River shook his head as if to ward off the thought. It wasn't something he wanted to admit to himself.

NOVA OPENED HER eyes and looked around. She felt dizzy and weak but alert enough to recognize that she was in a hospital. Judging from the royal blue curtain that walled off the space, which was big enough for a bed and a chair, she was in the emergency department.

It took her a moment to remember what had happened. Her memory cleared from its foggy state—someone had jumped her. Maybe two people. Nova squeezed her eyes shut, trying to remember exactly what had taken place at the de Leon home.

Bracing herself against the pain, she placed a shaky hand on her face, which still throbbed with a dull ache. Her eyes were sensitive to the lighting in the room. She closed then opened them a few times, trying to adjust her gaze. She heard someone moaning softly in the bed next to her. Not only could she hear every groan and the private conversation between the patient and family member, but she could also smell the vomit.

The sickening odor caused Nova's stomach to churn in rebellion. She swallowed the sourness that threatened to come up and silently commanded the stirring in her belly to calm down.

Nova glimpsed a couple of nurses in light blue scrubs walking past her room. Wincing, she put a hand once again to her forehead.

Out of the corner of her eye, she glimpsed a slight curtain movement.

Nova's eyes widened as she spotted River walking toward her, his close-cropped hair perfectly framing his face. His almond-colored skin seemed to glow in the sunlight, highlighting every chiseled feature. Despite the pain that spiked through her head, she couldn't help but admire how handsome he still was, just like she remembered him. "River... what are you doing here?"

"I told you I was coming to Charlotte, remember?"

"I do," she responded after a moment.

"I found you unconscious at the house."

Nova blinked. "You brought me here?"

"No. I called the paramedics," River responded. "Did you happen to see who hit you?"

"Everything happened so fast. All I know is that there were two people in the house. I had one down, and the other hit me with something. I don't know what."

"Nova…how long have you known Mateo and his wife were thinking about running?"

River's accusatory tone made Nova sit up in bed. "Mateo was upset, but I'd hoped I'd convinced him to stay in the program. There were intruders in their home. There is the possibility that they might have been kidnapped." She winced from the throbbing ache of her head.

"I don't think so," River responded.

She peered over at him. "Why do you say that?"

"Kidnappers wouldn't have taken the time to pack clothes," he replied. "Two pieces of luggage are missing and so is the vehicle. It looks like they *ran* off before the intruder arrived."

"We have to find them," Nova said as she slipped from under the covers. "I'll initiate a search for the SUV."

"You're not going anywhere," he said. "The doctor hasn't released you."

"I can't just sit here either."

"Do you have any idea where Mateo might have gone?" River asked.

"I'd say Los Angeles. He was really upset over the deaths of his brother and cousin. He wants revenge. As for Arya, she most likely went to her parents' home in San Diego. She's been really worried about them. From what I understand, she and her mother were extremely close."

Nova's gut twisted with guilt. She should have been watching them more closely. They were her witnesses, under her protection, and now they were missing. Her heart raced with worry for their safety, knowing how consumed with rage one had been and how anxious the other was about her family. It was all too much, a constant nagging that kept Nova on edge, unable to relax until she found them safe and sound.

He shook his head no. "I don't think she's with her parents. Since Juan's death, I've had someone watching them, and there's been no sighting of Arya."

Mateo and Arya's disappearance made her head pound even worse. "I hope you're wrong about this."

"I've been wrong about many things, but this isn't one of them," River stated.

Nova stiffened. She had a feeling he was referring to his past relationship with her. But she was too weak to mount up a defense, so she let the comment slide for now. She and River had more pressing matters that required their full attention.

Chapter Three

River was all business with Nova. "You know that Mateo called the DEA after an attempt was made on his life," he said.

"Yeah." She nodded. Mateo knew how far the cartel would go to get to him and yet he'd fled.

"He embezzled money from them. They won't forget that. So, why do you think he'd risk leaving the program?" River asked. "Do you really think it's about revenge for Juan's and Julio's deaths?"

"Obviously, you think it's something more," Nova responded. "What's your theory?"

"I believe it's because Mateo had something he assumed was important enough to bargain with. I agree with the agent who did the original interview. He suspected that Mateo withheld crucial information from us. If this is true, then it's possible that he's out there trying to negotiate for his and Arya's life."

"Randolph called to update me on your condition." Roy Cohen's voice made them both look toward the entrance.

The appearance of her supervisor at the hospital caught her by surprise.

Something's wrong. She could tell by the grave expression on Roy's face. His pale complexion almost matched the yellowish-blond color of his hair.

"What's happened now?" she asked. "Has another one of Mateo's relatives been murdered?"

"Not a relative," Cohen answered, closing the curtain behind him. "This time it was Mateo."

Shock coursed through her body. "*What?* When?"

Cohen shook his head. "Mateo flew to Los Angeles last night... And now he's dead."

After she found her voice, Nova said, "That's why I drove to Burlington. I wanted to assess the situation. I knew Mateo was upset over Juan's death. I wanted to make sure he didn't do anything like leave the program."

"Airport surveillance shows that he was traveling alone."

"I can't believe this..." She muttered a string of profanity under her breath. "I told Mateo to stand down..." After a moment, she asked, "Where's my phone?"

"Nova, you need to rest," River said.

"I need my phone."

He handed it to her.

She immediately called Arya's number.

No answer.

Nova tried it several times over the next half hour.

Still no answer.

She left a message saying, "Arya, this is Deputy Marshal Bennett. I need you to return my call as soon as possible." She knew Arya was the anxious type, and Mateo's death would only make her anxiety worse.

She looked over at River. "There's a chance that Arya stayed behind but she's gone into hiding somewhere. I feel in my gut that she's in trouble."

"She is in just as much danger as Mateo was," he agreed. "Arya may actually have knowledge of what her husband did for the cartel, or the cartel suspects Mateo told her everything."

Nova folded her arms and said, "She told the last DEA agent assigned to the investigation that Mateo had kept her in the dark. She thought her husband was an accountant for high-profile clients—not that he was involved in something illegal. According to her, Arya only discovered the truth when he decided to go into the program."

"Mateo gave us copies of cartel files, but I strongly feel he didn't give us everything. The last agent who touched the file felt the same way. Mateo knew where most of the bodies were buried, so he knew way more than he told us."

"You seem pretty sure about this?" Cohen interjected.

"I've known Mateo for a few years. He came up a few times in other investigations. From what I know about him, that was his character. He was stealing from the cartel, so it's not beneath him to try to blackmail Johnny Boy and Poppy. Especially if he thought he could get enough money to stay alive."

"Okay, you might be right about Mateo, but that doesn't mean he told Arya anything. Mateo told me that he kept her from his business dealings with the cartel."

"Nova, she's the only person Mateo trusted," River stated.

She slowly swung her legs to the edge of the bed and braced herself for the head rush. "I need to see the doctor. I have to get out of here." Nova pressed the call button.

"You should try and rest for a while," River said.

"I agree," Cohen commented.

"I told you both that I'm good," she responded. "We have to find Arya."

When the nurse came, Nova told her, "I need to see the doctor. I'm ready to get out of here. I'm in the middle of an investigation."

"He'll be here as soon as he's done with another patient."

"Thank you," she replied.

The doctor walked into the room.

"I'll be outside," River said.

"You don't have to leave," Nova responded. "This shouldn't take long."

The doctor conducted a series of neurological and cognitive examinations and then ordered an MRI.

"Don't leave until I get back?" she told both men. Nova suddenly didn't want to be alone. Her anxiety level was always high whenever she had to undergo any medical assessments.

"Sure," River responded, while Cohen nodded in agreement.

After the MRI, Nova was returned to her room, and River was nowhere to be found.

Disappointment washed over her that he hadn't kept his word. It was soon blocked by the memory that she'd disappeared on him. Maybe this was some form of payback.

"He stepped out to make some phone calls," Cohen said.

River hadn't left. Her body sagged with relief as she eased back into the hospital bed. She didn't want to examine that reaction too closely. River was here for work—it was nothing personal.

"CAN I COME IN?" River asked from the doorway a few minutes later.

"Yeah. C'mon in…"

The doctor swept into the room behind River. "You have a concussion… We want to keep you overnight for observation."

Nova shook her head. "No. I need to go home."

"You have to physically and mentally rest to recover from a concussion," the doctor said. "Although you have a minor concussion, if you try to return to your regular activities too early, there is a risk of another concussion. You should wait until all your symptoms are gone before resuming normal activities."

"How long can these symptoms last?"

"In many cases, symptoms of a minor concussion resolve within a few days to a couple of weeks," the doctor responded.

When he left the room, Nova eyed her supervisor and River. "Great. I'll be fine in a few days. I've always healed fast."

"Nova, you could've been killed," Cohen stated.

"I know. The good news is that I wasn't." She sighed in frustration. "I can't believe I have to stay here in this hospital."

"It's just one night," River responded.

Nova surprised him by asking, "Will you stay with me?"

He met her gaze before looking away. "I have to go back to the house and speak with the police."

River glimpsed a shadow of disappointment in her eyes before it disappeared.

"Oh. Okay," she said.

"I want to make sure I didn't miss anything earlier." He didn't know why but he felt the need to explain. "I'll come back here if it's not too late. In the meantime, you need to rest."

"What I really need is to get out of this hospital," Nova responded. "I'm so over it already."

River knew why she didn't like hospitals. They'd talked about it during the two weeks they'd spent together. He also despised this environment because it served as a constant reminder of vulnerability and mortality. Every sterile smell, clinical beep and antiseptic surface reinforced his discomfort. But pain of any kind was a sign of weakness, as far as River was concerned. In the thirty-five years he'd been in this world, he'd cried twice: when he realized his mother never wanted him, and at the death of the woman who did—his grandmother.

He knew Nova associated hospitals with her own fragility, stemming from witnessing the decline of her paternal grandmother when she was sixteen.

Turning up her nose, Nova uttered, "The smells...the white coats and scrubs..." She shuddered. "I just can't stand being in here."

"Don't give the nurses a hard time." River walked toward the curtain. "I'd better get out of here."

"Now you're the one running away," Nova muttered beneath her breath. Could she blame him? River had every right to be skittish where she was concerned. But they would have to put aside their feelings to work together.

BY THE TIME River returned to the hospital, Nova had been moved into a private room for the night. He took the elevator to the fourth floor and stood outside her door until a nurse asked, "Are you okay?"

"Yes, I'm fine," he responded. "She's resting, and I didn't want to disturb her."

"She's been expecting you."

"The other visitor...is he still here?" River inquired.

The nurse shook her head no. "He left when she was moved to this room."

River eased inside, careful not to disturb Nova.

She was asleep, almost buried under the thin bedcovers.

He'd never forgotten her mesmerizing brown eyes or the way his body reacted when he locked gazes with him. Her long lashes brushed the top of her cheeks, almost kissing the freckles sprinkled across the bridge of her nose.

Nova had come close to dying earlier. Although they

hadn't been on speaking terms, River didn't want anything bad to happen to her.

A soft moan interrupted his thoughts. Nova shifted her position but didn't wake up.

Silently, River slid into the chair meant for visitors and suppressed a shiver as the antiseptic smell of the hospital surrounded him. He hated this place, with its sterile walls and constant reminders of death. It brought back painful memories of his grandmother's final days, fighting a losing battle against cancer. And now he was here again, by Nova's side.

He couldn't let himself get too close to her. But for now, he would stay by her side until she woke up and he could leave this place once again.

While she slept, River reviewed the information he had on her witnesses. He and Nova shared a common goal. They both wanted to find Arya de Leon. Her husband had been a valuable informant for the DEA, providing them with crucial information on drug trafficking operations. However, upon further investigation, they discovered that there were significant gaps in his reports.

Files from certain years were missing, and it appeared that large sums of money could not be traced or accounted for. This raised suspicions and cast doubt on the validity of his testimony. The DEA team knew they had to tread carefully as they delved deeper into this tangled web of deceit and illegal activities. It would mean a win for the agency if River could fill in the missing pieces. Not to mention his career.

His last two investigations had resulted in significant busts. River felt he was on a winning streak and didn't want to lose focus. He wanted to prove something to himself and those who never thought he'd amount to much.

It was too bad Mary, the woman who'd given him up at birth, was gone.

He had been a very angry kid and was constantly in trouble for fighting and skipping school. And then he'd been recruited to play for an AAU basketball team when he was fourteen. The coach had watched him playing street ball and thought he showed promise.

River had flourished under the tutelage of his coach/mentor, eventually graduating with a 3.99 GPA. He'd attended college on an athletic scholarship, joining the DEA after graduation.

He and his former coach still kept in touch. The man was there for River when his grandmother passed away four years ago and again when Mary had died in March.

Nova turned from one side to the other, and River observed her for a moment, then looked away. He settled back against the cushion of the chair and closed his eyes. The events of the day were catching up with him.

NOVA SAT UP in bed, looking around. A smile tugged at her lips when she saw River across from her, sound asleep in what had to be the most uncomfortable chair.

Almost as if he'd felt her eyes on him, River woke up.

"Good morning," she said, trying to sound cheerful.

He brushed at his eyes. "G'morning. How are you feeling?"

"I still have a little bit of a headache, but other than that I feel fine." Nova gestured toward the chair he was sitting in. "How could you sleep in that?"

"It's more comfortable than it looks," River responded. "The nurse told me it converts into a cot, but I hadn't planned on falling asleep."

Nova moved to the edge of the bed and then swung her

legs outward. "I'm gonna take a shower. Hopefully, the doctor will come by soon, and I'll be able to get out of here."

She slowly made her way across the room.

In the bathroom, she stood close to the mirror, checking out the bruises on her forehead.

Nova removed the hospital gown and got into the shower.

The hot water didn't do much to soothe her aching body, but she hadn't expected otherwise. She just wanted a bath.

Two knocks reverberated through the bathroom door.

Nova turned off the water and then got out. "Yeah?"

"I was checking to make sure you're okay," River said through the door.

"I'm good."

"Okay."

Nova grabbed a towel and dried off.

She slipped on a T-shirt and a pair of leggings that were in the large handbag she had with her. Nova took a deep breath and then walked out of the bathroom.

"Do you know if my gun was recovered?" she asked.

"I have it," River responded.

Nova was relieved. "Thank you for keeping it safe."

She tried to hide her joy at being back in bed. She felt accomplished in not having to ask River for help. If they were on better terms, it was possible Nova wouldn't feel the way she did.

He hadn't been rude to her, but he was very distant. Even now, they sat in the room in a pregnant silence, waiting for the doctor to arrive.

River got up and walked over to the window, looking out.

"How long do you intend to be in town?" Nova asked.

"Until I speak with Arya."

"I'm not sure she'll be of much help to you, River. She

had nothing to do with anything," she responded, keeping her voice low.

Their conversation came to a halt when the doctor entered the room.

An hour later, Nova was released from the hospital.

"Thanks for having my car brought here," she said as River held the door open for her.

"Are you sure you can drive yourself back to Charlotte?" he asked. "You can ride with me."

"I'm good," Nova responded. "The headache is pretty much gone now. No dizziness or double vision. I'll be fine."

"I'll be following you. If you need help, just pull to the side of the road."

"Thank you, but I'm sure I'll be okay."

Nova didn't drive off right away. Her head was consumed with thoughts of Arya and her safety, trying to come up with ideas of where she could have gone. So far, nothing had come back on the license tag.

She was acutely aware that River was sitting patiently in his vehicle waiting.

When it looked as if he were about to get out of his car, Nova started the car and left the hospital parking lot.

He followed her to I-40.

Three and a half miles later, they took the exit to I-85 South. Nova noticed that River stayed at least two cars behind her. It was as if he was sending the message that he intended to keep her at arm's length.

Nova felt the stirrings of guilt and regret over how she had walked out of River's life without so much as a word to him. At the time, she didn't know what to say to the man she'd fallen in love with but hardly knew. She'd panicked, and the only thing she could think to do was run away.

Nova assumed he must have had regrets, too, because

she'd never heard from River afterward. His lack of communication validated her belief that she'd made the right decision. Still, she was bothered by the remoteness she'd glimpsed in his gaze earlier.

Could he forget what we shared so easily?

Swallowing her apprehension, Nova chewed on her bottom lip as she drove. As much as she wanted to forget, she couldn't. The first time she and River had made love was forever etched in her mind. It was when Nova realized she'd fallen in love with him. That realization had shaken her to the very core.

The intensity of her feelings for River scared her, forcing Nova to flee despite knowing she couldn't move on with someone else. The truth was that he wasn't a man who could be easily replaced.

Now he could barely look at or stand around her. Not that Nova could blame him, given how she'd left things between them.

I should have written River a note or something. He deserved better from me.

She couldn't undo what had transpired between them. Nova considered it a waste of time to dwell on something she could not change.

She wondered if he'd met a woman who loved him freely and without reservation. The thought didn't sit well with her, but she couldn't blame River. After all, she was the one who'd chosen to walk away.

An hour and forty-five minutes later, Nova walked into her town house. She'd half expected River to follow her all the way home or at least call to see if she was okay.

Silence. He didn't call or come by.

He's really over me.

Nova choked down her disappointment. Forcing River

from her mind, she navigated to her home office. Seated at her desk, Nova placed a quick call to check in with her supervisor. She pulled out a bottle of Tylenol from the side drawer and tossed one in her mouth, followed by sips of room-temperature bottled water.

Nova settled back in her chair, waiting a few minutes for the pain to subside.

A photograph fell out when she picked up the folder lying on her desk.

It was of Mateo and his wife.

Nova admired the locket Arya always wore around her neck. It was a lovely piece of jewelry. Her mother had one that was given to her by her grandmother, but she hardly ever wore it.

Nova pushed away from her desk and stood up.

She walked over to a painting and removed it to reveal a built-in safe. She opened it and tossed the file inside. She kept all the physical files on her witnesses locked up for security. The copies on her computer were all encrypted as well.

She thought back to what River had said about Arya. Nova had to find her before the cartel did.

Chapter Four

There had always been an undeniable magnetism between River and Nova, which probably explained why he was sitting in his rental car down the street from her town house. River wanted to make sure she'd arrived home safely. But he didn't want her to know that he cared this much about her well-being.

He hated seeing her again. It had taken him two years to get her out of his system. River certainly didn't want to work with her, but he had no choice. She was Arya's handler, and he needed her assistance finding the woman. He didn't doubt that Nova would do whatever she could to keep Arya safe and in WITSEC.

After an hour passed, River felt she'd pretty much settled in for the rest of the day, so he headed to his hotel. He had only planned to be in town long enough to talk to Mateo, but now that he was dead and his wife missing...River's stay would be extended. He knew Nova had initiated a trace on the vehicle owned by Mateo and Arya. In the meantime, he decided to comb the file once more.

He spent the afternoon watching hours of video taken during Mateo's interrogation. Outside of handling finances and laundering money for the cartel, Mateo had also assisted in securing stash houses where thousands of kilograms of cocaine were unloaded from tanker trucks and then reloaded with weapons and money headed to and from California, Mexico and Arizona. During his involvement with the Mancuso cartel, he had extensive knowledge of shipments of cocaine, fentanyl and other drugs worth several billions of dollars.

Mateo had been a valuable asset for the DEA; the wealth of information and evidence he had against John Boyd Raymond made him a coveted witness. The notorious criminal sat atop the FBI's Ten Most Wanted Fugitives list, hunted by every law enforcement agency in the country. But for the DEA, it was personal. They were determined to bring Johnny Boy to justice for the cold-blooded murder of two of their agents. For River, one of the fallen agents had been like a brother, fueling his burning desire for vengeance and driving him to do whatever it took to see Johnny Boy behind bars.

River ordered room service and then made a phone call to his partner.

"Hey, Kenny. Thanks for the information on Pablo and Ramona Lozano." He'd had his partner help with the surveillance of Arya's parents, and so far, there had been little movement from the couple. "Do me a favor and keep them under surveillance for a few more days. Their daughter may show up there. Let me know as soon as she does."

"How is Nova doing?"

"She's fine," River responded. He'd called Kenny to update him after Nova was taken to the hospital. "No real damage done. She's at home now."

"Did you two get a chance to talk things over?"

"About the witness...yes, we did."

"You know that's not what I was talking about," Kenny

responded. "You and Nova need to have a conversation about what happened."

"I told you that what Nova and I had is long over. I'm not about to rehash the past. The only thing between us now is our dead witness's missing wife."

"If you say so…"

"I do," River stated. "Hey, look…I need to get back to work. I'll check in with you tomorrow."

He disconnected with Kenny and called Nova, unsure why he couldn't shake the worry that clung to him. "I just wanted to make sure you're all right and see if you needed anything."

"I'm fine." Her calm voice reassured him, but he could hear the exhaustion. "I ate something and took my medication."

"Okay," River said, trying to sound casual. "Call or text me if you need me to pick up dinner or something."

"I will. Thanks."

After hanging up, he stretched out on the bed, his body feeling out of sync with the time difference. As he lay there, thoughts of Nova filled his mind. He tried to find comfort in shifting from one side to the other, but it was useless.

Giving up on sleep after an hour of restlessness, River sat up in bed and propped himself against the pillows. He returned to reviewing the files on Mateo, but they couldn't distract him from the nagging thoughts about Nova and their complicated past.

CLAD IN A sports bra and a pair of leggings, Nova sat down on the edge of her king-size bed. She pulled her golden-brown hair into a high ponytail before sliding under the covers. The headache was now a dull throb.

At 3:07 p.m. her phone rang, the ringtone identifying the caller as her best friend.

She sat up in bed to take the call. "Hey, Jersey…"

"You all right?" she asked. "River told me what happened."

"River called *you*?" Nova couldn't believe it.

"Yeah. I was listed as your emergency contact. He had called the precinct the day everything happened and left a message for me. I was working a case and didn't call him back until a few minutes ago. He told me you were home now. How are you feeling?"

"I'm good," Nova responded.

"Girl, what happened?"

"I went to check on my witness, and someone clocked me good," she responded. "River was meeting me there. He found me unconscious."

"Thank goodness he showed up in time," Jersey said. "I think it's interesting that you are working together again."

Nova didn't respond.

"Do you need anything? I just got off work, but I can pick up something for you to eat."

"River called not too long ago asking if I needed anything. I told him I was good. I can always have something delivered."

"That was sweet of him."

"Yeah. Don't read too much into it, Jersey."

"Well, reach out if you change your mind. I can run out and pick you up something."

"I probably won't be bothering you," Nova said. "I'm going to take a nap."

"Check in with me when you wake up."

"Okay," Nova responded.

As she settled under her soft, fluffy comforter, Nova reached over and placed her smartphone on the nightstand.

She sighed in relief, hoping that the darkness and stillness of the room would help ease her pounding headache.

Just as she closed her eyes, the shrill ringtone of her work phone broke through the silence. Her hand darted to grab it.

"Deputy Marshal Bennett speaking," she answered professionally. But all she heard on the other end was silence.

"Who is this?" Nova asked, growing suspicious and slightly irritated.

Still, no response came from the other end, just an eerie quiet that sent a chill down her spine. "Arya?"

The caller hung up.

Nova bolted upright and called the office to ask one of the techs to trace the call.

She released a short sigh of frustration, abandoning the idea of a nap. She couldn't afford to be down right now.

Headache or not, she was going back to work.

The only reason she'd tried to rest was because her boss had insisted. Her gut instinct told her that Arya had been the caller.

"Where are you, Arya?" she whispered.

Rubbing her temples, Nova reached for her phone and dialed the office to check on the progress of the trace. As she listened to the ringing, her mind wandered back to the missing woman.

"Deputy Marshal Bennett, we managed to trace the call." An agent's voice crackled through the receiver, snapping Nova back to reality. Her heart raced as she leaned forward, anticipation filling her. "It's from a burner phone."

"Where did it come from?"

"It's strange. The call was traced back to an abandoned house in Concord."

So, Arya's still in North Carolina.

"Send the location to my phone, please."

"Sending now."

Without hesitation, Nova got out of bed. She slipped a hoodie over her head and grabbed her keys, determined to find Arya and bring her back into the safety of WITSEC.

Chapter Five

As Nova approached the abandoned house, her heart quickened with unease. The air was thick and still, almost as if it held its breath in anticipation. In the distance, she could hear the faint whispers of the trees rustling in the wind, adding to the ominous atmosphere.

She scanned the wooded area, searching for any signs of life, but there was nothing—no cars on the street, no movement behind the windows.

Taking a deep breath, Nova exited her car and stepped onto the cracked pavement. With each step closer to the house, she could feel a strange energy enveloping her, making her skin prickle with goose bumps. She'd considered calling River, but decided to venture out alone. Her thoughts were centered on Arya and finding her.

The front door hung open, the lock broken and swinging on its hinges. She couldn't tell if someone had forced it open or if time had slowly eroded its strength.

Cautiously, she entered the darkened interior. "Arya?" she called out softly. "It's me, Nova. Please don't be scared. I want to help you. I can take you somewhere safe." Her voice echoed through the empty halls, but there was no response except for the creaking of floorboards beneath her feet.

As Nova ventured farther into the house, the atmosphere grew even more suffocating. The air seemed to thicken, making it harder to breathe. The dying light from the outside filtered through the cracks in the boarded-up windows, casting eerie shadows on the peeling wallpaper.

With each step, Nova's apprehension deepened and her temples throbbed. A shiver danced down her spine, and she wrapped her arms around herself for comfort, though it offered little solace.

The silence was deafening, broken only by the distant howl of a neighborhood dog. As Nova ascended the creaky staircase, she felt a strange pull drawing her toward a particular room. The door stood slightly ajar, inviting her inside like a siren's call.

Summoning every ounce of courage, Nova placed her hand on her weapon before pushing open the door.

Evidence of recent occupancy was scattered about the bedroom. A brand-new sleeping bag lay crumpled on the floor, still bearing the crisp folds from its packaging. Empty fast-food containers and their greasy remnants were strewn on the dusty window seat, along with a roll of toilet paper and depleted water bottles. It was clear that someone had slept here, but they were long gone now.

This current setting before Nova was a stark contrast to the woman she had come to know. Arya de Leon was all about five-star hotels, often clutching the locket she wore around her neck at the thought of staying anywhere less extravagant.

Her gaze drifted back to the sleeping bag, and she strode over to it. With a nudge from her shoe, the cover was thrown open, revealing a cell phone inside. Nova was confident that it was the one used to call her earlier.

She hesitated for a moment, her mind racing with questions. Was it Arya who had left the phone here? And why?

Nova's curiosity got the better of her, compelling her to pick up the device. As she held it in her hand, the weight of intrigue settled upon her.

The screen flickered to life, displaying a simple text message: Find me.

RIVER WAS CAUGHT off guard when Nova reached out to him. He had offered to help with errands or bring food but never expected to actually hear from her.

"I heard from Arya," she announced.

"When?"

"She called me a couple of hours ago but didn't say anything."

"How did you know it was her?" he asked. "How can you be sure?"

"I wasn't until now," Nova responded. "I had a trace put on the number, which led to an old abandoned house in Concord. I followed the trail and—"

"You did *what*?" River's mind was abuzz as he took in the news. Nova had risked her safety and well-being to find answers, and he couldn't shake off his worry for her.

"I checked out the house and found the cell phone. There was a message on it that said, 'Find me.'"

"Nova, where are you right now?"

"I'm in my car at a gas station. I'm heading home when I hang up with you."

"Be safe."

"River, I'm fine. I feel fine."

As Nova promised to head back home, River couldn't shake off the conflicting emotions swirling inside him—relief and concern for Nova despite everything that had happened between them. He shouldn't care as much as he did.

As the minutes ticked by, River found himself pacing restlessly. Their shared history weighed heavily on his shoulders. Nova had vanished from his life once before, leaving him heartbroken and confused. The wounds from their past were still raw, yet she had managed to stir up a whirlwind of emotions within him once more.

A gentle breeze blew through the open balcony door, rustling the drapes and bringing a momentary respite to River's racing mind. As he gazed at the bustling city life below, nostalgia washed over him, reminding him of the two beautiful weeks he'd spent in Nova's embrace.

His mind strayed to Nova's mention of the message that was on the phone.

Find me.

The urgency in Arya's message echoed in his head, but a flicker of doubt crept in. Why flee again without speaking to Nova if she wanted to be found? Was that message really from Arya, or was something more insidious at play?

FIND ME.

With Mateo dead, Arya was now in the wind on her own. Nova considered that perhaps she was scared the intruder was on her trail, which may be why she continued to run. Nova couldn't rest until Arya was back safely. With the weight of her father's legacy on her shoulders, she couldn't afford to fail.

She had driven to the office to speak with Cohen and to drop off the phone after speaking with River. He agreed to send a team of agents to the abandoned house.

She planned to return to the Burlington house with River to attempt to retrace Arya's steps, searching for clues that could lead Nova to her whereabouts. She intended to scour the house, meticulously examining every corner, hoping to find a hidden message or hint pointing them in the right direction.

"We will find you," she vowed. Her father had never lost a witness, and she wouldn't either. This would not be her legacy.

Nova couldn't shake off the concern in River's voice during their brief phone call, but she couldn't afford to dwell on it either. Her priority was Arya and making sure she was safe. Yet a small part of her was grateful for his genuine worry despite their tension.

In solitude, Nova realized that it may not have been the most sensible choice to venture off to an abandoned house alone. But her determination to find Arya had driven her to take the risk. Unfortunately, she'd returned home without any luck in her search. She felt both aggravated and anxious for Arya's well-being.

As the sun continued dipping below the horizon, casting long shadows across the quiet street, the weight of Nova's unsuccessful search for Arya bore down on her shoulders, exacerbating her frustration and unease. The abandoned house loomed in her mind, haunting her thoughts with unanswered questions.

How did Arya come across the empty home? Why did she stay in North Carolina instead of seeking refuge with her parents? Am I reading this all wrong?

What if it was something more?

Her phone rang, cutting off her thoughts.

"I hope you're at home resting," River said when she answered.

"I am," Nova confirmed. "At least, my body is resting. My mind is busy trying to figure out this phone message.

Cohen's sending agents to watch the abandoned house. I'd like you and me to return to Mateo and Arya's home in the morning. I want us to conduct our own search."

"Sounds like a plan," River said. "Anything on her vehicle?"

"Not yet."

"Do you want to meet me at my hotel?"

"Just come to the Marshals office. I'll be there in the morning."

"Do you still have the phone?"

"No, I took it to the office. I want it checked for prints."

"I guess I'll see you in the morning."

"See you then," she murmured.

They hung up.

Nova had gotten out of bed and walked through her house while talking to him, checking locks and arming the security system. Arya was still at the forefront of her mind.

She had to find her before the cartel did, no matter what it took. Nothing would stop Nova from keeping Arya safe.

THE EARLY MORNING sun cast a soft glow over the quiet suburban neighborhood as Nova and River parked their vehicle discreetly down the street from the de Leons' residence. The house, surrounded by neatly trimmed hedges and a white picket fence, appeared calm and unassuming.

As Nova approached the porch, she noticed the once lush and vibrant ferns drooping and wilting from neglect. The leaves hung limply, their once bright green color faded to a dull, sickly shade. It was as if the plants were crying out for help. Nova made a mental note to give them the care and attention they deserved before they left the house.

She adjusted the strap of her holster as she approached the front door. River followed closely behind. They exchanged a quick nod before Nova knocked on the door, the sound echoing through the stillness of the morning.

No answer.

She pushed away the thought of what had happened the last time she was here. Nova's instincts kicked in, and she reached into her pocket for the spare key.

With a swift turn, the door creaked open, revealing a dimly lit living room.

The air inside was tense as they stepped into the house.

Nova swept her surroundings, her eyes scanning for any signs of disturbance or anything that seemed out of place.

They moved through the house methodically, checking every room for any clues or indications of where Arya might have gone. Nova examined the study, rifling through papers and files. River focused on the kitchen, checking the refrigerator and cabinets for any signs of sudden departure.

As they explored, a sense of urgency grew. The unanswered questions fueled their determination to find Arya before it was too late.

Nova halted in front of a corkboard behind the desk, covered with pictures and notes. She traced her finger over a recent photograph of Arya, reminding herself of the stakes involved.

River discovered a plastic bag hidden between packages of meat in the freezer. "Nova, take a look at this," he called, holding up a small notebook he found inside.

The notebook contained cryptic notes and coded messages, hinting at Mateo's attempts to stay one step ahead of the cartel and law enforcement.

Nova's eyes narrowed as she scanned the pages, noting the dates and realizing that Mateo had been preparing for something all along.

"He never intended to stay in WITSEC," she told River. "He had money stashed in several banks in other countries."

"Looks like he never intended to testify. He and Arya were going to leave the country."

"We really need to find her," Nova said, determination flashing in her eyes.

With newfound purpose, Nova and River continued their search, determined to unravel the mystery surrounding Arya de Leon's disappearance and bring her back to safety.

The morning sun climbed higher in the sky, casting a determined light on their path as they pursued the elusive trail that would lead them to Arya's whereabouts.

LATER IN THE DAY, River went to the local DEA agency to check out a few things and to reconnect with a friend he'd met years ago when they attended college.

"I heard you were in town," Taylor said. "I was out yesterday when you called."

"They told me that you called in sick. You all right?"

"Yep, I'm great. My son was the one who was sick. He's getting over a stomach virus. My wife had to be in court yesterday, so I had to stay home and clean up the messes from both ends. Man, I'm traumatized."

River chuckled. "Poor you..."

Shaking his head, Taylor said, "You don't know the half of it."

They walked into the break room for coffee.

"So, what brings you to Charlotte? And where is your partner?"

"Kenny's back home working our investigation on that end," River said. "I came here because one of my witnesses is dead and another is missing."

"Any leads?"

"Not very many, but we're exploring all of them. I need a space to work."

"There's an empty desk behind me," Taylor offered. "You can plug in your computer there."

"Thanks."

River added copies of the information they found at the house to his file. He called his partner and discussed his findings. He and Nova weren't sure whether Arya was still in town, but there was no doubt that she would turn up in San Diego at some point.

Sunlight filtered through the blinds and lent an air of secrecy to his solitary pursuit. Every document, every line of text he scrutinized brought him closer to uncovering Mateo's slipup.

As time ticked by, River's anticipation ignited like a flame in the depths of his chest. A strong sense of determination coursed through his veins, driving him to unravel and destroy Mateo's intricate schemes of corruption. Despite the fact that their key witness was deceased, his information could still shed light on the inner workings of the drug cartel.

As River carefully examined the financial records, a peculiar pattern emerged. It seemed that Mateo had unknowingly left a trail—an intricate breadcrumb trail leading straight to his betrayal.

River's eyes widened with astonishment as he connected the dots, realizing that Mateo's slipup was not just a simple miscalculation but a meticulously calculated move to divert attention from his true motives.

As he delved deeper into the financial records, River's analytical mind pieced together the irregularities that had initially caught his attention. It was a web of intricate transactions, money funneled through various shell companies and offshore accounts. The path seemed convoluted at first, but patterns emerged; hidden beneath the facade of legitimate business dealings lay a complex network of bribery and embezzlement.

Still, there were gaps in the information. There were more, perhaps critical details on the cartel's business dealings that Mateo hadn't shared. The cartel's operations extended far beyond what he had revealed, and River was determined to uncover the truth.

He leaned back in his chair, his mind racing with possibilities. He reached for his coffee, taking a slow sip as he considered his next move.

Some of the handwritten entries were written by someone else. River assumed that Arya was the writer. Although he hadn't met them, his gut told him that the only person Mateo would've trusted with this information was his wife. If his theory was correct, then this was proof that Arya knew of her husband's relationship with the cartel.

He pulled out his phone and tapped out a message, fingers moving rapidly over the screen.

Can you meet me in thirty minutes? River sent the text to Nova, hoping she would agree to see him.

Sure. My place okay? came the reply.

Yes. He slipped his phone into his jeans pocket.

River took his time gathering his notes, making sure they were organized. He spent a few more minutes catching up with Taylor before heading out to his car.

River knew that Nova had more information about Arya than he did. He depended on her knowledge; they would have to work together to find the missing woman.

The lingering recollections of their ill-fated romance, the repercussions from their previous joint assignment, weighed heavily in the atmosphere, forming an uneasy knot in River's stomach. He desperately wanted to keep things strictly professional.

River pulled into the driveway and turned off the car's engine.

Nova was waiting for him by the front door, and she stepped aside to let him enter the foyer. "What's going on?" she asked.

"I just finished going through Mateo's file," River replied. "He gave us some useful information, but as I followed the trail, I'm convinced that he didn't give us everything. Considering his position, every financial transaction was done with his knowledge."

"I believe you," Nova said. "Their house had been searched—someone was looking for something. Apparently, they didn't find anything on Mateo when they killed him."

"He could've stored it somewhere safe, or he gave it to Arya," River stated. "I also found some handwritten entries that I believe were written by a woman."

"You think it was Arya?"

He nodded. "I do."

Nova eyed him. "Either way, she's not safe."

Their gazes locked, both understanding the urgency and danger that surrounded them. "That's why we have to find her," River declared, determination evident in his voice.

"Right now, all we have is a cell phone," Nova stated.

"What about the place where you found the phone?" River asked. "I would think that's where we'll find clues. The first of which is the phone—she knew you'd be able to trace the location. That's most likely why she called you and stayed on the line."

"The house was searched and nothing else was found," she announced. "The sleeping bag was taken into evidence, along with the food containers. There wasn't anything else there."

"There's only one way to find out for sure," River said. "Up for a drive?"

"Always. But it's going to be dark soon."

"I have a couple of flashlights."

Nova's cell rang.

She answered it.

He heard her utter a word of profanity. The call wasn't good news.

She ended the call, saying, "Arya's SUV was just found in a Target parking lot. They searched the stores in the shopping center. She's nowhere to be found."

Inside the car, River asked, "How is your head?"

"I'm good," Nova answered.

They parked down the street from the house in Concord and waited.

"How did she even find this place?" he wondered aloud.

"I have no idea," Nova responded. "I can't imagine her staying behind in North Carolina."

"Maybe that was part of Mateo's plan," he suggested.

She nodded in agreement. "So, what do you think? Should we head inside?"

"Let's do it."

The air was heavy with anticipation as they approached the dilapidated structure. The moon's feeble glow offered little visibility, casting eerie shadows upon each broken windowpane.

To River, the house stood as a forgotten relic of a bygone era, its secrets buried within its decaying walls.

Nova led him up to the bedroom on the second floor. "This is where I found the phone."

The sleeping bag was gone, but the rotting remains of

old take-out containers filled the room with a sour odor. She wrinkled her nose in disgust.

River glanced around the room with observant eyes. The walls were cracked and peeling, with remnants of old wallpaper clinging on for dear life.

"I told you that there's nothing here," Nova uttered in frustration. "Right now, all we have is a message on a phone."

"It's a start," he said. "Were there any other calls made?"

"No. It only had my number."

"Then she must have another burner," River suggested. "My partner is still surveilling her parents' home. No sighting of Arya as of yet."

Nova eyed him. "What do you think about flying out to San Diego? I think we should speak to Pablo and Ramona Lozano in person. There's a chance that Arya's on her way there. We'll check flights, but my gut tells me that she will most likely travel by car."

River hesitated a brief second before replying, "I understand your drive to see this through, but you need to consult with your doctor first. Changes in air pressure and cabin conditions during a flight could affect you after the concussion."

"I can't just sit around and wait for something to happen!" Nova snapped, her hands clenching into fists at her sides.

"I'm not saying you can't travel," River reassured her, his voice firm but gentle. "But we need to be cautious."

"I understand your concern, River," Nova said through gritted teeth, trying to rein in her impatience. "But Arya needs our help."

River watched Nova fidget with the hem of her linen shirt, a determined furrow in her brow. He could sense the familiar blaze of determination burning within her, but he also knew that caution was necessary in this situation. With Arya still on the loose, pushing Nova to take it easy was impossible.

Chapter Six

Nova wasn't interested in seeing her doctor. She was more than capable of taking care of herself. She didn't want someone telling her that she was grounded because she'd had a minor concussion. She intended to be on the plane with River heading to San Diego despite this. Arya had been missing for three days now, and Nova couldn't bear the thought of the woman being out there alone and in danger.

As she packed her bag with essentials for the journey, Nova felt a mix of anticipation and anxiety. She knew that finding Arya wouldn't be an easy task, but she was willing to go to any lengths to bring her home safely.

River, always the voice of reason, watched Nova with concern. "Are you sure about this?" he asked, his brow furrowing. "Your health is important, too, you know."

"I'll be fine." She brushed off his worries with a dismissive wave of her hand. "Besides, we can't just sit around and wait for something to happen. Arya needs us."

He openly studied her.

"I'm fine, River. You need to go back to the hotel and pack," Nova stated. "I want to be on the first flight out tomorrow." She sat down on the sofa and picked up her cell phone. "I need to call Cohen."

After speaking with her supervisor and assuring him

that she was fine, he backed River's suggestion to see her doctor.

She hung up and scheduled a video visit with her physician. Thirty minutes later, they discussed her travel plans.

"No headaches," Nova said. "No problem with my vision. I feel good."

When the appointment ended, River approached her cautiously, worry evident in his eyes. "Your health is more important than finding Arya right this moment. I'll be searching for her and we can get other agents on this case."

Nova looked up at him, a fire burning in her eyes. "You don't understand," she replied, her voice laced with determination. "Arya is my witness. I'm responsible for her. I can't just sit back and do nothing while she's out there, possibly in danger. I have to find her."

"All right." He nodded resignedly. "Your doctor didn't have a problem with it, and I can't stop you. Just promise me that you won't push yourself too hard."

Nova paused for a moment, contemplating River's words. She realized that he was right. She couldn't let her determination blind her to the importance of her well-being. Taking a deep breath, she said, "I promise," her voice softer now, filled with gratitude for his concern. "I won't push myself too hard, and I'll make sure to look after myself as we search for Arya."

River prepared to leave.

"I'll see you tomorrow at the airport," Nova said.

He stepped out, and she watched him get into the rental and disappear from the city streets.

As night fell, Nova was consumed by a whirlwind of emotions. The weight of uncertainty pressed down on her chest, but she refused to let it deter her from finding Arya.

She knew that time was of the essence, and every moment spent apart was another moment Arya could be in danger.

RIVER ARRIVED BACK at his hotel room shortly after 9:00 p.m. He and Taylor had eaten dinner across the street from the DEA agency on Randolph Road.

He was about to shower when his phone began to vibrate. He picked it up off the marble counter. "Hello."

He walked out of the bathroom and sat down on the edge of the bed.

"Hey, big brother."

A smile tugged at his lips. Despite his feelings about their mother, he shared a special bond with his sister. "Bonnie, how are you?"

"I'm okay. I'd like to know what's going on with you. I haven't heard a word from you since Mama's funeral."

River sank into a nearby chair. "I've been busy with work."

"She's been gone almost six months."

His jaw tightened. "I know."

"Do you think you'll ever forgive her?"

"I forgave Mary a long time ago, Bonnie." River had always addressed his mother by her first name. Mary was more like a sister. No, not even that. Mary was more of an acquaintance.

"She was sixteen when she had you, River. At that time, Mama didn't know anything about being a mother."

"I've heard it all before and I'm fine," he responded. "You don't have to worry about me."

"But I do worry. I know you feel like Mama abandoned you. I know she didn't raise you, but you were always in her heart."

"That's exactly what she did. None of it matters now."

River didn't want to talk about the effect his mother's rejection had had on him.

He was the result of his teen mother's relationship with an older boy who went off to college and never returned home. She'd never told anyone his name—just moved on with her life and without her son.

He swallowed hard, forcing down the bitterness that threatened to spill out.

"After Mama got married and had me, she wanted to get you, but Grandma wouldn't let her take you. She told Mama that you were more her son than anyone else's."

That was a lie. He'd heard his grandmother practically beg her daughter to raise him with his sister. Mary had flat out refused. She'd told her mother that she didn't want a boy, but River didn't want to hurt Bonnie with the truth. His sister adored Mary. "Bonnie, all I can say is that the damage was done long before then. Look, I can't unfeel the way I felt growing up without Mary's love. Like I said earlier…it doesn't matter anymore."

"I miss you, River."

"When I can get some free time, I'll make a trip to Sacramento to visit with you," he said.

"I hope you mean it."

"Bonnie, I mean every word. I'll call you and check in next week. I promise." Despite his feelings for their mother, River never let them affect his relationship with Bonnie, who was eight years younger. He loved his sister beyond measure.

He buried his emotions deep within himself, pushing away any thoughts of Mary and Nova. The painful rejections from both women still lingered in his mind, but River had a mission to focus on.

Finding Arya de Leon was his top priority, no matter

how much his heart ached for the love he had lost. He couldn't afford to let these distractions hinder him, not when so much was at stake.

River pushed aside the pain and focused solely on the task at hand, determined to succeed no matter the cost.

THE NEXT MORNING, Nova continued to try to contact Arya several times at the cell number she'd been issued by WITSEC. She arrived at the airport and met River at their gate, hoping that Arya had gone to her parents' house and they could speak to her soon. However, when Nova had called the Lozanos last evening, Pablo and Ramona denied their daughter was there. They both claimed they hadn't spoken to her in years.

The steady hum of airport activity surrounded Nova as she stared at her laptop screen, her eyes skimming words without registering their meaning. Frustration gnawed at her, a relentless companion echoing the turmoil within. She couldn't shake the feeling that the threads of Arya's disappearance were slipping through her fingers like grains of sand.

Beside her, River's silence mirrored the weight of the unsaid.

An electric current seemed to crackle between them, unspoken and undeniable. As Nova's fingers grazed the rough surface of her laptop, she could feel River's intense gaze piercing through her, causing her jaw to clench with unease. With a quick snap, she shut out the outside world, wanting desperately to escape the heavy tension that hung in the air. But even in this momentary respite, she couldn't shake off the powerful pull that River had on her.

Their boarding announcement echoed through the intercom, and Nova stood up, her movements precise, purposeful toward the gate agent. This journey held more than the promise of flight—it was a pursuit of answers.

The agent, indifferent to the weight of their mission, processed the documents with routine efficiency.

As they took their seats on the plane, the engines hummed to life, drowning out the doubts in Nova's mind. Leaning back, she glanced at River, their eyes locking in a silent pact. The aircraft taxied down the runway, hurtling them further into their investigation.

The plane transported Nova and River into the unknown, leaving their unresolved tension in the air like the turbulence that awaited them.

THE SCENT LINGERED, a ghost haunting River's senses with every breath. If only she hadn't worn that perfume. It wrapped around him like a relentless adversary, an uninvited companion on this mission. River's attempts to ignore it proved futile, each whiff a reminder of a vulnerability he wasn't prepared to acknowledge.

In the cramped confines of the plane, River fought to regain control. He couldn't afford distraction, not now. Not when the stakes were so high.

As Nova excused herself to make a phone call, River took a moment to collect himself. Leaning back in his seat, he closed his eyes.

"I can't let her affect me this way," he muttered, a vow to steel himself against the unseen forces at play. "I'm in control."

But as the minutes ticked away, doubts crept in like shadows. Was he truly in control, or was it a facade he clung to for pride? The truth whispered in the recesses of his mind, a nagging reminder that emotions were not easily subdued. As the flight wore on, the plane's hum became a backdrop to the internal struggle within River. He opened his eyes, glancing toward the empty seat beside him where Nova would soon return. The air still carried faint traces of her presence, a reminder that she held an inexplicable sway over him.

A sense of vulnerability gnawed at him. In this clandestine battle of wills, it became evident that the only person in control was Nova. The realization settled over him and River grappled with the unsettling truth—he was navigating uncharted territory. The compass of his emotions pointed directly toward her.

If only she hadn't worn that perfume. It was the one he remembered on her from their two weeks together, when he'd felt the rush of falling for her. He'd been so certain that feeling would last. After the heart-wrenching pain and betrayal he'd experienced the first time, River knew he couldn't risk opening his heart to Nova again. The thought of being vulnerable and potentially getting hurt once more was enough to send shivers down his spine. He couldn't bear the thought of going through that kind of agony again, and losing her a second time would surely break him beyond repair. No, it was safer for him to keep his heart guarded, even if it meant sacrificing the possibility of a future with Nova.

I can't let her affect me this way, he thought silently. *I won't let her do this to me. I'm in control.*

Was he, really? Because the way River felt right now... The only person in control was Nova.

Chapter Seven

Nova didn't relish having to endure the cloud of uneasiness surrounding them for the next five and a half hours. They had all this quiet time together to clear the air… It was time to tell him exactly how she felt. She cleared her throat. "I know things between us are strained, but I thought we could coexist. We're working a case. This isn't some social outing. We're supposed to be a *team* on this investigation. I don't have a problem working with you, but can you say the same about me? Because if you can't, then you need to just have the case reassigned to another agent."

"That won't be necessary," River responded. "I can manage my feelings while working with you, Nova."

"I apologize," she said. "I guess I'm letting my personal feelings affect my judgment and it was unprofessional. It won't happen again." Nova rubbed the right side of her temple, trying to massage away the hint of a headache. It was a subtle reminder that she'd suffered a concussion.

"I'm sorry if I haven't been my professional self either," he said.

Nova nodded, satisfied with where they'd left things. She took an aspirin and checked her emails. Then she settled in her seat and closed her eyes as she waited for the pill to work its magic.

"I don't remember you ever being this quiet."

She opened her eyes and looked at River. "I have a lot on my mind."

"Is this the first witness to do a disappearing act on you?"

"Yeah," she said. "And hopefully my last. I know that most of the people in the program are criminals and that they often struggle with what they perceive as mundane living. Some have difficulty leaving their previous life behind and often return to old habits. I know now that I was right to be concerned about Mateo."

"From everything I've learned about him, Mateo was a greedy man," River said. "He wouldn't have been happy with a simple life in some small town."

Nova couldn't disagree because River spoke the truth. Mateo was an intelligent man who'd decided to apply his accounting expertise to aid the cartel in cheating the government of tax dollars and helped them launder drug money.

She'd been a case agent for Mateo for the past eight months. Before that, Nova had worked a six-month protection detail for a federal judge who had been receiving death threats.

She stole a peek at River, who seemed interested in an in-flight movie. She pulled her iPad out and opened a book to read. She almost released an audible sigh of relief when the headache finally surrendered to nothingness.

THEY WALKED IN silence through airport exit doors to pick up their rental—Nova had chosen an SUV—and drove out of the parking lot ten minutes later.

"It's been quite a while since I was here in San Diego," she said, programming the Lozanos' address into her GPS. "Probably five years or so."

"I came down for a conference a couple of months ago," River responded.

Pointing to her left, Nova asked, "Hey, are you still crazy about In-N-Out?"

His expression suddenly became animated as he said, "I *love* In-N-Out. You know that's my spot."

Grinning, Nova maneuvered the vehicle into the drive-through line. They'd skipped breakfast and might as well eat on the way. They placed their orders and then pulled out into traffic again.

"How much do Arya's parents know about her situation?" River asked when they'd finished eating.

"They were allowed to say goodbye before they went into the program. So, they know she's in WITSEC. From day one, it was made clear that she wasn't to have any contact with them."

"That knowledge alone could get them killed," River said.

"I know."

He glimpsed the worried expression on Nova's face.

Glancing over at him, she said, "I hate that this is happening on my watch."

"Don't take it personally."

"It's hard not to do so," she retorted. "They got on my nerves more than once, but I wanted to see them thrive in this new life. Not everyone gets a second chance, you know…"

River nodded in agreement. "They have to want it for themselves, Nova."

"I know you're right." Her mind was working overtime as she tried to figure out Arya's next move.

"We're going to find her."

Nova gave him a grateful smile as she tried to ignore the cold knot in her stomach.

River saw Nova massaging her right temple. "Do you have a headache? Why don't you let me drive?"

"No, I'm good. We're almost to our destination."

Five minutes later, Nova pulled into the neighborhood. She put the vehicle in Park at the top of the street and turned off the ignition. Her eyes bounced around, searching.

He glanced around, too.

"Who are you looking for?" she asked.

"I wanted to see if one of our guys was still on surveillance," River responded. "Must have taken a break."

Nova finished off her bottled water.

He pointed straight ahead. "That's the house over there."

"There aren't any lights on," she observed aloud as she looked in the direction he was pointing. "You think they go to bed this early?"

"Nope," River stated. "The last time they were spotted was about a day ago. No one has been in or out since then. My partner said that they don't venture out much."

Nova got out of the car and slipped on a Kevlar vest.

"What are you doing?" he asked.

"I can't explain it, but I have a bad feeling about this. I felt this same way in Burlington." She already had her weapon in hand. She wasn't going to let anyone jump her a second time. "We need to make sure they're okay."

River followed suit, putting on his own vest, then walked behind her as she approached the back of the house. "Look at the back door," Nova said in a loud whisper. "Someone broke in."

She tried the knob, turning it gently. "It's unlocked."

Nova pulled out her phone and called the police before going inside.

They entered the house gingerly.

River tried a light switch.

Nothing.

Nova found the darkness thick and claustrophobic. It was like a hand closing around her throat. She pulled out a miniature flashlight.

"The power's been cut off," he said.

With her flashlight, Nova's eyes bounced around her surroundings. When she walked into the living room, she said, "I seriously doubt that Mr. and Mrs. Lozano left their house looking like this. We can safely assume that this house has been ransacked."

River nodded in agreement. "It looks like a crime scene."

"Do you think they've been kidnapped?" she asked.

He pointed upstairs. "It's possible. There's a packed suit-case up there that was probably left by mistake. They have security cameras in place throughout the house but the wires have been cut. I noticed it when I checked the garage."

"That's just great..." Nova walked back into the living room and was about to ascend the staircase.

A knock sounded on the front door.

"Is it the police?" Nova asked.

"Naw, it looks like he might be a neighbor," River said, peeking out of the front window.

"I came to see what's going on over here," a middle-aged man with a trim beard said when Nova opened the door.

She showed him her badge. "You took great risk coming over here after noting strangers in the house," she chided. "What if I weren't law enforcement? You could've been killed."

"I thought you were the police," he replied. "The people that own this place left town. Pablo called and told me that they were going away for a couple of weeks. He sounded scared." He looked past River. "What's going on over here?"

"Looks like there might have been a break-in," Nova said. "Did you happen to see anyone else near the house?"

"I never saw anyone outside of Pablo and Ramona, other than Yolanda, their housekeeper."

Nova and River exchanged looks. "I'm sorry, but I have to go back inside," he said. "Thank you for your help."

"Jerry Spotswood. That's my name." The man stepped off the porch and River swung the door closed.

Nova rushed up the stairs with River following close behind.

They proceeded cautiously through the house, their senses heightened by the ominous atmosphere that clung to the air.

With a shared nod, they approached the door of a room, the creaking floorboards beneath their feet betraying their presence. Pushing the door open slowly, they revealed a dimly lit guest bedroom. The space was a tableau of horror.

Their eyes fell upon Yolanda, her lifeless body slumped in the corner. Blood pooled around her, staining the white carpet a dark red. Nova and River entered, their guns drawn as they cautiously scanned the area for an intruder.

Then Nova rushed to Yolanda's side, checking for a pulse she knew wasn't there. Her heart sank as she realized they were too late.

Turning to River, she could see the same anger and determination she felt in his eyes. An innocent woman was dead, but they would not rest until they found those responsible.

As they combed through the room for evidence, Nova noticed a glint of metal under Yolanda's hand. Pulling back the woman's fingers, she discovered a small piece of jewelry engraved with a strange symbol.

River's voice broke through her thoughts. "We need to call this in. The killers can't be far."

But Nova couldn't shake the image of Yolanda's terror-filled eyes from her mind. She vowed to get justice for the woman, no matter what it took. "They didn't have to kill her."

"Johnny Boy doesn't believe in leaving witnesses behind," River responded, pulling out his phone. "I need to call my partner. I don't know what happened here, so I'm hoping he can help me make sense of this."

In the living room, she looked at the photos lining the walls and the mantel over the fireplace, paying close attention to the picturesque details. There were several framed photos of a house with mountains in the backdrop. Nova grabbed a few. She hoped they might explain where Arya and her parents may be hiding.

"Jerry lives across the street," River said. "I had Kenny check him out. He's been living there for the past ten years. As far as we can tell, he has no cartel connections."

"Was he able to explain what happened with the surveillance?" Nova asked.

"There was a disconnect. The team was taken off prematurely. My supervisor isn't happy right now. This is on us."

"It looks like Arya's parents packed in a hurry to me," Nova observed as she continued looking around. "But why? Is it because she warned them, or were they hurrying to get to her?"

"It could be both," River responded.

"But killing her parents won't force Arya out of hiding," Nova said.

"But it could *silence* her forever," he said. "It could make her too afraid to ever speak against them."

She nodded in agreement.

Nova could sense the frustration written all over River's face. She understood that it was weighing on him that the surveillance team had been abruptly removed from Arya's parents and now the housekeeper had been killed.

They heard the shrill scream of sirens in the distance.

Nova and River stood on the corner, watching the flashing lights approach. Whirring sirens grew louder, piercing the calm suburban ambience like a discordant melody.

Moments later, Jerry appeared, hastily jogging toward them with his trusty flashlight. His face etched with concern, he seemed to age before their eyes. His neatly trimmed beard was now disheveled, and sweat glistened on his furrowed brow.

Jerry abruptly stopped beside Nova and River. "What in the world is going on? I've been patrolling these streets for years—nothing has ever happened in this neighborhood… Well, just some teens wreaking havoc."

Nova laid a gentle hand on Jerry's trembling shoulder. "Yolanda's dead."

He gasped in shock. "I never heard a thing."

Minutes ticked by like hours as they waited in silence.

The flashing lights of the approaching police cars grew brighter, casting an eerie glow upon the once peaceful street. Neighbors began peering out the windows and leaving their houses, drawn by the commotion.

"This neighborhood will never be the same," Jerry uttered.

"I THINK WE should hang back and watch the house to see if someone comes back tonight," River said after the police and CSI team left. He wanted to catch the perpetrator who had taken an innocent life, but he also knew that the surveillance team had probably been pulled due to budget cuts. Should they take a chance and stay back to see if anyone returned to the crime scene? "It's a long shot, but that's all we have right now." He stood outside the vehicle, watching.

Nova nodded in agreement. "Let's do it."

It was after 10:00 p.m. It was just dark enough on the street to provide some cover for the surveillance. River had positioned the rental car well away from the house but close enough to see if anyone drove up. The view was excellent but discreet enough for them to keep from being seen.

Now and then, they caught movement in one of the windows at Jerry's house. He was watching the empty home as well.

"I still don't believe Arya knows anything about her husband's business dealings."

"Nova, she may not be as innocent as you'd like to think," River said, not understanding why she had so much faith in Mateo's wife. "I watched Arya's interview, and her answers sounded rehearsed to me, but I don't know the woman."

"Arya was probably nervous," Nova explained. "Her whole life was changing in a short period."

He opened the driver's-side door for Nova.

"Thanks," she murmured.

River walked to the other side of the car and got in.

"Do you really think Arya's parents plan to return to this house?" Nova asked.

"I'm not sure, but you'd think by now they know something's wrong," River responded. "Like the fact that their alarm isn't working. I'm sure the alarm company has tried to reach them. If they're not running, why not come home?"

"We can assume that Arya warned them, which is why they left town. We need to find them all. I don't want any more bodies turning up."

"I don't want that either," he said. River hoped that Arya's parents would be found alive and well.

Staring out the driver's window, Nova stated, "I really hope Arya's with her parents. If she isn't, then I don't know where to begin looking for her." She wanted to roll down the window so the breeze could wrap itself around her like a soft shawl on a cool evening. "We didn't really have any reason to think they were in danger. With Mateo dead, I can't figure why they'd want Arya or her parents."

He looked over at her. "The cartel isn't going to give up."

"I know," she responded with a sigh.

"Nova, whatever happens…this isn't on you," River said.

"That's what everyone says, but the facts are that Mateo and Arya went missing on my watch. I was responsible for them. If something worse happens and fingers are pointed, they'll be at *me*."

He could tell that Nova was taking this to heart. She was great at her job and dedicated to keeping her witnesses safe. River didn't want to see her begin to doubt herself. *That's when people start to make mistakes.*

Chapter Eight

Nova was becoming antsy just sitting in the car doing nothing. Her mind was all over the place. If Arya wasn't in San Diego, then where could she be?

Anywhere.

She bit her bottom lip, trying to remember if Arya had ever mentioned anything that would explain her whereabouts. The woman had often griped about living in North Carolina and openly expressed her desire to return to her life in Los Angeles.

"Do you think she would risk returning to LA like her husband did?" Nova posed the question.

River replied, "It's worth considering. At this point, we can't rule out any possibilities."

"I know a couple of people we should talk to—they might be able to help us," Nova said. "There's Kaleb Stone, a close friend of my father's. The night my dad was killed, he stepped in to provide security for a cartel witness determined to return home. He was on his way to the safe house... My dad had been shot... He was dead by the time Kaleb arrived."

"I actually know Kaleb. The last time I saw him was right after he left the Marshals."

"He opened his own security firm after he left."

"So, what happened to the witness?" River asked.

"He married her," Nova responded with a chuckle. "After she testified against Calderon and a few other high-ranking members of the cartel."

"Are you talking about the Homeland Security agent who was shot at with her partner a few years ago? Everybody thought she'd died, too."

"Yeah."

"So, she left WITSEC to go back to LA?"

Nova nodded. "There was a leak in the Milwaukee office. It was a mess, but after that, the Marshals changed some of the protocols regarding witness security. But now I'm wondering if we have a leak here. I'm still trying to figure out how they found the house in Burlington."

River settled back in his seat. "We are aware that Poppy and Johnny Boy were using bribery and blackmail to control individuals within various levels of law enforcement and the government. But there is a chance they obtained information by killing Mateo. His body was found without any identification, so it's possible they had accomplices visit his house."

"That's why I think we should talk to Kaleb and Rylee. They've been investigating the Mancuso cartel for the past two years," Nova said. "Since we're here in California, it won't hurt to meet with them."

"I'm open to it," River said. "Without Mateo alive to testify and if Arya doesn't have any information...my case against the cartel will fall apart. I don't want that to happen on my watch."

Nova placed a call to Kaleb Stone. "Hey, it's me. I'm in San Diego."

"Nova, hi. How long will you be here?"

"A few days," she responded. "If you and Rylee aren't

busy, I'd love for you two to come down. I want your feedback on a case I'm working with the DEA. It's concerning the Mancuso cartel."

"Rylee and I can fly down there tomorrow morning. I'll text you once I make the flight arrangements."

"Thanks a lot, Kaleb."

"I'll see you tomorrow."

Nova hung up, saying, "They're flying down in the morning to see us." She glanced around, then said, "I don't know about you, but I'm not looking forward to sleeping in this car."

"A couple of agents should be arriving soon to take over surveillance," River said. "We can head to the hotel when they get here."

The mention of a hotel reminded Nova of a similar situation two years ago. They'd been tracking a fugitive. The more time they'd spent together, the harder they'd found it to ignore their growing attraction, so they gave in to their feelings. Two weeks later, Nova had walked out of his life the day after they'd apprehended the guy.

"You okay?" he asked, cutting into her thoughts.

"Huh... Yeah, I'm good."

After the agents arrived, River had a brief discussion with them before he and Nova left the area. "There's a hotel not too far from here," he announced.

"That's fine," Nova replied. "As long as they have a comfy bed, I can sleep anywhere."

"I only stay at a certain hotel brand," River said.

She smiled. "You sound like Mateo and his wife."

River eyed her. "Are you saying that you don't have a favorite chain?"

"I do, but I'm also open to staying elsewhere."

They settled on any hotel under the Marriott brand.

Nova pulled into the first one that came up on the GPS. "This is the Mission Valley location."

"I'm fine with that," River said. "I've stayed here once before. It's very nice inside."

"I'm good with clean and comfortable," she said. "After a few hours' sleep, I'll be ready to return to work."

RIVER'S STOMACH COMPLAINED loudly enough to garner Nova's attention. "Sorry about that," he said.

She gave a tiny smile. "You're not alone. I'm hungry, too."

They got out of the car after pulling into the hotel parking lot. River grabbed their luggage and followed behind Nova.

Inside the hotel, they checked into separate rooms.

"I'm going to grab a bite to eat," River announced in the elevator. "When I get back, we can try to create some type of timeline leading up to Arya's disappearance."

"I need to eat as well. Why don't we order room service?" Nova suggested. "This way, we can keep working over dinner."

He didn't respond as thoughts ran through his head. Room service... How many room service meals had they enjoyed two years ago? Intimate dinners that had led to him telling her things about his past, about his feelings, that he shouldn't have...

At River's hesitation, she said, "C'mon... It's just a meal. We should be mature enough to eat together."

He chided himself for reading too much into the situation. Nova wasn't trying to make dinner more than it appeared to be—she just wanted to continue working while they ate. River couldn't deny that it was the best use of their time. "We can do that," he relented.

Nova unlocked her door and held it open for him to enter.

"Where's the menu?" River asked, leaving his suitcase near the door. He placed hers right outside the closet.

She pointed to a thin binder on the desk. "It's over there." After they flipped through, Nova called to place their order. While they waited, she let her mind drift back to the Lozanos and where they could be. Had they lied when they'd said Arya hadn't contacted them recently? If she had, she could've put the cartel on her parents' trail.

A knock at the door interrupted her thoughts. She answered and took the meals from the hotel server. "The food's here," Nova announced as she brought them in. "Perfect timing, because I'm starving."

She placed a covered plate in front of River. "I can't believe you were so hungry and then you just ordered a salad and bread."

"It's late," he responded. "I don't sleep well after a heavy meal."

"Heavy or not, I'm going to enjoy my grilled salmon burger and fries. I'm not gonna feel guilty about it."

River chuckled. "I hear you. Enjoy your meal."

A mischievous grin on her face, Nova held out a french fry to him, saying, "Here... I know you want one."

"What are you trying to do?" He gave her a sidelong glance. "Tempt me?"

"I just remember how much you love a good fry."

"I'll pass," River said.

Nova's smile disappeared and she dropped her gaze to her plate.

The air in the room had abruptly become stuffy.

"You wanted to discuss the case," he said. River loaded salad onto his fork, clearly not wanting to lose focus.

She cleared her throat softly. "Yeah. Where do you want to start?"

"From the beginning. Has Arya ever mentioned a place she loved visiting? When a witness runs, they may go to someplace familiar to them."

"She wanted to be relocated to New York or Chicago— we decided they were the wrong places to send them." Nova stuck her french fry into a puddle of ketchup. "We felt the smaller the town, the better for them."

"Her parents travel a lot," River said. "They could be anywhere."

Nova nodded. "We should check hotels. They have to sleep sometime."

River chewed, considering, and she spotted the bread-crumbs that had gathered near the corner of his mouth. Without thinking, she reached out to brush them away. The action took her back to a time when he welcomed her touch.

He jerked his head back as if stung.

"Crumbs," she murmured. "Sorry."

River wiped his mouth with a napkin.

Embarrassed, Nova concentrated on her food and waited for the moment of awkwardness to become a thing of the past. She hoped River didn't get the wrong idea. It had been a stupid move on her part, although it wasn't planned.

Her phone emitted a sound, notifying her of an incoming text.

Nova read it, then said, "Kaleb and Rylee should be arriving sometime after nine."

He nodded, and they continued their meal in silence. As the evening wore on, River rose from his seat. "I'm gonna turn in."

Nova wasn't ready for him to leave, but she refrained from voicing any objections as he quietly exited her room. They remained in a fragile space, the unspoken tension hovering between them.

Sitting on the sofa, Nova was caught in the present moment, no longer dwelling on the past. Eleven o'clock arrived, triggering memories of a night that weighed heavily on her conscience.

After a night of shared intimacy and whispered confessions, River had uttered those three powerful words, "I love you." Nova's smile had concealed the turmoil within, but his words had brought a sudden rush of panic. She'd sprung out of bed, fabricating an excuse about her mother needing assistance.

Fifteen minutes later, she'd returned, feigning calmness. River, ever observant, had asked about her mother. She'd assured him everything was fine, inviting him back into their shared embrace. But as they made love again, a shadow of unease had crept over Nova.

In the quiet aftermath, she'd slipped out of bed, tiptoed out of the room with her clothes and left without a trace. The memory now propelled her to River's door. She needed to confront the ghosts of the past to explain why she had vanished that night and left California for Charlotte.

Nova paused in the hallway outside his room to take several calming breaths. She inhaled deeply and exhaled slowly, then knocked on his door, hoping to bridge the gap between the present and the unresolved fragments of their shared history. At least if they discussed it, this would end the tension that was their constant companion.

"Has something happened?" River asked when he opened the door. He looked instantly concerned.

"No," she quickly assured him. "I...I need to talk to you."

His eyebrows rose in surprise. "About what?"

"About *us*."

River shook his head, the dim light casting shadows on

his face. "No… There's nothing to talk about, Nova. Besides, it's late and I'm exhausted."

"I just need to explain myself…"

"Nova, you leaving me like that… It was a cowardly move." His voice was laced with anger. "And after everything we'd been through."

Her heart swelled with pain and fear, her past mistakes coming back to haunt her. She desperately wanted to make things right with him before it was too late.

River's next words rang in her ears: "It's eighteen months too late."

Nova felt dizzy as tears threatened to spill from her eyes. "I…I didn't want to fall in love," she whispered, her voice trembling. "I'd just lost my father… Then I met you. Back then, I wasn't sure if it was a way to avoid dealing with my grief or if it was something more. I was confused, hurting, and just not in the right mental state for a relationship. I came here to say that I'm sorry for hurting you."

Nova turned away, suddenly needing space. She felt the weight of his gaze on her body as she walked away, fighting back the tears in her eyes.

As she went back to her room in silence, Nova tried to steady her breathing and calm the racing of her heart. She knew that River was right—they couldn't change the past. But she couldn't help feeling disappointed.

She lay in bed, feeling an emptiness in her chest where love should have been.

Chapter Nine

River couldn't believe Nova suddenly wanted to have a conversation. There was a time when he would have welcomed a discussion, but it was much too late for that now. It had taken him a long time to get over her. He wasn't about to let her dredge up that pain again.

He had never been the type of person who had scores of women chasing after him. River had always been considered the nerdy type. It didn't bother him to be called a nerd. He wore that label with pride.

Before Nova, there had only been one girl whom he'd dated for four years. While he cared for her, River had never been in love until the day Nova walked into his life. The time they spent together was one of the happiest in his life.

Until he woke up to find her gone without saying good-bye. Without saying anything.

River's pride wouldn't let him contact her once he returned to Charlotte. He spent much of his time chasing criminals. He didn't have any interest in pursuing women. He desired a simple, uncomplicated relationship. He'd dated a couple of women after Nova, but not for long. No one made River feel the way she had. No woman had come close. But that was another time and place.

River decided to call his sister. He didn't want to sit there in his room being pitiful or feeling sorry for himself. He wanted pleasant conversation.

When Bonnie answered, he said, "Hey, sis. I'm calling to check in as promised."

"I'm glad to hear from you. Are you traveling?"

"Yes," he responded.

"Any chance you'll be coming to Sacramento?"

"Not right now," River said. "I'm in the middle of an investigation."

"Oh."

He heard the disappointment in her voice. "You know the plane flies both ways. Why don't you come visit me?"

"I'd love that."

"Send me some dates and I'll fly you to LA. There's this new restaurant in Marina del Rey that I know you'll love."

"I can't wait," Bonnie said. "I need a vacation, too."

She'd spent the past two years taking care of their mother. Now that Mary was gone, Bonnie had returned to the hospital as a nurse.

"I mean it," River said. "Look at your calendar and get back to me. We'll spend some time together after I close this case I'm working on."

"I will," Bonnie responded. "Looking forward to it."

They talked for a few minutes more before hanging up.

The weight of the recent events pressed heavily on River's shoulders. The murder of Mateo, the agency's star witness against the Mancuso cartel, and the disappearance of Mateo's wife had thrown a meticulously built case into chaos. It was a setback that demanded a recalibration of his approach.

River stared at his notes, mapping out the intricate connections he had painstakingly pieced together. The photos of Mateo and his wife seemed to mock him, their faces a haunting reminder of the cost of this relentless pursuit.

His mind raced, searching for a thread to pull, a lead to follow. A flicker of determination sparked as River reached for his phone. Dialing, he waited for the familiar voice on the other end.

"Kenny, it's me. Did you manage to persuade Rico Alfaro to give up his supplier?"

"He claims he's willing to take the fall. My gut tells me he's been in cahoots with the Mancuso cartel."

River released a sigh of frustration. "We need to convince him that we'll go as far as putting the word on the street that he's a snitch."

His partner's agreement resonated through the line, and River hung up, his mind racing with possibilities. He needed to revisit every lead, every contact and every piece of intelligence they had gathered. He couldn't afford to overlook anything, not if he wanted to salvage what remained of the case and bring Johnny Boy to justice for Mateo and the deaths of his friend Jason and another agent.

River and Special Agent Jason Turner's friendship was forged in the face of danger and a shared purpose. They had stood side by side, confronting the ruthless Mancuso cartel, and with each mission they completed together, their bond grew stronger. From the moment they were introduced in the dimly lit corridors of DEA headquarters, there was an instant connection—a recognition that they were cut from the same cloth, driven by an unyielding determination to bring justice to those who sought to spread fear and chaos.

Their friendship went beyond mere camaraderie; they were like brothers, not only because of their shared experiences but also due to a deep mutual respect and trust. Jason had been there for River during his darkest moments, offering unwavering support and encouragement when the weight of their mission threatened to crush him. And River

had returned the favor, standing by Jason's side and willing to sacrifice his life to protect his friend from harm.

But then came the day when tragedy struck, shattering
their world and leaving River to pick up the pieces. Jason's
death at the hands of the Mancuso cartel was a devastating
blow, one that left River consumed with grief and anger.
The loss of his friend was like an open wound, a constant
reminder of the dangers they faced and the ruthless ene-
mies they were fighting against.

In the aftermath of Jason's death, the stakes were higher
than ever before. The Mancuso cartel operated without
consequence, their power spreading like a disease through
society. But River refused to let his friend's sacrifice be
in vain. He clung to hope that he would find a thread that
would unravel the cartel's empire and bring an end to their
reign of terror. For Jason's sake, he would stop at nothing
to put an end to the Mancuso cartel's tyranny.

After a shower, River sat in a chair, his legs propped
on the ottoman, watching television. His thoughts drifted
back to Nova. He wondered what she was doing right now.

River felt terrible for how he'd reacted when she came
to his room; it was an unexpected move on Nova's part—
one he had never seen coming.

He hadn't changed his mind about sending her away. It
had been the right thing to do. River couldn't afford to lose
concentration on the job he had to do.

THE FOLLOWING DAY, Nova ate breakfast alone in her room.
She hadn't bothered to check in with River because she'd
had enough of his attitude. Besides, she didn't want him
getting any closer to her. It would only make things more
dangerous for them both.

Nova took a deep breath and then a sip of herbal tea. She had a job to do, which required her complete focus.

Shortly after 8:30, the phone in her room rang.

Sighing softly, Nova answered it. "Hello…"

"Good morning. I was checking to see if you're awake," River said.

"Actually, I've been up for a couple of hours. I just finished eating breakfast."

"So did I," he responded. "What time are you expecting Kaleb and his wife?"

"Within the hour. Their plane landed thirty minutes ago."

"I'll come to your room whenever they get here," River said.

Nova didn't reply.

"Did you hear what I said?"

"I heard you," she uttered. "I'll ring your room."

Nova hung up before River could respond.

Deep down, she really didn't have a right to be angry with him. River was entitled to his feelings. Nova wasn't the type of person who carried grudges for years. She chose to either settle them or purge them. Her parents had always told her that life was too short to hold on to bad feelings.

When Kaleb and Rylee arrived, Nova called River. "Hey, they're here."

He was at her door within minutes.

"River, oh man… It's good to see you," Kaleb said when he entered the room. "It's been a long time."

"It sure has," he remarked. "*Kaleb Stone.* I hear you're a married man now."

"Happily married man," he said. "This is my wife, Rylee."

River shook her hand. "It's nice to meet you."

Nova watched River interact with Kaleb. He was smiling, his body more at ease. She wished he were that way around her.

She indicated the small kitchenette. "We can sit over there."

They gathered around the table to discuss the de Leon investigation.

Rylee sat beside her, saying, "Nova, I hope you know how much your father meant to me. I really hate that he lost his life trying to keep me safe."

"My dad died doing what he loved," she responded.

"How is your mother?" Kaleb asked.

Nova smiled. "She's great. Mom keeps busy by volunteering at church and a shelter for homeless women and children."

"Do you have any leads on Mateo's wife?" Rylee asked.

"Not really," Nova answered. "Her parents live in the area, so River and I flew out here to see if she was with them."

Kaleb looked at River. "What's the DEA's part in this?"

"We're hoping that Arya de Leon might have information critical to our investigation. We know Mateo didn't give us everything he had on the Mancuso cartel. I think it was because he was hoping for some type of leverage. He might have been planning to negotiate with Johnny Boy or Poppy for his life, or he was going to try to blackmail them. All this is speculation until we find Arya."

"If what you suspect is true," Kaleb said, "if Mateo gave evidence to his wife for safekeeping...that information could possibly help us dismantle the cartel."

River nodded in agreement. "Exactly." Especially now that their key witness was dead.

Nova knew that Rylee and Kaleb wanted to tear down the cartel just as much as she and River did.

"We're willing to lend our assistance and resources to you both," Rylee said.

Nova smiled. "Thanks."

"I was told by a CI that Manuel DeSoto…Mateo…tried to blackmail Poppy before he disappeared into WITSEC," Rylee said. "He claimed to have copies of deeds and information on all the properties and businesses owned by the cartel. He offered to sell it to her for ten million dollars. He said he'd go away, and they'd never hear from him again."

Nova nodded, familiar with the intel. "Apparently, Poppy didn't believe him," Nova responded. "That was such a stupid move on his part."

Shaking his head, River interjected, "Mateo only narrowly escaped when Johnny Boy discovered he'd been skimming money off the top. If Johnny Boy was the one targeting Mateo's family, Mateo might have sought him out for revenge."

She nodded, though she didn't spare him a glance. She didn't want to give Kaleb and Rylee the impression of tension between them.

"What happens when you find Arya?" Kaleb asked. "Are you putting her back in the program under a new alias?"

"I just need to find her," Nova responded with a slight shrug.

She suddenly felt like she needed some air. She stood up and walked over to the balcony. She opened the sliding glass door and stepped outside.

"Nova, you look troubled," Kaleb said when he joined her on the balcony.

"I keep thinking about Mateo and Arya. I can't help but feel as if I failed them somehow."

"Nova, Mateo's death isn't on you. He took it upon himself to leave WITSEC. He knew the risks, regardless of his reason."

She looked over at Kaleb. "River told me the same thing. But the reality is that Mateo was under my protection. I should've put him under twenty-four-hour security because I knew he was beginning to spiral out of control. I went out to see him, but it was too late."

"You didn't do anything wrong. At the time, he wasn't under a high-threat situation, Nova. There wasn't a need for additional security. Look, I know all too well how it feels to lose a witness. It's not a good feeling," Kaleb said. "I don't know if your dad ever told you, but that's why I left the Marshals."

She studied him. "He didn't."

"My witness left the program just like Mateo," he said. "It's what got him killed, but I took his death personally. I didn't want to lose another one, even if it was caused by their own actions."

"I'm beginning to feel the same way. After we find Arya, I'm not sure I'll stay with the agency. I joined the Marshals because I wanted to work with my dad..." Nova paused momentarily, saying, "I'm not going to lose Arya."

"We'll do everything possible to help you find her."

"Kaleb, I'm so glad you're here."

"Me, too." He placed an arm around her. "I want you to know that Easton would be so proud of you. I bet he's looking down at you with a big grin."

She glanced up at him. "I hope so. How is Nate?" Nova asked.

"My brother is doing well. I've been trying to convince him to leave Wisconsin and join me in Los Angeles. He's not trying to hear it."

She laughed. "How do *you* like living in California?"

"It's fine. I'm happy anywhere Rylee is," Kaleb responded.

"Kaleb, that's a nice thing to say," Nova responded, masking the pain in her voice. "I can see how genuinely happy you are with Rylee." She couldn't help but think of her short time with River and how it had left a lasting imprint on her heart. Despite trying to move on, memories of their time together haunted her.

"I'm surprised some man hasn't snatched you up yet."

"One-track mind," Nova stated. "I've been focused on my career. Besides, the badge intimidates some of the men I've dated. I'll probably end up with someone in law enforcement. They seem to be the only people who understand me."

Kaleb smiled. "I used to feel that way, too."

"And you ended up marrying someone in the field."

"That wasn't the deciding factor, though," he responded. "I would've married Rylee no matter what."

"That's great. Maybe one day I'll get lucky enough to find my Mr. Right. I'm not really in any hurry, though."

"You just have to be open to loving and being loved, Nova."

She smiled. "I hear you."

Nova really wanted to share her life with someone special. It was just that she hadn't met him yet. Well…she'd blown it with the man who'd come close. He would always hold a special place in her heart. She definitely had regrets. Nova wished now that she'd handled things differently.

Her chance with River had come and gone. No point in dwelling on the past. Life was meant to be lived looking ahead and not in the rearview mirror.

RIVER EYED NOVA'S interaction with Kaleb from across the room and wondered what they could be discussing. He'd never seen her like this. From the moment he'd met her, River had quickly learned that Nova was always sure of herself and liked to be in control. The woman outside with Kaleb seemed reflective and doubtful. He wondered what could have made her so upset.

"How long have you known Nova?" Rylee asked, cutting into his musings.

"A couple of years," River answered, trying to sound nonchalant. "We worked on a case together. I hadn't talked to her since. Until now."

"I see. Nova's father was my handler when I was in WITSEC," Rylee said. "My relationship with her actually developed after Kaleb and I got married."

She leaned down to open her laptop. "Have you conducted a property search?"

"I checked for listings under Mateo's and Arya's names. Nothing came up."

Rylee sat down at the table. "I'll run her parents' names and those of other known relatives. Maybe we'll get a hit. Arya could be hiding in one of the family properties."

Nova approached, trailed by Kaleb, and said, "I took some photographs from the Lozano house. Maybe we can find out where they were taken. There's nothing but dates written on the back of the pictures."

"I'll scan them and send them to the tech at HSI," Rylee said.

"It's worth a try," Nova agreed as she laid them on the table. "River and I have already conducted a property search. We have a list of places to check out. One of which is a house given to Ramona Lozano by her brother before he died," Nova said. "It's in Oceanside. I need to change out of these sweatpants. Then I'll be ready to leave."

River thought she looked nice in the tank top and navy sweats but decided to keep his opinion to himself.

"Kaleb, you can join me in my room while Nova gets dressed," River said. "I need to grab something before we go.

"I had no idea that you were with Homeland Security," River said as he and Kaleb walked across the hall to his room. "I thought you were done with this life."

"I thought so, too," he responded. "My brother and I were partners in a private security firm. I sold my shares to him after Rylee and I got married."

"Did you join HSI because of your wife?" River inquired.

"Partly. While I was trying to keep Rylee safe, it made me realize just how much I missed being part of the action.

"How long have you been working the Mancuso cartel investigation?" Kaleb asked.

"Not long. I inherited the case from another agent who left the job. I think it was given to me because of my recent investigation into the Torres cartel. But I have personal reasons for wanting this case—a close friend of mine was murdered at the hands of Johnny Boy."

"The Torres cartel... That was *you*?" Kaleb asked. "That was a huge bust. Great job, River."

"It was a team effort coordinated with HSI, ATF and LAPD."

"Still, it was good work. Man, don't sell yourself short."

"Thanks," River replied.

He wanted to ask about Nova but decided against it. Kaleb wasn't aware of their past and River thought it best not to bring up the subject. *Keep the focus on the job.*

Chapter Ten

"Kaleb looks happier than I've ever seen him," Nova said. She'd freshened up and was back in the kitchenette with Rylee. "I have to say that you two are so good for each other."

Rylee smiled. "I've never loved anyone as much as I love him."

"Did you fall in love with him while he protected you?"

"The first thing I noticed about Kaleb was those piercing gray eyes. We were initially attracted to one another, but at the time, our main focus was keeping me alive and out of the cartel's reach."

"I love a happy ending," Nova said.

"You sound like a romantic."

"Not at all," she responded. "When things get serious… I run." To be honest, there was only one man she'd run from. It was hard to put into words what was going on in her head back then. She'd just lost her father and felt like she couldn't catch her breath.

"Have you ever tried to figure out why?" Rylee asked.

"I don't know."

"Sounds like you panic."

Nova nodded. "The excitement of this intense connection clashed with the heaviness of my sorrow and left me feeling lost, like I was spiraling out of control. I didn't know which way was up, and every emotion seemed to blur together into a confusing mess. In the middle of all that chaos, it hit me—I hadn't really taken the time to grieve for my dad properly. His loss was this gaping hole in my heart, and instead of facing it, I let myself get swept away by the whirlwind romance. I was scared, Rylee, scared that I was losing myself in the middle of it all. I really messed things up between us and I don't know how to fix it."

"What happened?"

"I made the toughest decision I've ever had to make—I ran away. No words…no note…nothing."

"No…" Rylee offered a sympathetic look.

"Yeah, and I regret the way I left," Nova admitted, a wave of sadness flowing through her. "I should've stayed there and talked to him. I should've told him what I was feeling at the time."

"How long has it been?"

"Eighteen months."

"Do you still see him, or can you get in contact with him?" Rylee inquired.

"I've run into him recently," Nova said.

"I'm assuming it didn't go very well."

"There's a lot of tension between us." She turned to check her reflection in the mirror before saying, "I guess we'd better get going."

Rylee nodded, standing up. "Nova, I have a feeling everything will work out between you and River."

Turning to face Rylee, she asked, "How did you know I was talking about River?"

"Girl, you can cut the tension between you two with a knife."

"Really?"

"Yes." Rylee grinned. "But things will get better between you."

Nova picked up her black tote. As they walked to the front door, she said, "Rylee, I really hope you're right about me and River. I miss his friendship."

"Is that all?"

"No, but it's all I can expect from him now, and even that's asking a lot."

River and Kaleb were in the hallway waiting.

Nova met River's gaze; then she looked away almost immediately. He was such a handsome man. Her eyes traveled down to the white polo shirt and jeans he wore.

Ten minutes later, they were walking through the parking deck to the SUV.

They made the forty-five-minute drive to Oceanside.

While Nova sat in the back seat chatting with Rylee, Kaleb and River talked about how they met and the case that brought them together.

Nova watched the passing streets and immediately fell in love with the area's laid-back vibe. She especially liked the quaint little homes. Nestled in the coastal town was the military base Camp Pendleton. Her father had once been stationed there when he was in the Marines. Nova had been too young then to remember anything now about the base or the area.

The Lozano house wasn't too far from the Oceanside Pier. The exterior was painted in soothing shades of seafoam and aqua. From where they were parked, they could see the patio featured a firepit, lounge furniture and a grill. Nova imagined it was the perfect spot for evenings with family and friends to sit back and chill, watching picturesque sunsets, toasting marshmallows or making s'mores.

Her attention shifted to the house as they sat in the car across from the corner property, watching as a middle-aged woman walked out to retrieve the rest of the bags from the trunk of a car.

"Somebody's home. Possibly the housekeeper," Nova suggested.

River removed his sunglasses. "Judging from the groceries...Pablo Lozano and his wife must be here, too, and they're planning to stay a while."

Nova released the breath she'd been holding. "I think it's best I speak to the parents alone," she said. "River, you might intimidate them."

"Why don't I go with you?" Rylee suggested. "Two women won't seem so threatening."

Kaleb nodded in agreement.

She exited the car, and she and Rylee walked to the door.

Rylee rang the bell. "Here goes..."

"Hello," Nova said when the woman they'd seen earlier opened the door.

She and Rylee showed their badges and introduced themselves before Nova added, "We're looking for Mr. and Mrs. Lozano."

"They're not here," the housekeeper responded. "They left yesterday. They're traveling, and I don't know when they'll return."

"Do you happen to know where they went?" Nova inquired, wondering about the groceries.

The woman shook her head. "No, they didn't tell me anything. Just that they would be out of town for a few weeks. Mrs. Lozano said it was a much-needed vacation." She smiled gently before adding, "They haven't traveled much since they lost their daughter."

Rylee nodded. "Do they always leave without telling you where they're going?" she asked.

"They tell me only what they want me to know."

"Someone broke into the house in San Diego," Rylee stated. "Whoever it was killed the housekeeper."

The woman gasped. "Yolanda…"

"Yes," Nova confirmed. "We noticed the bags of groceries you brought into the house. It's a lot for a house no one currently lives in."

She looked from Rylee to Nova. "What do y'all want with Mr. and Mrs. Lozano? These are good people."

"Here is my card," Nova said. "I just want to make sure they're safe."

"Wait here…"

The housekeeper left for a moment before returning with a photo in hand. "I'm not sure where it is, but I think it might be in North Carolina. The Lozano family used to go there every summer. It belongs to one of Mrs. Lozano's cousins."

Nova's face lit up with a smile. "Thank you." The photo was different from the ones they'd found.

The photograph showed a beautiful, large lakefront home with white exteriors and a charming stone pathway leading up to the front door. The house was surrounded by lush green trees and a sprawling lawn that faded into the crystal blue lake in the background. There was a glimpse of a wooden dock extending from the backyard toward the water, lined with cozy lounge chairs and a small boat tied to its side. The clear blue sky and fluffy white clouds above completed the picturesque scene.

She climbed back into the car, unsure if they were getting closer or falling behind in their investigation.

RIVER PEERED AT NOVA, who sat in the back seat with Rylee. He'd been trying not to stare all morning. He yearned to unpin her hair, allowing it to flow free around her face, but quickly forced the image out of his mind. The only thing between them now was their missing witness and her parents.

"I emailed a copy of that new photograph to one of the techs at HSI," Rylee told the group. "Hopefully, they'll be able to narrow down the location for us."

Nova looked up at River, saying, "The housekeeper thinks Arya's parents are in North Carolina."

"Where?"

"She didn't know for sure, but we're thinking this is where this picture may have been taken."

River said, "That's great if it's in North Carolina, but it's a long shot. That backdrop could be anywhere."

"If it were just the beach, I might agree with you," Nova stated as she studied the photograph. "But look at those mountains... This house sits on a lake."

While waiting for the light to turn green, she handed the picture to River.

"I think you might be right," he said after returning it to her. He tried not to focus too much on the feeling of his fingers brushing hers as he'd passed the picture back. "Now we need some luck to find the exact location."

"Sounds so simple, doesn't it?" Nova smiled.

"Hopefully, my tech person will call back with some good news," Rylee said.

The traffic light switched to green, and they continued down the road, the anticipation palpable in the air. The journey to uncover Arya's parents' whereabouts had become a puzzle, and each piece could lead them closer to the missing woman.

As THE CAR rolled forward, Nova couldn't shake the sense of urgency that propelled them back to the East Coast, chasing elusive answers against North Carolina's landscape.

When they returned to the hotel, Rylee said, "I've been charged with putting together a multiagency task force. My team will be in this area for a meeting with the San Diego police and I asked them to stop by. They should be arriving within the hour."

"That's great," Nova said. "I'm looking forward to meeting them." She sat down and opened up her laptop. "While we're waiting for an address on that property, I'm going to go back through the phone records of Arya's parents. I want to see which relatives they have been in contact with. It looks like they may be trying to cover their tracks."

"It will help keep them alive," Kaleb said.

"But for how long?" River responded.

That was Nova's concern as well. Her heart raced as she realized the gravity of Johnny Boy's actions. The men he sent were ruthless and calculating, experts in hunting down their targets. She knew they would stop at nothing to find their intended victims, leaving a trail of destruction in their wake.

Fifty minutes later, there was a knock on the door.

"They're here," Rylee announced.

As Rylee introduced each team member, Nova took a moment to observe them individually.

Sabra Gomez stood with an air of authority, her dark hair pulled back in a tight bun and dressed professionally in a white button-up shirt and black blazer. Next to her was Tauren Gray, whose mixed heritage could be seen in his rich cream-colored skin and serious expression. He mentioned that he and River had trained together at the DEA Academy in Quantico.

Maisie Wells, on loan from LAPD, exuded confidence with her twist-out hairstyle and regal posture. Rolle Livingston from ATF had a neat ponytail that showed off his defined features, and FBI agent Harper Arness's short hair gave off a professional vibe.

Finally, there was HSI agent Seth Majors, who commanded attention with his tall stature and commanding presence, framed by clean-shaven dark brown skin and closely cropped black hair.

"Wow," Nova murmured. "Looks like you've put together quite a team."

"I wanted you all to meet because we share a common interest," Rylee stated. "We're currently focused on the Mancuso cartel."

"We heard the DEA lost a witness recently," Tauren said.

Nodding, River responded, "He was mine."

When everyone was seated, Nova said, "I was his case agent in witness protection, and now his wife is missing. We think she's gone into hiding. She's in danger."

"There's been some chatter about a missing package," Sabra said. "Maybe this is what they've been talking about. But something else is going on that they seem to consider more urgent. We've decoded some of the conversations originating in Mexico and discovered that the cartel has several tractor trailers leaving the Arizona/Mexico border. They're said to be carrying *lettuce*. In this instance, lettuce refers to cocaine. Several hundred kilos."

Nova knew that the codes and lingo used by drug traffickers were only limited by the imagination. Kilos had often been referred to as batteries, oranges, melons...

"Johnny Boy has been on a pretty good run," Rylee stated. "It's time we stop him."

"How does this man manage to keep eluding arrests?" Harper asked. "Even Calderon was apprehended eventually."

"Because he's smarter than Calderon ever was." Nova's

jaw clenched as she replied, her eyes burning with determination. "Johnny Boy knows how to stay under the radar,
never getting too comfortable or predictable." She couldn't
help but secretly hope that he would slip up, a glimmer of
desperation creeping into her tone. They needed a break
from this endless game of cat and mouse.

Rolle interjected, "We all know he has a pretty good
system going. His life is like a shell game. Johnny Boy has
several body doubles, just like Raul Mancuso did. Ninety
percent of the time, no one knows where he or the doubles
are. The difference between Raul and Johnny Boy is that
he didn't hire these look-alikes to fool the Mexican and
US governments—they're in place to fool the people closest to him."

Nova said, "According to Manuel DeSoto, outside of
Poppy, only a few people can speak to Johnny Boy in
person—and the families of those with that privilege live
in luxury at Johnny Boy's expense. It's how he rewards
their loyalty."

"Naw...it's not a reward. That's all about power," Rolle
stated. "Johnny Boy wants the people around him to know
that not only are their lives in his hands, but their family's
lives are, too."

River nodded in agreement. "My witness told the DEA
that Johnny Boy had one of his lieutenants killed because
the man brought a personal phone to a dinner hosted by
him. He's always been paranoid about anything that might
be a tracking device, a recorder or a camera. The only
known picture of Johnny Boy was taken when he was nineteen and booked for a murder in Jamaica. He sat in jail for
about a week. During that time, all the witnesses to that
murder ended up dead, so he was released. They couldn't go

forward without a witness, and his alibi was solid. Johnny Boy disappeared after that."

"How do we know that the man arrested in Jamaica wasn't one of Johnny Boy's doubles?" Harper asked. "Maybe the real Johnny Boy murdered the witnesses. Think about it... His fingerprints disappeared... If it wasn't for my witness, we wouldn't have what information we have now. Johnny Boy is still pretty much a shadow."

"I have a man in custody right now...Rico Alfaro...but he's not saying a word," River announced. "He fears Johnny Boy more than doing life in prison."

"He can't elude us forever," Rylee stated. "We will dismantle his routes truck by truck—come down hard on his people until someone is willing to talk."

"What will y'all do with this new information you've decoded?" River asked.

Nova wondered the same thing, but he'd beat her to it.

"The team is heading to Arizona this afternoon. They'll connect with local ATF and DEA agents to assist with intercepting the trucks," Rylee responded. "We just scored a win when we seized fifty pounds of cocaine in a shipment of what was supposed to be packs of coconut flour a few days ago, and we're hoping for another."

"Johnny Boy might be in Arizona then," River said. "I heard he likes to be nearby if there's a problem. He wants to know the person responsible for any mistakes."

"If this is true, then he isn't focused on Arya," Nova responded.

River eyed her. "That's because he's got people out there searching for her. Trust me...he's not letting up."

Seth checked his watch. "We need to pick up Max."

"Who is Max?" she asked.

"Oh yes, we have another team member," Rylee announced. "Max. He is Seth's K-9 partner."

"What kind of dog?" Nova wanted to know.

"He's a Belgian Malinois," Seth answered. "He's six years old and the best partner I've ever had. Max is a dual-purpose dog trained for patrol and narcotics."

"Where's Max now?" she asked.

"He's getting some much-needed grooming," Seth stated. "My sister owns a shop down here, so we dropped Max off before coming here."

After a few more minutes of discussion, Rylee's team left the hotel.

"I wanted you all to meet because I hope that we'll continue to work together in this war against the drug cartels," Rylee stated.

"What did you have in mind when you mentioned working together?" Nova asked.

"I meant that I'd like for you and River to join the team. Nova, you'd have to relocate to Los Angeles. I'll understand if this is not something you're interested in doing right now."

She glanced over at River. He seemed as surprised as she was by Rylee's offer. Nova didn't know what he would decide, but she knew what she would do—she wanted a change. Relocating wasn't a problem because Nova loved the West Coast and could see herself living here full-time.

It would also place her and River in the same city. She didn't know how he would feel about it, but it didn't matter because this was about her career. She wouldn't let their past get in the way of her aspirations.

Chapter Eleven

River's eyebrows rose in surprise over Rylee's job offer.

He was even more shocked when Nova said, "I'd be interested in joining. I've been trying to figure out my next move after Arya is safe, and I really believe this is it."

Rylee smiled. "That's great. We can talk about this in detail after we find Arya."

River sat quietly, observing the women as they talked. He was stunned by the idea of Nova moving to Los Angeles. While the task force sounded interesting and like a great opportunity, he loved his job and wasn't looking for a change. He wasn't opposed to helping if needed, but he was finally up for a promotion he'd been wanting—now wasn't the time to leave.

He personally didn't think it was a good idea for Nova to relocate to Los Angeles. It was too close for his comfort. It was a big enough city to keep them from running into one another. However, because they were both in law enforcement, he and Nova were bound to move within the same circles.

I can't make Nova's career moves about me. No point in worrying about something that might not happen.

The sound of her laughter was like a siren's call, luring him back to the warmth and comfort of their past love. But as he watched Nova laughing with Kaleb, River couldn't help but feel a twinge of fear in his heart. A fear that if he let her back into his life, she would once again leave him broken and alone. The familiar excitement at the sound of her laugh quickly dissipated as he remembered the pain and heartache she had caused before. He knew deep down that letting her back in meant risking his heart all over again, and he wasn't sure if he could survive another shattering blow.

He couldn't deny that Nova still had an effect on him, although he'd never admit this truth aloud to anyone. River struggled with admitting it to himself.

Nova walked over to where he was sitting. "What did you think of Rylee's team?"

"I've known Tauren a long time, but the others... They were cool," he responded.

She nodded. "I thought they were an impressive group of people."

Nova didn't spare him so much as a glance when she walked past, crossing the room to where Rylee was sitting. They were looking at something on the laptop computer.

River got up to make a phone call. He strode to the door, opened it and walked across the hall. The case he was calling about was in his room. Although his focus was on finding Arya, he still continued investigating the other assigned cases.

He had to return to Nova's room afterward. They were going to discuss the next course of action to find the Lozanos and Arya. He also placed a call to local police to send someone to check out one other house in San Diego that belonged to Arya's grandparents. It was currently listed for sale.

When River returned to Nova's room, he was met by her frosty stare. Working in a tense environment wasn't good for either of them. If they weren't careful, this tension between them could turn into something more toxic.

River didn't want that, and he was sure Nova didn't either.

"HEY, NOVA... I don't want to get into your business, but are things cool between you and River?" Kaleb inquired while they were sitting in chairs on the balcony. They had taken a short break.

Nova had come out to watch the sun go down. She wanted to experience a California sunset.

"Why do you ask that?" She wondered if Rylee had mentioned their earlier conversation to him.

"I noticed that you two don't seem to have much to say to one another outside of your investigation. Things between you seem kinda strained."

"Rylee mentioned the same thing earlier," Nova stated. "You might as well know what happened... Eighteen months ago, River and I worked on a case together. We spent two wonderful weeks together. Things between us started happening so fast that I could barely breathe and panicked. Kaleb...he made me feel things I'd never felt before. I didn't know what to do, so I left without saying anything to him."

"And now?"

"As you can see...he's not exactly fond of me." Her heart ached at the very thought, but she wasn't going to let it show.

"You know that River's responding out of hurt, Nova. If he really didn't want anything to do with you, I doubt he'd be here."

"That's the irony. I was actually trying to save him from heartache, but maybe he needs more time to erase the pain."

"Have you tried to talk to River about what happened?" he asked.

Nova shook her head as terrible regrets assailed her. "He's done a really great job of discouraging any personal conversation. You know Dad used to be the one who gave me relationship advice. I wish I could talk to him about this."

Kaleb embraced her. "I'm sorry Easton's not here, but you can always come to me, Nova. I'll do the best I can. Your dad was my go-to person for relationship advice as well."

"I feel like I've failed him in some way," she said. "He never lost a witness. I knew Mateo and Arya were headstrong. I should have…"

"Don't torture yourself like this. It doesn't do you any good."

Water welled up in her eyes and overflowed, rolling down her cheeks.

Nova pulled a tissue out of her pocket and wiped away her tears. She clenched her jaw to kill the sob in her throat. "I don't know why I'm getting so emotional."

"Our jobs are stressful, and you're still grieving. Sometimes, we all need to sit down and have a good cry."

With a deep breath, she forced herself to head back to work, trying to impose an iron control on her emotions.

Kaleb excused himself and went inside to speak with his wife.

"Are you okay?" River asked when she walked back inside. "You looked like you were crying."

Nova was surprised by his question. "I'm good. I just had an emotional moment over my dad."

"I know you must miss him very much. Are you up to discuss a plan of action? If not, we can do it later."

"No…of course. We can do it now."

Nova grabbed a water bottle and a snack bag of peanuts from a basket in the kitchenette, taking them to the table.

Rylee stepped away from them when her phone rang.

"We found it," she said after hanging up. "The house in the photo is in the Lake Glenville area. Another relative."

"Arya never once mentioned that she had family in North Carolina," Nova stated. "We never would've been placed there. She intentionally withheld that information. I know that she and Mateo vacationed there for the past two years." Shaking her head, she uttered, "Those two..."

River looked up from his file.

"That's probably where Arya's been all this time," she said. "She may have felt it was the safest place to go."

He agreed. "Lake Glenville is about three and a half hours from Charlotte."

"We should book seats on the next flight to Atlanta," River said. "It's two and a half hours from Lake Glenville."

Nova agreed.

Kaleb and Rylee prepared to head back to the airport.

"It was so good seeing you and Kaleb," Nova said. "Thanks for everything."

Rylee stood with her hand on the doorknob. "I'll be in touch within the next week or so regarding the task force."

"Great! Because I'm really looking forward to hearing more about it," Nova responded. "I'm ready for something new."

"We're booked on a flight leaving tonight at seven," River announced.

Rylee said, "Kaleb and I want to take you to dinner before you head to the airport."

"Fine by me," Nova responded with a smile.

She glanced over at River, who said, "Sure."

Nova quickly packed her suitcase because they were heading to the airport right after they finished eating. River went back to his own room to do the same.

After checking out and putting the luggage in the SUV, they decided to eat at the restaurant in the hotel.

"This is a nice place," Rylee said.

Nova glanced around. "Yes, it is…"

She was saddened by Kaleb and Rylee's leaving. They were the perfect buffer between her and River. She wasn't looking forward to being alone with him again.

"I GUESS THIS wasn't a completely wasted trip," River stated shortly after the plane took off. "Unfortunately, Yolanda was an innocent victim in all this."

Nova agreed. "We probably wouldn't have found out about the house in North Carolina otherwise."

"I hate to put a negative spin on this, but there's a chance that Arya or her parents might not be at this house either."

"I know, River," she said. "But we'll cross that bridge when we get to it." Nova felt the tension rising between them like a thick fog, suffocating and uncomfortable. They were being very careful to keep space from each other even though they were seated beside one another.

"So, you're thinking about leaving the Marshals?" River asked, his voice laced with skepticism.

Nova gave him an icy stare. "I've given it serious thought… What about you?"

His response was a dismissive shake of his head. "Not interested. I'm happy where I am."

She clenched her jaw, struggling to keep her emotions in check. They needed to talk about what had happened in their past, no matter how painful it may be. But last time she'd tried, it hadn't gone well.

Nova sighed, feeling frustrated and unheard. "I just hate all this tension between us," she finally said, her voice low and strained.

River's expression softened slightly. "I didn't mean for things to turn out this way. I don't think I've been rude to you."

"You haven't exactly been warm and fuzzy either," Nova retorted, her tone sharp with hurt.

"I never meant to hurt you," River answered, his words genuine but guarded. "I just don't want things to get out of hand."

Nova's heart sank at his admission. So, he didn't trust himself around her. She couldn't blame him after what had happened between them.

"Just so we're clear," she said, keeping her gaze fixed ahead. "I am capable of keeping my distance and staying professional."

"I know that."

The comment ended things on a bittersweet note, both silently agreeing to put aside their issues for the sake of the investigation. But as River pulled out a bag of potato chips and offered some to her, Nova couldn't help but feel a sense of unease and sadness linger between them. Would they ever be able to repair their fractured relationship fully?

Only time would tell. She shook her head at his offer of a snack.

"You sure you don't want any?" River asked. "Because I've seen you staring them down. I'm pretty sure I heard your stomach growling, too."

Nova knew he was trying to lighten the mood. She decided to accept his peace offering. "It was probably your stomach you heard. Considering you only ordered a salad at dinner," she teased.

"C'mon... It's been a while since we shared a bag of potato chips."

"It's been a minute," she responded while settling back in her seat, her unease slowly dissipating.

Nova eyed the bag of chips again, then reached inside.

"I knew you couldn't resist." River smiled.

Giving him a mock roll of her eyes, she took the bag out of his hand.

"I can't believe that you're really thinking about leaving the Queen City," he stated. "When we met, you talked about how much you loved Charlotte."

She nodded. "I do love it there, but I want a more productive role in helping to take down the Mancuso cartel. They're responsible for my father's death. I want to make sure he didn't die in vain."

His eyes widened in surprise. "You never told me that. I don't think you ever mentioned how he died."

"I didn't want to focus on the tragedies in my life back then," Nova responded. "My dad and I... We were close. Losing him is harder than I ever imagined it would be. I feel like there's a hole in my heart."

"I understand," he responded. "I felt that way when I lost my grandmother."

"I have his text messages saved. I read them when I need to talk to him."

He smiled. "I think about all the conversations I used to have with my grandmother. There are times when I can almost hear her voice."

As they talked about the people they'd lost, Nova sank deeper into her seat while trying to stifle a yawn.

"Why don't you try and get a nap in?" River suggested. "We will hit the ground running as soon as we land."

"I really hope we find them this time," she murmured.

"We haven't lost yet."

"We haven't exactly gotten anywhere either." She paused

a moment, then said, "River, don't mind me. You know I'm not a pessimist. This whole thing with Mateo and Arya…" Nova gave herself a mental shake. "You know what… I'm good."

"I know you're frustrated," River said. "I am, too. It's an unspoken part of our job description."

She gave a short chuckle as she stuck a pair of AirPods in her ears and selected a playlist to enjoy. She resolved to let the music revitalize her spirit. When the plane landed, they had to move quickly. They couldn't afford to waste any time heading to Lake Glenville. She hoped fervently that Pablo and Ramona Lozano would be at the house along with Arya.

RIVER TOOK WHAT he considered a power nap during the final hour of the flight. Turned out it was what he needed, because he felt rejuvenated by the time the plane landed in Atlanta.

They rented a car and drove to Lake Glenville, the coastal town located eight miles from Cashiers, NC, in a mountain rainforest.

"It's beautiful up here," Nova said, looking out the passenger-side window.

"It looks like the perfect place to visit if you're a lover of the outdoors," River remarked. He wasn't, so while the landscape was indeed a beauty, it wasn't his thing.

Nova took a sip of her water. "I remember you saying that you weren't the camping or fishing type."

"I'm not. I love the beach, but I've never cared much for the mountains."

She chuckled. "I'm not either. I'll take the beach any day. I did read that there are three waterfalls here."

They made a left turn into a quaint neighborhood. Following the directions of the GPS, River turned right on the first street they approached.

"This is the house that was in the photograph." Nova's voice was a velvet murmur as River slowly passed the home. "It's the one with the dark blue shutters."

River felt his heart race and swallowed hard. "Yes, that's it."

They parked down the street.

"I'm thinking we watch the house for a bit instead of just rushing up to the door," River said. "If they're in there, we don't want to spook them."

"After what they've been through, don't you think seeing a strange car in the neighborhood with two people sitting in it might spook them more?" Nova responded. "I think it's better for us to get out and talk to them."

Shrugging, River said, "Okay. We'll try it your way. Do you think we should wear our vests?"

"Not this time."

They got out of the car and made their way up to the house.

Nova rang the doorbell a few minutes later. She released a soft sigh of relief when the door opened a sliver and Ramona Lozano peered through the crack.

Looking from River to Nova, she asked, "May I help you?"

"Mrs. Lozano, I'm Deputy Marshal Nova Bennett. Your daughter may have mentioned me." She held up her badge. "Is your husband home with you?"

The thin woman looked as if she were about to faint. She ran trembling fingers through her short hair. "Yes, he is. Is he in some kind of trouble?"

"No, he isn't."

Her brow furrowed. "Then why are you looking for him?"

Nova glanced over at River, then back at Ramona. "You know I'm not here about Pablo. I've been searching for the two of you and your daughter. You all could be in danger." She identified Arya by the name she was given at birth.

Nervous, Ramona glanced away. "I'm afraid I don't know where she is. I—"

"Look, I know she's been in contact with you, Mrs. Lozano," Nova interjected. "I'm sure you've heard by now that Yolanda was murdered in your home. The people after you are not playing games. You're all in grave danger, and I'm here to help."

The woman released a shaky breath. "Ava called to warn us that we were in danger, but I haven't heard from her since then, and I don't know where she is."

"Mrs. Lozano, I only want to keep your daughter safe."

Clutching her necklace as if it were a lifeline, Ramona responded, "If I hear from her, I'll let you know if you leave your number with me. All I want is for Ava to come home to us. We miss her terribly. I don't know what that dreadful husband of hers has gotten her into…"

"I want you to know that I'll do everything in my power to keep Arya safe," Nova reassured her. "But I need to find her first."

Ramona gestured for them to enter. "You can search the house, but she's not here." River accepted her invitation to verify that they were alone in the home while Nova sat down in the living room with Ramona.

"Ava said she couldn't tell us where she was—only that we had to leave California," Ramona explained. "We heard about Mateo's family, and then Mateo… Her father and I did as she asked. We left our home and came here." Clutching the gold cross around her neck, Ramona sighed. "Poor Yolanda. I told her that she should visit her family in Mexico. But she wanted to help. We knew someone might be watching the house, and we didn't want anyone to know we'd left. She thought she'd be safe."

"They were either looking for you and your husband... or trying to find your daughter. Don't you see that *we* can protect all of you?" Nova paused momentarily, then added, "If you do hear from her, tell Arya I found her message and I'm on her side."

"I will," Ramona responded. "Thank you."

"My daughter told us to leave and go where nobody would find us," Pablo said when he and River joined them in the living room. "We figured we'd be safe here."

"It wasn't easy locating you," Nova stated. "I must confess that I took some of your photos, and they led us here. Are you sure you can't give us a clue as to where we should look for your daughter?"

"I can't help you," Ramona said, averting her gaze. "I'm sorry."

Nova understood the fear and desperation that gripped the Lozano family. She respected Ramona's decision to keep quiet, even though it made their task more challenging. Her heart went out to them, but without more concrete information, finding Arya would be like searching for a needle in a haystack.

Chapter Twelve

They walked back to the car and got inside.

"It's obvious that Ramona Lozano isn't going to tell us anything because she wants to protect her daughter," Nova said. She was frustrated and needed to vent. "I thought telling them about Yolanda's murder might scare her into telling us where to find Arya, but she's sticking to her story."

"You don't seem convinced," River said.

"I'm not sure what to believe," she responded. "Arya was worried enough to warn them to leave their home... Surely, she'd check in. She'd want to know that they're safe. At least, that's what I would do."

He nodded. "I agree. So, what do you want to do?"

"We should hang around and see if they suddenly have visitors."

They sat there for the next couple of hours.

"There hasn't been any movement coming or going," River said. "There's a café two blocks from the neighborhood. Why don't we pick up something to eat?"

Nodding, Nova said, "Works for me."

They made the trip in silence and River pulled back into the neighborhood. "What's weighing so heavily on your mind?" River asked as they returned to their surveillance spot and started to eat in the car. "You look like you're trying to figure something out. I can almost hear your brain working."

"I was thinking about Mateo," Nova explained. "I think he wanted money to disappear, and this was the only way he thought he'd be able to get it. Unfortunately, now Arya has a target on her back."

"From what I know of Johnny Boy, he'd eliminate Mateo's wife and her entire family to play it safe."

"My gut tells me that Ramona knows where Arya's hiding," Nova said, pulling her hair into a ponytail. "I wish I could get her to trust me."

Glancing around, River said, "Everything seems normal around here. No perceived threats in the area—that's a good thing."

"It is, but I'd feel better if we just sit for a while longer to see if anything happens."

"I don't have a problem with that," he said with a slight shrug.

Nova swallowed hard. She was quickly becoming tired of the runaround. She didn't mind the chase if she were getting results. Right now, she didn't see anything but disappointment. They needed to find Arya, and soon.

RIVER AND NOVA continued to watch the house after dark, but nothing seemed amiss.

Nova pulled out a small bottle and spritzed some of the liquid on her neck.

"Arya's endgame is to be reunited with her parents," he said while trying to ignore the tantalizing scent of her fragrance. She'd opened a window and her scent now wafted to him. "We just have to figure out how they're going to make that happen."

Nova craned her neck and stared at the house. "I really

thought they'd pack a suitcase and take off as soon as we left. Maybe Ramona was telling the truth. Maybe she doesn't know where Arya's hiding."

"The day's not over yet." A few more minutes passed in silence and he tried to think of a conversation starter while they were sitting there in the vehicle. There were so many things River wanted to say to her, and much he didn't want to say. His emotions were conflicted since Nova had come back into his life. It brought back memories of Mary and the way she'd rejected him. The trauma of that experience shaped the man River had become, especially when it came to love.

Nova would never know how hard it was for River to be vulnerable enough to share what he was feeling with her. She'd made him feel safe and then she destroyed that safety. After their relationship ended, River had vowed to never show such vulnerability to anyone ever again. He viewed love as a weakness—one that could be easily exploited.

He chided himself for going down that path. They were on assignment, and making sure the witness and her parents remained unharmed was the priority. Right now, nothing else mattered.

River eyed the license plate of a black truck that passed them.

Nothing was remarkable about it, but it held his attention for the moment. He watched to see if the vehicle slowed as it neared the Lozanos' house.

It kept moving without slowing down.

"Something wrong?" Nova asked.

"No. Just checking out the truck that just passed by. It wasn't anything."

The tags were local. River kept looking to see if it passed by again, but it didn't. Nothing to send off any red flags, but his experienced senses were on alert.

NOVA STRUGGLED TO maintain a professional front, but keeping her mind off the handsome River was a challenge. She wondered how he could be both sexy and frustrating simultaneously. Those kissable lips of his reminded Nova of their time together in the past. Memories that she didn't want to dredge up. Memories she regarded as precious.

They were only precious to her, Nova realized.

The garage door to the Lozano house went up, cutting into her thoughts.

She glanced at the clock. It was one o'clock in the morning.

Pablo walked briskly, carrying a travel bag to the SUV. Ramona followed behind.

Nova nudged River, who'd seen it, too.

"Looks like Arya's parents are about to leave."

"Let's find out where they're going," River said as he started the vehicle.

Nova nodded. "Pull in front of the driveway so they can't leave."

The black truck that cut them off came out of nowhere. River made an abrupt stop to avoid a collision. Nova's body was pushed back and then thrown forward. Her instincts immediately sounded the alarm in her mind. Trouble loomed on the horizon.

"That's the same black truck that passed earlier." River's voice was tense, carrying the weight of recognition. "I remember the license plate. It's an ambush."

Nova's heart raced, and she drew in a deep breath, attempting to steady the nervous energy that flooded her. Anxiety surged as she mentally mapped out the potential outcomes. There was no avoiding it; they had to face this danger head-on.

In a swift, practiced motion, Nova slipped on a vest before emerging from the shelter of the SUV.

"US Marshals," she yelled with authority as she swung open the passenger-side door. "Get out of the truck with your hands up."

On the opposite side of the vehicle, River stood, gun drawn, moving cautiously toward the driver's side of the suspicious truck.

Nova repeated her command, scanning their surroundings, and that was when she noticed another truck strategically parked in front of the Lozano home, effectively blocking any chance of escape.

Pablo and Ramona Lozano were trapped.

The only thought on Nova's mind was finding a way to reach Arya's parents and get them to safety.

Just then, the passenger-side door of the vehicle that cut them off suddenly swung open, and a dark-skinned man with dreadlocks leaped out, brandishing a weapon aimed directly at her.

Instinct took over, and Nova fired off a shot with precision, hitting her target.

River swiftly closed the distance between them, pulling her to safety just as another assailant opened fire in her direction. He responded in kind, unleashing a round of gunfire.

The driver of the black truck, undeterred by the chaos, seized the opportunity to escape, accelerating around the other car with reckless speed.

Shots echoed through the air from the other vehicle before the driver shifted to Reverse and backed down the street.

River aimed and fired his weapon at the SUV.

Nova cautiously made her way to the bleeding man on the ground. She kicked his gun out of reach, then knelt to see if he was dead.

The Lozanos' SUV was bullet-ridden, its metallic frame

reflecting the faint glow of a single light bulb hanging from the ceiling. The passenger-side door hung open at an awkward angle, revealing torn upholstery and shattered glass.

Nova felt lightheaded. "Nooo!"

Ramona lay motionless on the cold concrete floor beside the vehicle, her chest rising and falling in shallow breaths. Pablo's lifeless body was sprawled out in front of the car, his limbs twisted at unnatural angles and blood staining the ground beneath him. The unmistakable scent of gunpowder lingered in the air, a grim reminder of the violence that had taken place.

She rushed toward them.

River ran behind her.

"Pablo Lozano is dead," he said, kneeling beside his body with his fingers over the pulse point.

Ignoring the tightening in her stomach, Nova checked on Ramona. "She's still alive." She pulled out her cell phone. "But she needs to get to a hospital." Nova called the shooting in and requested an ambulance.

Ramona opened her eyes. Her voice barely above a whisper, she said, "Please h-help…my d-dau…my daughter." She arched her back, winced and closed her eyes, probably trying to block out the pain.

"Mrs. Lozano, don't try to talk. The paramedics are on the way," Nova said "They should be here soon." She sent up a quick prayer, asking God to keep the woman alive. She didn't want Arya to lose both parents. One was devastating enough.

"Ava… Miami… GPS…"

"I'm going to do everything I can to help her."

"My h-husband…" Ramona murmured before losing consciousness.

Nova heard the wailing of a siren in the distance and released a short sigh of relief. She'd done what she could to help Ramona and now it was up to the medics.

While they waited for the EMTs, she peered inside the Lozanos' SUV.

Nova checked the GPS, took a photo of the address input for Miami. "So, you were planning to meet up with Arya," she whispered. "I knew you weren't telling me everything."

Police officers quickly arrived on the scene, followed by an ambulance.

River went over to talk to the police while she stayed with Ramona.

"She's been shot," Nova told the paramedic, ignoring the officers who were going over the details of what had happened with River. "One bullet grazed her arm and the other one…it's below her right breast. She's unconscious."

They placed the injured woman on a backboard and transported her to the ambulance.

"C'mon," Nova said. "We're going to Miami. That's where they were headed."

"You think Arya's there?"

She nodded. "Before she lost consciousness, Ramona asked me to help Arya and said the address was in the GPS."

Something flickered in River's eyes but disappeared as quickly as it had come, leaving Nova to wonder what he could be thinking.

"What is it?" she asked.

"I'm just wondering why she chose Miami."

"I don't know," Nova said. "But I'm calling the Marshals and having her mother placed under round-the-clock security."

River nodded, wrapping up with the police while Nova

called Cohen to update him. When she disconnected, she and River made their way back to their vehicle.

"Miami... I find it interesting that Arya would go there since there's tension between the Mancuso and Mali cartels in Miami," River said. "Johnny Boy's been trying to establish a firm presence down there."

She'd heard something about that. "The Mali cartel hijacked and burned more than a dozen stash houses belonging to the Mancuso cartel in Florida a year ago," Nova said. "The fighting between the two organizations was so bad that they had to impose a curfew in certain areas. There's definitely bad blood between those two."

"Maybe that's what Mateo had planned all along," River said. "If negotiating with Poppy and Johnny Boy didn't work, then it's possible he intended to sell information to the Mali cartel for protection."

"Only he didn't count on being murdered."

River nodded in agreement. "Exactly."

"He never learned his lesson," Nova said. "Let's hope Arya does."

Chapter Thirteen

Nova sent up a silent prayer for Ramona Lozano. She'd already called the Marshals office in Miami, giving them the address for Arya's known location and requesting round-the-clock protection. She and River would get there as soon as they could, and when they finally found her, Nova planned to be the one to convince her to come back into the program. One question lingered in her mind. "How did they find Arya's parents?"

"I don't know, but I'm glad we were there," River responded. "If we hadn't been, Arya's mother might be in the morgue with her husband."

"She's not out of the woods yet," Nova pointed out.

Her phone rang, and she answered quickly.

"The marshals are at the hospital," she announced after ending the call. "At least we know Ramona's safe. She's under twenty-four-hour security. As soon as she's stable enough, she'll be taken someplace safe to recuperate." Nova paused briefly, then said, "Looks like you've been right all along. The cartel must consider Arya a huge threat. There has to be a reason why. They must see her as more than a potential loose end."

River nodded. He made a call, then got off the phone, saying, "She's been assigned to a Victim Witness Coordinator. I'm expecting a callback from the federal prosecutor."

Nova couldn't help but express her disgust at such a heinous act. "Arya's going to be devastated over her father's death, but hopefully, the news about her mother will be a brighter note."

"My partner is going to meet us in Miami," River announced.

She grinned. "I'm surprised Kenny is still putting up with you."

River gave her a sidelong glance. "Did you really just say that?"

"The two of you fuss like an old married couple," Nova said. "Did y'all ever check into couples counseling like I suggested?"

He chuckled. "Whatever…"

IN THE DRIVER'S SEAT, Nova glanced over at River, who seemed deep in thought. She could tell from his body language that her nearness brought him discomfort. He always seemed to stand with his arms crossed as if to protect himself. Whenever River had his laptop out, he carried it close to his chest like a physical barrier. Even now, he sat with his back so straight that Nova couldn't imagine he was relaxed in that position. She tried a couple of times to strike up a conversation, but River gave her one-word responses.

They were both exhausted, so it didn't bother her that he wasn't being very talkative. However, Nova desperately wanted to bridge the gap that had formed between them. She was at a loss on how to do so. It was her fault that their relationship had crumbled, and she couldn't shake off the weight of guilt.

Despite everything, she knew that their priority right now was protecting the witness from the deadly drug cartel. If only they weren't in this dangerous situation, she could focus on repairing their broken bond.

As they crossed into Florida, Nova welcomed the short break. Her mind and body were drained from constantly being on high alert.

River offered to take over driving for the rest of the journey to Miami, and Nova didn't protest. Part of her wanted to stay awake and keep an eye on things, but exhaustion eventually caught up, and she drifted off for a quick nap.

Nova woke up to River softly humming a tune beside her. Blinking away the remnants of sleep, she looked out the window and saw they were parked in front of a small roadside café. The warm Florida sun was casting a golden glow over everything, lending an air of tranquility to the scene.

Stretching her limbs, Nova took a deep breath and turned to River. "How long have we been here?"

River glanced at her with a smile. "Just about half an hour. You seemed so peaceful—I didn't want to wake you."

Nova nodded gratefully, her heart swelling with affection for him. She realized that despite their strained relationship, there was still an unspoken connection between them.

"I feel refreshed. I can take over if you'd like to get some sleep." Nova glanced at the clock. "You haven't been to sleep since we left North Carolina."

"Let's grab something to eat, and I'll see how I feel after," he responded.

Stepping out of the car, Nova couldn't help but notice the way River's hand grazed against hers. It sent a thrilling rush through her body, but she pushed those feelings aside as they entered the café. She needed to focus on Arya and avoid getting lost in this unexpected attraction. The more time they spent together, the more Nova's resolve wavered, torn between duty and desire.

RIVER WAS DOING everything he could to maintain a professional distance around Nova. But after her statement, he realized it wouldn't be as easy as he'd imagined.

Memories of the last time they'd worked together came flooding back. River tried to force them back into the deep recesses of his mind. There wouldn't be a repeat of what had happened two years ago. River vowed he wouldn't succumb to the weakness he felt whenever Nova was in his presence. His self-control was much stronger now, built up by the heartbreak she'd inflicted upon him.

Nova wanted to move forward as if nothing had happened, but it wasn't that easy for River.

He glanced over at her. She was on the phone. She'd periodically checked in on Ramona Lozano to learn her prognosis. The last time she'd called the hospital, Ramona was in surgery.

"How is she?" he asked when she hung up.

"She's out of surgery and is expected to recover fully," Nova responded. "At least I'll be able to tell Arya that her mother will be okay despite her father's death."

River met her gaze. "I'm really sorry about your father."

"I miss him a great deal. My mom and I are also very close, but I am... I was a daddy's girl for sure. He was my hero."

"Is your mom still in Wisconsin?" River asked.

"Yeah," she answered, giving a slight nod. "She'll never leave Milwaukee. Since I left, she's visited me several times, but she loves her hometown. I tried to convince her to move to Charlotte." Nova turned in her seat. "I know you were very close to your grandmother."

"Adelaide was my heart." Memories of his time with her floated to the forefront of River's mind. "She didn't miss any of my games when I was growing up. She was the team mom... She hosted a lot of the meals..."

"She sounds wonderful," Nova said. "I didn't know my paternal grandparents—they disowned my dad for marrying a Black woman. But my mother's parents...Bessie and Isaiah Chapman... They gave me so much love that I don't feel I missed out on having the other set in my life."

"You can't miss what you never had," River responded. "That's what people say, but it's not true. I missed the love of a mother."

"I—"

He cut her off. "Let's change the subject." River hadn't meant to show more of his vulnerability, and he wouldn't open up to her about his relationship with his mother. They had crossed into a red zone. He had to get them back on course.

"Sure," Nova said.

River relaxed his body. They were once again in the safe zone, and he wouldn't stray from it again.

Nova moved her body into a more comfortable position. They were less than twenty minutes away from their destination. "Arya rented this place under her mother's name," she said, closing the laptop.

"I'm not so sure that was a smart move," River responded. "Since the cartel went after her parents."

"I emailed my supervisor about her mother. I'm hoping we can get Ramona into the program with Arya."

They took the exit SW 11th Lane, where the house was located.

River received a call from his partner.

"Kenny's already there," River announced when he ended the call. "Arya's in the house alone. She's expecting us.

"Nice location," River said as they passed through the small community of luxury homes.

Staring out the window, Nova said, "Mateo and Arya sure love the finer things in life. I thought she was going to faint when I took them to their house in Burlington. She kept saying it was much too small. They had a square-footage requirement of at least six thousand square feet."

"Okaay… What kinds of jobs did they have in the program?" River asked with a chuckle.

"She worked in a dental office," Nova said. "She was

the office manager. Her husband worked second shift at a medical-supply warehouse. Their incomes wouldn't have supported the type of housing they desired."

"We're here," River announced.

A pair of Arya's signature rosebushes led up to the porch.

Nova and River exited the vehicle and walked up the steps of the two-story house to the front door, which opened before they could knock.

Arya was standing in the doorway, immaculate from head to toe, but her eyes were lined with shadows, and she looked as though she hadn't slept in days. "Finally," she breathed as she guided them into the house. "I was beginning to worry you wouldn't find me." She led them into the living room.

"You didn't make it easy for me to find you," Nova began. "I found out from your mother."

"I thought my parents would be here by now. Do you know if they left already? They aren't answering their phones."

"Something's happened..." Nova began.

"What?" Her eyes grew large, and her voice trembled with fear.

"Arya, you might want to sit down."

But Arya refused, shaking her head frantically. "Nooo... Just tell me."

Nova took a deep breath and spoke the words that would shatter her world. "Someone from the cartel showed up at the house in Lake Glenville," she said gently. "Arya, they shot your parents."

She began crying.

"I'm so sorry. We couldn't save your father, but your mom is alive. Ramona's in a hospital under guard."

"It's all my fault," Arya sobbed. "I never should've involved them. Mateo told me to warn them and have them go to the vacation house and stay there until I was safe in Miami, and they could follow. But the day I left Burlington, I returned to the house because I'd forgotten something—I could see that someone had broken in, so I left."

"How did you end up at that abandoned house in Concord?"

She dropped down on the love seat. "Mateo found it. It's where I was supposed to stay until he returned." Nova and River sat across from her as she continued, "We were going to leave the country, but when I never heard back from him, I knew something must have gone wrong. I had a bad feeling... I knew he'd been killed. I didn't know what to do, so I called you. Then I was too scared to tell you where I was, so I left the phone behind." Arya shook her head. "I don't know how the cartel could track my parents down—they were careful in covering their tracks."

"They must have put some tracking software on the car or maybe they hacked your parents' phones," Nova suggested.

"If so, then it definitely won't be hard for them to find me, too," Arya said. "I spoke with my parents at least three or four times since leaving Burlington. It was because I didn't want them to worry." She chewed on her bottom lip. "Nova, I've really made a mess of things. Now my father is dead." She started crying again.

Nova leaned forward. "None of this is your fault."

Arya stood and paced across the hardwood floors. "Nova, I need to see my mother."

Nova shook her head. "I'm sorry, but it's unsafe for you to go there. The doctor will keep me updated on her progress."

"What if they try to kill her while she's at the hospital?"

"That won't happen."

"Why not?" Arya asked, knitting her trembling fingers together.

"Because they believe that she died along with your father," River interjected. "Your mother is being moved to a secure location under a temporary assumed name. US marshals are guarding her. Arya, she's safe."

Tears rolled down her cheeks. "I can't even bury my father."

"Your father will be cremated," Nova said. "Meanwhile, I'm working to get your mother into the program with you."

Arya appeared surprised. "You're not kicking me out?"

Shaking her head, Nova responded, "I'm giving you a second chance, but this time you will have to comply with the rules of WITSEC, and if you're holding on to evidence the DEA can use, you *must* turn in everything to Special Agent Randolph."

Arya averted her gaze. "I don't have anything. Mateo took it with him when he went to LA."

The hitch of her voice told Nova the woman was lying. Why?

"Arya, those are the terms," Nova stated. "It's not negotiable. We both know that Mateo was too smart to carry anything on him."

"I can't give you what I don't have. You can search my things for yourself." A lone tear ran down her cheek. "I wasn't involved in my husband's business. I just want a few minutes to myself to mourn the loss of my father. Can you give me that?"

Nova nodded. "Sure."

"I'll be in my bedroom."

"That went better than I thought it would," Nova said when she and River were alone in the living room. "She denies any prior knowledge of Mateo's business with the cartel."

"She knows more than she's telling us," River stated. "It's possible the information could also be somewhere in a bank, but I doubt it. Mateo didn't trust banks. He told the DEA how he'd hidden money in the walls of his office and the bottom of his freezer."

"Most likely, he was hiding that money from the cartel since he was stealing from them," Nova responded. "Didn't he turn over his computer to the DEA?"

"Yes," River responded with a nod. "Mateo was a smart man. I wouldn't be surprised if he had another computer hidden somewhere."

Kenny walked into the house after surveilling the perimeter of the property just as Nova said, "I'm going to check on Arya. I need to make sure she isn't trying to escape out the window."

"I don't think you have to worry about her," Kenny replied. "When I arrived, she appeared relieved. I believe she is grateful for the company and support during this situation."

"How is she?" River asked when Nova returned from checking on Arya. Kenny had picked up dinner for them from a popular chicken eatery.

"She says she's not hungry. Right now, she's still very emotional," she said. "Mateo and her father dead, her mother in the hospital, and the stress of being on the run. It's a lot to have to deal with. I was able to convince her to lie down and try to rest. She's worried that if the cartel was able to find her parents, they might be headed here."

"It's possible."

"I know," Nova responded.

"Does she have her cell phone?"

"Kenny took it from her," Nova said. "He turned it off."

"That's good to hear," River responded.

"He's camped outside her door right now," she stated. "I volunteered to take the next watch."

They found a movie to watch on television.

Nova stretched and tried to get comfortable. She snuggled up in one corner of the sofa.

When River glanced over at her, she was fast asleep. He'd known she wasn't going to last too much longer.

Smiling, he gave her a gentle nudge. "Why don't you go to one of the guest rooms? You're tired."

She sat up. "No, I'm good."

"No, you're not," River said. "Nova, you're exhausted."

She wiped her face with the backs of her hands. "I told Kenny that I'd keep watch so he could get some sleep."

"I can hold it down for now."

"Okay, but I just need a couple of hours," Nova stated.

Pointing toward the first-floor guest bedroom, River urged, "Go get in bed."

She refused. "No, I'll stay out here. Besides, I'm much too comfortable to move right now."

Grinning, he handed her a throw.

Nova smiled at him. "Thank you."

River settled back, keeping a watchful eye on their surroundings, as Nova drifted into a well-deserved rest on the sofa, the glow of the television casting a soft light on the room.

The night unfolded in a hushed ambience, punctuated by the occasional distant sounds of the city. He found a moment of respite, even amid uncertainty and danger.

NOVA WOKE UP with a start. She looked around, asking, "What time is it?"

"Almost two a.m.," River answered from across the room. He was in the dining area, working on his laptop.

"Oh, wow... I didn't mean to sleep so long."

"It's fine. You needed to get some rest, Nova. You're not a robot."

"Neither are you, River." Standing, Nova said, "I'll keep watch now. It's time for you to get some sleep."

He didn't argue. "I'm going to take a shower first. Wake me at six."

"Will do," she responded. "Where's Kenny?"

"He was in the kitchen a few minutes ago," River said. "He may be upstairs."

River opened the door to the first-floor bedroom and went inside, heading straight to the bathroom.

From where she sat, Nova could hear the steady down-pour of water hammering the ceramic tiles inside the glass-enclosed shower.

She got up and navigated to the kitchen, needing something else to focus on than a wet, naked River Randolph. The hinges on the pantry door whined as she opened the door. She wasn't looking for anything specific but found cases of bottled water, various snacks, pasta and spaghetti sauce. In the refrigerator, Nova saw an assortment of cheeses, pepperoni, sausages and other meats.

Before she even turned around, Nova knew he was there. River was standing in the doorway, dressed in nothing but a pair of gray sweatpants. His look was so electrifying that it sent a tremor through her.

"Looking for a late-night snack?" he asked.

"Naw," Nova responded, averting her eyes. "I was just being nosy. What about you? I thought you were going to bed."

"I just came to get a bottle of water."

She retrieved one from the fridge and tossed it to him.

"Thanks," he said.

"Good night."

"What are you about to do?"

She swallowed tightly. "I'm going upstairs to check on Arya. I'll take the position outside her room."

He nodded. "I'm going outside to check the perimeter before I turn in."

Nova went upstairs and peeked in on Arya, who appeared to be sleeping soundly. Satisfied, she sat in the chair outside the room with her iPad. Might as well catch up on some reading, she decided.

She couldn't fully concentrate because of the handsome man in the room below. Seeing him in those gray sweatpants had struck a vibrant chord with her. She hadn't wanted to tear her attention from River but had forced herself to do so. Arya wasn't entirely out of danger yet.

Chapter Fifteen

"Where's our witness?" River asked the following day when he walked out of the bedroom. Although he hadn't slept eight hours, he felt completely rested in half the time.

"Probably still in bed," Nova responded as she removed four slices of bread from a toaster. "I haven't seen her at all this morning."

She walked the short distance to the fridge and retrieved the butter. "Kenny was down here a moment ago."

"You've got it smelling good in here."

She glanced over her shoulder at River. "You sound like you're surprised. I've been cooking since I was twelve. I'm a foodie, so I had to learn how to cook."

He held up his hands in mock surrender. "I didn't say a word…"

Nova went halfway up the stairs, then shouted, "Arya, if you intend to eat, you'd better come on down while everything is hot."

Arya entered the kitchen, saying, "I prefer to have breakfast in bed. I'm in mourning."

"I'll fix you a plate. You can take it upstairs if you want."

"I'm tired of tasteless food." She picked up a bagel. "I bought them like four days ago. Why can't we go to a real restaurant?" Arya whined.

"Because you're in hiding," Nova responded. "You're not out of danger yet."

"I'm so sick of this. This isn't how my life is supposed to go."

Nova shrugged. "Then you should've chosen a different one."

She glared at Nova. "Why did the feds take all our money? Why couldn't they leave us with at least a million?"

River could tell that Nova was struggling to keep her temper in check.

"It wasn't *your* money," River stated.

Arya rolled her eyes. "Mateo told me we would one day have our life back. He said we'd be rich again. That we could live anywhere in the world—it was our choice. We were going to buy a luxury yacht and live on it. Nobody would've been able to find us because we'd sail around the world... This just isn't fair."

"You should be grateful that you're still aboveground," Nova said. "Your life is in danger, Arya. We're not concerned with your social status. And while we're here, we're not your servants. We are here to keep you safe. Try to remember that."

Pouting, Arya rolled her eyes heavenward. She put a piece of toast on her plate, then stuck her fork into a sausage. "It would be nice to have an omelet now and then."

"Feel free to make one," Nova said with a grin to lighten the mood. "If you're cooking, I'll take one with spinach and tomatoes. Arya makes the best veggie omelets."

"I'm just saying... I feel like I'm owed something, Nova. I lost my husband because he went to the DEA for help, and now he's *dead*."

River opened his mouth to speak, but Nova touched his arm. When he met her gaze, she gave a shake of her head.

It was her telling him to take it easy on Arya.

After breakfast, they settled in the living room with Kenny posted at a window upstairs. Nova sat beside Arya on the leather couch while River sat in a chair across from them.

"I'm telling you that my husband wouldn't have given me any files or documents. Maybe he stored them in a safe somewhere, but only he would have the key."

They'd been trying to find out what the de Leons could be hiding but were getting nowhere. River decided to choose a different line of questioning. "I'm curious. What made you decide to come to Miami?"

Shrugging, Arya responded, "I don't know... I just thought I'd be safe here."

"In a city run by the Mali cartel?"

"Has nothing to do with me. I don't belong to any cartel."

She tried to keep her expression neutral, but River didn't miss the way she fidgeted on the couch.

"Your husband was a prominent figure in the Mancuso cartel. Was he going to switch sides?"

Arya shrugged once more. "I don't know."

River eyed her. "I decided to look into your mother's family, and one of your uncles was an attorney for the Mali family."

He heard Nova's soft gasp of surprise. He hadn't yet shared this piece of information with her. River had only found out that morning. He'd decided to look when he recalled that the owner of the property in North Carolina had a Florida mailing address.

"I don't know anything about that," Arya responded, her hands folded in her lap. "I mean, my uncle was a lawyer. He had his own law firm. No idea who his clients were."

"I have a feeling that Mateo knew all about him."

"My uncle died a long time ago." She met his gaze. "I

want to help you, but whatever my husband knew died with him, I'm afraid."

"Do you expect us to believe you had no help getting to Miami?" River demanded.

"I followed Mateo's instructions. That's all."

"Did you contact anyone outside of your parents?" River pressed.

Arya shook her head no. "Just the rental agency."

"Using your mother's identification," Nova said.

"It's all I had to work with. I don't have pay stubs or a job anymore. I needed a place to stay."

"Why don't we take a break?" Nova suggested.

River sighed, feeling frustrated with the lack of progress in his interrogation. He glanced at Nova, noting the sympathy in her eyes. She had always been compassionate and willing to give people the benefit of the doubt. But River knew better. He had seen firsthand the deceit and manipulation rampant in the criminal world.

Gesturing for Nova to follow him out of the room, he stepped into the foyer. Nova joined him, and they leaned against the wall, the air tense as their gazes locked in a silent conversation.

"We're not getting anywhere with her," River finally said with frustration. "She's hiding something. I can feel it."

"AGENT RANDOLPH THINKS I'm lying," Arya said when Nova returned to the living room alone.

"Are you?" Nova inquired, fixing her with a penetrating gaze.

"No, I'm not," she retorted with a mixture of frustration and desperation.

"He's not the only one you have to convince," Nova stated, her tone indicating the gravity of the situation.

"What do you mean?" Arya's eyes widened with curiosity and a hint of fear.

"Johnny Boy. He knows your death was a lie... He's coming for you."

Arya's face lost color as she stammered, "Th-that's why I think it's time to leave Miami. Nova, just let me get a ticket to someplace far away. I'll disappear for good."

Nova shook her head, a heavy sense of responsibility settling on her shoulders. "He will hunt you down unless you help us put him in prison."

"Johnny Boy is unstoppable!" Arya exclaimed, her fear palpable. "Can't you see that?"

"We can't let fear dictate our choices. If you run, he wins. We need to stand up to him, expose the truth and make sure he pays for what he's done."

Arya looked torn, caught between the terror of facing Johnny Boy and the uncertainty of trusting Nova and the team to protect her. The gravity of their choices weighed heavily on them both, their fates entwined in this dangerous game that could only have one outcome—life or death.

Nova found River in the kitchen.

"How did it go?" he asked.

"She's scared."

"She doesn't trust that we can protect her," River stated. "We'll have to remind her that she and Mateo were safe until they left WITSEC. Johnny Boy knew exactly how to get Mateo to leave the program. Arya is not safe on her own."

"I agree." Nova sighed. "But how do we get her to trust us?"

SHORTLY AFTER MIDNIGHT, a vehicle parked across the street.

"There's a black SUV outside," Nova yelled from the home office. She watched with growing concern. "The doors are opening, and two guys just got out. River, they're *armed*."

"I'll get Arya," he said while taking the stairs two at a time.

Kenny went out the door leading to the back of the house. They were likely going to attack from both the back and front of the house.

Nova stood at the window, studying the men even as she slipped on a Kevlar vest. They didn't look familiar. The taller of the two was dressed in a black sweat suit, the expression on his face threatening. The other wore a black knit cap and leather jacket. He seemed intent on hiding his face.

River ran to the porch armed and ready while Nova went to the front window with her Glock pointed at the two men. River ordered them to halt.

Instead, the first assailant took aim.

The quiet street soon erupted in a deafening noise. Bright muzzle flashes and the sound of automatic gunfire filled the neighborhood, the bullets causing a couple of the windows to explode.

Nova ducked for cover, then fired at the would-be intruders, hitting the tall one. He collapsed on the sidewalk.

From the side of the house, Kenny took a shot at the other and wounded him in the arm. The man dropped his gun and stood with his good hand up in the air. Kenny approached to make an arrest.

Nova ushered Arya, who was in a Kevlar vest as well, downstairs and through the door leading to the garage. Her adrenaline was high, and she was ready to take on any threat.

She heard rather than saw the garage door going up.

Kenny gestured for them to leave. "Get out of here," he said. "I will take care of this." She slid into the vehicle beside Arya in the back seat while River got into the driver's seat.

"Arya, get down on the floor," Nova said.

The cartel gunman now lay on the ground with his hands stretched out. Kenny stood over him with his gun still in hand.

Arya was crying. She glanced over her shoulder and said, "How did they find me?"

"I wiped the address off the GPS in your parents' car, so I don't know, but I can promise you that they won't be able to find you again," Nova responded. "We're going off the grid."

River glanced into the rearview mirror at her as they drove away. "What do you have in mind?"

"I'm going to call Kaleb and Rylee. We could use their help."

"We need to change cars, too," he said.

She punched in a phone number.

They passed two police cars speeding toward the house.

"Kaleb, I need a favor," Nova said when he answered. "I need a safe place to take Arya de Leon. Someplace outside of Miami. She's been compromised." They could lie low and regroup using one of the houses that wasn't even on the Marshals' radar.

"Rylee's going to send Rolle to meet you in Jacksonville," he responded. "We'll let you know the address within the hour."

Nova looked over her shoulder at Arya. She sat in her seat, staring out the window blankly.

Maybe the poor woman is in shock.

"It's going to be a long night," River said.

"I'm glad we're all here to experience it still," she replied with a smile.

"I don't want to die," Arya said. Anguish colored the tone of her words.

"We're going to make sure that doesn't happen," River

stated. "We want you to live out the rest of your life without fear."

"I think I will always be afraid."

Nova was struck by how helpless Arya looked right now, and compassion washed over her.

She pulled a cap out of her backpack and held it out to Arya. "Put this on and keep your head low. I wouldn't put it past Poppy or Johnny Boy to have someone monitoring street cameras."

Arya twisted her long hair into a tight bun and secured it with a black scrunchie that was on her wrist. She put the cap on her head, then slipped on a pair of dark sunglasses.

Satisfied, Nova looked to the front.

"What about Kenny? He's going to meet up with us, right?"

River nodded. "I'll send him the location as soon as we get it."

THEY MADE IT safely to Jacksonville.

"We're supposed to meet Rolle at an IHOP off Stanton Road," Nova stated. She released a soft sigh of relief when they arrived. Rolle was there waiting for them as prearranged.

"Good to see y'all," he said when Nova got out of the SUV. "We're switching vehicles, so I'll take the keys to your SUV."

River handed them over. "Here you go. What are we driving?"

"This," Rolle responded while pointing to the car parked next to the SUV.

"Wow...nice..." River walked around the gray Mercedes G 550.

Rolle looked at Nova and asked, "You have the address for the safe house in Alabama?"

"Yeah," she responded.

"Then you're all set. Oh…" He pulled an envelope out of his pocket. "Kaleb sent this. He said that none of you should use credit cards. *Cash only.*"

Nova opened the envelope to reveal two thousand dollars in denominations of hundreds, fifties and twenties.

"Thanks for your help," River said.

"No problem. I was in Atlanta to visit my mom. Rylee called and I got on the first flight down here."

"Sorry for disrupting your vacation," Nova said.

"It's all good. I'm flying back home in a couple of hours. I had a day with my mom, so I'm good for another six months."

Nova glanced at River as they walked toward the car. "Why don't you get some rest and let me drive?"

He shook his head. "I'm good," he said before getting in and starting the car.

Nova sat down on the passenger side. "You just want to get behind the wheel of this Benz. I remember you telling me this was your dream car."

He chuckled. "I just thought you might want a break from driving."

"I'll take over in a couple of hours," she responded, settling into her seat and closing her eyes. "Wake me when you want me to take over."

"We're less than eight hours from Birmingham. I can make it."

"Good," Arya uttered. "I'm beginning to feel claustrophobic being in a car for so long."

Although Nova didn't voice it, Arya had more serious concerns than being cooped up in a car. The cartel had no intentions of giving up their search for her.

Chapter Sixteen

"Are you sure this is the right place?" River asked. He stared at the stunning brick home nestled in the prestigious Greystone neighborhood.

"This is the exact address that Kaleb gave me. 5430 Rosemont Circle in Birmingham."

"This house is gorgeous," Arya murmured. "*See*, this is the kind of place I should have in WITSEC."

"Not gonna happen," Nova responded with a chuckle. "The only way you get this type of house—you'll need a high salary to afford this lifestyle."

"Why couldn't I keep some of the money Mateo—"

Nova dismissed her words with a slight wave of her hand. "You already know the answer to that."

Arya sighed. "It isn't fair."

Kenny pulled up, parked and got out. River entered the house ahead of everyone and turned off the alarm. The main level featured a large gourmet kitchen with Corian countertops, a double oven, an eat-in area and a formal dining room. He navigated to the door leading to a screened-in porch with an open deck. The house was gated all around and separated from the other houses behind them by trees. He was pleased to see there were cameras and motion lights.

He joined Arya and Nova in the great room.

Nova pointed toward a hallway. "The master suite is over there," she told the men. "It has dual vanities, a jetted tub and a huge shower. Kaleb texted me some details on the way over."

"That's the room I want," Arya said.

River, Kenny and Nova all looked at her.

"No?"

"No," Nova stated. "Pick a room upstairs."

Listening to the interchange, River knew she was correct. Arya would be safer up there than on the main floor.

"This really sucks," Arya grumbled.

"I'll check out the second level," River said.

"I want to check out the grounds," Kenny stated.

River nodded and followed Nova and Arya upstairs, where they found four bedrooms, each with its own bathroom.

Arya chose the largest one, which came as no surprise.

"How long will we be here?" she asked.

"As long as necessary," Nova answered. "We're waiting on a new ID for you and a new location."

"And my mom will be able to come with me?" she asked.

"We're working out the details," Nova responded.

"Can't I go someplace exotic? I've had enough of small towns. I stand out like a sore thumb. I don't believe it's safe for me."

River returned downstairs and conducted a quick search of the kitchen to see if he had everything he needed in terms of cookware.

"What are you doing?" Nova asked when she strolled into the kitchen.

"I'm making dinner tonight," he announced. "Just checking to see if we have the cookware."

"Write down what you need and Kenny or I will pick it up," she offered.

River recalled the last time he'd made dinner for Nova. It was their last night together. He'd taken her to a restaurant owned by a friend of his. The restaurant was closed on Mondays, so they were the only people inside. She'd kept him company while he prepared their meals.

River forced his thoughts back to the present. This wasn't some romantic gesture on his part. He cleared his throat softly, then said, "Kaleb really came through with this house. It's a nice place."

She nodded. "He did. I already hate having to leave it."

He could feel her watching him as he typed up a shopping list for Kenny.

After a moment, she said, "I need to check in with my supervisor. Then I'm gonna check on Arya."

"I'll let you know when dinner is ready."

NOVA FOUND ARYA sitting on the edge of a king-size bed. Grief was etched all over her tear-streaked face.

"How are you holding up?" she asked.

The woman inhaled deeply. "I'm trying to put on a brave front, but I really miss my old life. I miss my father and Mateo... I'm scared all the time."

"We will do everything possible to make sure that you and your mother stay safe."

"Mateo told me he was going to fix everything so that the cartel would leave us alone."

"Did he tell you how he was going to accomplish this?" Nova inquired.

Arya hesitated, then said, "Agent Randolph was right. Mateo went to California to try and negotiate with the cartel. He said that if that didn't work, then he planned to give the Mali cartel information on the Mancuso operations in exchange for money and protection... I had a bad feeling about it, but Mateo... He just wouldn't listen to me."

"Why didn't you call me? I could've tried to talk some sense into Mateo."

"Because he made me promise not to say anything. He said we'd be gone before you realized it. Mateo said he had a plan." Arya started to cry again. "I—I t-told him not to trust those p-people. When he didn't respond to my texts or calls, I called my mother to tell her and Papi to go to the house on Lake Glenville. I thought they'd be safe there since no one knew about it."

"The cartel may have been listening to your mother's calls," Nova said.

Arya wiped her face before asking, "Can you call the hospital to check on my mother?"

"I can do that." Nova picked up her phone, connected with the nurse in charge of Ramona's care and spoke to her for a few minutes.

"Your mother is resting, and she's doing great," Nova said when she ended the call.

Arya released an audible sigh of relief. "Thank goodness." There was a brief pause before she spoke again. "Special Agent Randolph... He's very handsome, don't you think?"

"Let's focus on what's really important," Nova said. "Like telling him everything you know about the cartel."

RIVER HAD NOVA sample the chicken enchiladas after retrieving them from the oven.

"I'm impressed," she said. "Where did you learn to cook like this?"

"Trial and error," River responded. "Along with several cookbooks."

"Well, the enchiladas are delicious."

Nova helped him prepare the plates and carried them to the table.

After Kenny blessed the food, Arya sliced into her chicken enchilada and stuck a forkful in her mouth. "This is really good. Have you ever considered that maybe you're in the wrong line of work?"

"Cooking is a way to relieve stress. I'd never want to make it a career," River said. "I love my job with the DEA."

Wiping her mouth on a napkin, Arya said, "I was furious when Mateo told me he worked for the cartel. I always thought he should be working for some huge corporation. He was very intelligent. He could've worked anywhere he wanted."

"You really didn't know anything about Johnny Boy or Poppy Mancuso until you went into witness protection?" River asked.

Averting her gaze, Arya responded, "I didn't. Mateo didn't take me around his clients or business associates."

He glanced over at Nova, then turned to Arya again. "Your husband mentioned pulling all-nighters in his interview. You were never suspicious when he didn't come home? Most accounting jobs are Monday through Friday, and while some accountants work late, it's usually during tax season, and they aren't in the office all night long."

"Of course I was," Arya answered. "I thought he was having an affair. We fought about it all the time." She picked up her napkin and wiped her mouth again. "Can we change the subject, please? I don't want to talk about this anymore. Not right now."

River picked up his water glass and took a long sip. Arya's body language indicated that she wasn't being completely honest with him.

He was also finding it hard to keep his emotions at bay. It had been a long time since he'd been around Nova, and River wasn't prepared for how she made him feel.

Just being here in this room with her sent a course of electricity within him. River tried to shake off this feeling of being so alive, but he failed miserably. The part he thought had died rose in him suddenly and refused to be ignored.

After they finished their meal, Kenny volunteered to clean the kitchen and, surprisingly, Arya offered to help him.

When they were done and had gone upstairs, River and Nova settled in the loft.

"Kenny's going to come up and relieve you at midnight," River announced. "I'm probably going to crash. I'm tired."

"You should," she responded with a smile. "Thank you again for such a delicious dinner. It was a lot better than the pizza I thought we'd be eating tonight."

River met her gaze and couldn't look away, feeling that there was a deeper significance to the visual interchange. He pulled Nova toward him and kissed her, surprising them both. Heat sparked in the pit of his stomach and ignited into an overwhelming desire.

He kissed her a second time; his tongue traced the soft fullness of Nova's lips. His mouth covered hers hungrily until he released her, saying, "I'm sorry. I never should've done that. I have no idea what came over me."

Nova chuckled. "If we'd had wine, we could blame it on that."

"I suppose we could pretend that the kiss never happened," River suggested.

She gave a stiff nod. "Yeah, we could do that."

His senses reeled as if short-circuited, but he tried to

display an outward calm despite the physical reactions to his desire for Nova. "Maybe we should get back to the reason why we're here."

She agreed.

"I really didn't mean to ravish you like that."

Nova placed two fingers to his mouth and said, "We're fine, River. I have no illusions that the kisses meant anything to you."

"That's not…"

"Good night, River. I'll see you in the morning."

Instead of going to bed like he'd planned, River went down to the office.

He checked the security camera footage displayed on the monitor. He was sure they were safe and hadn't been found, but he intended to stay cautious.

He checked every area more than once.

After conducting a walk-through to make sure the windows and exterior doors were securely locked, River turned on the alarm system before going to the great room. He sank down on the sofa to watch television. He kept the TV volume low.

River felt himself drift off and forced his eyes open. He got up, went to the office, then checked the security cameras once more before navigating to the bedroom to shower.

Afterward, he considered going upstairs to check on the women but pushed the thought away. He didn't want to face Nova just yet. River had given in to his emotions earlier, but it couldn't happen again. He didn't want a repeat of the last time they were together.

Chapter Seventeen

Positioned in the loft across from where Arya lay sleeping, Nova remembered the kisses she'd shared with River over and over in her mind for most of her watch.

She squirmed uncomfortably in the chair she was sitting in. Her back was starting to ache, and every now and then there was numbness in her legs.

Nova stood up and stretched.

She thought she heard movement below and crept over to the railing, looking down. She watched as River strode to the narrow window beside the door and peered outside. He'd changed into a pair of light gray sweats. The socks on his feet cushioned the sound as he walked across the marble floor.

She descended the stairs, whispering loudly, "Is everything okay?"

River turned to face her and said, "I thought I saw lights through the trees. It looked like the vehicle was coming here, but then it turned around. Nobody's out there."

Alarmed, Nova walked over to a window and glanced out. "Are you sure?" Kaleb's brother, Nate, owned the safe house and the adjacent properties on both sides. She was confident that the cartel couldn't have discovered their location.

River nodded. "I am."

She relaxed. "That's good to hear."

"Why don't you go back up there and get some sleep?"

"I'm good," she said while trying to stifle another bout of yawns. "You were supposed to be resting."

"I wasn't as sleepy as I thought," River said. "If you want, you can take the master suite down here and I'll keep watch."

"Kenny should be up taking over shortly."

Nova was touched by his concern but didn't allow herself to think it could be something more. What they'd shared two years ago had been nice. She cherished the memories of their time together, but the reality was that they would both do their jobs, and when Arya and her mother were safe, she and River would say their farewells and that would be the end of it.

"You really need to get some rest," Nova said.

"I will at some point." He smiled, and she couldn't deny the sudden warmth she felt being on the receiving end of that smile. "Good night, Nova."

"Good night."

"I HAVE SOMETHING to tell you both," Arya announced when she came downstairs the next morning.

"What is it?" Nova asked as she poured herself a cup of herbal tea.

"I think it's time I told you the truth," she said, settling across from Nova at the breakfast table. "It's true. Mateo had enough stuff on the cartel to cause some serious damage."

Nova nodded. "What made you change your mind?"

"It finally sunk in that Johnny Boy isn't going to stop until he finds me."

Nova rested her hands on the table. "I'm not going to let that happen, Arya."

River and Kenny joined them a few minutes later.

"Arya wants to talk to you both," Nova stated.

She nodded. "I know all of you will do what you can to keep me safe, but Johnny Boy means to kill me. At least you'll know everything if that happens."

"I meant what I said," Nova told her. "We are going to protect you with everything we have."

Despite the danger seemingly all around them, this was the very thing that Nova had trained for—she was willing to risk her life to save Arya. She'd followed her father's path to become a marshal because it was admirable work. Nova also thought it took courage to enter the witness protection program—having to be separated from loved ones, often living in strange cities, then having to lie to everyone and look over a shoulder for the rest of the individual's life. Arya was doing the right thing.

Nova took a sip of her tea. "The best chance for being safe is following my instructions, Arya. And by telling River everything you know."

Arya carefully opened the silver locket hanging from her neck and extracted a small, black micro SD card. She held it out to River with a determined look in her eyes.

Nova couldn't believe it—all the evidence to bring down the cartel was in his hands.

"It's all there. Some of the information you already have, but there was a whole lot more that my husband didn't give the DEA all those times he met with them."

"I knew it," River exclaimed.

Nova left Arya alone in the room with River and Kenny. She went to the office and eyed the quad split screen, checking the multiple security cameras on the property. Although she was confident that they wouldn't have any unwanted visitors, Nova wanted to be prepared if there were any signs of suspicious activity on the property. Her Glock was loaded and ready.

She made another call to the hospital requesting an update on Ramona Lozano.

"Mrs. Lozano's wounds are healing nicely," Nova was told.

Arya's mother had been moved to another location, which would be safer for her. "Have there been any calls asking about her?"

"No, ma'am."

"That's good to hear."

Nova found a couple of articles online about the deaths of Pablo and Ramona Lozano. She printed them. She wanted to prepare Arya before she found them herself.

RIVER SLIPPED THE SD card into his laptop while Arya picked up an apple and took a bite out of it. He'd spent the past hour being filled in on what Arya knew and now he wanted to dive into the evidence. His eyes widened as he realized that all the evidence they needed against the powerful cartel was contained on that small card.

As he scrolled through the files, Arya said, "You now have everything, Special Agent Randolph. More financial records, lists of properties owned by the cartel—even drug shipments."

"Mateo kept meticulous records," he said. River was relieved to have this information and someone else who could testify.

"So, what do you think?" Nova asked when River entered the office an hour later. "Can you use any of what she gave you?"

"We have some solid and damaging evidence," he answered. "I can see why Mateo tried to blackmail Poppy.

This information could potentially topple a huge part of her dynasty. However, it's going to be a challenge getting to her since she's hiding on a private island near Ecuador and there is no extradition to the United States."

"I believed Arya when she told me that Mateo kept her out of the loop. She lied to me."

"She was protecting her husband."

"I'm beginning to think she knew all along that Mateo worked for the Mancuso cartel."

"I've always believed that," River said.

"Where is she?" Nova asked.

"She's still in the dining room with Kenny."

"I checked in with the hospital. Her mother's doing well."

"You should tell her," River said. "I need to make some phone calls. Mind if I sit in here?"

Nova pushed away from the desk. "It's all yours. By the way, I checked the security cameras—nothing unusual." She placed a hand on her weapon.

"Keep an eye on Arya," River said. "I'll be out shortly."

Nova left the office.

He called his supervisor first, then the federal prosecutor to update. "I have great news. I have the rest of the information DeSoto didn't turn over to us earlier. I'll email everything over to you in a few minutes."

River was grateful to Nova. He knew that she was part of the reason Arya had agreed to come forward.

Chapter Eighteen

After Arya went to bed, Nova and River sat down on the stairs.

She'd been wanting to have another conversation with him, but thought it best to wait for an opening. He gave her that when he said, "I keep thinking about the night you came to my hotel room. You could've talked to me about your feelings, Nova. You didn't have to run away. Your silence and absence spoke volumes."

"I realize that I handled things wrong," she responded. She wanted to be completely honest with River. "When we first got together, I didn't think either of us was looking for anything serious."

"So, you were just in it to have a good time—nothing more?"

She looked over at him. "I'm not saying that at all, River."

"Then exactly what are you saying?"

"We lived over three thousand miles apart. I really didn't have any preconceived notions about what was going on between us. I knew that neither one of us wanted a relationship that might interfere with our jobs—remember we talked about that? It's probably why I honestly never expected you to make any type of declaration. Especially so soon."

"To be honest, I surprised myself when I said it," River

confessed. "I have to admit that I never expected things between us to become so passionate. It scared me, too, but I was willing to take a chance with you. I thought you felt the same way."

"That's why I regret leaving. I wish more than anything that I'd just talked to you that night."

"I wish you had," he responded. "I've had to deal with rejection all of my life and it's not been easy for me to trust someone with my heart." River wished he could rescind the words that had just come out of his mouth. He hadn't meant to share his personal pain with her. Not like this. He didn't want her pity.

She reached over and took his hand in her own. "I'm really sorry."

River gave a slight shrug. "You don't have to apologize."

"Yes, I do," Nova insisted. "You deserved better than what I gave you."

"I appreciate that you didn't lie about your feelings."

"You must know that I cared deeply for you, River. And since we're being honest... I didn't realize just how much until after I left."

He gave a wry smile. "It's all in the past now."

Nova swallowed hard, then said, "I've really missed talking to you."

River eyed her. "Same here."

"Do you think we can try being friends?" she asked.

"Sure. If that's what you want."

She nodded. "I'd really like that."

His cell phone rang. "I need to take this call." River stood up and walked down the stairs.

NOVA SAT THERE wondering if he was going to come back upstairs. When ten minutes passed, she got up and moved to the loft.

At some point, she must have fallen asleep, because when Nova woke up, it was around 2:00 a.m. Kenny was seated in a chair across from her. He was watching something on his phone.

He glanced over at her and smiled.

Nova got up and checked on Arya, then crept down the staircase. She was hungry.

She was surprised to find that River was still up.

"When I finally got off the call, you were asleep," he said.

"I'm really glad we had a conversation," Nova responded while looking for something to snack on. "I know it doesn't change anything."

"It doesn't change things, but we don't have all that tension between us any longer." He opened the refrigerator. "There's some fruit, cheese and crackers."

"You must be snacky, too."

"I had an apple. I finished it just before you came down."

Leaning against the counter, Nova asked, "River, what did you mean when you said you've been dealing with rejection all your life?"

His expression became unreadable. "It's nothing."

"Please don't do that. *Talk to me.*"

"My mother never wanted me," he announced. "After I was born, she left me with her mother. She was only sixteen at the time, so my grandmother raised me. She got married when she was twenty, but even before that...I don't remember having a real relationship with Mary—that was her name. I think back then she was like a sister to me."

Nova's heart broke at the thought of River having to grow up feeling rejected by his mother. She couldn't imagine what that was like. "And you two were in the same house?"

River nodded. "There were a few times when she'd help me with my schoolwork... She'd buy me a toy every now and then, but that was it. After she got married, Mary and her husband had a baby girl. They loved Bonnie dearly. I think Mary always wanted a girl."

"She never came back for you?" Nova asked.

"No. I was never in Mary's heart. I was only an inconvenience to her."

"Did her husband know that she was your mother?"

"My grandmother told him. He welcomed me, but Mary told him that her mother refused to part with me."

Nova hurt for River. "I'm so sorry."

His gaze downcast, he shrugged in nonchalance. "It's fine. I had a wonderful grandmother and she loved me until the day she died."

Nova reached for his hand, which had settled near hers, then thought better of making contact. They were still in a fragile state. "But I'm sure it hurts that your mother rejected you. Is she still alive?"

"Mary died about six months ago."

"Did you attend her funeral?"

"I did, but only because Bonnie said she needed me to be there with her," River responded.

"You and your sister have a good relationship, then?" Nova inquired.

"Yes, we do. I'm thankful that Mary didn't try to discourage my getting to know Bonnie. I love my sister."

They walked across the hall to check the security cameras.

"So far, so good," she murmured. "I spoke with Sabra earlier, and from what she's gathered from cartel conversations, Johnny Boy is furious with his men for losing the package." Sabra was a tech on the task force Rylee had put together, and her intel had been helpful.

"That's pretty much what I expected," he responded. "That SD card Arya handed over is a definite threat to his organization. I feel good knowing that he's most likely losing sleep over this."

"I'm with you there," Nova said. "Every time I think of Calderon in prison for the rest of his life plus one hundred and thirty-five years…it makes me really happy. Although he didn't actually shoot my father, he is still responsible. I wonder how he feels about being so easily replaced by Johnny Boy as Poppy's right hand."

"You have a right to your feelings, Nova." River paused a moment, then asked, "Are you wanting to leave the Marshals because of your father?"

"That's a part of it."

River wrapped his arms around her, drawing her closer in his embrace. With her body pressed to his like this, he felt blood coursing through his veins like an awakened river.

Their eyes locked as their breathing came in unison.

Nova tried to ignore the aching in her limbs and the pulsing knot that had formed in her stomach.

Without a word, River swept her up, weightless, into his arms.

He carried her to the first-floor bedroom, where he eased her down onto the bed.

He unbuttoned her blouse, but before River could go any further, he abruptly pulled away, saying, "I'm sorry. I can't do this to myself a second time."

His rejection was like a bucket of cold water, washing over Nova and cooling her ardor.

"It's okay," she said while buttoning up her top. "I understand."

But the truth was that she didn't understand at all.

Nova looked up at him, noting his pain-filled gaze. "You're just not ready."

"You are such a beautiful woman. I…"

"It's okay." She shrugged. "Why don't we just keep this at friendship?"

He nodded. "I'm sorry."

"Stop apologizing, River. It's not necessary." Nova wanted him to know that he didn't need to protect himself from her. Not this time. "I've always cared about you."

"Let's not do this…"

"We're supposed to be having an honest conversation." She really wanted him to hear her heart through her words.

"And I'm speaking in truth."

"So am I," Nova said. "I just need you to listen and hear me."

"I can't do this right now," he responded. "I'm sorry."

He walked out of the bedroom.

"No," she whispered, "I'm sorry."

RIVER WOKE UP from a dream about Nova that had quickly become erotic. He turned from one side to the other, trying to escape thoughts of her, but it wasn't meant to be. She was still heavy on his mind.

He had thoroughly enjoyed spending time with her in the early morning hours. For a moment, River had been able to forget that so much time had passed between them. It felt like old times.

Nova never did anything to try to impress him—she was comfortable in her own skin, which was a quality he greatly admired.

When River thought of how he'd reacted last night, he felt like a heel for running out on her. He should have just explained that he felt it was best to have a platonic relationship. He never should have gotten involved with her on a personal level. From the moment River saw her that first time, he'd known that his life would never be the same.

"I should have kept it business between us," he whispered. "From the very beginning."

It was too late then and it was too late now.

River was still in love with her.

Chapter Nineteen

Nova hoped to avoid River, but he opened the door to the room he'd slept in just as she walked by.

"Good morning," she said, not looking at him. "I'm glad you finally got some sleep."

"I'm sorry about last night."

She shrugged in nonchalance. "Forget about it. I have." Nova wasn't about to let him know how much his rejection hurt.

His eyebrows arched a fraction at her words. The air suddenly felt thick with tension between them as they went downstairs.

River followed her into the kitchen and tried to make small talk, but Nova didn't have much to say.

"Nova…"

"I mean it," she interjected. "Let's just forget about it."

"It's not that easy for me," he responded.

"That sounds like a *you* problem," she said, walking over to the refrigerator and retrieving the carton of eggs. She was embarrassed and just needed some distance.

River left the kitchen without another word.

Nova was relieved because she needed some time alone to process her feelings. She could no longer deny that she was falling in love with him.

She cooked several slices of bacon, scrambled six eggs and made four slices of toast. When everything was ready, she went upstairs.

Nova ran into Arya coming out of her bedroom. "I was just coming to tell you that breakfast is ready."

She stopped by the office. "Breakfast is ready," she told River and Kenny.

Ten minutes later, they all sat at the table, eating in silence.

River was the first to finish his food.

Pushing away from the table, he said, "I'll be in the office if you need me."

She nodded, then reached for her glass of orange juice and took a sip. Kenny left a moment later.

"Nova, I'm sorry for lying to you after everything you've done to keep me safe," Arya said when they were alone. "Mateo really thought he could get the cartel to back off. He went to Los Angeles to meet with Poppy. He figured she'd do anything to get that information back."

Wiping her mouth, Nova said, "Like I told you before, you should've come to me. If you had, I would've done everything I could to keep him safe, even if it meant holding him in custody."

Arya leaned back in her seat. "I have to live with the choices I've made for the rest of my life. I've lost two important men in my life. I pray I don't lose my mother. I don't think I could bear it."

"If there's anything else that you know about the cartel, you should tell River and Kenny."

"I will," she responded. "Because there is more."

Stunned, Nova met her gaze. "Are you telling me that you're still withholding evidence?"

"I've given him all the files. I just didn't tell him everything that I know yesterday."

"This isn't a game, Arya."

"I know that."

Nova called out for River and Kenny to join them.

"What's going on?" they asked in unison.

Arya appeared slightly embarrassed before admitting, "I need to tell you—"

"If you're going to confess that you knew he was working for the cartel, I figured as much," River interjected.

Kenny put his phone on the table. He was recording the conversation.

"I've always known about my husband's relationship with members of the cartel..." She glanced over at Nova before adding, "That's because I urged him to work for them."

Nova's mouth dropped open. She hadn't expected to hear anything close to this.

"You have to understand..." Arya continued. "My parents weren't supportive when my husband and I married. They didn't think he was good enough for me and refused to give us any financial support. We were so poor at the time, and I didn't want to live that way. I knew my uncle worked for the Mali cartel and I wanted what my cousin had... Glitz and glamour...fancy parties and private jets. I wanted it all."

Arya clasped her hands together and hid them in the folds of her ruffled maxi skirt. "My husband was a small-time drug dealer when we met in college. My friend connected him with her boyfriend and soon he was working for the Mancuso cartel. After he graduated, he moved up the ranks and started handling the money." She paused a moment, then said, "My background is also in accounting, although I also had a real estate license. On occasion,

I'd help him reconcile the books, usually around the end of the year. I'd also help him find opportunities to launder the money."

Floored, Nova glanced over at River, who said, "What you're telling me is that you also worked for the cartel."

"Yes," she responded. "I found property for them. The cartel owns a building on Front Street in Los Angeles. It used to be a clothing store. There's nothing there now, but according to the paperwork filed at the end of the fiscal year, it's bringing in over a hundred thousand in sales each month."

"Are you telling us that they're laundering money through a store that's closed?" River asked.

Arya nodded, then said, "That's not the only one. They have several businesses like that—empty storefronts that show a profit on the books. They buy lots of commercial properties. Houses, too. They also have several legitimate businesses. A nightclub on Sunset Boulevard, a couple of hair salons and beauty-supply stores. They own several shell corporations, but the largest is Grupo Worldwide Holdings Inc."

Nova sat there listening to the woman she'd believed to be an innocent victim in all this.

"Have you ever been around Johnny Boy?" River inquired.

"Once," she responded. "And I'm sure it was really him. Not one of the fake Johnnys."

"Why do you say that?" he asked.

"Because he had a tattoo of his father on his chest with the initials *CR* below it. Six months before they discovered we were stealing from them, we were invited to a pool party at one of his houses. The host was supposed to be Johnny Boy. Only he wasn't the host. He was just another guest.

At least, he pretended to be one. I'd drunk a lot and had to go to the bathroom, and when I came out, I glimpsed this guy in one of the bedrooms with some girl. He didn't have on a shirt. That's when I saw the tattoo. It's pretty large."

"Did he see you?" Nova asked.

"I don't think so. I got out of there as quickly as I could, because if he had, I'd probably be dead already."

"Why didn't you tell us any of this before?" River asked.

"Because Mateo was trying to keep me safe," she responded. "I hope you get Johnny Boy. *I hope he dies.*"

"Is there anything else you can tell us?" Nova inquired.

"I've told you everything. The rest is on that SD card." Arya paused a moment, then said, "I never even told Mateo about seeing that tattoo. I couldn't risk anyone finding out that I could identify Johnny Boy. I want to stay far away from these people—they've destroyed my life." She looked at River. "I don't want to have to testify."

"We can request anonymity," he responded. "If granted, none of the defendants will know who you are."

"If you can really do that, then I will testify to what I know," Arya said, "but I'm hoping that with the information and evidence you have in hand, you won't need me at all."

"I can't make any promises. I will need to speak with the federal prosecutor about all this."

"I understand."

"Arya, we will do everything we can to ensure you're safe," River said.

Arya glanced at Nova. "I hope you'll be able to get my mom into the program with me. If she's with me...we can completely disappear together." Arya stretched, asking to retreat to her bedroom for some rest. River nodded.

After she left, Nova said, "If Arya never told Mateo

about the tattoo, then Johnny Boy may have no idea that anyone outside of his small circle knows about it."

"I'm glad she finally decided to come clean." River shook his head. "I had no idea just how involved she was. She worked for the cartel."

"Makes sense to me why they're after her," Kenny said.

Kaleb called Nova later that afternoon. "We've heard some chatter. Johnny Boy isn't a happy man these days. He wants his lost package found. He's now offering bonuses to the person who finds it."

"Arya knows too much. She can also identify Johnny Boy. She's going to need round-the-clock security until his arrest."

Kaleb agreed.

The next few days went much the same. Cohen gave his approval to keep Arya in Birmingham for now. After breakfast, Arya rehearsed her new backstory in the WITSEC program; they took an hour and a half for lunch, then more practice to perfect her new identity. After dinner, Arya spent an hour or so with River and Kenny, discussing her time in the cartel.

Nova thought about how much she would miss working with the Marshals Service, but she was super excited about the next chapter in her career. Her eyes strayed to River.

If only she had someone to share it with.

River went outside after Arya went upstairs to her room after dinner one night.

Nova found him sitting on the patio half an hour later. They hadn't talked about what had almost happened a few nights ago or how it made her feel.

"I realized something from the other night," she said. "I fully understand how you must have felt when I left without saying anything to you. I want to apologize for that, River."

He met her gaze. "Apology accepted."

He was still peering at her intently. Nova saw the heart-rending tenderness of his gaze. She secretly hoped that River would ask her to stay outside a while longer, but he didn't, much to her disappointment.

"I'll see you tomorrow morning," she said.

"G'night."

Nova tried to swallow the lump lingering in her throat.

She was falling in love with a man who would never be able to return that love. The thought shattered her heart into a million little pieces.

RIVER STOOD OUTSIDE the room Nova was in. He'd been there for almost ten minutes before finally deciding to knock.

She opened the door, then stepped aside to let him enter.

"Tomorrow, Arya and I will travel to meet with the marshals transporting her mother," Nova announced. "Her documents will arrive in the morning. I don't want to prolong this any longer."

River nodded in understanding. "She won't be in your custody after that."

"I know. I might even miss her."

They stood staring at one another with longing. There was no denying that they shared an intense physical awareness of each other.

Without warning, River pulled Nova into his arms, kissing her. He held her snugly.

"I'm so glad you're here."

He gazed down at her with tenderness. "I will be here for as long as you need me."

Parting her lips, Nova raised herself to meet his kiss.

His lips pressed against hers, then gently covered her mouth. River showered her with kisses around her lips and along her jaw. As he roused her passion, his own grew stronger.

This time, it was Nova who slowly pulled away. She took him by the hand and led him over to the edge of the bed.

They sat down.

"Being around Kaleb and Rylee reminds me of how much I'm lacking when it comes to love," Nova said. "I've never admitted this to anyone, but I get lonely sometimes."

"So do I," River confessed. "Growing up, I used sports to take my mind off how lonely I felt. Now I use work."

His closeness was so male, so bracing.

River stroked her cheek. "What are you thinking about?"

"You want the truth?" she asked.

He nodded.

"I was thinking about how long it's been since I've been this close to a man. How long it's been since I've kissed a man or made love." She raised her eyes to meet his. "It's been a while."

"Same here," River murmured.

"I'm not trying to seduce you," she said quickly. "I meant what I said about us being friends."

"I was thinking about hanging around in Charlotte for a few more days when we get there. I can change my plane ticket. That is if you don't mind showing a friend around the city."

She broke into a grin. "I don't mind at all."

He reluctantly and quietly made his way to the door and eased it open. "Good night."

It was getting harder and harder to walk away from Nova.

Chapter Twenty

Nova's mission was a simple, protective security detail: take Arya to the checkpoint, hand her off to the next set of marshals who would settle her in her new location, and head back to Charlotte.

They were nearly in Tennessee—Nova had accompanied another marshal in moving Arya securely to the handover point. "How is everything going?" River asked when she called to check in while at a gas station.

"It's going. I've considered taping Arya's mouth up a few times," she admitted. "We're about thirty minutes away from the destination."

He chuckled. "Exercise patience, beautiful."

"I'm trying," Nova said. "After the handoff, I'm heading straight to the airport. I'll get home close to six."

"I'll see you then."

His words brought a smile to her lips. "Same here."

When she hung up, Arya said, "I knew something was going on between you and Special Agent Randolph."

Nova didn't respond. She slid back into the passenger seat, next to the marshal who was transporting them.

When they passed the sign welcoming them to White Water, Tennessee, Arya said, "I don't think anybody will ever think to look for me here. I've never even heard of this place. It looks kinda depressing."

"That's the idea," she responded. "We don't want anyone to find you."

"What is there to do in White Water? And where is there
to shop to find *real* clothes? I'm not a Target kind of girl."

"The town is close to Memphis," Nova responded. "It's
a thirty-minute drive. But, Arya, you really must be careful. You can't forget for one minute that Johnny Boy wants
to silence you permanently."

"That's good to know about Memphis." Arya looked out
of the passenger window. "As for that murderous Johnny
Boy...I hope somebody kills him."

"Thanks to you, we now have a good shot at finding the
man."

"I wish I didn't have to have another handler."

Nova hated having to turn her charge over to someone
else, but it was for the best. "You'll be fine, and I think you'll
really like him," Nova reassured her. "Just follow the rules...
You and your mom will be safe."

Arya nodded. "It's been a painful lesson to learn."

Nova glanced over at the marshal who was driving them,
and smiled. She truly hoped Arya was serious.

"I appreciate you letting me pick out my new name.
I've always loved the name Ariel. *Ariel Ramos.* I love it."

"Glad to hear it," she replied with a smile.

"Will my mother be there when we arrive? Sorry...I
mean my aunt Rosa."

Nova looked out the front passenger window. She'd been
checking periodically to make sure they hadn't picked up
a tail. "If not, she should be arriving shortly."

"I can't wait to see her."

Nova released the breath she was holding when they
arrived at the designated meeting location. She opened

the door. "Stay inside," she told Arya. Hand on her duty weapon, she walked around to check the perimeter.

Deputy Marshal Hightower, who'd driven them, remained near the vehicle.

They were the first to arrive.

Nova walked back to the SUV and got back inside. "They should be arriving soon."

"You don't think anything happened to them?" Arya asked.

"Nothing outside of traffic, maybe."

An SUV like the one they were in pulled up a few minutes later.

Arya reached for the door handle. "Why aren't we getting out?"

"Just wait," Nova uttered.

Hightower got out of the vehicle first and walked over to talk to the driver of the other SUV.

"You can get out now," she confirmed.

Nova escorted Arya over to the waiting vehicle, which held Ramona. Nova's eyes watered at the emotional reunion between mother and daughter, who would now live as aunt and niece.

When they were back in the SUV, she said, "Drop me off at the airport in Memphis, please."

Nova eagerly anticipated going back home and reuniting with River. She was thankful for the opportunity to mend their friendship, but she wasn't expecting too much. After all, she was the one who had left. But she'd apologized for the past. Now it was up to River to take the next step.

Despite her reserve, Nova threw herself into River's arms the moment he arrived at her house. "I'm so happy to see you."

She'd called him as soon as her plane landed, then rushed home to shower before his arrival.

"Same here," he responded, sweeping her into his arms. His mouth covered hers hungrily.

Nova gave herself freely to the passion of his kiss before stepping out of his embrace to say, "Let's get business out of the way first. Your witness and her mother are safe and secure in their new location." She handed him a business card from her pocket. "Here is the contact of her new case agent. For the next two weeks, they'll have twenty-four-hour security and stay in a safe house before moving to their new home."

"Thank you," he said.

"Where's Kenny?" she asked.

"Hanging out with some of the local DEA agents. He wanted to enjoy himself before his flight back to LA."

Nova chuckled. "I'm sure. It feels good to breathe finally," she said. "I like Arya, but I'm thrilled that someone else is responsible for her. She's more cunning than I ever thought."

"I agree."

"And right now, she's the only person who can potentially identify Johnny Boy."

Nova poured two glasses of red wine, then handed one to River.

After preparing plates laden with cheese, crackers, pepperoni and hot-and-spicy chorizo, they sat down on the sofa.

"I don't feel like I can fully relax until Johnny Boy's off the streets," Nova said. "Poppy will still be out there somewhere, though. Once I close out this WITSEC case, I'm turning in my resignation and going after them both."

River took a sip of wine, then bit into a cracker covered with cheese and pepperoni. "You'll be a great asset to Rylee's team."

"I think so," Nova responded.

River's phone rang.

"You've got to be kidding me..." she muttered, sitting up. "Tell Kenny he has terrible timing."

"It's not him," he responded.

Nova nodded and gave him some privacy. She went to her office and quickly checked her email.

River appeared in the doorway moments later. "Johnny Boy's been located. Kenny and I have to catch an early flight to Arizona in the morning."

She couldn't contain her excitement. "Where is he?"

"He's hidden in some remote hideaway between Arizona and the Mexican border," River stated. "Kenny and I will participate in his capture as part of the Native American Targeted Investigation of Violent Enterprises Task Force. They're called NATIVE for short."

Nova knew of the group. Her father had first told her of the elite group of Native American trackers working within US Immigration and Customs Enforcement. The team patrolled their portion of the border between Arizona and Mexico in the fight against drug and human trafficking. "You'll be working with the Shadow Wolves, then," Nova said.

"You know about them?"

"My dad told me about them. Have you worked with them before?"

"I have," River said. "One of their team members, Ray Redhorse, is a good friend of mine."

"How do you know that it's really Johnny Boy?"

"We don't, but it's the only credible lead we have, so

we're going to pursue it," he responded. "Thanks to Arya, we should be able to verify if it's him or not."

"I'm going with you," Nova announced. "I want to be there when you take Johnny Boy down. He killed my witness."

"Nova…"

"Don't try to stop me, River. This is important to me."

After a moment, he nodded. "Clear it with Cohen. You will have to follow my lead."

"I can do that," she agreed. "Just let me go up and grab my bag. I keep one packed and ready to go."

As they headed out the door fifteen minutes later, Nova couldn't shake the dull sense of foreboding she felt.

"You just getting back?" River asked Kenny when he answered the door to his hotel room.

"Yep." He glanced over at Nova and grinned. "You tagging along?"

"I intend to do my part in taking down Johnny Boy," she responded. "It got personal when he killed Mateo."

Kenny nodded in understanding. "I feel you."

River quickly packed his travel bag, then set it on the floor across from the king-size bed. He was glad to have Nova along on this operation. She was calm under pressure and a great shot. He trusted her instincts.

But there was more.

For so long, River had believed he didn't deserve love, but Nova made him feel otherwise. Maybe once this was over… He stopped the thought from forming. He didn't like making too many plans when he was about to go on an operation like this. River wasn't worried about the outcome—he had confidence in his abilities and the team he was working with. But he knew all too well how things could go left in the blink of an eye.

He preferred to take it day by day.

Catching Johnny Boy would be a massive victory for the DEA and his career. River looked forward to the day he could look the drug trafficker in the face. There would be one less threat on the streets. He was smart enough to know that another would rise for each one they took down, but River would never stop fighting.

He glanced over at Nova. "Let's get out of here."

Downstairs in the lobby they waited for Kenny, who was still packing.

Fifteen minutes later, they were headed to the airport.

The drive was filled with a tense silence. River could feel the weight of their mission hanging in the air, suffocating any casual conversation they might have had. Nova stared out the window, seemingly lost in her own thoughts, while Kenny fiddled with the radio, searching for a distraction.

As they arrived at the airport, the atmosphere shifted. Energy crackled around them as travelers hurried by, oblivious to the dangerous game River and his team were about to play.

They made their way through security without incident, blending seamlessly into the bustling crowd.

River couldn't help but steal glances at Nova as they navigated through the maze of corridors. Something about her drew him in—the way she carried herself with unshakable determination, her unwavering loyalty to their cause. But it was more than that. Her presence offered him hope amid the darkness they were about to face.

They reached the gate just as their flight was boarding. River watched as the flight attendants checked tickets and passengers shuffled onto the plane. He could feel the anticipation building within him, knowing that this mission held the key to everything they had been fighting for.

River noticed a subtle shift in Nova's demeanor as they handed their tickets to the flight attendant. Her usually steely gaze softened, a flicker of vulnerability betraying her facade of strength. It was at that moment that he realized she was just as weighed down by the gravity of their task as he was.

The team settled into their seats.

River glanced out the window, catching a glimpse of his reflection in the glass. His face, worn with determination and sacrifice, revealed the toll of this impending fight on him. He wondered if there would ever be a time when he could be free and wouldn't have to bear the world's weight on his shoulders.

As the plane taxied down the runway, Nova turned to River, and their eyes locked briefly, a silent understanding passing between them.

They were in this together, no matter what lay ahead.

THE ENGINES DRONED ON, drowning out the noise of the doubts and fears that echoed within Nova's mind. The plane accelerated, and soon, they were airborne. The turbulence rattled the cabin, but she found solace in the chaos. It reminded her that even amid uncertainty and upheaval, she could still find her footing.

With each passing minute, their destination grew closer. They were heading into the heart of darkness, where victory awaited them or... Nova couldn't shake the feeling that this mission was different from all the others they had undertaken before.

She leaned closer to him, her voice barely audible over the whir of the engines. "River, this isn't going to be an easy fight. So far, Johnny Boy has been two steps ahead of us."

He turned to face her, his eyes filled with conviction.

"I know," River replied, his voice steady, although laced with concern. "But we've trained for this. And I've got you watching my back. I'm not worried."

Nova nodded, taking comfort in his unyielding confidence. River had a way of grounding her, reminding her that they were stronger together than apart. She squeezed his hand, their fingers intertwining in a silent promise to face whatever awaited them.

The once turbulent skies began to clear as the plane pierced through the dense clouds. The sun's golden rays spilled into the cabin, casting a warm glow that breathed life into Nova's troubled soul. It was as if the Lord offered His blessings for the mission ahead.

She was excited to meet the Shadow Wolves team, a group of elite operatives chosen for their unparalleled expertise in covert operations. Each member had their unique skills and backgrounds, but together they formed a formidable force, ready to face any challenge that came their way.

They landed two hours later.

A DEA agent based in Arizona picked them up and transported them to the base of their operations. The Shadow Wolves contingent and agents from the DEA and ATF awaited them.

"Are Redhorse and his team sure it's Johnny Boy?" Kenny asked in a low voice.

"As sure as any of us can be," River replied. "He was sighted in Sells, Arizona. Ray told me he could sneak into an area where cartel members were supposed to be on watch—instead, they were sleeping. He said he got close enough to get a pretty good look at the man. He believes that it's Johnny Boy. Not some look-alike."

"You're saying that he was basically in the cartel's camp,

and nobody saw him?" Nova questioned. "He'd have to be a *ghost*. Johnny Boy's too paranoid to sleep that deep."

"Ray's team nicknamed him Fade because of his uncanny ability to become a part of the scene without being detected," River said. "It means ghost or spirit, so you're right. I wouldn't be surprised if he slipped a sleeping aid in their coffee or something."

"Regardless, that's impressive," she responded.

"Wait until you see the Shadow Wolves in action," River said. "They can look at desert vegetation and tell how recently a twig has been broken, a blade of grass trampled by a human, or how many smugglers there are and which direction they were headed. I guess it's because they grew up comfortable with nature and know how to hear silent things and see the invisible in the desert."

"Wow," she murmured. "They have some serious tracking skills."

"Passed down from the elders, according to Ray," River said.

Nova looked up at him. "What about modern technology?"

"They have night-vision goggles, but it's been a while since I was on a task force with the Shadow Wolves," River answered. "What equipment they had back then didn't come close to the high-dollar toys the cartel can afford. But regardless of expensive technology, there still needs to be a person in the field. This is what the Shadow Wolves do well. They rely on traditional methods of tracking."

The room designated for the briefing was dimly lit, the air carrying a tangible air of anticipation. Nova fell into step behind River and Kenny as they made their way to a table situated in the middle, flanked by other law enforcement officials. The atmosphere buzzed with a mix of hushed conversations as everyone prepared for the critical briefing.

As Nova took her seat, she stole a glance at River. The presence of two additional US marshals entering the room brought a reassuring sense of unity. Cohen, her supervisor, had worked his magic with some last-minute negotiations to secure permission for Nova's involvement. Her father's collaboration with the local agency had played a crucial role several times in the past. Still, Nova's proven performance during the prior investigation with River had truly tipped the scales in her favor.

The dynamics of the room shifted subtly as the briefing commenced. Maps were spread across the whiteboard, detailing the intricate web of the upcoming operation. The plan unfolded like a chessboard, each move considered, calculated and executed with precision.

Nova's attention remained focused, her mind absorbing the details and contingencies. The room became a hive of activity, with agents discussing tactics, sharing intelligence and preparing for the challenges ahead. The collective expertise in the room allowed for a well-coordinated effort, a symphony of skills coming together for a common purpose.

One by one, the agents filed out of the room, each grabbing their tactical gear and checking their weapons before heading off to complete their final preparations.

Chapter Twenty-One

Nova stared out the window, taking in the rugged, mountainous landscape dotted with mesquite trees and cacti, as she, River and Kenny headed to the cartel's known location in the desert. The muted browns, yellows and greens were interrupted by occasional pops of vibrant red desert flowers. In the distance, a few humble buildings could be seen, signaling the location of tribal lands.

"I can see why the cartel would choose this terrain near the border," Kenny said. "It's wide-open land."

"It's desert," River responded. "Since Calderon's arrest, nearly half of the Mancuso drugs are now coming through Mexico and across the international boundary through the Tohono O'odham reservation."

They arrived at their destination twenty-five minutes later.

A muscular man approached and River conducted introductions between Nova, Kenny and Ray Redhorse.

Ray introduced his team. "We have another member," he said. "Ben Chee...he's out following a *sign*."

"What type of sign?" Nova asked.

"We use a technique called *cutting for sign*. Cutting is how we search for and evaluate a sign. This includes footprints, tire tracks, thread or clothing."

Nova listened with interest. "River said that you were able to sneak into a cartel camp once, and nobody saw you."

Nodding, Ray replied, "I'd been tracking them for a few hours. I waited until they made camp and fell asleep. Their spotter didn't even see me."

"You really are a ghost," Kenny said.

Nova nodded in agreement. She was in awe of Ray Red-horse and glad to have the Shadow Wolves accompanying them on this operation.

Ray chuckled. "I just try very hard not to get caught."

"The last time I was here, Ray made this incredible jack-rabbit stew," River said. "I'd never tasted any rabbit and wasn't interested in trying it, but he talked me into it. He cooked it over an open fire, which had a smoky flavor. It was *delicious*."

"I told River he'd starve if he didn't eat it," Ray responded with a chuckle.

"You made something else... It tasted like asparagus."

"Oh, the buds from a cholla cactus."

"The man is a ghost and can cook," Nova stated. "Now I'm really impressed."

"You haven't seen nothing yet," River responded.

RAY REDHORSE DROVE his truck slowly, with River, Nova and Kenny riding along. He kept his window open and carefully examined the ground as he drove.

"Anyone coming north had to travel this path," he explained.

Ray suddenly stopped and got out of the truck. He crouched down to study what seemed to be scrapes in the sand. "Looks like they tied carpet strips to their shoes. They're trying to hide their footprints."

"How long ago?" River asked.

"Most likely late yesterday." Ray pointed to a print. "See

that groove? A rat probably made it during the night. The traffickers could be far away by now."

Kenny sighed. "We missed them."

"This desert is huge," Ray said. "Traffickers don't rely on a specific route. They have a labyrinth of routes to utilize. The cartel uses spotters in the mountains to warn traffickers when to change their route."

"So, then we take out the *eyes*," River stated.

"The cartel will send a replacement," Ray responded. "We can take them down all day, but like ants…they'll just keep replacing them."

They all got back into the truck.

Ray drove down another path.

Fresh tire tracks shimmered in the sunlight, while older footprints overlapped with insect trails.

The three men got out of the truck a second time.

Ray fingered a burlap fiber snagged by the thorns on mesquite bushes. He held it to his nose, sniffing it. "This came from a bag filled with marijuana."

They scanned the area before climbing back into the vehicle. Ray drove around the mesquite bushes. "It's getting worse out here. Lately, we've had some problems with machine gun–wielding thieves lying in wait to steal drugs from the traffickers," he said. "And a couple of cartels fighting over ownership of certain routes."

"I see you have your friend with you," River said, referring to Ray's M4 assault rifle.

"I never leave home without it."

River glanced over at Nova. "How are you feeling about all this?"

"All I can think about is capturing Johnny Boy and his many minions. The Mancuso cartel robbed me of my father and a witness. I want to take down as many of them as possible."

"I understand," River responded. "They took out two DEA agents... One of them was like a brother to me."

The fire burning in her eyes mirrored his own. River knew they were kindred spirits fueled by a desire for retribution and justice. They both wanted nothing more than to dismantle the Mancuso cartel piece by piece.

"Nova," he said solemnly, "we will get Johnny Boy."

She nodded in agreement, her face etched with determination.

It was close to two o'clock when the joint task force spotted a ramshackle shack hidden amid the rocky terrain of the Arizona desert.

The air was thick with tension as they cautiously advanced, their weapons drawn and senses on high alert.

"All right, move in," barked Ray Redhorse, his voice terse with urgency.

With practiced precision, the team spread out, each member taking up a strategic position around the weathered structure.

River cautiously pushed it open.

Nova scanned the area, determined to see everything and everybody.

As they stepped inside, the pungent aroma of marijuana assaulted her senses, mingling with the musty scent of decay that permeated the air. Stacks of crates lined the walls while the floor beneath their feet was littered with discarded debris.

"Spread out and search the premises," ordered Ray, his eyes scanning the room for any signs of movement.

They heard a noise outside.

Two men tried to escape, from the sound of it, but had been apprehended.

"This is just the beginning," Ray declared, his voice resonating with determination.

As the sun began to dip below the horizon, their mission had been a success. They had taken down several scouting locations and captured those involved in trafficking.

But there was one crucial element missing.

Johnny Boy.

The team had been on the lookout for him, with no luck. However, their persistence paid off when they uncovered a massive stash of marijuana linked to the notorious Mancuso cartel. One of the men decided to talk after the agents seized 3,400 pounds of marijuana from the shack he was guarding.

"*Puedo ayudarle*...eh... I can help you," the scout repeated nervously, his eyes darting between each agent in the room. "I know where Johnny Boy is hiding."

Those words caught River's attention. "Where is he?"

The scout fidgeted nervously, knowing this was his only shot at survival. "*Acuerdo*...deal... I want deal."

River stepped closer, his gaze never wavering from the scout's face. "Speak quickly," he commanded. "Tell us everything you know about Johnny Boy and maybe we can offer you a chance at redemption."

The scout hesitated for a moment, his mind racing as he weighed his options. It was evident that fear wrestled with his desire to escape the clutches of the cartel. Finally, he gave in to his desperation and whispered, "Okay. I'll tell you..."

AFTER MIDNIGHT, River and a team of DEA agents and police officers were on the road to the small town of Pima,

Arizona. The scout had given up Johnny Boy's location—a community in the desert outside of town. The Shadow Wolves had remained behind at the arrest site to continue monitoring movement in the desert.

"Wow...look at this place," said Nova when they arrived at their destination. "There's a grid-tied solar system, a greenhouse...all miles away from the nearest neighbor."

River glanced around. This was the perfect place to hide because it was so secluded. The three-story house was situated on eight or nine acres. There were orchards with apple, peach, apricot, pomegranate and pear trees. Nearby was a large fenced garden area and a metal shop warehouse. He'd heard that Johnny Boy was vegan and preferred to grow his own food.

His gaze returned to the home with the elaborate entry. "It's a beauty. It'll be a shame to have to shoot up this house if it comes to that."

They were a safe distance away from the property, waiting for the command to infiltrate.

"What do you think a place like this would cost?" Nova asked.

"At least a couple million," River responded. "The floor plan showed an Olympic-sized pool, a tennis court and a basketball court. There's also a hair salon and barbershop on-site. The guy has everything he needs."

"I'm surprised there's no guardhouse or men on roofs with guns," Kenny interjected.

"My guess is that he's trying to blend in around here," River stated. "The guns are in the house and that building over there...trust me."

He and other law enforcement fanned out around the house and perimeter as they set out to capture and arrest Johnny Boy. There was still the chance that he might have fled already like a thief in the night, but River pushed the thought away.

We have to make sure we have every avenue covered.

River and the team crept to the porch steps of the house. Nova flanked him on the right.

He glanced over his shoulder, ensuring everyone was in position before gesturing to the officer to his right who was holding the ram waist-high.

River instructed the others to assume their positions, then gave the door a hard knock and yelled, "This is the DEA. *Open up.*"

No response.

River repeated the order sharply.

Again, nothing from inside.

He signaled to the officer standing behind him, then moved out of the way.

The officer drew the ram back, then swung it toward the door.

It didn't open.

He struck the door again, getting the same result.

River had enough experience to realize that the door was most likely barricaded on the inside. He also knew that they'd lost the element of surprise. Whoever was in the house had time in which to prepare a defense.

The officer repeatedly battered the door, forcing it to give way. It would open a few inches, but then immediately slam shut.

River swallowed his unease and stood directly in front of the entrance. He was able to steal a glance into the house for a split second, brief snapshots of figures moving about. He soon realized he was seeing a person—no, it was two people.

The officer slammed the ram once more.

River caught sight of a man with a shotgun aimed directly at the door.

"Gun," he yelled, ducking and pushing the officer out of the way just as a loud noise erupted from the interior of the house, leaving a hole in the door. Another round of bullets tore through the wood, forcing River to jump off the porch and into a cluster of bushes for cover. He glanced around, searching for Nova. She was safe, having taken cover behind a nearby tree.

He looked back at the house and caught a real glimpse of Johnny Boy—just as gunfire rang out all around him.

River felt a flash of raw pain and knew he'd been hit. Still, he drew his weapon and began firing into the house.

Out the corner of his eye, he saw one of the agents run to the left corner of the house. Another moved quickly to the right.

River touched his left side. His fingers were covered with warm blood. The wound throbbed as he felt blood spread across the front of his shirt.

I'm losing too much.

River tried to speak but couldn't think clearly. Everything started to spin, moving him toward a cloud of darkness.

In the distance, he heard someone saying, "We have an agent down..."

Nova rushed to his side. "We have to get you out of here. Hang on, River."

"Ken..." River managed.

"I'm right here," his partner uttered.

"No... Nova..." Every word took effort and all of River's strength.

"Don't try to talk," she responded. *"I'm here."*

Burning pain ripped through him.

"Where's the ambulance?" Kenny yelled. "*Call* them again."

River heard another round of gunfire nearby.

"Stay with him, Nova." Crouched low, his partner took off toward the side of the house.

A circle of darkness swirled around River, growing larger each minute until he couldn't see anything else. Waves of pain washed over him. He groaned with each wave.

Just before he was carried away on a sea of unconsciousness, River heard the loud shrill of sirens.

Chapter Twenty-Two

The journey from the perilous scene to hospital was a blur for Nova. As the medical team rushed River into surgery, she found herself directed to the waiting area, the weight of worry settling heavily on her shoulders.

The setting was different but it still reminded Nova of the night her father was killed by a cartel member.

"I can't lose him," she whispered, her words a silent prayer as she sat amid the sterile stillness of the hospital waiting room, every passing moment an agonizing eternity.

Time stretched until the door swung open, and a doctor entered.

His solemn expression carried the gravity of the situation, but his words brought a glimmer of hope. "Agent Randolph's surgery was a success. They were able to remove the bullets. Thankfully, no major areas suffered any real damage. He should be waking up anytime now. He'll be moved into his room after that."

Nova's sigh of relief was audible, the tension releasing from her like a held breath. "I'm relieved to hear it," she acknowledged, gratitude welling up as she realized that River had emerged from the brink of danger.

When Nova was finally allowed to see him, River lay sleeping, surrounded by the quiet hum of medical equipment.

She pulled a chair beside his bed and sat down, her gaze never leaving his face. The harsh fluorescent lights of the hospital room felt softer in these quiet moments, and Nova waited patiently for him to wake up, in a silent vigil by his side.

The steady beep of the heart monitor filled the room, a reassuring rhythm as she watched over River and hoped that he would awaken soon.

The room became a sanctuary of quiet anticipation. In this space, the echoes of worry were replaced by the promise of recovery and an unspoken bond forged between them.

RIVER OPENED HIS EYES, blinked several times, then opened them again. No doubt he was still feeling woozy from the anesthesia.

"Hey, you..." she said, relief and happiness flowing through her.

He turned his head. "Nova..."

"I'm here," she responded with a tiny smile. "You really scared me out there."

"I'll be fine," River said. Still feeling groggy, he closed his eyes. He opened them a few minutes later. "I'm sorry if I drifted off."

"You're good," Nova said. "Don't try to stay awake for me. I'm not going anywhere."

"Did we get Johnny Boy?"

Nova didn't want to be the one to tell River about the trafficker's escape. In the rush of the shoot-out, her only goal had been getting River the help he needed. But Kenny had called to fill her in that they hadn't made an arrest. "Kenny is on his way. He should be here soon."

When the nurse entered the room, Nova stood up. "I'm going to the cafeteria to get something to drink. I'll be right back."

"You don't have to leave," River said.

"I know. Don't worry. Not going far at all."

Nova walked out of the room just as Kenny stepped off the elevator.

"River just asked about Johnny Boy," she said, meeting him halfway. "I think you should be the one to tell him what happened."

He nodded, looking exhausted. "After all River's been through, I wish I could give him some much better news."

"The nurse is in the room with him right now," Nova stated.

"How are you holding up?" Kenny inquired.

"I'm relieved that he's still alive."

"Me, too." Kenny passed her, heading to River's room.

As she made her way to the elevator, Nova glanced up to see a tall man with long dreadlocks, a bouquet in hand, weaving through the corridors. His movements seemed purposeful, and a chill crept up Nova's spine.

Johnny Boy.

Instinct kicked in, and she followed him discreetly. He was so intent on his purpose that he never once looked in her direction. She was grateful her badge was hidden inside her pocket and that she'd removed the jacket that would've identified her as law enforcement.

Nova's eyes never left the bouquet, trying to see if it concealed potential danger.

The man moved with an eerie calmness, scanning room numbers with predatory intent. The dreadlocks swung with every measured step.

Nova's heart pounded as he drew closer to River's room.

When he produced what appeared to be a weapon from beneath the flowers, determination eclipsed her fear, and she stepped forward, calling out his name.

"Johnny Boy!"

He turned sharply, eyes narrowing as he saw Nova.

In that tense moment, the bouquet became a weapon. He threw it at her and fired a shot.

Nova's instincts propelled her into action; she lunged for cover. The bullet missed, leaving only the echo of gunfire in the hospital hallway.

Amid shocked screams, her eyes quickly bounced around to see if anyone had been shot.

Dropping the flowers to the ground without hesitation, Johnny Boy made a break for the stairwell, his hurried steps resonating in the hallway.

Nova, fueled by adrenaline and fierce determination, sprinted after him. The hospital staff, caught off guard by the sudden chaos, looked on in shock.

As Johnny Boy reached the second floor, Nova closed the gap.

Hospital security, alerted by the commotion, sprang into action. Responding to the urgency, they swiftly intervened, creating a human barricade at the bottom of the staircase.

Johnny Boy's escape route thwarted, Nova cornered him, her eyes locking on to his as she took aim.

"Drop the weapon!" she ordered.

His eyes darted around, taking in his situation.

The armed security closed in, acting in synchronized precision.

Smirking, Johnny Boy did as she instructed, then held up his hands in surrender.

Nova stood breathless, her gaze fixed on the man in custody. She was thrilled to see him in handcuffs.

When he was taken away, the hospital gradually returned to its usual hushed atmosphere, the threat extinguished, but the echoes of the confrontation lingered in the air.

"What happened?" Kenny asked when Nova returned to River's hospital room. "I heard gunshots."

"Johnny Boy was here," she announced. "I think he was planning to take out River."

"Where is he now?"

"In police custody. I called Special Agent Scott. I'm going to meet him at the precinct, but I wanted to check on River first."

"He's still groggy from the anesthesia and pain meds. I expect he'll probably be out until morning."

River opened his eyes just as Nova approached the hospital bed.

Nova could tell he was struggling to stay awake. "Stop fighting it. Go to sleep, River."

"No... I need to talk to Kenny."

"Here I am, partner."

She planted a kiss on his cheek. "I have to go."

He took her hand in his. "You will be back, though?"

"Yes. I'll get back as soon as I can."

"Hey, buddy," Kenny said when River woke up a second time. "You don't look so great."

"Just tell me that my getting shot was worth it," he responded. "Is Johnny Boy in jail?"

"He's in custody now." Kenny paused momentarily, then said, "He came to the hospital. Nova saw him and interrupted his plan."

"I thought I heard gunshots. Was I dreaming, or did that happen?" River asked.

"Naw, it was real. Right out in the hallway. Luckily, no one was hurt. Nova's on her way to the precinct now."

Nova's genuine concern, her quick actions in saving him, melted the final wall around River's heart. *Once I fully recover, she and I must sit down and talk.*

It was still a struggle for him to stay awake. "I need to close my eyes for a bit."

"You go right ahead," Kenny said. "I need to make some phone calls."

He fell back to sleep as he heard the door shut.

Chapter Twenty-Three

Nova wore a huge grin on her face as she exited the police precinct in the early morning hours.

The man captured at the hospital was not just another doppelgänger. The tattoo on his chest left no room for doubt—he was indeed John Boyd Raymond. His fingerprints had regrown, providing further evidence of his true identity. She silently thanked Arya for informing them about the tattoo and its significance.

Johnny Boy's arrogance was astonishing. He sat there smirking and laughing at them, unfazed that he was in custody or that he would be doing serious time for all the many crimes he'd committed.

He flat out refused to entertain any conversation, repeatedly saying, *"Lawyer."*

She'd left the interrogation room in frustration, wanting to get back to River.

She was looking forward to sharing the news that Johnny Boy had been arrested. He was Poppy's number one—his being in custody would shake up the cartel.

A sense of foreboding washed over her.

Maybe Johnny Boy didn't seem worried because he had a backup plan. There was a chance that River was still in danger.

Upon her return to the hospital, a palpable urgency to secure River's safety gripped Nova. Approaching the front desk with resolute determination, she flashed her badge and asserted, "I need Agent Randolph moved to another room immediately." Her tone conveyed a seriousness that couldn't be ignored.

The nurse behind the desk, eyes a mix of concern and fear, nodded in response. "Yes, ma'am."

Nova headed to his current room, passing a man with a cell phone to his ear, positioned a few feet away from the nurses' station. He was dressed in a pair of jeans and a Western-style shirt with cowboy boots. She homed in on him as she quickly approached River's room.

Both Kenny and River looked at her when she entered.

"What's wrong?" he asked.

"I requested to have you moved." Nova paused a heart-beat, then continued, "Johnny Boy's been arrested, but I'm not convinced that you're out of danger."

River nodded, looking less groggy than the last time she'd seen him. "See if it can be arranged for me to be flown to a hospital in Los Angeles."

A nurse came in to check his wounds and change his bandages, putting a temporary halt to their conversation.

"Has anyone been asking about me?" River asked.

"Not that I know of," the nurse replied. "Just so you know...we were instructed not to confirm that you're a patient here."

"That's great," Nova said. She showed her badge, then added, "I want the names of any nurses or doctors who will be caring for River. They are to be the *only* ones to come into his room."

"I'm working a double shift, so it will be me until seven a.m. tomorrow morning."

"I won't be leaving your side," Nova announced.

Kenny chuckled. "I had a feeling you'd say that. Can't say I'm surprised at all."

The rest of the morning passed without incident, and Kenny left the room to pick up some lunch for him and Nova.

She got up to go to the bathroom, leaving the door open just a tad in case River called for her.

Just after she washed her hands, Nova heard the door to the room open and close.

The nurse had checked on River at noon. The doctor wasn't expected to come back for another round until later in the evening.

Nova eased to the door and peeked into the room.

A lone figure moved stealthily toward the bed.

It was the man she'd seen earlier. Somehow, he'd been able to sneak into the room. He must have been watching the room and assumed River was alone after Kenny left.

Nova quickly assessed the situation. This man was bigger and stronger, but she wasn't about to leave River vulnerable to his attack. She fervently prayed that her boxing and self-defense lessons were about to pay off.

Using her foot, Nova eased the door open wider.

The man turned around, surprise evident on his face.

Nova saw the needle in his hand and wished she hadn't left her gun in her tote beside the bed.

He gave her a menacing look, then lunged at her.

Nova dodged and shoved the man off balance, forcing him to drop the syringe.

But it wasn't enough. He recovered, then sent a punch in her direction.

Agony tore through her as Nova took a hard hit to her right shoulder.

She cocked back her uninjured arm and threw a jab as hard as she could. It connected with his jaw. Kicking out, Nova connected her foot into the man's knee, bringing him down.

Nova squeezed her eyes closed as she tried to breathe through the pain ripping from her shoulder and down her arm. The tendons in her left hand were on fire, but Nova wasn't about to let up. She punched the attacker's face again, then a third time.

In the distance, she heard River talking, but she couldn't understand what he was saying.

She had no sense of time or place as she put all her energy into knocking the man unconscious. Nova had no awareness of when Kenny rushed in with hospital security.

Someone—she didn't know who—pulled her off the man.

The room was soon filled with hospital staff. Some were checking on River while others placed the man on a gurney, handcuffed him and pushed him out of the room.

"Nova," River called out. "You okay?"

Kenny assisted her over to the chair. "You should let them look at your shoulder."

"I'm good," she said. "He landed a solid punch. I'll be sore for a few days but that's about it." Her gaze was on River. She evaluated him, making sure he was okay. Satisfied that River was safe, Nova lowered her eyes, searching the floor. "Kenny, over there... He came in here with a syringe."

Kenny slipped on a pair of gloves from a nearby counter before picking it up. "I'll send this to our lab."

Nova's eyes traveled back to where River lay in bed. "You sure you're okay?" he asked again.

She nodded. "I'm good."

But the truth was that she was anything but okay. Nova could have very easily taken that man's life to save River. But this time it had nothing to do with her sense of duty as a law enforcement officer. It was different because she was protecting the man she loved.

RIVER WAS MOVED into a new room with twenty-four-hour security. The doctor felt he was too weak to be moved to a hospital in California.

Nova hardly left his side for the next two days. River was concerned that she wasn't getting enough rest.

"You should go with Bonnie to the hotel," he told her. His sister had arrived this morning. He was glad that she and Nova were getting along so well.

"I'm good. Don't you start worrying about me," Nova assured him. "Focus on getting better so we can get you home."

She sank into the visitor chair. "I can tell you're feeling much better. You're starting to get bossy."

He tried to laugh but it hurt.

They talked for a little while until River noticed she could barely keep her eyes open. Ten minutes later, she was sound asleep.

River eased out of bed and held on to the portable IV stand for support. He crossed the short distance to the bathroom.

His business done, he made his way back to bed, sagging with relief when he eased his body under the covers.

Bonnie had tried to convince him to use the portable urinal for another day or so, but his pride just wouldn't let him. He'd argued that he needed to move around to regain his strength. Right now, he was out of breath and in extreme pain. The medication helped to take the edge off, but the sheer effort it took for him to get out of bed and go to the bathroom—it almost wasn't worth it.

River felt bad that he hadn't helped Nova fend off the attacker who'd come into his room, but she'd managed well. He could only press the call button and hope someone would arrive in time. He'd tried to pull the chair closer to the bed in hopes of getting to the gun he knew was inside the tote.

He knew that Nova had had the same goal—she'd wanted to retrieve her weapon but couldn't. Still, she'd managed to subdue the man.

River had done a silent assessment of his own, making sure she wasn't seriously hurt. He caught her wincing every now and then, but Nova had refused to be examined. She kept telling the nurse and the doctor that she was fine. He felt that was because she didn't want to leave his side—she was in what he called *guard* mode.

Later that evening, River signaled to his sister and Kenny to give him a moment alone with Nova.

"Kenny, we haven't had a chance to talk," Bonnie said. "Why don't you take me to dinner? I don't mean to the cafeteria either."

"I'd love that, actually," he responded with a grin.

"Did I miss something?" Nova asked when she and River were alone.

"Kenny met my sister a few years ago," he responded. "As far as I know, it's not been anything outside of harmless flirting here and there."

"Oh, okay."

"Nova...you saved my life. Thank you."

"I was just doing my job." She shook her head. "No, that's not true. River, all I saw was that the man I loved more than life itself was in danger. He was going to kill you and I had to stop him."

He couldn't help but feel a swell of pride and love for her

in that moment. She saw him as the man she loved with all her heart. And in that instant, as his life hung in the balance, she risked everything to protect him. He couldn't believe how lucky he was to have someone like her by his side, willing to sacrifice herself for his safety.

"I wondered what was going on in your mind. I'd never seen you filled with such rage. Kenny had to pick you up to keep you from punching the man to death. He deserved it, as far as I'm concerned."

"I'd do it again," Nova said smoothly.

He gestured for her to sit on the bed beside him.

"You're supposed to be resting."

"What's the plan? I know you're working on something in that brain of yours."

"As soon as you're strong enough to fly, I'm taking you to Los Angeles to continue your recovery."

River nodded in approval. "Sounds good to me."

"I meant to check to see if he had any ID on him."

"Kenny most likely took care of all that," River said. "I'm just glad nobody else got hurt." He paused a moment, then added, "I wish you'd let someone check out your shoulder. I know it's bothering you."

Nova eyed him. "I'm good. My shoulder is a bit sore and my hand's swollen but not broken. That's it."

"You'd tell me the truth, wouldn't you?"

"Yeah."

River took her left hand in his. "I heard what you said, Nova. I would prefer to have that discussion when I'm not under the influence of pain meds."

She smiled. "I can wait."

FIFTEEN DAYS LATER, River was out of the hospital and home. Nova had finally convinced him to take a nap. He'd been up most of the morning after a follow-up visit to the doctor. Her gaze traveled her surroundings. The dove-gray walls and deep navy-colored drapes provided a rich backdrop while soft music floated throughout the house. River had a fantastic view of palm trees, the beach and the Pacific Ocean.

He had contemporary furnishings. The dining area was large enough for a table of six and overflowed in the open great room. She especially loved the teal-and-silver color scheme of the kitchen.

"Did you decorate this place by yourself?" Nova asked when he woke up an hour later.

He nodded. "Yeah, I did."

"You have a really nice home."

"Thanks. When are you going to start looking for a place out here?"

"I don't know," Nova responded. "Right now, I just want to make sure your recovery goes well. I must confess that I have zero nursing skills, but I'll make sure your bandages and the area around the wound are kept clean and dry. The doctor says you're healing nicely."

He smiled. "You'd probably do a better job than I would."

Nova rearranged his pillows so River could sit propped up.

"Thanks," he said.

"Your doctor said you could use an ice pack on the bandage to help with swelling. Do you have one?"

Nodding, River replied, "There's one in the freezer."

She picked up her iPad. "Let me check my notes. I want to make sure I'm not missing anything."

"Nova, you can relax." River chuckled. "You're doing great."

She released a short sigh. "Are you in any pain?"

He shook his head no. "I'm fine."

River patted the empty space beside him. "Sit down and talk to me."

"You should get some rest," Nova stated.

"I will."

"When you were shot…it reminded me of the night I lost my father." Her eyes teared up. "I'd never been so scared."

River took her hand in his own. "When I thought I was dying, all I could think of that night was you and how much I wanted to see that beautiful smile of yours. I was filled with so many regrets. I promised I'd make some changes if I was given the chance."

"Like what?" Nova asked.

"I've spent most of my life afraid to give my love to anyone for fear of rejection. Then I met you."

"And I broke your heart."

"That's all in the past," River said. "Back then, it might not have worked out. I think we were both trying to sort out our individual issues. Now we're older and wiser…"

"I'd like to think so," Nova responded.

"Back then, I thought we had something. Then I realized that you weren't ready for a relationship. I do believe that you cared for me, but I also believe that you aren't ready to make a commitment."

"I panicked, River, but that's all changed now," Nova said. "I want to be with you. Can't you see that?" She kissed him. "What we have is worth fighting for," she whispered.

His voice cracked with emotion as he asked her, "But can you handle the tough times that come with love? Will you stay and fight when things get difficult?"

She tightened her grip on his hand and looked into his eyes. "I already proved it when I risked my life to save yours," she said firmly.

He needed to hear it from her own lips that she was willing to stay and fight for their love.

Nova met his gaze. "You know that I love you. I'm not afraid anymore. River, I'm so sorry for the pain I caused. I would rather cut off my own hand before I ever hurt you again."

When he didn't respond, she said, "River, I'm the only woman for you."

"That you are," he confirmed. "I've never met anyone who makes me feel what you do. There was a time when I wanted to forget you, but I couldn't. My heart wouldn't let me. *You* wouldn't let me."

"Then I need to hear *you* say that you're ready to give me a second chance."

"I'm ready to take another chance at love..." River said. "With you."

Epilogue

Six months had passed since Nova decided to relocate to Los Angeles, leaving Charlotte behind and embracing a new chapter in her career with Rylee's task force, whose sole focus was targeting high-level drug cartel organizations such as the Mancuso cartel. She felt a sense of freedom that she never had with the Marshals.

She found herself thriving in the fast-paced environment, fueled by the adrenaline of her work and the camaraderie of her fellow agents.

Amid the chaos of their demanding jobs, Nova found solace in the arms of River. Their relationship had blossomed in the months since her arrival, growing stronger with each passing day as they navigated the highs and lows of their shared journey. Together, they forged a bond built on trust, respect and a deep-seated love that defied the odds.

The sound of Kaleb's voice cut into her musings.

"We received intel that Poppy has a new number one," Kaleb stated. "They're being very secretive about this one."

"Well, it's only a matter of time before we find out who he is," Rylee responded confidently.

"Nova, I know that this is never going to bring your father back, but it might help," Kaleb said after the meeting ended.

"It won't, but I'd still like to make as many of the Mancuso cartel members pay for what they've done," she responded.

"I'm alive because of Easton," Rylee stated. "If I have anything to say about it, we'll keep chipping away at Poppy's organization until we get to her."

Grinning, Nova shot back, "I'm here for it all."

"That's it for now. Operation Reckoning is live…"

* * * * *

INTRIGUE

Seek thrills. Solve crimes. Justice served.

Available Next Month

Protecting The Newborn Delores Fossen
The Perfect Murder K.D. Richards

....

A Colby Christmas Rescue Debra Webb
Wyoming Undercover Escape Juno Rushdan

....

Killer In The Kennel Caridad Piñeiro
The Masquerading Twin Katie Mettner

6 brand new stories each month
INTRIGUE
Seek thrills. Solve crimes. Justice served.
MILLS & BOON

Keep reading for an excerpt of a new title
from the Medical series,
THE REBEL DOCTOR'S SECRET CHILD by Deanne Anders

PROLOGUE

EXCITEMENT VIBRATED THROUGH Brianna Rogers as she followed the office manager, Sable, into the crowded conference room. With her arms loaded down with boxes of donuts, Brianna looked across the table at all the people she'd soon be working with. She'd done it. In just a few months, she'd be working as a certified nurse midwife. The opportunity for a residency at Nashville's Women's Legacy Clinic was one that she'd never imagined receiving. It was known as the premier women's clinic in the city, so the experience she'd receive here would be priceless.

As the door opened and a silver-haired man with kind blue eyes came in, the room went quiet. Bree rushed to her seat. She had only met the founder of the clinic, Dr. Jack Warner, once during an interview, but she admired the practice he'd built and especially the home for pregnant women in need of a safe place to stay that he had founded.

He took his seat at the end of the table then reached for the tablet Sable had told her contained the itinerary for the meeting.

"First off, I'd like to welcome two new colleagues. I

hope you've all met our new resident midwife, Brianna Rogers. She's a recent graduate of Vanderbilt and came to us highly recommended."

A man yelled, "Go Commodores," from across the room, taking the attention off her, something she appreciated. One of the midwives, Sky, waved at her from down the table. Bree waved back. Even with the unwanted attention, she was already feeling at home here.

"Also, I want you to welcome Dr. Knox Collins, who will be filling in for Dr. Hennison, who, I'm sure you all know, just welcomed another baby boy."

Bree's heart skipped a beat and her arms and face prickled with tiny pinpricks. No. It was impossible that he could be there. A roaring in her ears started as her eyes scanned the room, stopping when she saw a man with laughing gray eyes and a devilish smile that should have come with a warning.

Never in her wildest dreams would she have imagined herself stuck looking across the table at the man who had broken her sister's heart and left Bree to pick up the pieces. Especially since one of those pieces had been a newborn baby. She'd never forget the first time she'd heard that name. It had been when her phone rang. She hadn't spoken to her sister in months and was so happy to see her name on the display.

Suddenly, she was back there, eight years earlier. Brittany, her voice overflowing with a happiness Bree hadn't heart in years, laughing as she told Bree the news. "It's a girl, Bree. A beautiful baby girl. I have a daughter. You're an aunt."

Stunned, Bree didn't know what to say. Brittany had been pregnant? How was that possible without Bree knowing about it?

"Well, aren't you going to congratulate me?" her sister asked.

"Of course," Bree said, recovering from the shock of her sister's words. "Where are you?"

Bree listened closely as her sister explained how she'd gone into labor early and the baby was still in the hospital.

"Who's the father?" Bree asked, unable to hold back the question any longer. Brittany had been known to hook up with some less than desirable types in the past.

"It's Knox Collins, Gail and Charles Collins's son. But you can't tell anyone. Me. This baby. We mean nothing to him. He's messed up, Bree. He drinks and parties all the time. I don't want that for my daughter. Promise me you won't tell anyone, Bree. Promise me."

Bree had no choice but to agree. If Brittany thought the man would be a bad influence on her daughter, she had no choice but to believe her. She'd ask for more information the next time her sister called her.

But the next call she received wasn't from her sister. Instead, it was from the hospital. She could hear the woman's voice. "I'm sorry, Ms. Rogers, but there's been a terrible accident."

She told the woman that she was wrong. She'd just spoken with her sister only hours earlier. Her sister couldn't be gone.

She remembered holding her niece in her arms for the

first time, knowing it should have been Brittany standing there to take her baby home. Not Bree.

Overwhelming grief had threatened to overtake her then, but she pushed it back. Just like she had when she'd realized she was suddenly responsible for her sister's newborn baby. There was no time for grieving. Because if she let it take hold of her, she'd never climb out of the dark pit of it. She'd never be able to take care of the child who had no one else. Just like Bree had no one else but that child.

The noise of the room rose, bringing her back to reality as everyone around her stood up to leave.

Looking down the table she saw Knox accepting the greetings from the clinic's staff. How was it that he stood there, smiling and happy, going on with his life while her sister's life was cut so short?

Bree shook her head. No. She wouldn't let herself go there. Ally had to be her first priority. The little girl had given Bree a reason to keep on going for years now, to keep pushing to better herself so that she could provide a good life for her niece. And there was no way she was going to let some hotshot rebel doc like Knox Collins get in her way.

Subscribe and fall in love with a Mills & Boon series today!

You'll be among the first to read stories delivered to your door monthly and enjoy great savings.